ROBIN SCHONE

"Combining the erotic with the romantic, Robin Schone
tests the boundaries of romance fiction."
—*Literary Times*

CLAUDIA DAIN

"Claudia Dain's emotionally charged writing . . .
will take your breath away."
—*New York Times* bestselling author Sabrina Jeffries

ALLYSON JAMES

"Ms. James is able to capture what it feels like to discover
that sex can be fun and intimate and loving."
—*Fallen Angel Reviews*

SHILOH WALKER

"[Walker writes] some of the best erotic romantic
fantasies on the market."
—*Midwest Book Review*

PRIVATE PLACES

ROBIN SCHONE

CLAUDIA DAIN  ALLYSON JAMES  SHILOH WALKER

B
BERKLEY SENSATION, NEW YORK

THE BERKLEY PUBLISHING GROUP
Published by the Penguin Group
Penguin Group (USA) Inc.
375 Hudson Street, New York, New York 10014, USA
Penguin Group (Canada), 90 Eglinton Avenue East, Suite 700, Toronto, Ontario M4P 2Y3, Canada
(a division of Pearson Penguin Canada Inc.)
Penguin Books Ltd., 80 Strand, London WC2R 0RL, England
Penguin Group Ireland, 25 St. Stephen's Green, Dublin 2, Ireland (a division of Penguin Books Ltd.)
Penguin Group (Australia), 250 Camberwell Road, Camberwell, Victoria 3124, Australia
(a division of Pearson Australia Group Pty. Ltd.)
Penguin Books India Pvt. Ltd., 11 Community Centre, Panchsheel Park, New Delhi—110 017, India
Penguin Group (NZ), 67 Apollo Drive, Rosedale, North Shore 0632, New Zealand
(a division of Pearson New Zealand Ltd.)
Penguin Books (South Africa) (Pty.) Ltd., 24 Sturdee Avenue, Rosebank, Johannesburg 2196,
South Africa
Penguin Books Ltd., Registered Offices: 80 Strand, London WC2R 0RL, England

These novellas are works of fiction. Names, characters, places, and incidents either are the product of the authors' imaginations or are used fictitiously, and any resemblance to actual persons, living or dead, business establishments, events, or locales is entirely coincidental. The publisher does not have any control over and does not assume any responsibility for author or third-party websites or their content.

PRINTING HISTORY
Berkley Sensation trade paperback edition / August 2008

Library of Congress Cataloging-in-Publication Data

Private places / Robin Schone . . . [et al.]. —Berkley Sensation trade pbk. ed.
    p. cm.
  ISBN 978-0-425-22172-3
  1. Erotic stories, American.   I. Schone, Robin.

  PS648 .E7P75 2008
  813'.60803538—dc22   2008001065

PRINTED IN THE UNITED STATES OF AMERICA

10 9 8 7 6 5 4 3 2 1

CONTENTS

THE DECIDEDLY DEVILISH DUKE

Allyson James

To Forrest, my own devilish duke.

ONE

An Entertainment at Cards

Surrey, 1835

Michael Beaulieu, the Duke of Bretherton, was contemplating the hideous pattern on his teacup when he heard Amelia Lockwood's voice. It was a low, sultry voice that ten years ago could make his cock hard by whispering his name. Doubly so when accompanied by Amelia's red-lipped smile and a lazy look in her deep blue eyes.

Michael lifted his gaze to see Amelia on the other side of the ostentatious drawing room speaking to his host, the idiotic Preston Lockwood. Amelia, the woman he'd driven away ten long years ago with his arrogance and stupid high-handedness, the woman who vowed she hated him and never wanted to see him again. He'd quit England right after that and hadn't returned for a decade.

Now he learned a disturbing fact—her voice could still make him hard.

Amelia did not notice Michael. He had chosen a seat partially concealed by a carved wooden screen, some monstrosity a curio seller had passed off to Lockwood as Oriental. Likely it had been made in Wapping. He'd chosen the chair because he did not want to be here.

Michael had come to Preston's house party only because an old friend had begged him to accompany him.

Damn it all, I despise the man, Nathan Fuller had pleaded. *But I've got to go because I need his backing in my election. Do come and make it bearable. No one's seen you in a decade. . . . They've forgotten all about that business. . . .*

They hadn't of course. He hadn't missed the looks of blatant curiosity from the hoi polloi of Surrey, the excited buzz that the beautiful debutante who'd driven him away had arrived in her widow's weeds.

He'd been politely listening to an elderly gentleman, a well-traveled man as weary of inane London as Michael was. He'd found the gentleman's tales interesting until Amelia's voice cut through them, and then no amount of money could have pulled his attention back.

"Preston," she was saying in that blood-heating voice. "We should speak of this privately."

What the devil was she wearing? A prim, dark blue bodice buttoned up to her chin, long sleeves hiding her arms to her wrists. The last time he'd seen her she'd been in gauzy lace, a bodice cut low across her shoulders and breasts, the top two buttons undone so a man could slide his finger, or his tongue, into the enticing crease.

Now London's most sought-after debutante was dressed like a nun. An impoverished nun.

"If you have anything to say, coz, say it here," Preston drawled. "I keep no secrets from my friends."

Idiot. Preston Lockwood was cousin to Amelia's late husband, Basil Lockwood. Amelia was supposed to be in some remote country village; why she was here looking brittle and out of place was beyond him.

The elderly gentleman noticed his interest. "Oh, my dear chap, I must be boring you exceedingly."

"Not at all," Michael said, almost sharply. "I just wondered why she was here."

"Mrs. Lockwood?" The gentleman lifted grizzled brows. "Preston Lockwood was her husband's only heir, and she's dependent on him. Probably asking for money, poor gel."

Her high color and the rage in her eyes told Michael she wasn't having much luck.

Michael quietly excused himself, rose, and moved so he could hear her, deliberately staying out of Amelia's line of sight.

"You know my conditions," Preston said, spreading his hands. He was surrounded by a group of men dressed identically to him, fops in expensive frock coats and waistcoats, style sacrificed for costliness.

"Your conditions have nothing to do with Basil's will," she said crisply.

Preston shrugged. "But he is dead, and I am alive, and I am your trustee."

"The word *trustee* implies trust."

"You always were clever, my dear. I have no idea why you came all this way to see me. My conditions were clear."

Amelia's lips went white as she glanced again at his friends. "I truly wish to speak of this in private."

"This is private enough."

Michael tasted rage, the same that had kept him alive in places where no one cared that he was the oldest son of a duke or English or rich. Preston wanted witnesses to whatever he planned to do, likely knowing that alone in a tête-à-tête, Amelia could best him.

At the same time, Michael admired the proud tilt of Amelia's head, the glistening coils of dark hair that would be a silken weight when taken down. Ten years and Michael still wanted her with powerful intensity. He wanted her in his bed, her limbs tangled in his sheets, her body opened for him, her lips parted for his kiss.

He saw the same lust reflected in Preston's eyes, and his rage flared.

"I shall make a bargain with you," Preston was saying. He reached to the table next to him and lifted a pack of cards from the green baize surface. "A game of piquet, will that suffice? I know you and Basil loved an evening of piquet."

"What of it?" she asked in suspicion.

"We shall play, and if you win, I will give you your money with all conditions waived. If you lose—you do whatever I say." He let the pack ripple through his fingers. "If you refuse to play, you leave my house as destitute as you entered it."

The man was stupid in his arrogance. It sounded as though Preston was denying her funds from a trust her husband set up for her. She could have a solicitor on him in a heartbeat.

If she could still afford a solicitor—her clothes spoke of genteel poverty with no pennies left over to hire someone to recover her money. Besides many a solicitor or man of business might simply tell her to marry Preston—ladies were supposed to let gentlemen take care of them.

Amelia's shoulders moved with her sharp breath, but she stood her ground. Good for her.

"Very well," she said.

Beneath Michael's rage, he wanted to laugh. She must have noted the same thing he had observed during the weekend house party, that Preston couldn't play cards worth a damn.

Unless, of course, he planned to cheat.

Michael walked forward. Preston's friends noticed him with startled looks and retreated. Michael had a nasty reputation. A man who'd lived in exotic places, disappearing for years altogether, then turned up looking like a gypsy in Eastern garb with a daughter in tow, got talked about. Whispers of duels in Cairo's streets, a Turkish harem, discovery of a great treasure, murder . . .

"An interesting bargain," he said, pretending not to notice Amelia's head jerk around, her azure eyes widen. "Except that you have no head for cards, Lockwood, and you know it. I suggest you let me sit in for you."

Amelia's gasp was audible. So was Preston's. The man probably *had* been meaning to cheat.

"Why should you do this for me?" Preston asked. An excellent question.

"I'd like something in return, of course."

Still Michael did not look at Amelia, who was glaring at him in palpable rage. She hadn't forgiven him yet, and he couldn't blame her one bit.

"What?" Preston asked nervously.

"I will name my price when I've finished the game."

Preston gnawed his lip. He knew damn well Michael was the better player, having lost plenty already to him since the house party began. His indecision was comical.

One of his friends broke in. "We should let the lady decide. Who will you play, Mrs. Lockwood?"

"No, no," Preston said petulantly. "This is my game, and Amelia has agreed to it. Very well, Your Grace, you may take up the cards for me."

He stuck out his hand, not to Amelia, but to Michael. She was a prize, a woman to win, not a person.

Michael took the man's hand, hiding his smile when Preston flinched at his extra-firm grip.

"Done," Michael said.

TWO

Playing for Keeps

This could not be happening. Michael Beaulieu could not be here, looking so brown and exotic, walking back into her life to take over again. He was ten years older, still tall and hard faced, with glittering green eyes and a hawklike nose, still with the arrogant curl to his lip. He was a duke now, a man with a grim reputation, one of the richest and most powerful men in England.

He hadn't changed at all.

She knew she could have bested Preston. Basil had taught Amelia cards so well she could have won and walked away with the two thousand pounds Preston owed her.

Why did Michael have to charge in and guarantee that she'd lose? He didn't like Preston—that was obvious from the derisive way his cool green gaze flicked over him. So why? Did he hate her so much he wished her on Preston? He'd raged at her ten years ago, but the heat in him seemed to have turned to ice.

"Shall you sit, Amelia?" Preston said, pulling out a chair at the card table.

Amelia stared at the chair and his pudgy hand, not wanting to go anywhere near him. Michael smoothly cut him out of the way, gripped Amelia's elbow, and guided her to the seat.

The heat that rushed through her at the contact unnerved her. She hid it by settling herself, trying to draw a calming breath. She'd been tricked into this game, but she determined to play her best and win it. After that she could turn her back on Preston—and Michael—forever.

Michael took the cards Preston handed him, examined them closely and demanded a fresh pack. One of Preston's toadies produced another one, and Michael proceeded to remove the unneeded cards with his strong, tanned fingers.

Amelia remembered those fingers sliding along her bare neck, tilting her face for his kiss the day he'd first come to propose to her. They'd stood in her father's apple orchard, and he'd brushed his lips across the corner of her mouth, tart apple on his breath.

She shut away the memories. She needed her wits to play this game and win it, but watching his calm fingers shuffle the cards, his lashes flicking as he did so, made her mouth dry.

Blast the man for still being so handsome. Preston, the same age as Michael, had a receding hairline, watery eyes, and a stomach going to paunch. How dare Michael still be muscular and tall, his hair wavy and thick, his eyes intense?

Michael set the shuffled pack in front of her. "I will deal. That gives you the advantage."

"No, indeed," she retorted. "We shall cut for it, as per usual."

"As usual? Have you and I played before, Mrs. Lockwood?"

His eyes sparkled as wickedly as ever. Her thoughts flashed to that faraway night she'd made her debut and to Michael cutting across the ballroom while everyone melted before him, his green eyes holding that same look of determination.

She gulped and said hastily, "As is usually done. You know what I mean."

Michael's lips curved into his slight smile, and he gestured for her to cut the deck. Her fingers shook as she exposed her card, the seven of hearts.

Michael drew the jack of clubs, which he showed her with a cool expression. The lower draw became the dealer, because as Michael had said, the dealer was at a disadvantage. The other player got to call his or her points first, and could win the game without laying down a card if he received a good enough hand.

Amelia gathered up the cards, which were still warm from his touch. Shuffling and dealing at least let her regain some of her composure.

The clash between them had been long ago and far away, she told herself. It had ended badly, but both of them had married and become different people. Michael had an eight-year-old daughter, she'd heard, half-French, half-English. A wild child, people said, in outlandish clothes and with no schooling.

"Shall we say the best of five games?" Michael asked calmly as he picked up his cards.

"Yes, yes," Amelia said, flustered.

Each game of piquet went to a hundred points, or *cent*, usually taking several hands to do so. If she could win three games quickly, she could end this ordeal.

Preston and his friends leaned to look as Amelia fanned out her cards. A good hand with quite a few face cards and aces, she noted with satisfaction.

Michael raised his brows as he contemplated his hand. "Carte blanche," he announced.

He meant he had no face cards at all and so received an immediate ten points. Drat.

Michael discarded three cards and picked up three from the pile. Amelia exchanged two.

"A point of four," Michael said once he'd arranged his cards again.

Amelia relaxed a little. He'd just revealed that he had four cards all in one suit, but she had five in the suit of hearts, so he'd get no points for it. "Not good," she said with a little smile.

"A *quart*." That meant he had four in sequence in one suit. Drat again.

"Good," she said glumly, since she didn't have a sequence of four herself. She tried not to grimace as he wrote down four more points.

"*Trio*," he said. "Kings." He had three of a kind of kings, beating her three of a kind of tens.

"Good," she said with a sigh.

In all Michael began the game with nearly twenty more points than she had. But that was simply the luck of the deal. When the real play began, she had all kinds of strategies to best him. She'd learned the game well—in the long winter nights with Basil there had not been much else to do.

Michael laid down his first card, the ten of hearts. She countered with the jack and took both cards. Despite the desperation of her situation and her old rage at Michael rekindling, she felt the tingle of competition, the love of the game. She wanted to win, and not simply to gain the money Preston owed her.

She caught the glint of challenge in Michael's eyes. He felt the same drive, the same need to win. No, he hadn't changed a bit. But she would show him that she was up to his challenge now, and match him.

His brows twitched as she continued to win cards from him. Despite burying herself in the soggy countryside while he roamed the sun-soaked deserts of Egypt, she could hold her own. She'd make him know that.

"You play well," he remarked. "Your husband taught you?"

"I taught *him* a thing or two, Your Grace."

A smile touched his mouth. "I believe you, Mrs. Lockwood."

Her face heated. "I can't imagine you played much piquet with Arab sheikhs."

"You would be wrong. I became friends with a sheikh who

loved whist and piquet and other such games. We spent many a night in play."

And the sheikh had a harem, I believe. Gossip surrounding Michael and his exploits had been fierce.

Michael's eyes glinted as though he guessed what she was thinking. She snapped her attention back to her cards.

"I cannot imagine what possessed you to play, Your Grace. Or what your prize will be. Something sufficiently humiliating?"

He laid down his last card, a seven of spades. "Would I humiliate you, Mrs. Lockwood?"

"You would," she said as she took the last trick and wrote down her points. "I knew you well, Michael."

He chuckled, a dry sound like the sands of the Arabian dunes. "Then you will have to play your best. I intend to win."

He would not make it easy for her, and he would not be intimidated. He'd sit there warming her blood with his smiles and his green eyes, and he would give her no quarter. No, he hadn't changed a bit.

She picked up her cards and tried not to grimace. Not as good a hand, but she could do something with it.

The curious, gaping guests surrounded them, but Amelia's focus narrowed to the cards and Michael's hands and body across the table. Diamonds, spades, hearts, clubs—and Michael's strong fingers and his green, green eyes.

His skin had burned brown, with white patches in the corners of his eyes as though he'd become accustomed to squinting in the sun. His shoulders were broad under his formal coat, the material stretching as though his body wanted to burst out of it. No doubt he'd gotten used to Turkish dress—loose trousers, robes, and turbans.

She imagined him standing under the bright sky, wind molding his clothing to his body. She remembered how hard his muscles had been, tight under his English clothes. He'd always worn the softest, most expensive cashmere evening coats, heaven for her to run her fingers along as he escorted her from dance floors.

Everyone had thought they'd be a match. Michael, in his consummate arrogance, had taken it for granted, and he'd walked over everyone, including Amelia herself, to get it. In his own way, he'd been as bad as Preston. And here he was, taking over her life again.

"Four," Amelia said coolly, fanning out her cards.

"Not good." The corners of his mouth turned up.

Damn.

"*Tierce,*" she tried again—a sequence of three in a suit.

"Not good."

"*Quatorze.*" Four of a kind, worth fourteen points.

"Not good."

She gave an exasperated sigh. "Is anything good?"

His glance was wicked. "You tell me."

"Save the banter for your club, Your Grace, please."

"I have to take my banter where I can get it. White's does not approve of my appearance or my friends."

She glanced at him curiously as he wrote down his points. "You are a duke. Certainly they would forgive you looking like a barbarian."

"Oh, they'd never deny me membership. But the old gentlemen put their quizzing glasses to their eyes as though I were something they stepped in. One is not allowed to be too exotic."

He meant that he'd not been forgiven for turning his back on his father and country to live in Arab lands in a tent with goats. And a harem. And then turning up again looking rather like a wild sheikh himself. She could imagine the conservative old gentlemen at White's rather looking at him askance.

He won that hand, and the game, reaching a hundred points before she did. They started another, tension tightening inside her.

The room quieted as they played hand after hand, Amelia creeping ahead in points, then Michael matching and pulling ahead. It would be close.

If she'd played Preston, she would have won by now, and she knew Michael knew that. He betrayed it with every glance, every satisfied smile when he wrote down his points. He played with the intensity and patience of a man stalking wild game, not about to give up until he got what he wanted, just like he had ten years ago.

By the time they reached the hand that would win the last game, all of Preston's guests and most of the servants had gathered to watch. Michael had won two games, and Amelia had won two. It fell to Michael to deal, so Amelia would call her points first.

Her hand was good. She had plenty of face cards, but not all of them, so Michael would not have carte blanche. She had four clubs and four diamonds, four queens, and four nines.

She called her points, and at almost every declaration, Michael said, "Good," which meant he didn't have better. She started with thirty-six points to his ten.

She laid down the first card, her nine of hearts. He lost by laying down the seven. Her heart beat faster as she laid down her next nine.

Michael played cannily, getting rid of his low cards and enticing her to lay down her high cards so that he could save his best for last. He kept glancing at her, his green eyes hard. Preston leaned over the table until his nose nearly brushed Michael's cards, and Michael turned impatiently away from him.

Amelia laid down her last card, the queen of hearts. Michael had already played the ace, so he couldn't top it with that. Eight cards lay in the discard pile, untouched. If Michael did not have the king, she'd win a point for the trick plus a point for taking the last trick, which would push her to one hundred and let her win the game.

But if Michael had the king, he'd win the trick and the game, and enough points to take him past one hundred. Preston would win, and she'd either be tied to the bloody man or destitute. Was this Michael's revenge, served cold after ten years?

Michael smiled at her, and her blood turned to ice. It was the smile of a man who'd cornered his prey, who was about to see the fruition of nights of patient stalking.

Preston pressed a chubby hand to his mouth. The rest of the room held its breath.

With a negligent flip, Michael turned over his last card.

The eight of clubs.

Amelia had won.

THREE

Michael's Price

"No," Preston cried in anguish. "Oh, damn you, Bretherton, you told me you played better than I do."

"And I do." Michael turned from Amelia, whose red-lipped mouth hung open in astonishment, and pinned Preston with a hard look. "But the lady played like fire. I believe you owe her a sum of money. Will you take a bank draft, Amelia?"

Her chest in the ugly dress rose sharply. "What? Oh, of course. A draft will do."

Preston was spitting fury. "Not fair . . ."

Michael stood up, easily topping him by a foot. "The game is finished. You gambled and lost. A gentleman pays his debts or faces ruin."

Preston's face mottled red. Michael guessed that if any other man had implied that Preston wouldn't—or couldn't—pay, he'd find himself called out. But the Duke of Bretherton was a dangerous man, and everyone knew it. "Very well," he almost whispered.

The crowd drew apart, voices swelling as they talked about

what had just happened. Gossip would spread like wildfire to every corner of England by tomorrow.

Michael put his hand under Amelia's arm and firmly guided her from her chair. She came unresisting at first, then as her wits returned, she glared at him and tried to wrench away.

"No," he said in her ear. "We are leaving. Now."

Without giving her time to argue, he propelled her to the nearest door, through the anteroom beyond, and out into the main hall. By the time he heard a query rise in the drawing room, he had Amelia down the stairs and out the front door, a footman chasing them with their wraps.

Fog swirled across the gravel drive, cold and dank even in summer. Michael's valet, Merriman, ever watchful, sprinted away to fetch the chaise.

Amelia remained rigid beside him, not arguing or making a scene, though she had a perfect right to. Only when the carriage halted in front of them, its door emblazoned with the ancient Bretherton crest, did she speak. "What about my two thousand pounds?"

"Was it that much?" he demanded. "Bloody idiot."

A footman wrenched open the carriage door and jerked the stairs down. Michael half-guided, half-pushed Amelia into the vehicle, then leapt in beside her and let the footman slam the door.

"Don't worry about your money," he said. "I'll see that Preston has it delivered into your account."

Amelia pulled her shawl closer, hiding the dress, but it didn't do much good, because the shawl was just as hideous. She regarded him with blue eyes that could still take his breath away, even though there was as much anger in them now as a decade ago.

"You cheated," she said.

He assumed an innocent expression. "I beg your pardon?"

"You let me win the game. Why did you?"

To keep Preston's filthy hands off you, he wanted to say.

"Nonsense, you are an excellent player," he answered, keeping his voice calm.

Her warm presence next to him was distracting. He longed to flatten her against the carriage wall and slant his mouth over hers, but he knew he had to go carefully or he'd lose her again.

"At the end of the game, you had the king of hearts," she said. "Preston tried to look into your hand so you turned away. I saw it." She gave him a piercing look. "But when you put down the card, it had miraculously become the eight of clubs."

"Had it? How extraordinary."

"You cheated, Michael."

He gave her a cool look. "You would have preferred Preston to win?"

"If you had let me play him without interfering, I could have easily won."

He shook his head, voice going hard. "No, you would not have. He would have cheated, far more egregiously than I did. I wanted to make certain you walked away with your two thousand pounds."

She stared at him with lips parted, her face dull red in the shadows.

He brushed his thumb over the back of her gloved hand, pleased that she started at the pressure. "Before you try to steel yourself to express gratitude, I should tell you my price."

"But you lost the game."

"I never said my price was a condition of my winning. It was a condition of playing in Preston's place."

"You quibble. . . ."

"I always choose my words carefully. My price is you, Amelia."

The carriage jerked on the rutted road, and Michael caught her, her body pressing satisfactorily against his. Her blue eyes were sinfully beautiful. She'd make a wonderful mistress, a woman made to pleasure a man. He knew she'd shoot him before she'd agree to that, but what richness to teach her. . . .

"No," she said. "I won't let you do this to me again."

"You need me," he said in a rough voice. "I know your husband died and left you dependent on Preston. I know Preston wants not just money but you. I know you have no protection."

"I have my two thousand pounds."

To a man of Michael's wealth, it seemed a pathetically small sum. "Which will not last forever."

She sat rigidly within his embrace. "You have not given up, have you? You have walked back into my life as determined to take it over as before. Only this time, you find me in a much more precarious place."

"I don't want you to be," he said swiftly. "That is why I'm offering you marriage. Be my wife, Amelia. As you should have been all those years ago."

She stared at him with eyes he'd not forgotten in all his travels and adventures, his exploits, his women. Being this close to her made him ache like fury. The surprise of seeing her, the joy of discovering she was as beautiful and irrepressible as ever, and realizing that his wanting had never gone away, had pushed his body to the breaking point. He needed release and relief.

"Marry me now," he said. "You need a place to live, I need a wife to keep every ambitious mama in London away from me. My daughter needs a mother. We will help each other."

"Very convenient," she said, voice shaking.

Of course it was convenient. It was an excuse to have her come home with him on the moment. He needed . . . something. He was swimming in chaos and searching for an anchor, to what, he did not know.

"Say yes, Amelia."

Her dark brows climbed. "I see ten years in the Arabian deserts has not dampened your arrogance."

"It wasn't all in the Arabian deserts. I spent some time in Greece and Russia, as well."

"We wander from the point. Where are you taking me?" She

peered through the glass at the fog, but night had fallen, and there was nothing to see but swirling mist.

"To London. I have a house there."

"Ah, the monstrosity in Park Lane. I read of it in the newspaper."

"The Bishop of London is a friend of mine. He will give us a special license and marry us tonight."

"What if he is not at home?"

"Then we'll wait for him."

She moved a little, which brushed the side of her breast against him. "Why are you doing this to me?"

"Because I want to keep you from the clutches of idiots like Preston Lockwood. I will give you money and position and leave you the hell alone if that's what you want."

"What I want is something I can't have."

Michael didn't like the bleak note in her voice. He couldn't stop himself catching her face in his hands. "Let me do this, Amelia. Let me make up to you for what I did. You will have the power of my name and a hell of a lot more than your two thousand pounds. You might hate me, but I don't care."

He couldn't read what flickered through her eyes. Perhaps it was anger at him, perhaps at Preston for driving her into this corner. Clearly he'd stirred up the passion and the rage that had swirled inside the beautiful Amelia ten years ago, because her eyes flashed fire.

"All right then, Michael," she said. "I will marry you."

He tasted triumph, but Amelia didn't look one bit cowed. Michael realized, as the carriage entered the streets of London, that he might have won the game, but the battle between them had just begun.

TWO nights later, Amelia lay in her bed in Michael's exotic house, alone. Michael had married her at the bishop's house after his proposal then brought her home to Park Lane and left her there, bidding his housekeeper to look after her.

Amelia wasn't certain what she'd expected—at the very least for him to try to come to her bed. He hadn't disguised his triumph that he'd gotten her into his power after ten years of waiting, but then he'd gone off in the night and hadn't returned.

The servants who'd come with the house when Michael bought it from another peer seemed relieved Amelia had arrived. They didn't know quite what to make of a duke who filled his home with foreign curios but never stayed to enjoy them. Even his daughter didn't live there, stopping with some of Michael's friends in Cheshire.

"I don't know what I feared when Merriman told me His Grace had brought home a wife," the housekeeper confided. "A wild woman from Egypt or an African native, I thought. But when I brought your tray in the morning, there you were, quite sensible and English. Begging your pardon, Your Grace."

To Amelia's dismay she learned that Michael had turned the running of the household entirely over to her, and the staff now wouldn't do a thing without Amelia's say-so. She sensed quickly that they needed her to tell them what to do, because Michael had never given them any guidance.

Not that he'd given her any, either.

She sat up in bed that third night, unable to sleep. She'd thought Michael wanted her—*her*—as he had ten years ago when he'd run roughshod over everyone to get her. But that was long ago, they were both much older now, and perhaps he'd simply decided to assuage his guilt at finding her dependent on someone like Preston by giving her a respectable marriage. He'd said in the carriage he needed someone to look after his house and daughter and keep matchmakers away from him, and he'd apparently meant it.

She thought of the stories of his harem and wondered if he'd found the equivalent in London—perhaps that was what kept him from home. *I have no business being jealous*, she thought. She'd made the cold decision in the carriage to marry Michael for safety, accepting him, faults and all.

So why was she fuming that Michael ignored her? Plenty of women would love a husband who gave them as much money as they wanted and the running of the household, then stayed out from underfoot.

She swung back the covers and got out of bed, feet finding her slippers. At least Michael's house was interesting, filled with exotic gold, ebony, and bejeweled curiosities from Egypt, Arabia, Greece, and Africa.

She could lose herself studying them, items from a world she'd never see. Michael didn't lock things away behind cases—the entire house was strewn with them, including a gold bust of a beautiful Egyptian woman on the stair landing.

Halfway down the hall she heard a noise from Michael's bedroom. Her bedroom was not next to his; his was two doors from the top of the landing, hers farther back in the wing. He'd never take a chamber right next to the landing, because he'd always been slightly nervous about heights. That little fact made him more human to her, one of the only things that did. The rest of him was pure arrogant aristocrat, expecting to be master of everything.

A vertical slit of candlelight showed that his door was ajar. A soft groan reached her, and she froze.

She knew what the sound meant—she'd been married, with married servants in a house with thin walls. Dear God, he hadn't brought one of his harem *here,* had he? But that would be Michael all over, a man who did what he wanted and said *damn your eyes* to anyone who got in his way.

Amelia crept to the door and put her eye to the inch-wide crack. Michael was alone and naked. He stood at a right angle to the door, one foot propped on a gilded chair.

Firelight kissed his brown skin, gleaming off the curve of muscle from shoulder to waist. The flickering light touched his hip and a tight round of backside that she longed to brush with her fingers. Would his skin feel as smooth as it looked?

A lovely, lovely view for any woman, but no woman watched but Amelia.

His hand was moving on the length of his cock, his fingers snapping against his palm as he completed each stroke. His face twisted with the feel of it, his brows drawn as though he were in pain. His sun-streaked dark hair grazed his shoulders as he tilted his head back.

Heat flared through Amelia's veins. She'd never seen a man do this, had heard of it denounced as an abomination and a sin. But no one who watched Michael's tall, hard body sway in pleasure as he pumped himself through his fist could call him an abomination.

He continued to pull on his shaft, which was thick and dark and shining with oil. She wanted to touch him. Her arrogant, high-handed Michael, a man who took what he wanted, regardless, who had stormed back into her life and taken over. She should hate him, be glad he left her alone, and instead, she was dying to touch him. She caught her breath.

At the tiny sound Michael's eyes snapped open. He looked straight at the crack in the door then turned around, betraying no panic that he'd been caught.

"Amelia," he said, letting go of himself and reaching for his dressing gown. "Please come in."

FOUR

Lessons in the Night

Amelia pushed open the door and slipped inside, closing it all the way behind her. She stopped in front of him, while he gazed down at her with green eyes that hid his emotions. Almost.

She shouldn't want to touch him. She wanted to keep hating him with the fierce, sharp anger she'd carried since that day in the apple orchard. But it was an old wound, and he was her husband now, and he belonged to her. Wonderful thought that this beautiful male was *hers*.

She caught a flash of uncertainty as she pushed open the lapels of the robe and put her hand on his heated skin. He was like a living statue, every muscle in perfect proportion, a gift from a divine artist. His dusting of golden-brown curls caught on her fingers, and she felt the hard ridges of his pectorals, the tight point of his nipple.

He groaned and seized her hands. "Stop."

Not what he'd said in her father's orchard. Then he hadn't wanted to stop for anything.

"Amelia." He squeezed her fingers. "You should go back to bed."

"I find that I don't much want to," she said.

"I am a wicked, wicked man. You know that." He lifted her fingers to his mouth. "And I will want wicked, wicked things. Things you never dreamed of."

She swallowed, the heat of his lips unnerving. "I had a husband. I know about . . . the marriage bed."

"You see, you can't even say it. It isn't the marriage bed I want, Amelia, a dutiful wife doing what she must. I want your body. Nothing less than all of it, to touch, to pleasure." He leaned closer. "To fuck."

Her chest constricted. No one but Michael had ever said that word in her presence, would ever dream of saying it *to* her.

"My poor love," he said. "I am corrupt from head to foot, and you are innocence itself. Perhaps I should have left you alone."

His eyes were cool and unreadable. He could go from warm and smiling to cold as ice in a heartbeat.

Before she could stop herself, she asked, "Are these wicked things what you learned in your harem?"

He gave her an incredulous look, then the frost left his eyes and he laughed. "Ah, the harem story. It is trotted out whenever I leave a room."

"Is it true?"

"No, my dear. In Arab countries a man is expected to care for, feed, and clothe every wife and concubine he obtains. If I had such an entourage, I certainly couldn't have left them behind. I'd have been responsible for them." He gave her a wink. "Tell no one. I enjoy hearing the stories."

"Oh."

"You sound disappointed. Have I lost allure because I didn't bed fifteen women at once?"

Her face heated. "Of course not. Don't be ridiculous."

"Funny thing about gossip, my love. While everyone is slavering over shocking stories without a grain of truth, they miss the true stories, which are much, much worse."

She sensed darkness close behind his amusement. "What stories?" she asked, curious in spite of herself.

"I will tell you someday. Stories that will curl your hair." He touched the ringlets at her forehead. "Suffice it to say I learned all manner of things. From women—and from men."

It was tempting to slip back to the old days, when he flirted with her and teased her mercilessly, and she flirted shamelessly back. Being the center of his attention had been heady, and if she wasn't careful, she'd be the same oblivious fool again.

"It is a spectre, is it not?" she asked softly. "What is between us? I vowed I'd never forgive you."

His amusement abruptly died. "Damn. I always did admire your forthrightness."

"We are both older now, less impetuous. We should talk about it, and clear the air."

He growled. "No, we shouldn't. I was young and an idiot. You bested me despite all I tried, if you remember, and I slunk away with my tail between my legs. End of the matter."

"And yet here I am—your wife."

His green eyes glittered. "Is that what you think this is, a perverse form of revenge?"

"You did seem happy at the bishop's house, once the deed was done. Triumphant even."

"Who the hell wouldn't be? You were the most beautiful woman in all of England, and you haven't changed an iota. Everyone wanted you, and you condescended to let *me* kiss you. Can you blame me for beating off the rest of the pack to get to you? And now, finally, I have you."

She flushed under his flattery, remembering. What woman wouldn't have been swept away by the attentions of handsome Lord Michael Beaulieu, heir to a dukedom? He'd been the most eligible bachelor in England, and Amelia had been proud to catch his eye.

Pride. Her downfall. When she realized all he had done to get her, that she was his prize, her happiness had turned to ashes.

She'd been lucky that Basil Lockwood was able to marry her right away.

Now Michael had caught her, and who was to say he was any different, even after ten years? He'd certainly heaved Preston aside and dragged her away, taking over her life as surely as he had taken it over long ago.

His hands were hard on her shoulders, but she refused to fear him. She touched his chest again, tracing his fascinating nipple with her fingertip.

His eyes darkened. "You have no idea how seductive you are, do you?"

She looked up at him. "In a cotton night rail and woolly slippers?"

"Especially in that, little innocent. You are still innocent, aren't you? You went to your husband's bed, of course, but did he teach you?"

Amelia thought about Basil, his hesitation and shyness. Basil never would have dreamed of standing straight and tall and naked in his bedroom, running his fist around his own shaft.

"Did you love him?" Michael asked, his voice low and rough.

Basil had taken care of her, given her peace of mind. He hadn't been an overly affectionate man, but he'd been a good one.

"Yes," she said.

"Good. I'm glad you did. I don't expect you to love me, but I want you to let me love you. To teach you."

Her heart thumped. "Teach me what?"

"This." He parted the velvet robe and let it slither to the floor.

Amelia gulped. Michael was strong and beautiful, his sun-bronzed skin so unusual in gray England. She imagined him standing on desert sands, letting the sun kiss his body with its morning light, a wild and beautiful man England had never been able to tame.

She let her gaze run over him, from the unshaven whiskers on his chin, down the chest dusted with gold hair to his hard abdomen and the long, thick member below it. She'd never before seen a man's stem. Basil had always come to her in the dark, and the act had been quick, sweaty, and unremarkable. Basil had been a kind man but lacked the raw sensuality of Michael.

Michael's shaft lifted straight from his body toward her. It was long and hard, still gleaming with the oil he'd slicked on it, dark red and moving a little with his pulse. The flange was a soft ridge, the tip with a fascinating slit that for some bizarre reason she wanted to lick.

"Touch it," he said.

His half-smile told her he didn't think she'd do it, but she refused to be timid. This was her marriage as well as his.

She reached out and brushed one finger over the hot skin of his shaft.

Michael groaned, the cold entirely deserting his eyes. "Are you trying to kill me?" He took her hand and wrapped it around his length, his strong fingers making her hold him fast. "Either touch me with certainty or not at all. Else I might explode."

It was like holding the thick branch of a tree, but one hot and alive. His erection lay heavily in her palm, his skin smooth and fiery hot.

"Show me," she said.

He moved her hand, his firm fingers on top of hers. "Like that."

It was strange to be standing here in the firelight, with him bare, his dressing gown like a puddle of darkness on the floor. The two of them together after ten long years, but instead of arguing about what had gone on before, they stood in the firelight while she stroked him in silence.

She touched him as he showed her, liking the warm, sleek feel of him. The wiry hair at his base curled around her fingers, the tip watery smooth against her hand.

"You see?" she breathed. "Not so innocent."

"You are." His words were soft on her face. "I know you've never touched a man before."

"Well not—*here*."

"Not where? Say the word, Amelia. Remember the one I taught you long ago?"

She recalled the wicked lessons he'd given her in the orchard. He'd made her feel naughty, whispering words in her ear to make her blush. Rather than being ashamed she'd delighted in it.

He leaned his forehead against hers. "Say it, Amelia."

"Cock," she whispered.

His groan was louder, and suddenly her arms were full of his tall, naked body.

FIVE

The Taste of Pleasure

God, he loved the taste of sweet, sweet woman, her innocent mouth that formed the naughty word. He'd desired Amelia when he'd been twenty and she eighteen, but that was nothing to how much he wanted her now.

Amelia wore nothing under her night rail, a fact that made his body throb. He opened her mouth with his, forcing his tongue inside, and she didn't resist.

He raked his hands through her hair, pulling apart the braid, loving the satin feel in his fingers. He wanted to lay naked beneath her and have her spill her hair over him. He wanted her astride him, her eyes half-closed in pleasure, her hair falling around them like a curtain.

Too fast. She'd never even kissed like this before. He could tell she wasn't used to a man licking the roof of her mouth, running his tongue along her teeth.

"Suckle me," he said against her lips.

"What?"

"Suck my tongue."

He licked her full bottom lip then pushed his tongue into her mouth. She tentatively sucked the tip.

"Mmm." He pressed the nape of her neck, encouraging her. She suckled some more, starting to understand.

He kneaded her back with his hands, splaying open the braid until her hair tumbled loose. His cock responded to her working mouth as though she sucked there instead.

He broke the kiss and smiled. "Like that. Did you enjoy it?"

"Yes," she said.

"This is why I am a wicked man, Amelia. I've learned so many things since you last saw me, and I don't want to stop until you know them all."

She looked dazed but also intrigued. "What sorts of things?"

"Are you afraid of me?"

"Of course I am not."

"That only betrays your ignorance." He undid the top buttons of her night rail, trying to ignore the warm scent of her beneath.

She reached for him again, her lips poised to take his. She wanted to learn.

Instead of kissing her, he yanked the nightgown open to her waist, making her gasp. He rested his hand between her breasts, feeling her heart beating swift and hard.

"You can tell me to stop," he said. "You can tell me you wish to go back to your room. The door is unlocked, the way open."

"I don't want you to stop."

"But you don't know what I'll want to do."

She drew a breath. "If you go too far, then I will tell you to stop."

He leaned his forehead to hers and gave her a feral smile. "It doesn't work that way. I might not be able to stop until too late. A wise woman would leave now."

"I am your wife, Michael. I am supposed to share your bed."

"*Share my bed.*" He wanted to laugh. "Sharing a bed implies something calm and tame. What I want to do is neither calm nor tame, and it doesn't necessarily involve a bed."

He kissed the side of her neck, drawing her skin between his teeth in a gentle love bite. She made a small noise in her throat that drove him on. She might hate him for what he did all those years ago, but she couldn't resist him now.

He licked the hollow of her throat, kissing his way lower to her full breasts.

When he'd kissed her in the orchard, he'd licked the tops of her breasts where her stays had pushed them above her lace-lined bodice. He still remembered the color of the lace—pale yellow with patterns of roses.

Ten years later, her breasts were fuller and rounder, the nipples as large as copper coins. He licked the heat between them, then sucked one nipple into his mouth.

She tasted of warmth and velvet, salt and goodness. Her nipple filled his mouth, the tip hard against his tongue as he suckled her.

Amelia pulled him to her, letting him suck and nip and lick as much as he wanted. The more he tasted the more he wanted.

He slid his hand between her legs, pressing her quim through the cloth. She wasn't ready for all he wanted to do, play his fingers through her hair, tease her button, slide his fingers into her cleft.

But they had the rest of the night. He had an appointment with his man of business at ten the next morning—until then he was free to teach Amelia.

"Michael," she murmured. "Why were you touching yourself before I came in? I've heard that men do that, but I never truly believed it."

He smiled into her skin. "I needed release, knowing you were down the hall, sleeping, all warm and delectable. I was burning."

"You were?"

"My love I've waited a decade to have you. Of course I'm burning."

He wanted her in the worst way, but this time he wasn't going to be stupid about it. Last time he'd expected her to fall to his feet in gratitude, like the fool he'd been. This time he'd teach her slowly and carefully, like taming a bird to his hand or a spirited horse to trust him.

"I liked watching you," she said, flushing. She didn't want to like it, but she couldn't help herself.

Michael warmed. She'd always been a woman of fire, daring and eager, and if he hadn't been an arrogant idiot, he could have had her warming him every night of his life.

"Did you, love? Would you like to help me release?"

She gave him a curious look. "How?"

"You learned to suckle my tongue. Would you like to do that to my cock?"

Her gaze dropped to his still rampant organ, bare and waiting. She wasn't a shy woman, thank God. Her hesitation had to do with her past anger at him, her anger at finding herself bound to him again, not maidenly jitters.

"I think so," she whispered.

"Be certain. You choose."

Amelia stepped away from him, her night rail open to the waist, revealing the lush, beautiful woman inside. Her hair was a mess, her eyes large and dark. "Yes."

His whole body pounded. "Come over here then."

Michael led her to the bed. A padded bench with scrolled arms stretched across the foot of it, a handy place to sit down and put on one's boots. He made better use of it now.

He seated Amelia on it, facing him, and stood in front of her. Her gaze fixed gratifyingly on his stem, its tip pointed to her lips. She might still hate him, but his body fascinated her.

When he released her shoulders, she leaned forward and tentatively kissed his tip.

White heat flashed through him at the butterfly touch, and he clenched his fists until his nails creased his palms. God, what she could do to him. He wanted to fuck her mouth, then lay her back on the bed and drive into her. He wanted her to scream for him, to run her nails down his back and twine her legs behind him while he pumped himself into her.

But her eyes as she contemplated him stopped him. She was not a practiced courtesan or a woman to be used. She was Amelia, his first love, the most beautiful debutante in London, the woman he'd move heaven and earth for.

He would protect her from everyone and most of all from himself.

"Lick it," he said, his voice raw. "Get used to me."

She ran her tongue around his tip, her touch light, and he couldn't stifle a groan.

She pulled back a little. "Do you like that?"

"Yes," he said tightly.

Amelia gave a satisfied smile, a woman learning her power. That was what she never understood, how much power she had over him, how much she always had. She'd thought herself overpowered by him, but she hadn't realized how much the reverse was true.

She blew lightly where her tongue had moistened him—an odd sensation, but he liked it.

She licked him again, becoming bolder. She held him steady with her fingertips while she learned him a little at a time.

"You taste . . ." She leaned back while she thought. "Like buttercream."

"Buttercream?" He wanted to laugh. "Are you sure? I don't recall being iced like a pastry." Although that gave him some fine ideas. . . .

"Not exactly like it *tastes*. But smooth and satisfying. How it *feels*."

"I think I like that."

She continued her exploration. He watched her eyes as her gaze flicked over him, her mouth as her red tongue licked and teased and tickled. As she became bolder, she leaned forward and nipped his tip, her teeth sharp.

Michael sucked in his breath. "Dear God, Amelia."

"Did I hurt you? I don't know, you see, how sensitive . . ."

He stilled her words by circling her lips with his tip. "Take me," he begged. *"Please."*

Mystified, she parted her lips and let him ease inside her mouth.

Slowly, he growled at himself. *Don't hurt her.*

At first she merely held him inside her mouth, her tongue moving on him as it had when she'd licked him. He let her do that for a while, closing his eyes with the intensity of it. He so needed this woman.

"Suck," he said softly. "Like you did when you kissed me."

She did, gently pulling him. His head rocked back of its own accord, his body arching hungrily to her, as though he'd never felt the like.

He'd had women. While the harem story was an exaggeration, Michael had never wanted for female company, before or after his marriage. A young, wealthy Englishman abroad attracted attention, and he'd let himself drown in it. Satisfying his body helped him forget that Amelia hated him, that she'd had very good reason to hate him.

But when he'd seen her two nights ago, standing like a proud angel in Preston Lockwood's house, it hit him in his gut that he'd never stopped wanting her. Ten years, and his longing hadn't ceased.

He never truly meant to coerce her into this room and have her sitting at the bottom of the bed sucking on his cock. But, damn, he was glad he had.

He threaded his fingers through her hair, stopping himself from thrusting hard into her mouth. A man didn't do that to his newlywed bride. And right now, in this darkened place, Amelia was his world.

She knew how to pleasure him, in her innocent way. Tongue and lips working, fingers stroking him, she explored from his tip to his tight balls. Urgency rose in him, and he wanted to come. The thought of her swallowing him down was unbelievably erotic, but no. . . .

No.

He wrenched himself out of her mouth, leaving her staring in shock, and grabbed the towel he'd brought for his own relief. Wrapping it around himself, he shuddered into it, releasing his seed.

Amelia's shocked look turned to disappointment. "Oh, then we will not be able to complete . . ."

Dear God, what kind of man had Basil Lockwood been? Michael swept Amelia off the bench and deposited her on the bed. She landed with a thump, her hair swinging, her face flushed in confusion.

Her night rail slid from her shoulders, baring her chest and upper arms, a lovely, lovely woman. He could tup her all night, and be instantly randy for more.

"How could a man be anything but ready for you?" he asked her. "Take off the nightdress and get under the covers, my sweet wife."

He tossed aside the towel and raked back the covers. She hesitated a short moment then skimmed off her night rail and burrowed quickly under the blankets.

Michael climbed in beside her, tangling his legs in hers. He liked the feel of her smooth hips and thighs backing into his, the curve of her waist under his hand. He spooned her into him and nibbled her ear.

"A good way to share a bed, I think."

She looked over her shoulder, not saying anything, but Michael sensed what she was thinking.

"Don't worry love," he said. "I only want to make you feel what you made me feel. You don't have to do a thing."

She looked mystified. He realized she had no idea what he meant, had no idea what sweet release was. His estimation of her husband dropped another notch.

He wrapped one arm firmly about her waist so she couldn't wriggle away, then eased his hand between her legs. He used the back of his thumb to tease her berry until it swelled, feeling her warm to him.

She gasped, but in delight. "What are you doing?"

He chuckled in her ear. "That's pleasure, love. Sweet, pure pleasure. Want me to do more?"

"Yes, please," she said, her voice breaking.

He rubbed and tickled her, first gently then with more power. She opened to him like a flower, her body arching to his touch, her gasps turning to moans of delight.

She was wet and slick as his fingers glided and danced, her hair at her cleft thick and warm. Some daring women shaved themselves for their lovers—his wife had—but he liked Amelia's wiry hair, which tickled his fingers.

He took her to climax, and when she reached it, he knew she didn't understand what was happening. Her eyes opened in surprise, and she bucked and rubbed against his hand, her body knowing what it wanted.

He rolled her onto her back, his body also knowing what it wanted. Michael thrust himself quickly inside her, no need to ready her. Her gasps turned to sobs of need, and he caught the cries in his mouth.

A few more thrusts and her tight, hot body did its work. He squeezed his eyes shut and spilled his seed for the second time that night.

"Michael." Amelia looked at him, eyes wide, as though needing him to explain.

He withdrew, spooning her against him once more. "Hush, love," he said. "Time to sleep."

She said nothing, but her hand tightened on his. The look she gave him with her beautiful eyes nearly broke his heart. He kissed her cheek, then lay down behind her, holding her close.

Whether she fell asleep immediately or not, he never knew, because oblivion took him almost at once. The release of being with Amelia had been greater than any he'd ever had, and it left him exhausted.

When he awoke in the morning, Merriman was throwing back the velvet drapes, letting sunshine stream through the windows.

Michael sat up in bed, seeing nothing in it but scattered pillows. Amelia had gone.

"She's 'aving breakfast, guv," Merriman said, his dark eyes twinkling. He threw the dressing gown at Michael. "She looks neat as a pin. I'd say ye need to do better next time."

AMELIA was determined to say nothing to Michael when he entered the breakfast room. Not one word, not one look to bring to mind the way she'd screamed in his bed.

She'd never experienced anything like it. The time spent in his bedroom last night taught her that she'd not known what bodily relations with a man truly were.

What she'd had with Basil had been . . . nothing. The entire act had embarrassed him, and he'd avoided it whenever he could. She realized that now.

Michael embraced it wholeheartedly. He'd shown her what she believed in her heart to be true—that bed did not have to be humiliating or shaming. It could be beautiful and joyous.

She purported to hate Michael, angry at how he'd ruined her life and sent her running from him. But she knew that she'd never fallen out of love with him, and now that Michael had returned to take over her life, she was letting him.

Amelia heaped her plate with food from the sideboard, finding herself exceedingly hungry. She'd seated herself and started in when Michael entered.

She looked up, her fork stopping halfway to her mouth. Last night he'd been naked and untamed; this morning he was every inch an aristocrat. His black suit hugged his trim body in a fine feature of tailoring, the ivory moiré waistcoat emphasizing his narrow waist.

His large hands bore only two rings, the signet ring of the Duke of Bretherton on his right and a wedding band, one of a pair he'd given her the night of their hasty marriage—Merriman had been dispatched to fetch them for the ceremony—on his left. The twin band resting on Amelia's hand felt suddenly heavy.

On his way to the sideboard, Michael said, "Good morning, my dear," and pressed a kiss to the top of her head. Loading his plate with food, he took his place on the other end of the table.

The ostentatious dining room was so huge that he sat a long way from her. Floor-to-ceiling windows with lace curtains looked out toward Hyde Park, giving the house a countrified feel in the middle of the city.

Michael leafed through a newspaper the correct butler had deposited on the table, like any other husband would do of a morning. Her man in the night with the wicked eyes had gone.

"Sleep well?" he asked behind the newspaper.

Amelia nearly choked on her buttered toast. She put it down and wiped her mouth. "Yes."

A page turned softly. "You rose early."

"I had many things to do."

"As do I. Much business that will take me all the way to the City and back."

Amelia looked at her plate. He'd disappeared from the house for two days and now he was leaving again. There was so much between them they needed to say, but she had such a horror of becoming a scolding fishwife that she remained silent.

At the other end of the table, Michael suddenly threw down the newspaper and got to his feet. "I can't do this."

Amelia looked up in surprise. "Do what?"

"Behave like the country parson and his wife." He stalked to her end of the table, scraped back a chair, and sat down, leaning elbows on knees. "As though there is no passion between us. All the time I keep imagining you licking butter from my naked body."

SIX

A Visit to a Man of Business

$\mathbf{A}$melia went hot. "There would not be much left for the toast."

He laughed, the exotic man with the sinful green eyes returning. "I would not give a damn."

Amelia was not used to desire, not used to anything but the ordinary. No one in Basil Lockwood's house had ever expressed emotion; even Preston, as sniveling as he was, had been merely annoying. No dramatics.

Michael displayed all his emotions; he always had. He might claim he'd run through his wild oats out in the world and was ready to settle down in England again, but she saw that deep down he hadn't changed.

He'd quit England in rage, had married a woman and watched her die, had sired a child. But still he smiled at Amelia with the recklessness of his boyhood, the recklessness that had caused their parting.

She wondered what his marriage had been like. His wife had been Russian, she'd heard, the youngest daughter of a baron or some such, who'd run away from home. She'd married Michael in a far-flung Baltic province and fled with him to Alexandria.

Michael leaned forward and kissed her, a long, passionate kiss that tasted of marmalade and coffee. Fire stirred in her. She'd never stop wanting him, and she wondered what kind of woman that made her. *A lucky one,* something inside her whispered.

As Michael eased away, she saw the footman replenishing the trays on the sideboard, pretending not to notice what they did. Good footmen were to perform like automatons, but when this one turned away she saw his amused smile.

Michael touched her cheek as the footman departed. "No need to blush so in front of the servants. We are married after all. Convenient, isn't it? We can live in the same house day after day, share the same bed night after night, and no one will say a word against us."

"There will still be talk," she pointed out. "I imagine once news of our marriage gets round, we'll face much speculation."

His look turned evasive. Amelia had learned during her marriage to Basil that bringing up an unpleasant or embarrassing topic sent men scuttling away to do something—anything—to avoid serious talks about it.

"Ah, but we are elderly now," Michael said. "Thirty and stodgy. What we did in the heat of youth is interesting; the marriage of an elderly widow and widower is far less so."

Amelia wasn't so certain. Michael's leaving England and Amelia's hasty marriage to Basil Lockwood had been the talk of the Town for some time. She'd buried herself in the country to still wagging tongues, hoping everyone would forget about her.

"I'd like to meet your little girl," Amelia said to change the subject.

Michael snorted, but looked relieved that they were pursuing a different topic. "No you wouldn't. *Little girl* is too sweet an appellation for my Felice. She's a hellion." Pride flickered in his eyes. "I hope my friend Fuller's wife has at least managed to comb her hair. I'll take you to see her—but not right away, I fear. Too much business to keep me in town."

Amelia couldn't stop her question. "What sort of business?"

She braced herself for a husband's answer: *Nothing to concern yourself with, my dear. Men's work.* Basil had said that often enough.

"Settlements," Michael answered promptly. "I am a duke now, in control of vast funds, lands, tenants, and livestock. A glorified sheep and cattle farmer, in truth, but then, most peers are. I have been attempting to set up a trust for Felice so that she'll be a rich woman in her own right when she comes of age. My man of business has a blind spot when it comes to this idea—he believes a woman should dutifully give everything to her husband upon her marriage. But what if the husband is a blackguard?"

Amelia hid a smile. Michael looked the essence of a worried father who would distrust any man who glanced at his daughter. She wanted to remind him that her father had felt the same way about Michael, but thought it wouldn't be politic at the moment.

Michael clasped her hand, never minding the butter on it, and pulled it to his lips. "The other piece of business is to work up settlements for you, so when I am carried to the mausoleum on the ducal estate in Cheshire, you won't have to play cards with someone like Preston for your bread. I promise that will never happen to you again."

In a flash, he'd become the generous Michael who thought nothing of tossing gold guineas at beggars. Even the beggars laughed at him for his extravagance.

"Come with me," he said. "Leave the running of the house to Mrs. Coleman; she's used to it. Together we should be able to twist this man of business around our fingers."

Ever after, she was glad she'd gone with him, although she could never have guessed that a simple appointment with a man of business would nearly lead to the destruction of her marriage. But with Michael handsome in his rich suit and his smile and warm eyes, and remembering the incredible way he'd made her feel the night before, she readily accepted.

APPOINTMENTS with men of business were generally dull, and this one was no exception. The best point, in Michael's opinion, was Amelia sitting next to him like bright fire.

The man of business, Mr. Holderness, was punctilious, exact, and dry. Michael easily talked him into generous settlements for Amelia—a house for use in her lifetime, money in trust for herself and for any children she might have, a large allowance while he was still alive.

Michael would give her more, jewels, horses, whatever Amelia wanted, and put them in trust so no one could take them away from her. He was very aware that women could easily lose all they had if legal provisions for them weren't nailed down.

When they turned to the question of Michael's daughter, Holderness became more difficult. He was of the old school that believed if a person didn't wear trousers they had no business controlling money or making decisions or even thinking. Perhaps Holderness's own wife was a terror, Michael mused, and he had to take out his feelings on the rest of the fair sex.

Holderness balked when Michael mentioned putting income-producing land in trust for Felice for her lifetime. He balked again when Michael wanted Amelia named as Felice's guardian—and the guardian of any children Amelia and Michael might have together—in the event of his death.

"Er, it is more customary, Your Grace, to name a *gentleman* of one's family to look after one's children," Holderness said in his whispery voice.

"It might be customary," Michael stated, "but I cannot imagine any person better suited to the task than my wife."

Holderness looked utterly baffled and cast an imploring glance at Amelia. "Perhaps, Your Grace, you will want to wait in the outer room. My assistant will give you tea, anything you like. Men's business is dreadfully tedious."

"Her Grace is fine where she is," Michael said with a growl.

Amelia touched his wrist. "I think he means he wants to speak privately with you, Michael."

"I ascertained that. Say what you need to say, Holderness. I keep no secrets from Her Grace."

Holderness looked pained, but cast Michael an *on your head be it* glance. "I hate to embarrass you, sir, but there is some question as to the—legitimacy—of Lady Felice."

Michael let his voice cool. "Baroness Anne-Marie and I were legally married in Wallachia."

"Which is unfortunately part of the Ottoman Empire."

"I made bloody certain it was legal. I wanted to rub my father's nose in it. I have the documents."

Holderness winced, if anything looking displeased with this answer. "Would you mind if I examined them?"

Michael looked exasperated. "I don't have them *with* me. In any case, what does it matter? Felice is a daughter, not a son and heir to the dukedom, and I can give any unentailed lands to whom I wish."

"That is correct." Holderness drew a wheezing breath. "Are you certain, Your Grace, that you do not wish to claim that your daughter, Lady Felice, is illegitimate? That the marriage never took place?"

Michael grew colder. "No, I don't wish to claim she is illegitimate, because she is not. Please change the subject; you are distressing my wife. Who, by the way, I also married legally. I may be impulsive, but I am also careful."

Holderness cleared his throat and shifted a paper on his uncluttered desk. "It pains me to say this, Your Grace, but I received a letter this morning that casts doubt not only on the legitimacy of the first marriage, but also doubt about the lady's death. So you see, if you can prove that your first marriage is legal, this letter unfortunately means you have committed the crime of bigamy."

SEVEN

Preston's Revenge

Amelia's mouth went dry. It was her nature to become quiet when faced with upsetting business, and she became more quiet and still than she had in years.

Michael, on the other hand, flushed with rage, the dangerous temper that had destroyed what they'd had years ago.

"I may have been a hotheaded youth," he said, mouth tight. "But I assure you, my first wife died in Constantinople. I was at her bedside."

Holderness looked unhappy as he shifted papers again. "I am afraid the letter writer claims he can produce the lady. She has been living in Cheswick this past year and only came forward a few days ago when she heard of your marriage to Amelia Lockwood."

"Who wrote this letter?"

"May I speculate?" Amelia broke in.

Michael glanced at her, his green eyes cold as ice. "Ah." He twirled his walking stick between gloved fingers. "I will guess, too. Preston Lockwood."

Holderness gave the barest nod.

"Then it is easily solved. Lockwood has a grudge against me for marrying Amelia. I suggest you disregard this letter."

"Under ordinary circumstance I would, Your Grace. But he has put together compelling proofs, has sworn testimony from gentlemen other than himself, and there is the lady in Cheswick."

"It is a farce, Holderness," Michael said. "I can always prepare a suit against him for libel."

"I would not do so, Your Grace."

"Damnation, man, you are supposed to protect me from this sort of thing. It is why I employ you."

Holderness cleared his throat, slightly shocked at Michael's language in front of Amelia. "There is a way, Your Grace, a discreet way. One that will stay out of the newspapers."

Michael waved a hand. "Enlighten me."

"Offer the lady a sum of money to disappear again or to state that she was coerced to lie."

"Pay her off, you mean? Damned if I will. She is not Anne-Marie."

"Whether she is or not is not important. We need to keep her silent."

Michael pressed his hands together until his gloves stretched tightly across his knuckles. Amelia saw in him the young man she'd known before, the one who'd paced like a wild animal when he realized that all his machinations could not force Amelia to marry him. He'd been so certain she couldn't escape. He'd kicked a fence post to pieces and marched away when he finally concluded that he'd lost.

"Would you like a fence post, Michael?" she asked him now.

He rounded on her, eyes like green fire, but he spoke to Holderness.

"My *wife,* as usual, takes things with aplomb. Pay the damned woman; keep the scandal away from me and mine."

Amelia gaped. He was giving in?

And then she realized—he was afraid. He was anticipating that everything he wanted, everything he had, would crumble to nothing like it had before. He lived his life on quicksand, moving constantly so as not to fall and drown.

"There has to be another way," she said to him. "Please do not let Preston win. I'd be very annoyed to watch him gloat."

Michael snatched up his walking stick and held his hand out for Amelia. "Do what you have to do, Holderness. We are leaving."

He obviously did not expect Amelia to argue with him. She let him lead her out, but once they were alone in the carriage, she turned to him. "Michael, you know that if you pay her, and someone gets wind of it, they will think you guilty."

Michael glared out the window, not looking at her. "I can offer this woman, whoever she is, a hell of a lot more money than Preston can dream of. She'll keep quiet and toddle away."

"Why not fight and prove it's a lie?"

He looked at her, eyes grim. "Because the chances that I can find someone who knew Anne-Marie when she was alive are slim. Felice was a tiny child—she doesn't remember her. Anne-Marie's family is far away in Russia, and they washed their hands of her long ago. People will believe the worst of me, and you know why."

He thumped back into the squabs, folded his hands over his walking stick, and contemplated rainy London. But his eyes before he turned away had told her everything. Michael didn't give a damn what the world thought of him, but he feared that Amelia wouldn't believe his innocence in the matter, and that bothered him.

Ten years ago Michael had tried to force her to marry him, behaving like a stage villain the moment her father had died and left her unprotected. She'd been the most sought-after debutante of the Season, and hotheaded Lord Michael had wanted her. She'd realized later, after she'd stopped preening herself for catching his eye, that he wanted her so no one else could have her. She was going to be his prize, and he was going to taunt the world with her.

Three days ago he'd stormed back into her life, coerced her into marrying him, and seduced her without compunction. Everything he'd done justified her perception of him, and Preston's lies were the crowning glory.

Michael assumed she'd believe that he'd abandoned his wife in Constantinople and pretended her dead in order to get away from her. That he wanted an English son and heir now that he was duke, so he conveniently suppressed Anne-Marie and married Amelia, thus gaining a respectable woman to be his duchess and mother to his heir.

"Tell me about her," she said. "About Anne-Marie."

Michael glanced up, then resolutely stared out the window again. "Not much to tell. She was Russian, as hotheaded as I was, and unfaithful to me from the first day we married."

"Oh. I'm sorry."

He snorted. "I was unfaithful, too. You know how I was—it's one of the reasons you told me to go to the devil. We quarreled more often than not and spent nights away from home. She had Felice, then a year later died of a wasting disease. She'd gone a bit mad at the end, but I held her hand that last day and watched her die."

Amelia's heart squeezed at the bleakness in his voice. "I'm sorry," she said again, truly sympathetic. Michael hadn't deserved such grief.

"Of course I can't prove that," he said. "I'd sent all the servants away, and in any case, none of them spoke a word of English."

"What about Merriman?"

"Afraid not. I found him in Cairo after Anne-Marie's death. A Cockney seeing the world, he said. Pickpocketed his way across the world more like. I had a baby under my arm at that time, and he helped play nursemaid." Michael paused, and pain crossed his face. "I am not even certain whether Felice is mine—Anne-Marie had many affairs and never bothered to conceal them from me. That's the real scandal, if Preston had only taken care to find it."

Amelia looked at him in surprise. "You did not know whether she was yours? And yet, you took care of her. . . ."

"I couldn't leave the child to starve or be sold, could I? She might not be mine, or she might, but either way, it's not the poor brat's fault."

Amelia's heart began to warm. "That was good of you."

"You'd not think so if you heard what she says of me. If you are expecting a sweet, grateful little angel, think again. She's the devil's child."

"Which means she's yours." Amelia smiled. "You are decidedly devilish yourself. I look forward to meeting her."

He grimaced. "I'll remind you of that when you flee from her, screaming. She bites."

"So do I," she said softly, thinking of how she'd nibbled on him the night before.

His head swung around, his green gaze spearing her. "Don't."

His expression was hard and impenetrable, but she understood. He feared false devotion as much as he feared she'd hate him. He didn't want to live a lie.

"Very well." She sat back in her seat, turning to study the rain.

But something between them had changed. If Michael had been the kind of man able to abandon a wife, he would have abandoned the child as well. Felice was a daughter, which meant she not only would not inherit the dukedom but she'd require a dowry, likely an extravagant one. It would have been much easier and cheaper for Michael to leave her behind, especially when he wasn't certain who'd fathered her.

The idea of Michael trying to care for a baby alone in the middle of Egypt made her want to smile. Someday she'd make him tell her those stories.

For now, he was certain that Amelia had not forgiven him, that she'd married him because he'd again pushed her into a corner, only this time she'd been unable to escape. Preston's ruse this morning would give Amelia grounds to try to have the marriage invalidated, and she saw in Michael's eyes certainty that she'd take it. He was afraid he'd lost her again.

But Amelia had gone through ten years of healing and growing and understanding. She'd lived with a man who had been quiet and a little dull, but also caring and compassionate, teaching her the value of such things. Her own overweening pride had been dampened.

What Michael had done in the past had been deplorable, but he had changed. His proposal ten years ago had been the act of a powerful, covetous, selfish man; this time, it was an act of protectiveness, and she saw the difference.

Michael remained stone silent all the way home, but Amelia's heart had lightened.

WHEN they reached the house, Michael went out again, this time not saying where. Amelia's lightheartedness turned to frustration and worry. Had he gone to confront Preston? Or this woman in Cheswick?

Amelia could cheerfully have shot Preston for what he'd done, but she reasoned that murder would only make things worse. She only hoped Michael wouldn't contemplate it.

To keep her mind off things, she buried herself in her tasks for the day—receiving the seamstress and trying on several of her new dresses, discussing menus with Mrs. Coleman, answering letters from the bolder ladies of the ton who wanted to claim acquaintance.

She also had a few shopping tasks that she wanted to undertake, and startled the servants by doing them herself—in the carriage with footmen and a maid in tow, of course. Mrs. Coleman said in a horrified voice that Her Grace should let others shop for her, but Amelia wanted to take care of some of the things personally.

By one in the morning, Michael had not returned. Amelia sent Merriman to bed, saying she'd stay in Michael's room and wait for him.

"Right you are, missus," Merriman said cheerfully. "I shall be snoring loudly in me attic."

Amelia liked Merriman, a cheeky Cockney and not a properly trained servant. He'd stuck with Michael through thick and thin, and even though Amelia was now in charge of the staff she wasn't about to dismiss him.

Amelia set everything out, changed into her dressing gown, and lay down on the bed, hoping Michael would arrive before she fell asleep. But the long, worrying day after the exhilarating night left her tired, and she drifted off, to be awakened much later by a resounding crash.

She sat up straight. The candles had guttered, and in the dying firelight she saw Michael standing amid the ruins of her preparations, swearing under his breath.

She leapt from the bed. "You've knocked over my card table."

"Why the devil is it in the middle of my bed chamber?"

"I will explain later." Amelia bent to retrieve the cards and the box that was still fastened with string. "Help me right it, and perhaps we can salvage something of my hard day's work."

EIGHT

Amelia States Her Case

Michael let his coat and cravat fall as he stared at Amelia. She wore a pretty silk dressing gown, new he guessed, and she was about to ruin it in her struggles to right the delicate-legged card table.

"Amelia, sit down. Let me do this."

He lifted the card table from her grasp and set it on its feet then righted the chairs. Amelia collected cards, a small box tied with string, and spent candles from the floor. "I expected you a bit earlier, you see," she said.

"I am surprised you expected me at all. Why aren't you in bed?"

She turned a reproachful look to him. "Why should I sleep while you are wandering London, worrying about Preston's lies? I care nothing for what he says. He was always insufferable."

"Because his lies will hurt you." His body throbbed with her nearness and the lithe way she moved. She was bare under the dressing gown, he was certain. "If the world thinks our marriage not valid, then I've ruined you."

"You do not need to explain it to me so exactly; I do understand the implications of Preston's claim."

Michael seated himself on the padded bench at the end of the bed and pulled off a boot. He tried, and failed, not to picture how Amelia looked sitting here last night, her night rail open while she took his cock between her lips.

"I have been all over London trying to find one person who might have been in Alexandria or Constantinople while I was married," he said. "Then trying to find someone who might know someone who was. The trouble with people who roam the world is that they're very rarely at home." He threw the boot aside and pulled off the other.

Amelia watched him, hands on hips. Her dark hair flowed to her waist, sweetly unbound. "You should leave such searching to your man of business. You'll wear out your boots."

"You heard Holderness. He is satisfied with paying off this woman and shutting Preston's mouth."

"So were you, I thought."

"If that is what it takes, yes. But I'd still like to have a trump card in case Preston tries to thwart me."

Amelia sat down at the card table. "Well, there's nothing more can be done tonight. We can have a nice game of picquet before the morning."

"I'd rather you went back to your chamber. The less we are together, the fewer tongues will wag if this gets out."

Amelia shuffled the cards with her slender fingers. "I was raised to be a dutiful wife, obedient and uncomplaining." She lifted a stubborn blue gaze to him. "But I am afraid I can be obedient and dutiful no longer, at least not tonight. Play cards with me, husband. I want to show you something."

"It is far too dangerous for you to stay in this room."

"I'm not afraid of you."

He stepped behind her chair and tilted her head back so she

looked up at him. "You should be, my love." He tightened his grasp. "I may not choose to let you go."

"I am not going anywhere."

Her eyes sparkled with determination. He couldn't resist bending to kiss her eyelids, letting her lashes tickle his lips.

That led to kissing her mouth, tasting her upside down. Her chest rose, the loose dressing gown letting him see her soft depths.

She began to pull away from him, and he snapped to his senses and stood up. "You see? Far too dangerous."

"I am not leaving, Michael. Do sit down and play cards with me. It is important."

She had some bee in her bonnet, he decided. He'd humor her, but only for a while.

He made himself let go of her and dropped into the chair on the opposite side of the table. "What is all this about?"

"A simple game, my dear. We are both good players, so it will be an entertainment."

He watched her smooth the cards and tried to restrain his wanting. "To divert us from our present troubles?"

"Partly." She set the deck down, one finger touching the top card. "But the prizes will be interesting."

"Prizes?"

"When we played before it was for money and marriage. Tonight we will play for other things."

"Explain yourself before I combust, please."

Her gaze flicked to him. "You seem in no imminent danger. A game goes to one hundred points. The first to reach it will ask for a favor from the other. Anything we wish." She cut the deck and touched the pile of cards to her lips. "To make it even more interesting, anyone who has *pique, repique,* or *capot* will gain additional favors."

Suddenly hot, Michael unbuttoned his waistcoat then undid the hooks holding his shirt closed. A *pique* was scored by the player who gained thirty points before the dealer declared a single one. *Repique* happened when either player could declare thirty points before the cards were laid down in play, and the other had no points. Both situations were uncommon. *Capot* was difficult as well—taking every trick in the game.

The near-despair he'd felt all day suddenly lightened. Amelia was proving herself fine at coming up with distractions.

"And what exactly do you mean by *favors?*"

She sent him a secret smile. "You will simply have to win a few hands and find out."

"Careful, love. Be so careful how you use that smile."

"It is useless to try to frighten me, Michael," she said. "I am determined."

His own feral smile returned. "Oh, love, such a challenge. I pray you do not regret it."

⁂

AMELIA hoped she did not regret it, either. The bleakness in his eyes when he'd come in had wrung her heart, and the wicked glint she saw now made her feel better.

But as he continued to watch her she grew a bit nervous. She saw the dangerous man in his eyes, the hunter who stalked his prey.

He took his cut of the deck, getting a lower card than hers, so the deal fell to him. She picked up her first hand with shaking fingers and noted she could make quite a few good calls.

Of course, with this game, she really couldn't lose.

"A point of five," she announced. Five cards in the suit of spades.

"How high?"

Her highest spade was a queen. "Queen."

Michael's lips twitched. "Not good."

So he had five in a suit as well with either the king or ace as his high card. She swallowed. "A sequence of four."

"How high?"

She wet her lips. "King."

"Good," he conceded.

At least she'd get four points. Amelia wrote them neatly on the sheet next to her.

"*Trio*," she said. "Tens."

"Not good." He grinned. "I like this game so far."

"When you gathered the cards from the floor, did you tamper with them?"

"What a suspicious lady you are. No, I did not slide any queens into my pocket."

He declared his point of five and his *trios*. Amelia obtained another point for starting the play.

As the game commenced she learned that at Preston's house party, Michael had been going easy on her. Now he played like a man driven, forcing her to throw down cards she'd intended to hold back while he won trick after trick. He wanted the *capot*— winning all the tricks in the hand.

"By the by," he mused, "what is in your box?" He nodded to the still-wrapped package at the edge of the table.

"You'll learn that when you lose to me and I ask for a favor."

"Ah."

And suddenly she won a trick. She took it with an exasperated sigh. "Don't cheat."

"Not cheating—I made a bad play."

"Michael."

He gave her an innocent stare. "Yes?"

"It is cheating if you deliberately let me win. Like at Preston's."

His expression hardened. "Damned if I was going to let him win. You needed that money, and I'd never have let you go to him."

Her heart beat faster, and she felt suddenly awkward. "It was good of you."

"It wasn't good of me. I wanted you as much as I ever did. Ten years ago I imagined you'd be pathetically grateful enough to marry me, and I thought so this time, too. Proving I'm still a complete fool."

"But I did marry you, as you can see," she said.

His eyes flickered with emotion. "I am not ridiculous enough to believe that it was for any great love of me. You did not exactly swoon and fall into my arms."

Her heart squeezed, but she spoke briskly. "Oh, do lay down a card, Michael. I have played the seven of hearts. Can you beat it? Or shall I wait until you retrieve the losing card from your sleeve?"

"When I win, you will regret your complacency, I promise you." He tossed down the king of hearts and won the trick, but he'd have won far more points if he hadn't thrown away a play.

Still Michael had fifty points, and she had a long way to go to catch up. She was dealer next, so he'd call his points first.

This time Michael wasn't kind. He discarded and picked up new cards and arranged his hand, calling points she couldn't match or beat. She was still able to squeeze in some points so he couldn't *pique,* but he proceeded to win every trick and take his extra forty points to win the game.

"On the bed." His voice was dark and brooked no argument.

Amelia calmly straightened her cards and rose, but not fast enough for Michael. He caught her around the waist and tossed her onto the bed on her back, then crouched over her and yanked her dressing gown open. She wore nothing beneath.

His hair hung over his face, his eyes nearly black in the shadows. She couldn't read exactly what was in them, but the animal-like glitter unnerved her.

"You are still dressed," she said.

"I had noticed."

"You are supposed to claim your favor," she pointed out.

"This is my favor. Lie back and spread your legs."

She lay flat, her fingers clenching the bedcovers, unable to move. She wanted this; she'd longed for this, but now she went rigid, the reality of him overwhelming her.

His impatient fingers parted her thighs, and he dipped his head to lick across her abdomen, his tongue lingering in her navel. His lips traveled down until they pressed right against her quim.

She gasped. Michael was right—she was too innocent. He had knowledge that far surpassed hers, and he'd likely think her plans tonight were amusing and naïve.

Michael slid his hands under her buttocks and lifted her slightly, then he pleasured her with his mouth. He moved his tongue all over her quim, dipping inside her cleft, flicking it over her swelling bud.

He did not let her rest. He covered her quim with his mouth, licking, nibbling, biting. She arched to him again and again, pulling his hair until he shook her off, but he didn't stop.

He took her to the edge she'd fallen over last night, and kept going. He plunged his tongue in and out of her as though he made love to her with it, then he trailed kisses across her thighs and came back to close his teeth over her nub.

"Please, Michael." She panted. "You have to let me—breathe."

He lifted his head, his smile so sinful that her words died on her lips. "Beg for mercy, love. Go on. You won't get any from me."

"Why not?"

"Because you're mine—I won you fair and square."

He lowered his head to her again, his mouth doing beautiful things. A darkness washed over her, and she lost all sense of time and place. Nothing existed but the bed beneath her and Michael and the incredible madness he made her feel.

When he finally stopped, she was gasping and groaning, holding tightly to the bed as though she'd fall if she let go.

He pressed a final kiss to her quim and lifted himself to lay beside her. The huge hardness behind his cashmere trousers rolled against her thigh, but still he didn't take off his clothes.

"I want to teach you some more words," he said.

"Words?"

His chuckle was dark. He took her hand and guided it between her legs, resting it on her hot and swollen cleft. "Do you know what this is?"

Wonderingly she touched the hard wet point between her legs and shook her head.

"Cunny." He said the naughty word as though there was nothing wrong with it. "Say that, love."

She blushed, which was ridiculous after what she'd just let him do. He pushed her fingers across her opening, and she closed her eyes in pleasure. What he made her do was very bad, wicked even for a married woman. Courtesans knew these things; wives did not.

"Cunny," she said.

"Very good. Remember what you said about me yesterday? You called me decidedly devilish, and you are right. You were right about me all those years ago when I did my best to take away everything you had, and I haven't changed."

"You have."

"So, my sweet." He went on as though he hadn't heard her. "Any time you want me to pleasure you, you must ask me in the right manner, or I won't know what you mean. If you want me to taste you, you say, *Michael, please lick my cunny*. Or pussy. Either one will do. Otherwise I shall refuse."

"I can't . . ."

"You can, love, if you put your mind to it."

"I mean, I can't take much more of this. I'll never be able to finish the game."

She tried to withdraw her hand, but he twined his fingers through hers, forcing her to explore herself. She felt her wiry hair and the hot, slick folds of her cleft. The tingle in her body was nowhere near what she'd had when he'd pleasured her with his mouth, but the daringness of it made her feel wicked.

"Don't be afraid to learn yourself," Michael said. "There may come a time when I ask you to pleasure yourself for me."

And she'd had no idea anyone did *that*. She had a feeling if she'd given in to his demands years ago, she'd know a great deal more now.

To please him, she tentatively poked her forefinger inside herself. It was strange and a bit unnerving to feel her own body, but Michael's fingers there with hers made it worth it. She passed her other hand over her breasts, the areolas silken, the nipples hard as pebbles.

"You see?" he asked, his eyes almost luminous. "Your body is beautiful, love. Treasure it."

"I always thought myself too plump."

"Not so. You are exactly right."

"I will reserve judgment. May we resume cards now?"

He kissed her, long and slow, his mouth tasting of himself and her all mixed up. "Of course."

He helped her sit up and arrange her dressing gown as though they were about to enter a ballroom together. Of course, at a ball, he wouldn't cup her backside as he helped her to her feet or scrape her to him for another long, tongue-tangling kiss.

Or perhaps he might.

She felt the tension rise in the next game, in spite of the languor his pleasuring had given her. Now that she knew what was at stake, she wanted to win. So did he. On the second hand, she played hard and got a *capot*—winning every trick.

"I do believe," she said as she wrote down her forty points, which put her far ahead of him. "That this entitles me to a favor."

Michael ruffled the deck through his fingers. "True."

He looked delectable and sensual, with his shirt open to the waist and loosened at the cuffs and his hair mussed. A lover risen from his lady's bed. *Her* lover.

Hands trembling, Amelia unknotted the string that held the box closed and pulled off the lid. Inside lay an assortment of chocolate, the finest bonbons made by a Parisian chocolatier, the sweet shop in Berkeley Square had assured her.

Michael's eyes widened slightly. They were ordinary bonbons, nothing odd about them, but she saw his intake of breath.

She smiled at him, pretending calm. "Please remove your clothes, Michael."

NINE

Sin and Chocolate

Michael had always prided himself on his control, never letting the woman in his bed gain the upper hand. He was the pleaser and taught them what he liked, not the other way around.

Amelia sent all that to the wind. Michael's heart hammered and his hands shook so much in his eagerness he wasn't certain he could get his clothes off. His last few shirt clasps went flying across the room to ping into the fireplace.

He unbuttoned his trousers and kicked them off and got out of his underclothing. Finally he was bare. He turned to the bed, but Amelia's palm was on his chest, fingers splayed, as she gently pushed him back onto the chair.

"Stay there."

Michael sat down, the fabric of the chair prickling his backside. The sensual feel only heightened his readiness, and he hoped he could contain himself long enough to let her do what she wanted.

Amelia kept her dressing gown closed, smiling a little as her gaze roved Michael's body. Michael leaned one elbow on the table and parted his legs, letting her look.

His body was tight, blood pumping rapidly, a dark feeling pooling in his abdomen and cock. That member swelled high, thick and dark, and Amelia's gaze lingered on it gratifyingly. She touched her fingertip to her lower lip as she looked, which nearly drove him mad.

Before he burned up from the inside out, she pulled her gaze away and dipped into the box of chocolates. She held one bonbon between her palms a moment then placed the chocolate between his lips.

Michael sucked it into his mouth, liking the rich silkiness on his tongue. While he savored it, Amelia rubbed her chocolate-coated fingers down his torso.

He jumped in surprise, then groaned in sheer pleasure as she leaned to lick it off.

"Dear God, Amelia." He swallowed his bonbon as he watched her busy tongue take chocolate from his skin and tight-as-hell nipples. Her teeth scraped one, and he drew a sharp breath. "What did I do to deserve you?"

"You could have forced me, ten years ago. You could have ruined me utterly, and you chose not to."

She straightened, her eyes triumphant, and reached for another bonbon.

He was going to die. He'd expire right here as she rubbed chocolate on him, and he'd go out a happy man.

"So now I'm a saint?"

"Not exactly. What you did was fairly horrible, and when I saw you at Preston's I thought you still the same. But I'm changing my mind."

Amelia held the bonbon as she had the first, then she tucked the chocolate into his mouth and grasped the full length of his cock. He closed his eyes as she smeared chocolate on him, and curled his tongue around the sweet she'd just fed him. He tilted his head back and swallowed just as she began to lick him clean.

He wasn't quite sure what she meant about changing her mind about him, but he was damn glad. *I never meant to hurt you,* his thoughts bled. *I loved you and wanted you, and thought I had to master you to get you.*

She suckled and licked, her head moving as she devoured the chocolate from his skin. He laced his fingers through her hair, reveling in its satin softness. He liked imagining the diamonds he'd give her glittering in it.

He'd spend the London Season with this beauty on his arm, the tedious sessions in the House of Lords made easier knowing he would return home to her. Every day would be an adventure, every evening an adventure of a different kind. He'd love her and cherish her and make up for causing her so much pain.

Amelia kissed the tip of his cock as she withdrew. Michael couldn't bear to be without her mouth on him, and he grasped her shoulders, feeling desperate.

"One more," she said.

How could she be so serene? He was aching, needing to roll her onto the carpet and fuck her until he released.

But he'd hold himself back, play it her way. Innocent woman, her games more erotic than any courtesan's because she did it for her own joy. She was not paid to entertain him; she did this because she wanted to.

He'd never understood the difference before. His first wife had been little better than a courtesan, having been mistress to an Italian count and an English army colonel before she'd lit upon Michael. Still raging from what had happened with Amelia, he'd insisted on marriage.

A fool and his dignity are soon parted, he thought. Anne-Marie had humiliated him at every turn, paying him back for everything he'd done to his sweet Amelia. She'd taught Michael hard lessons.

Amelia took up a third bonbon, but this time, she did not feed it to him. Instead she laid it carefully on top of his cock, balancing it near his tip.

"No . . ."

Amelia swirled her tongue around his flange, loosening the chocolate, then scooped the bonbon into her mouth and ate it.

He caught her face between his hands and slanted his mouth

across hers. He tasted the deep bite of chocolate and the smooth-
ness of fondant.

Michael lifted her to his lap, his hands parting her dressing
gown to let him touch the woman beneath.

She tried to turn away. "We have more of the game to play."

"I think I've already won this game."

"You're cheating, again."

He nuzzled her cheek. "We haven't much of the night left. I
don't want one of the maids banging in here to stir the fire while
we're sitting naked holding our cards."

"That is a point."

He pushed the dressing gown from her shoulders, letting the
silk folds slither to the floor. He used his fallen cravat to scrub the
remains of chocolate from his staff, then he turned her in the chair
to straddle him.

Her eyes widened. "This is not the bed."

"Good heavens," he said in mock surprise.

"Don't tease me."

"But I adore teasing you."

He lifted her slightly then repositioned her to slide her onto his
hungry, slick cock.

Dear God. Last night when he'd entered her, they'd both been
on the edge of release, and he'd pumped into her and finished
quickly. Tonight he felt the slow goodness of her, her warm sheath
squeezing him like a fist.

"*Yes.*" He drew out the word.

Amelia's eyes half-closed, her hair skimming around him. He
turned his face to it, loving it against his skin.

"Ride me," he said. "Rock on me."

She moved her hips tentatively and he guided her. She began to
feel it, little cries escaping her lips. He lifted himself to thrust into
her, catching her rhythm and matching it.

He loved this position, where he could control what they did
while enjoying the long, slow build. She'd obviously never done

this before—he imagined Basil had gone to her in the dark, done his duty perfunctorily while she lay on her back, and slipped away again.

How could any man not revel in every part of her—every stroke of skin, every kiss, every inch inside of her? Her naughty look when she'd brought out the bonbons made him both want to laugh and to seize her and devour her. He'd never get enough of her.

He was high inside her now, her quim swallowing him. He wanted to drown in her. His body was flushed with warmth, though his flesh rose in goose bumps.

This woman filled his heart and his body and the empty spaces in his soul. And he filled *her,* he thought with an evil smile. He wanted to fuck her and fuck her, and wake up the next morning and do it all over again.

Her cries were incoherent as she rocked on him, her nails drawing creases in his back. He clenched his teeth against the tiny pain and kept thrusting. The chair skidded a little on the carpet.

He reached for the box of bonbons and drew one out. He put it lightly between his teeth, and then he pulled her down for a kiss, both of them biting the chocolate. He swallowed his half, then licked the chocolate from her lips.

She smiled at him, eyes languid. He fed her another piece of chocolate, and this time, she licked *his* lips clean.

He loved her for a long time, swaying and rocking in the chair, playing with the chocolate or just kissing her. She was mastering kissing, learning how to use her tongue to engage his or to tease his lips and mouth.

His climax built, but he held it back, wanting to stay forever inside this woman. Tomorrow he'd have to face uncertainty. Tonight he had her.

But his body had other ideas. Amelia arched against him, far gone in pleasure, her nipples hard little nubs against his chest. He groaned out loud as he suddenly came, unable to stop himself.

As he did so, he reached between them and caught her berry

between his thumb and forefinger. She moaned, bucking against him, squeezing him tight.

When his vision cleared, she was smiling at him, and he felt nothing but the warm goodness of her.

"You see," he said, his lips barely able to move. "Many things are possible in a chair."

WHEN Amelia awoke later, it was still dark. The fire burned low and only a few candles had been lit.

She lay in the warm nest of Michael's bed, feeling stretched and pleasantly tired. Michael had carried her there after they'd finished in the chair, then he'd touched and kissed her until she'd fallen asleep.

She raised her head. Michael sat at the card table, dressed in shirt and trousers, contemplating the cards in his hand as though they held the answer to the mystery of life. He hadn't fastened his shirt, which gave her an enticing glimpse of his dark chest.

Amelia slid out of bed and pulled on her dressing gown. She sat across the table from him on the chair in which he'd loved her.

"What time is it?" she asked sleepily.

"Just after six. Don't worry, Merriman never comes in before seven."

He wouldn't look up from the cards, his green eyes focused sightlessly on them.

"Merriman knows how to attend to your every whim," she observed, for want of anything to say.

"He's been good to me. He'd been rotting in a Cairo jail for pickpocketing—horrible place. They were going to cut off his hand. I got him out of there and out of the city, and he's repaid me in loyalty ever since. He's not very servile, but that's not what I want from him."

"Cheeky, I think him."

"Yes. Damn cheeky."

He fell silent, and Amelia watched him anxiously. "What are you thinking?"

Michael shuffled the deck again and began to deal the cards. "We can play again," he said, not looking at her. "If you win, you may leave me, and I'll hold you blameless. I will pay for your keep and take care of everything so you won't be bothered. I know you never wanted this."

Her breath nearly stopped. "What are you talking about?"

"When I stepped up to you at Preston's I was the last person you wanted to see. The look in your eyes when you turned to me cut right through my heart."

She shook her head. "You're mistaken."

"You knew I hadn't changed. I was ready to stride in and take you, damn anyone who got in my way."

"It was different."

"Was it? How?"

Amelia fell silent, remembering.

Amelia had made a shining debut at eighteen, daughter of a baron, lovely, poised, with a doting father and a large dowry. She was declared a diamond of the first water, a catch. She'd done everything right.

Lord Michael had set his sights on her from the beginning. He was the only son of a duke, rich as sin, and already had a wild reputation. Amelia had been flattered by his attentions and preened herself about it. He'd followed her to every ball and soiree, dancing attendance, loudly proclaiming his intention to have her.

She'd liked him—mostly when he came to visit her father's Surrey house and they'd walk the grounds and talk. Away from the London crowds he was personable and charming, not playing the wealthy, arrogant lord.

Amelia knew she was somewhat to blame for it all going wrong. She'd started to like her power over him, and she began coy games with Michael, telling him she was thinking of accepting this gentleman or that one. Michael would grow furious and redouble his efforts to cut the others out.

It had been enjoyable at first, both of them proud and spirited and good at the game. Amelia spurned his first proposal, smiling at how angry it made him but a bit unnerved at his temper at the same time. She'd planned to accept if he asked her again, but he became broody, not dancing with her or trying to stay at her side, but watching her from afar, a calculating look in his eyes.

Then Amelia's father died and left her destitute. His debts had been insurmountable, bad investments ruining him. He'd tried to live on credit until his luck turned again, but his death ended that hope.

Amelia's admirers hastily withdrew, teaching her painfully that her charms for them had been purely monetary. Then when her father's man of business had come to see her, she'd learned of Michael's revenge for her refusal.

Her father had been ill for some time and had not told Amelia. Michael had come to Amelia's father and quietly bought up his unentailed property, paid off his debts, and gotten rid of his unwise investments. Her father's entailed property would go to his heir, a distant cousin, but the rest of the money Amelia's father willed to Michael, with the understanding that Michael would marry Amelia and keep her with it.

After the funeral, Michael took Amelia out and explained things to her. He owned her. Everything her father would have left to her, Michael now controlled. She had no choice but to marry him, proud lady who'd thought to thwart him.

Amelia had been furious and devastated, her grief at the loss of her father making her more so. Michael's green eyes had glittered in triumph, knowing he'd won his prize.

Amelia might have swallowed her anger, but some charming people who'd come to comfort her had told her that Michael had several mistresses in London and hadn't any intention of giving them up after he married. Hadn't Amelia had a lucky escape?

She'd seen everything in a blinding flash of pain. Michael had wanted her, not loved her. He'd hunted her, like he would stalk game. He'd marry her, install her in his house, and return to his mistresses, pleased with himself.

So she told him that dull, kind Basil Lockwood, their neighbor fifteen years older than she, had already proposed to her, and she'd accepted.

The incredulous look on Michael's face had almost satisfied her. He'd gone hideously red, the cords on his neck standing out, his large, powerful fists clenched. He'd raged at her, destroying the fence post, shouting horrible things. She'd returned words of cold fury.

And then he'd stopped. Just stopped, like a water pump draining dry. Without another word, he'd turned and walked away. He'd snapped off the branch of a tree as he passed it, a sound like a shot. He'd walked out of her life, and her heart had burned doubly with grief.

She'd heard the next day that he'd packed his things and quit England altogether. She learned much later still that Michael had gifted all the money he'd taken from her father to Basil Lockwood, who in turn had willed it to Preston. Basil, like Michael's man of business, had believed that women should be taken care of by men and not have money or property of their own.

"I still own your father's house," Michael said now, still contemplating the cards. "Did you know that?"

She nodded, her throat tight. "Yes, I knew."

"I will make it yours as part of the settlements. Perhaps you would prefer to live there."

She shrugged, her skin cold. "This house is convenient for the London Season. Perhaps we could spend a few summer months at my father's old house."

He looked up. "You'd live there with me?"

"Of course I would."

He laughed a little, his face weary. "Do you know that after I left England I kept expecting a letter from you telling me you'd forgiven me. First I wanted it so I could send it back to you in shreds and pretend I was indifferent to your forgiveness. Then I wanted it because it dawned on me what a fucking idiot I had been."

She clasped her hands on her lap. "So was I, thinking myself so clever to have handsome Lord Michael wrapped around my finger. I refused your first proposal to prove my power. My father explained to me what a horrid little creature I'd been, and he was right."

Michael seemed not to hear her. "I thought I had to chase you, to master you, instead of simply telling you I loved you. Your father should never have let me do what I did, but I convinced him you were too stubborn to accept me without some incentive. So he helped me."

"Of course he wanted me to marry you—you were going to be a duke. He always wanted me to rise in the world; I believe he promised this to my mother before she died."

Michael studied her, a tired man who realized he couldn't run away from himself. "It was all so unnecessarily stupid."

"We were bloody fools," she murmured.

"And I've done it again. I knocked aside Preston to play the card game instead of simply taking you out of there and helping you. I wanted to show everyone I still had my power."

"I could have refused to marry you," she pointed out. "It was my choice."

He shook his head, pushing his hand through his already mussed hair. "And I've been seducing you, hoping that you'll fall in love with me in spite of everything." He looked directly at her. "Amelia, I am so sorry."

"I've liked our . . . bed games."

He smiled a little. "Do you think I haven't? You are the most luscious, beautiful woman in the world, and I want more than anything to stay in bed with you the rest of my life. But I refuse to coerce you any longer. I suggest you retreat to your father's old house, have a place to yourself. We don't have to obtain a legal separation—I think both our reputations will be the better for not doing that—but I will leave you alone, I promise."

Amelia stared at him, tears blurring her eyes. She sprang from her chair and flung herself onto his lap.

"No. I don't want to leave you."

"I think it best you do. Preston's accusations will stir up gossip, in any case, and it might be a while before I can suppress it."

She gave him a defiant look. "All the more reason for me to stay with you. To prove I know you married me without hindrance."

He kissed her. Not a hungry kiss, but a kiss of sorrow. She started to return it with passion, but he broke away.

"We ought to clear up the mess," he said. "Before we shock Merriman."

Without waiting for her reply, he slid her to her feet and began straightening the things they'd strewn all over the table and bed. Amelia helped him silently. She'd tried to reassure him with her declaration and with her card game that she was willing to make this marriage work, but she wasn't certain she'd succeeded.

When Merriman entered, Amelia slipped away, letting her tears flow once she was out of sight. She would not let Michael send her away—she would have to show him that a woman who'd buried herself in the country for ten years knew something of courage.

Thinking of the tenderness on his face when they'd made love in the chair made her tears flow again, but also strengthened her resolve. She knew exactly what she needed to do, and she had many plans to make.

TEN

Trumps

Michael disappeared after breakfast, which had been an uncomfortable meal. He'd hidden behind his newspaper and did not volunteer his plans for the morning. Amelia had the feeling he'd evade her questions, so she did not bother asking any.

Once Michael was off in one of the several conveyances he owned, she found Merriman. "I need you to help me," she said. "And not tell His Grace you are doing it."

Merriman raised his brows. He was a short man with a shock of black hair and blacker eyebrows that dominated his face. He used the eyebrows with much enthusiasm.

"Not tell 'is nibs?" he said doubtfully. "That's against me religion, that is. Did 'e tell ye how 'e saved me life from the mad Saracens? 'Sides, he's likely to shoot me if I cross 'im."

"He will not shoot you, and if you do not help me, I will tell my maid you are the admirer who is sending trinkets to her room. She is most curious to discover who is doing it."

Merriman whitened. "Ye wouldn't."

"I would."

Merriman made a noise of despair. "Now, missus, that's black-mail, that is."

"Yes," Amelia said, smiling.

"All right," he conceded. "But if 'e does shoot me for it, you make sure I'm laid out proper and tell me old mum it was you what got me killed." He shut off the dramatics and gave Amelia a conspiratorial look. "What ye want me to do?"

MICHAEL did not return until very late, and Amelia nearly burst keeping her secrets, but she kept them. She greeted him with a kiss that he did not return and took his coat to hand to the footman.

She led him to the drawing room where she tried to kiss him again but broke off when Merriman entered to bring Michael brandy and Amelia some tea. Merriman kept his head down and gave Michael only monosyllabic answers to his questions, until Michael became exasperated.

"What the devil is the matter with you, Merriman?"

"Nofink, sir, nofink at all." Merriman shot Amelia a glower, then collected his trays. "A touch under the weather is all."

Michael frowned, but did not pursue it.

Amelia sat facing him in her armchair, her feet flat on the floor, her hands in her lap. So might any wife greet her husband at the end of a day. She asked him brightly, "Were your errands productive, dear?"

Michael paused in the act of sipping his brandy. "Moderately. And yours?"

"Oh, I kept myself busy."

His green eyes narrowed. "I see you come out with weapons drawn. What have you been up to?"

"Nothing. Womanly occupations."

"I hope it involved preparations to remove to Surrey."

"No, I have decided to remain in London."

Michael opened the humidor next to him and took his time

choosing a cigar. He delicately bit off the end and bent forward to light the cigar in the flame of a candle. Amelia waited with ill-contained patience until he sat back and casually drew the smoke into his mouth.

"I thought wives were supposed to do what their husbands told them," he said, the smoke curling out with his words.

"I informed you I was tired of being obedient. Especially when I know you simply want me out of the way."

"I was not anticipating an argument."

"Then you do not know me as well as you thought. You want me in Surrey precisely because I do argue with you—you know I will argue with whatever it is you intend to do. Tell me."

He sighed, blue-gray smoke shrouding him. "I confronted Preston, hoping to call his bluff, but he agreed to produce this woman for me. I know he expected me to offer him money, so I offered him none. He'd run to the newspapers as soon as I tried to bribe him to silence, and the journalists would take it as proof of my guilt."

"Exactly why I should stay in London."

Michael tilted his head back and spoke to the ceiling. "And here I thought I'd married a prudent and logical woman."

"I am being prudent and logical. Trust me, it is most logical and necessary for me to stay. When does Preston say he will show you your supposed wife?"

"Two days from now, at his house." He stopped. "Do you know, Amelia, that part of me fears he really does have Anne-Marie? I know it is impossible, but at the same time, I can't help it."

Amelia rose and went to him, sliding onto his lap. He held the cheroot out of the way, but she liked its scent clinging to him. "We'll face him together and stop everyone spreading vicious stories about you. Preston will be our least important battle."

His hand stole around her waist. Michael's eyes were flint hard, and she knew he would continue to argue and cajole for her to go away, but he'd subsided for now.

Amelia stroked his cheek, loving the rough feel of the whiskers that had grown since Merriman shaved him that morning. Her father had taught her how to shave when he didn't have a manservant, and she'd learned to do it well. She'd offer to take over the task from Merriman tomorrow.

The idea of rubbing warm soap over Michael's face and carefully shaving him made her shiver in delight. She'd lean over him, nestling his head between her breasts, and he'd watch her with his light green eyes.

"I've never smoked a cheroot," she said in a low voice. "Will you show me how?"

His gaze flicked to her mouth, his hand tightened on her hips, and he drew a long breath. "Oh, Amelia . . ."

TWO days later, Michael rode in his most ostentatious ducal coach to Surrey to call upon Preston Lockwood, Amelia at his side.

He'd lost every argument about packing her off to either Surrey or his ducal estate in Cheshire, mostly because he knew she was right. Her suddenly leaving town would scream that Michael believed Preston's story about Anne-Marie still being alive.

It had been two days of hell. Not because of anticipating this visit, but because Amelia kept him hard and hot every waking hour of the day and night. He didn't want to touch her until they resolved things, but he couldn't keep his yearning at bay.

Then he *would* teach her to smoke a cigar, how to use her lips and tongue on it in the most enticing ways. He'd teach her to drink brandy by filling his mouth with it and having her kiss him. Then he'd buy more chocolates and eat bonbons off *her*.

Michael's mind went to darker places. What they'd done so far had been fairly innocuous, but there were even more entertaining games he could play with her. He thought of the discreet shop he'd visited in the Strand the other day, where he'd seen delicate jeweled manacles. There were so many more ways he could take her, and he'd teach her every one. . . .

He yanked his thoughts back to their unpleasant errand. Any more speculation and he'd have her splayed across the seat, her legs wrapped around him and her skirts rucked high. He turned to her and swiped his tongue through her mouth, then regretted it because his cock went rigid.

Amelia's eyes were dark in the shadows, but she smiled, as hungry as he was.

The coach jerked to a stop, and the footman pulled open the door. They'd arrived at Preston's house, the place where Michael had played cards for Amelia's heart. Nearly every window was lit up, and with an inward groan, Michael realized Preston was hosting another house party. He'd likely promised his friends and neighbors that the entertainment would be the humiliation of the Duke of Bretherton.

Amelia's hips swayed into him as they walked into the house, her hand on his arm. He held her close to him, not intending to turn her loose among Preston's friends.

Preston was indeed hosting another card party for his foppish sycophants plus minor members of the ton. They raised quizzing glasses and lorgnettes, excited to be entertained, as Michael and Amelia strolled past.

Preston Lockwood pushed through the crowd to welcome them personally. "Ah, Amelia, you are looking well." His greedy eyes roved Amelia up and down—not looking at her body, Michael realized, but calculating the expense of her gown and the jewels on her neck.

"*Her Grace* is very well," Michael said. "I have business to discuss with you, Lockwood, the only reason I am here. Where may we withdraw?"

Michael did not wait for Preston to deny his request. He stepped around him, Amelia in tow, and began to open doors until he found a moderately-sized sitting room.

Preston hurried after them, followed by four of his toadies. Michael eyed them coldly as Preston closed the door.

"In *private*, I believe I said."

"I want witnesses," Preston returned.

"Of course you do." Michael turned to Amelia. "Perhaps, my dear, you would like to wait somewhere more comfortable?"

"No, indeed," Amelia said at once.

Preston looked distressed. "Do go, Amelia. This is men's business."

She gave him a belligerent look. "This is to do with my marriage, and I am staying."

Michael did not want her here. If they'd faced Preston alone, he wouldn't have minded so much, but he didn't like Preston's identically dressed fops watching with bright eyes. He also saw the futility of arguing with Amelia. If he wanted her gone, he'd have to carry her off over his shoulder.

"Then sit down, my love, and we will get this over with." He held out a chair for Amelia, and she sat gracefully. Michael arranged himself behind her and rested his hand on her shoulder.

At least he had a card up his sleeve. Several days of research and running all over London had helped come up with a solution. Holderness, his man of business, had been useless—it was time to sack him.

Preston pretended to look sorrowful, but his lips quivered in excitement. "Very well, we'll get on." He snapped his fingers at one of his friends who grinned and left the room.

Michael gave Preston a lazy smile. "I am afraid I know that the woman you plan to produce is an imposter."

Preston laughed. "Of course you'd say that, Bretherton."

"Her real name is Susan Brown, and she comes from Norfolk. Was an actress several years ago, then retired to have a child."

He had the satisfaction of seeing Preston splutter to halt. "It doesn't matter," Preston said when he recovered. " 'Twill be your word against mine. All I have to do is cast suspicion on your marriage to Amelia and it will be over. I am only trying to protect my cousin. You coerced her into a marriage she didn't want, and I imagine she'd be happy to get out of it."

"You imagine wrong," Amelia said softly.

Michael's voice went hard. "End the farce, Lockwood. Retract your accusation, pay Mrs. Brown what you owe her, and we'll all go home."

Amelia was looking up at him, eyes shining. "That was quite clever, Michael. Much easier than what I did."

Michael's stomach tightened in misgiving. *"Easier than what you did?"*

"Merriman helped a great deal. You ought to give him a rise in wages."

A dozen scenarios swam through Michael's head, none of them good. No wonder Merriman had been looking guilty of late.

"Amelia," he said carefully. "What did you do?"

She smiled and looked wise, but before she could answer, Preston's friend flung open the door and came panting inside.

"I couldn't get her to come with me," he gasped.

"What are you talking about?" Preston began.

Through the open door, Michael heard raised voices, the indignant bleating of a woman and the strong, strident tones of a man.

"What the devil?" Preston exclaimed, and bolted from the room.

Amelia started to follow, looking worried, but Michael pulled her back. "Amelia, what—did—you—do?"

Her eyes sparkled with excitement. "Do not be cross with me, Michael. I only meant to help."

He stood still, breathing hard, his heavy hand keeping her from fleeing. "You—and Merriman?"

"Indeed. He was most helpful running up and down London for me. You will not like this, but I found a man who had been your first wife's lover."

Michael was so surprised, he released her. He watched, dumbfounded, as she scurried across the room, not to flee from him but to see what was going on in the drawing room.

A short, slender blond woman—Susan Brown—stood with

hands on hips, facing a tall, lean man in military dress who towered over her. The man had tanned, weathered skin and was handsome in a raw-boned way, with close-cropped brown hair and piercing blue eyes.

The army man flicked his gaze to Amelia. "You are correct, Your Grace—she is not Anne-Marie Moldava. Anne-Marie is dead, God rest her soul." He turned hard eyes on Preston. "You, sir, shall answer to me for this."

The blond woman planted her hands on her hips. "What about me wages?" she shouted at Preston. "Ye promised me wages to pretend to be this Anne-Marie lady."

Amelia smiled at Michael, her blue eyes starry. "Michael, allow me to introduce Lieutenant Colonel Sebastian Courtland of the Twenty-second Foot."

Courtland's gaze sliced over Michael. "Your Grace."

The two men were of a height, Michael staring back into blue eyes as cold as his own. Anne-Marie's lover. Bloody hell.

"Amelia," Michael said.

"Merriman helped me find him," Amelia said, as calm as if they were at a country garden party. "Preston, this man was well acquainted with Michael's first wife and quite incensed when he heard what use you meant to make of her memory."

Preston was now trying his best to become small and inconspicuous, difficult for a man of his circumference. Even his sycophants looked at him askance.

Michael gave Courtland a conciliatory nod. "It was good of you to come forward."

"I did not do it for you," Courtland answered coldly. "I have heard of you and know you for a blackguard. I did it for the lady." He made a slight bow to Amelia. "Now, perhaps you will take her from this house and leave me to deal with Mr. Lockwood."

"And me," Susan Brown's voice rang out. "*What about me wages?*"

"Happy to oblige you both," Michael said, feeling more lighthearted than he had in a decade. "If Preston cheats you out of your money, Mrs. Brown, you send word to me. Amelia, shall we go home?"

Merriman appeared out of nowhere with their wraps, grinning like a monkey. Michael sent him a severe look. "I will deal with you later."

"Right ye are, guv."

As they filed out the front door, Michael's friend Nathan Fuller was descending from his carriage, on time for his performance. "Where are you going?" he asked, bewildered. "I have Mrs. Brown's sister in my coach."

Mirth boiled up inside Michael. "I'm afraid you've missed most of it, Fuller. But please do me a favor and take Mrs. Brown's sister inside for their tearful reunion. It should be worth it."

Fuller looked mystified but nodded. "Only too pleased to help. But aren't you staying?"

"No, my old friend." Michael put his arm firmly around Amelia's waist. "I need to have a chat with my wife."

"Right." Fuller turned away, grinning.

Amelia was warm by his side, and Michael led her quickly to the carriage that Merriman had called. Before lifting her in, he slanted a hot kiss across her mouth, laughing.

ELEVEN

Bretherton Hall

Amelia thought Michael would demand an explanation once the carriage started, but as soon as they were out of the drive, he dragged her to him and began unfastening and unbuttoning her gown.

"Michael," she tried.

He took her face between his hands and kissed her hard. "Don't ever do that again."

"Do what again?"

His green eyes blazed. "Run around London doing business with men like Courtland. It's dangerous."

"Merriman did most of the running," she said. "I only spoke to Lieutenant Colonel Courtland yesterday."

"I've met men like him on my travels—they are hard and unpredictable."

"Like you." She smiled.

"'Tis no laughing matter, love."

"Neither is losing you." Her smile vanished. "I did not do this to prove how brave I am, nor how far I'm able to twine dangerous men around my fingers. I did it to save our marriage. I didn't want Preston to win."

"I was working plenty hard to save it, Amelia."

"Quite secretively," she reminded him. "While you tried to send me off to Surrey."

"I planned to take care of the matter then join you there."

"Well, it is resolved now. What is the harm?"

Michael growled. "The harm is you dealing with things like this. Leave any sordidness concerning me alone."

"It concerned me as well." Her smile returned. "And I did want to see Preston's face when he was caught."

"I will flog Merriman," Michael muttered.

"No, you will not. He was most helpful. I sent him 'round to the army clubs to chat with valets and batmen and discover whether any of their officers had spent time in the Near East eight or ten years ago. Fortunately only a few men fit that description, and of them, only Courtland had known Anne-Marie. He agreed to meet with me to hear what I had to say, and he was very upset at Preston." She stopped, saying the next part hesitantly. "I believe he loved Anne-Marie very much."

"Did he, poor chap? Anne-Marie was not one to repay love with kindness."

"Did you love her?"

Michael hesitated a fraction of a second, then shook his head. "I thought so at the time, but I know now I never loved her. We were too much alike for love. Why she agreed to marry me is anyone's guess—a lark probably or perhaps to taunt her family. They were rather stuffy."

"I'm sorry," Amelia said softly.

"It was a long time ago." His arms tightened around her. "If nothing else, she gave me Felice."

Amelia remembered his worry that Felice was not even his, and she realized he loved Felice regardless. It took a man with a good heart to do that.

After a moment Michael said, "I concede I rather enjoyed seeing Preston's reaction myself." He gave her a fierce kiss. "But
please don't do anything like that again."

"I'm your wife," she said. "Your helpmeet. That means *help*
and *mate*."

"In this marriage I coerced you into." He withdrew a little, still
with his arm around her, but she felt the change. "I resolved to
work long and hard for your forgiveness, but I realize I have no
right to. I don't even deserve to ask forgiveness of you."

She rested her head on his shoulder, liking how warm and
strong he was. "I was just as proud and arrogant as you were all
that time ago. I can't blame you being furious with me. I'd strung
you along like a vixen, so self-satisfied."

He looked down at her in surprise. "Is that how you saw yourself?"

"Oh, yes. Perhaps I didn't realize it then, but all the attention
went to my head. I was a little beast."

"You were the most beautiful woman I'd ever seen. And in ten
years, you've grown only more beautiful."

Her heart warmed. "You are kind."

"It isn't kindness; it's simple truth. I loved you madly, but I covered it well with arrogance and idiocy. I thought I had to best you
to prove to the world that I could. Why I thought you'd bleat with
gratitude I have no idea."

"I am grateful. You saved me from Preston, and you've given
me hope that you and I can start over again."

His eyes went bleak. "Why would you want to start over with a
wreck like me?"

Amelia touched his face, loving the flick of his eyes as his gaze
was drawn to her mouth. "Simple. I love you."

He studied her for a long moment, chest rising and falling with
his breath, then he seized her and kissed her. He opened her
mouth, doing amazing things with his tongue.

She smiled under his lips. "I am looking forward to reaching home."

His grin was pure Michael—feral and delightful. "Never mind reaching home." He pushed her skirt up, his strong hands skimming her legs to her bare thighs. "Up on the seat with you. I am going to show you how much we can do in a carriage with an hour's drive ahead of us."

Michael lifted her to the cushions on her hands and knees, his touch gentle despite his strength. She wasn't certain what to expect, but she felt cool air on her bare bottom, and then Michael hard and heavy between her thighs.

The carriage was large and sumptuous with soft pillows and carpet on the floor, but the seat was a tight fit with both her and Michael on it. Amelia didn't mind as Michael's weight came across her back, then he was filling her, sliding straight into her slick quim.

She wanted to scream, but bit it back, not wanting the coachmen or footmen to hear. Michael laughed in her ear, the wicked, wicked man, as he *fucked* her in his own coach.

"Michael." She moaned, trying to hold back her climax. "I love you. I love you so much."

The words seemed to galvanize him. He pumped into her, his staff so very thick and hard. He rutted her like an animal, and at the same time it was so beautiful.

"I love you," she repeated.

"Stop," he said hoarsely. He groaned, taking her furiously, his fists heavy on her back. "No—not—*yet.*"

His scalding seed filled her, even though he was trying to hold back, not wanting this to end.

He backed out of her and scooped her onto his lap, kissing her face, his hands all over her body. "Say it again. Please."

"That I love you?"

"Yes. Say it over and over, as many times as you like. I'm a bad, bad man and I need you to love me so much."

She stilled his frantic hands and brought them to her lips. "I love you, Michael."

He suddenly gazed at her as though she'd stuck a knife into him instead of told him how she felt. She saw fear and anguish and terrible hope in his eyes. She said it again.

"I love you."

His arms went around her hard, and he buried his face in her neck. "I've always loved you. Loved you when you spurned me and when I tried to take over your life, and when I ran away from England, pretending I didn't care. I loved you when I came back, and especially when I saw you standing in front of Preston like a shining light. I knew I'd do anything to have you back."

"I wanted you, too. I wanted it to be real this time."

His next kiss was relentless. "When we get home . . ."

"Yes?" she asked eagerly. "When we get home?"

"I won't be merciful."

"Excellent."

"Even if you say you love me, I won't give you quarter."

Amelia shivered in anticipation. "I look forward to it."

Michael shot her a mischievous grin, his eyes filled with love. "It will be the most vicious game of piquet you have ever played." She started to laugh, and he added, voice dark, "But the prize will be the most exquisite pleasure you've ever known."

"A most interesting challenge, Your Grace." She put her arms around him and kissed the tip of his nose. "I can't resist."

A week later Michael entered his huge house in Cheshire to see a demon barrel down the stairs and run straight into his legs. *"Papa!"*

He saved himself from falling by swinging her into his arms. "Hullo, little hellion."

Michael kissed his daughter's cheek, then took in her snarled hair, dirty face, and torn dress. "You look horrible. Did you not know we were coming today?"

"My governess told me. She made me dress up all proper, but Bill in the stables wanted to show me the new foal. . . ."

Michael knew what that meant—Felice scrambling to keep up with the stable boy in her best clothes, not noticing or caring about muddy straw or dirty floors as she crawled over them. Likely she'd petted all the horses and let them drool on her as well.

Felice gave him a mud-smeared kiss. "Can we go back to Egypt, Papa? They won't let me wear boy's clothes here or ride astride or do as I like."

"A little polish won't hurt you, demon. And anyway, what would your new mama think of you?"

Felice kicked to get away from him, and he set her down. "Where is she?"

She ran to the front door just as Amelia ducked inside, untying her bonnet. Felice stopped short when she saw Amelia, and Michael held his breath.

Felice looked Amelia over, hands behind her back, as though she examined a priceless statue. "She's very beautiful. You have good taste, Papa."

Michael relaxed, the tricky threshold crossed. "And if you wash yourself thoroughly, she might even let you touch her."

"Don't be silly." Amelia knelt and opened her arms. "I've been anxious to meet you, Felice."

Felice didn't hesitate. She leapt forward and flung her arms around Amelia's neck.

Amelia hugged her for a long time, her eyes moist. Then she set Felice down, giving her a sunny smile. "Clean up for tea, and we'll have a nice chat. I've brought you all kinds of presents."

"The last thing she needs." Michael rolled his eyes.

Amelia gave Felice a conspiratorial look. "We won't share them with him."

Felice laughed. She shot her father a very Michael-like wink, then dashed away, shouting at the top of her lungs. Her harried governess came to the top landing and took her away.

Amelia peeled off her gloves, highly amused, then she gave Michael an incredible gift.

"I'm not sure why you doubt she's yours, Michael. She looks just like you."

Michael's throat went tight. "Does she?"

"Of course she does. The same nose, the same chin, the same smile. She might be your twin when she winks like that."

Michael's world spun. For years he'd hoped that Felice belonged to him, that it was true he had someone to call his own, but the uncertainty had always gnawed at him. Anne-Marie had cuckolded him and lied to him so continuously he hadn't been certain of anything. Amelia had just wiped out that uncertainty in a few words, without knowing she'd done something momentous.

Oblivious of his shock, Amelia went on. "And she'll have a new brother or sister next spring."

This time, Michael's throat closed entirely and the only sound that came out was a strangled croak.

Amelia gave him her beautiful, full-lipped smile. "My dear Michael, what did you think would be the result of all those games of piquet?"

She was laughing at him—the decidedly devilish Duke of Bretherton—as he stood with his mouth hanging open. Her laughter echoed to the high ceiling, ringing from the portraits of long-dead dukes and duchesses who looked down their noses at her.

Michael had always thought of this house as a grim mausoleum—now with Amelia and Felice and a new child, it would be a place of laughter and joy.

Amelia's laugh turned to a shriek as he caught her around the waist and spun her off her feet. He kissed her with all the wicked passion he could muster, until dark desire rippled through them both. Amelia's kiss tasted of sweetness and spice, overlaid with the smooth chocolate they'd done fine things with on the carriage journey up here.

Amelia smiled down at him and kissed him back, the love in her eyes making Michael complete at last.

A NIGHT AT THE THEATER
Claudia Dain

ONE

Drury Lane, London 1782

Zoe Auvray was in the almost comically ordinary position of being an actress without a role and without the immediate prospect of one. Naturally she found nothing at all comical about being without a roof and with barely a morsel in her belly, but she was French, and what was more, Parisian, and she could therefore look at her current circumstances with a somewhat cynical and amused gaze. Also naturally she fully expected to exit her present circumstances at the first opportunity. Tonight ought to do nicely.

Zoe, in London for less than a month, had made one remarkable friend and one stellar enemy. It was her enemy, Miranda Sinclair, a rather ordinary player in a less-than-ordinary play being even now acted upon the Drury Lane stage, who was responsible for Zoe being without a part. Miranda, an obvious allusion to Shakespeare and certainly not the name with which she had been born, could not act, but she could pose. Men did seem to enjoy watching Miranda move through her various poses, both on and off the stage, which accounted for her current success. But a success at posing was not at all a long-term thing, and so Zoe, who was more skilled at acting than Miranda, had lost her role.

Zoe, naturally, had no proof that Miranda had been the cause of her dismissal. Some things were just too obvious not to be true. Miranda, as did all avowed enemies, deserved a lovely and just retribution.

Zoe knew just what form her particular retribution upon Miranda would take, which put her in mind of her remarkable friend, Sophia Grey. Sophia was a courtesan of youth, beauty, and a rather brilliant strain of ruthlessness that Zoe found particularly fascinating, not to mention amusing. Their friendship, an alliance based on their mutual benefit, the most solid foundation for any friendship to begin, was predicated on their clear and unwavering understanding that men must serve as their platform into a much better, that is to say, much richer way of life.

In this, it was quite impossible for two women to be more aligned in purpose.

They sat in graceful poses in Sophia's box, looking down at the theater crowd below and around them. The Theatre Royal at Drury Lane was very popular as Richard Brinsley Sheridan would allow only the most entertaining plays to be produced there. The theater itself was built along very pleasant lines, though the sound quality, particularly where it involved bass voices, could have been improved. As a more than spectacular soprano, Zoe was highly aware of these sorts of details in theater design. However, the important details of this evening were that they were well displayed in Sophia's box facing the stage and they were well turned out, compliments of Sophia and by way of one of her previous protectors.

Sophia was wearing a perfectly lovely gown of golden ivory silk faille with an ivory serpentine floral motif and gold thread brocade. It was completely perfect for Sophia with her black hair and dark eyes and was delightfully augmented by a choker of diamonds and sapphires with earrings to match. Sophia looked what she was; a very successful, very beautiful, very expensive woman.

Zoe, courtesy of Sophia and her endless generosity, was wearing a borrowed gown of rosy beige silk faille with woven floral bouquets on an ivory ground. It was sumptuous and made her look equally so. Around her throat she wore a necklace of garnets and sapphires, also borrowed.

Sophia was beautiful in precisely the way that Zoe was not, which made her even more ideal as an ally obviously. Sophia was darkly sophisticated, coolly elegant, and seductively mysterious. Zoe was, without being hobbled by ridiculous modesty, blatantly sexual, amusing in the precise way that men found compelling, and lushly formed. And she could act, which was a very necessary ingredient when dealing with men. It was for these very reasons that Miranda had managed to get her sacked. It was for these very reasons that she would make her way very well into London's best and deepest pockets.

Zoe, if it was not already perfectly obvious, was going to take a lover. She would keep him for as long as he served her every need, which did not predict any sort of protracted relationship, but it should be pleasant enough for as long, or as short, as it lasted.

What could be more pleasant?

"Westlin is available as I have quite done with him," Sophia said, waving her fan languidly. "You could do worse, though barely. He has quite deep pockets and has a dismal ability to protect them. Quite the perfect choice, if one discounts his character."

"Perhaps. If other avenues close to me. I might consider him as an avenue of last chance."

"Quite precisely how he should be considered," Sophia said, her gaze skimming over Westlin as he stood talking somewhat heatedly with a most beguiling looking man of the most elegant proportions. "If he had not left me equipped with a healthy annuity and a house on one of the best streets in Town, I should find it difficult to say anything positive about him at all."

"He sounds almost repellant," Zoe said, with a smile.

"I am being most restrained as it is perfectly obvious upon the slightest contact," Sophia said, without an answering smile, "that

Westlin is completely repellant." Sophia had almost no sense of humor at all where it pertained to the brooding Lord Westlin, which was a fascinating response to the man who had provided for her so substantially. "But if Westlin is not to be for you, is there another man whom you would like to tempt? The theater throngs with them tonight, as indeed it does every night. London, for all its sophistication, is a most predictable city."

"And the men of London?" Zoe asked. She had been in London for almost a month; Sophia for over a year. In that time, surely a city must divulge its secrets to even the least discerning. Sophia was anything but the least discerning. Sophia Grey was without a doubt the most discerning and observant woman Zoe had ever known.

"As predictable as the men of any country. They want one thing above all else and answer to its every whim. It is," Sophia said, with a smile, "so very convenient for women of a certain sophistication, is it not?"

"Very convenient," Zoe agreed.

Women of a certain sophistication. Yes, she was that now, but it was a new condition, not even a year old. She had stumbled upon what she thought must be a very ordinary path to have reached her current destination; namely that of a woman of lost virtue, forced to make her way alone upon the world stage. It was a very melancholy recitation of facts, which was why she seldom allowed herself to think of it. Things were as they were. They did not change by either tears or tantrums.

"What of the Marquis of Melverley?" Zoe asked, pulling her thoughts back onto the necessary path, the path to food and shelter.

"Completely debauched," Sophia said swiftly, "and without the inclination for generosity."

"How unpleasant."

"Very," Sophia agreed, with a smile.

"He is not even well featured. How completely unaccommodating of him."

"He does have that reputation."

They were near to laughing now, which was such a delight. One might be destitute, but that certainly meant that laughter was even more of a necessity.

"And he? Who is that? He is well featured, though his coat lacks distinction," Zoe asked.

"That," Sophia said softly, "is my reason for being at Drury Lane tonight. Mr. Edward Jackson, the one responsible for Emma Chester's current position, or lack of one."

Ah, yes, Zoe had heard of Mr. Jackson. It was common knowledge, at least in certain circles, that Emma Chester, sweet, lovely, and entirely virginal, had succumbed to the very oldest and most profoundly hackneyed of seductions. She had fallen in love.

Perhaps the real truth of it was that she had been convinced she was in love. Certainly, as the story went, Mr. Jackson, the man who had so artlessly deflowered her, had showed no indication that he had ever loved Emma.

It was all so completely ordinary and so completely like a man.

Sweet words, an ardent look, a torrid kiss, up go the skirts and there you are: ruined. Which was not at all how it had happened to her, but she had been in enough plays to know how the scene was written.

"But what are you to do with Mr. Jackson?" Zoe asked.

"I am to make him pay, darling Zoe," Sophia said silkily. "I shall make him pay all that he can bear. And then just a bit more."

"In cash?"

"If possible, but mostly in humiliation and, if possible, in rejection. I am almost completely certain that it shall be possible. Just look at him. Is he not ideally suited for humiliation?"

Zoe looked. Mr. Jackson was a man in his physical prime and possessed of physical beauty of the tall, blond, blue-eyed sort. He was, to be sure, London's idealized standard of high-born loveliness. Zoe found him singularly unappealing. It was clear that Sophia did as well, though perhaps for different reasons. Zoe had known Sophia just long enough to understand that Sophia would do very much indeed for a friend. If Emma Chester had been misused by Mr. Jackson, then Sophia would think it only her duty to punish Mr. Jackson in every conceivable way. It was an initial impression about Sophia, to be sure, but it was a strong impression, and Zoe had learned that first impressions were entirely reliable. If she had only listened to her instincts a few months ago, she would not be in her current circumstances. And that was all the proof she would ever need to never doubt them again.

"Then your evening is planned. You have your man and your method. Is there anyone whom you can recommend to me? I would so like to have things settled as quickly as possible," Zoe said, which was a considerable understatement as she had nowhere to spend the night and she hadn't eaten anything more than a pastry in two days, until Sophia had taken her in just that afternoon and they had formed the only plan open to women of their particular skills.

Sophia, though comfortably fixed by Westlin, understood her situation well enough and looked at her sympathetically.

"I will repeat my offer, darling Zoe. You can stay with me for as long as is required for you to find your own nest. I know what it is to be without . . . everything," Sophia said, with an almost comical shrug. "I have a house. I have an income. I have complete ease in sharing what I have won from the men of London."

"I do appreciate your generous offer," Zoe said, taking Sophia's hand and squeezing it. "I feel I must provide for myself, dear Sophia. Besides, if we live together, it would invite the wrong sort of speculation."

"A bawdy house?" Sophia asked. "That might be amusing actually. Just think of what the gossips would say."

"You do not fear gossip?"

"Fear it? No, I use it. Gossips do all the work for me, darling Zoe. My reputation is built on it and it is in great measure why I can live as richly as I do. Tonight, in sparring with Mr. Jackson, I will add to my reputation and the gossips will do the rest."

Zoe felt in that instant how very unsophisticated she was in comparison to Sophia. Perhaps after a year in London, she would as well let gossip carry her ship, but now she was still too new at this to want to be discussed in such a way, even by strange and unknown people in a strange city.

"However," Sophia said, speaking from behind her fan, "if you would build a nest, I would strongly suggest that you look to the Duke of Aldreth. He is married to a woman of supreme refinement. He is fabulously wealthy. He is almost devastatingly handsome," Sophia said, which truly did give all the particulars in a very logical order.

Aldreth was a duke, which was as high as a woman could possibly go unless she wanted a prince and no one wanted princes anymore as they never had any ready money.

Aldreth was married and was therefore almost required to feed his passions elsewhere, particularly as his wife was refined. There was almost nothing worse in the bedroom than refinement.

Aldreth was able to give her the sort of life she wanted, perhaps even deserved.

Aldreth was handsome, which surely never hurt in these matters. Zoe was not so sophisticated that she could perform without some spark of attraction. She was very new to the entire experience of selling herself and she was very afraid that it showed.

"He sounds perfectly lovely," Zoe said. "But why have you not snared him for yourself, Sophia?"

"Because I have decided upon another course entirely, Zoe. I do believe I am going to marry. It is time."

Most odd. Women in their position did not often marry, at least not well. Zoe could not imagine Sophia not marrying well. Sophia wouldn't consider marriage if not done well.

"Have you chosen the man?"

"I haven't quite decided yet," Sophia said. "What do you think of . . ." Her voice trailed off. "Him?" With the smallest flick of her fan, Sophia indicated a scrumptious looking man. He was tall, dark, elegant. And he was in heated conversation with the Earl of Westlin.

"Who is he?" Zoe asked from behind her fan.

"The Earl of Dalby," Sophia answered. "He dislikes the Earl of Westlin almost as much as I do. Doesn't that speak well of him? He clearly has marvelous taste."

"Does he know you?" Zoe asked.

"Not yet. But he will," Sophia said, with a smile. "I shouldn't be at all surprised if Westlin was spilling out every thought in his head about me even now. Just look at Westlin's face. He looks positively livid. I blush to admit that I am the only one who can drive him to that particular strain of distress. Can you see how his nostrils are as white as chalk, the freckles almost visible from here? I perfected that."

Zoe looked down at the men below them. The theater was packed almost to capacity, the players on the stage nearly shouting to be heard above the noise of the audience. There was nothing quite so tempestuous as a theater crowd, which made it an ideal place to shop for men. They did like to bustle so, shoving and shouting. Zoe was so grateful to be sheltered in Sophia's box, a box for which Lord Westlin had paid out the Season. It was going to be so lovely to have a wealthy man see to all her needs. She did so hope that the Duke of Aldreth was going to be agreeable about it.

"But why do you want to marry, Sophia?" Zoe asked. "Your wants are seen to brilliantly and you have the freedom to enjoy having your needs attended at will."

"I've done everything else, darling," Sophia said, watching Westlin and Dalby snarl at each other with obvious enjoyment. "Why not give marriage a try?"

TWO

"Still lusting after your ex-mistress?" asked the Earl of Dalby of the Earl of Westlin.

Westlin did not so much as bother to turn and face Dalby. Westlin and Dalby had a history and a not altogether pleasant one. Westlin, as it happened, had married the woman Dalby had asked to marry. That was years ago now, of course, but one did not forget slights of that particular sort, especially as Westlin had not so much as looked at Harriet until Dalby had decided she would make the perfect wife. And she would have, for him. From all reports, which were scarce as Harriet rarely left Westlin's estate, she was miserable as Westlin's wife. Small wonder. Westlin was and ever had been the most stiff-necked man Dalby had ever known. That Harriet, whom he remembered as being of an exceptionally sweet nature, should be married to Westlin was completely horrid.

"Hardly," Westlin answered. "I've tasted all I want of that particular sweet. I'm here to cleanse my palate, if you take my meaning."

"Which is why you can't take your eyes off her," Dalby said pointedly.

All of London had watched the explosion that had accompanied Sophia Grey's removal of Westlin from her life. Things of that sort did not often happen. In point of fact, Dalby could not remember when it had ever happened before. Westlin, as these things went, had all the advantages as well as all the money. Sophia, it was perfectly obvious, had the bollocks of a bull elephant.

She had thrown Westlin out of her bed.

It was singular. It was wonderful. Of all people, a woman of uncertain pedigree had taken Westlin down a peg. The only way for Dalby to have been more pleased was if he had taken a hand in things himself, helped things along, as it were.

Dalby had come to the theater tonight with the half-formed thought of meeting Sophia Grey. Everyone spoke of her and the rumors about her spun wildly from dusk to dawn, the most popular story of late being what she had done to the Earl of Westlin. Dalby could not imagine why he had not yet met her, though knowing how Westlin managed his women, he likely had kept Sophia sequestered.

She was a beautiful woman, though possessed less of beauty than of dignity. It was an odd pairing of attributes. Some might even say it would be impossible for a woman of her reputation to possess any semblance of dignity. Yet she did. It was in her very carriage. She was tallish and slender for a woman, her hair black to match her eyes, her brows black slashes on cream white skin. Her mouth was wide and her nose was narrow. She had the look of French nobility and one of the rumors was that she was of a noble French house that had lost the bulk of its assets in the Seven Years' War.

"You hadn't taken her up for long, had you? She ran off quickly enough. I suppose even money can't keep a woman who won't be kept," Dalby remarked.

"I was done with her," Westlin said stiffly.

"That's not the story as I heard it. In fact, it's not how it's going down on White's book."

"I don't particularly care to have my name on White's book," Westlin said, avoiding Dalby's gaze.

"Then you should stop brawling with your mistresses," Dalby said. "The story, as it's going round, is that Sophia marked you as she left you. Something about a knife? Is it true she carries a blade?"

"She's a proper savage, isn't she?" Westlin said in a hoarse undertone, his pale skin flushed pink, his nostrils flaring white.

"Yes, that's the rumor that's been making the rounds," Dalby said in pleasant contemplation, watching Sophia as she slid her way past a throng of men, each one of them snared by the swish of her burnished gold skirts and the absolute disdain she showered upon them. What man could resist disdain in such a compelling package? "Is there any truth to that? Is she part Iroquois?" For that was another of the many rumors galloping about Town concerning Miss Grey, that she was an Indian of the Iroquois nation. An interesting notion, though he could not quite credit it.

"You think we shared pillow secrets?" Westlin snorted. "Hardly, yet she's a complete savage, as far as I'm concerned."

"Yes, you would say that," Dalby said. "Where did she mark you, Westlin? The wager at White's is that it's in a very vulnerable spot and that you bled copiously. It's being whispered that you can no longer perform, which would explain why your mistress jumped your bed for another. Perfectly logical, I might add."

"I hope you bet your estate, Dalby. You'd lose it. I would so enjoy telling Lady Westlin about your fall into penury."

"Oh, do you still speak to her? How convivial," Dalby replied. "I would have thought that by now Harriet would have nothing to say to you."

"Believe me when I tell you that Sophia will have nothing to say to you, Dalby."

"Not even if I ask her? I'm certain that she'll tell all. All women love to boast of a victory, particularly against a man, don't they?"

"I'd wager against that," Westlin said, his blue eyes blazing. "Sophia has peculiar ideas about men and women and what she'll do and not do."

"She wouldn't speak against you?" Dalby said. Did Sophia actually still have some feeling for Westlin? Was this nothing more than a spectacular lovers' spat? It was almost unthinkable. He wouldn't believe it.

"I'd hardly know that, but I do know that Sophia does not deal in details."

"What the devil does that mean?" Dalby asked.

"Ten minutes in her company and you'll know well enough what I mean. The woman is shrouded in mist. She'll let no one see her fully, which is just as well, I say. She should keep to the shadows. She belongs there, not out in Society with the rest of us. She's not like us," Westlin said, under his breath. "She's nothing like us."

"What did you do to her, Westlin?" Dalby asked, the mood suddenly thick. "What did you force upon her?"

"She was mine to do with as I willed. I paid for her, didn't I?" Westlin said smoothly, his tone defiant.

"Such skill with women." Dalby breathed slowly, thinking of the woman he might have married and how poorly Harriet's father had chosen for her. "The mind reels."

"If you think you'll fare better, try her. She'll slice your balls off. We'll see what appears on White's book then."

"You would wager on her? Has Miss Grey not taught you yet that she will best you?"

"The wager now is whether she will best you," Westlin said, his intense blue eyes gleaming. "Find out what I did to earn her anger, if you can."

Dalby swallowed in disgust.

"I will not wager on her."

"Afraid?"

Dalby could feel his blood roaring through his chest, his fists eager to pummel Westlin's arrogant face.

"I will find out where she cut you, Westlin; that is our wager."

"Fine, if that is all you are willing to risk. Find that out, if you can. I'll be watching."

"Do that," Dalby said, turning from Westlin to follow Sophia through the crowd. "I'm quite certain you'll enjoy the experience."

THE Duke of Aldreth had it all and he found it a surprisingly dissatisfying experience. It was not what he had been led to expect while drooling in the nursery. He was titled, healthy, wealthy, and married to one of the beauties of the day. Martha Whaley, one of the famed Whaley sisters, had been the most sought after of her sisters and indeed of all women of that particular Season in Town and he had won her for himself.

Aldreth, quite logically, had loved her, still loved her in the way that dukes love their duchesses. Martha was beautiful, agreeable, and accomplished. Martha had delivered him of a daughter, Amelia, not the heir he needed, but a pretty child all the same. Martha was very agreeable, certainly, and that applied to the bedroom. Her duty before her as clearly as his was before him, an heir must be achieved. The problem, in its most basic form, was that Martha was not at all accomplished at childbirth. Amelia had very nearly killed her. The next child likely would.

He found he had very little eagerness to bed his wife when her death was to be the likely result.

No, things had not turned out at all as he had supposed they would when his future had been laid out before him by his father, the first Duke of Aldreth.

Naturally his father had made huge sacrifices and taken monumental risks to earn himself a dukedom, and as such Aldreth was expected, and indeed had been trained from childhood, to carry on. He was to fulfill his obligations to his station in a responsible and noteworthy manner. He was to make no hard enemies. He was to make useful friends. He was to increase the wealth and protect the estate and he was to do this for the reputation of his father and the future of his son.

His father, as was usually the case, was dead. His son did not yet exist. Aldreth found himself in a state of flux and mist where all his instruction and his primary duties were as insubstantial as cloud.

He had a good wife, but he could not make good use of her.

Martha, no stranger to the duties of station, bore the burden much as he did, which is to say, in silent misery. She had, however, just last month and while still in bed recovering from the birth of Amelia, taken him figuratively by the collar and poured out her heart to him. Her heart, she made clear, was full of love and respect and not a little guilt. Her heart insisted that he find a feminine companion to see him through. Her heart would beat more easily if he could find one woman to align himself with, discreetly, ever discreetly, rather than avail himself of the scores of women who prowled the night. She understood his needs. She understood his sensitivity in not often visiting his needs upon her.

It had been a most uncomfortable conversation, particularly as authored by his wife.

He had kissed her and left her. He had not known what to do beyond that. He was certain that, in time, he would think of something. He had not. To be fair, he had not wanted to think about the situation as it stood, for what was the solution? He had a duty that he could not or would not shirk, his temperament and training being what they were. The Aldreth dukedom as fathered by the Cavershams must go forth. His wife must be protected.

Things being as they were, Aldreth avoided his wife as a forced habit and, to amuse himself, had formed a fast crowd to run with. He was rarely amused, another disappointment in a carefully planned life. Take, for example, Mr. Jackson. Mr. Jackson, untitled and with a perfectly ordinary fortune at his disposal, kept fast company and had built a fast reputation in order to do so. Mr.

Jackson, stupidly, was perfectly content to be a part of any party that existed solely to pursue pleasure, even if he could not truly afford it.

Aldreth, who suffered Jackson's presence because he was too lethargic to abandon him, found this remarkably pointless to the extent of being ridiculous. Jackson, if he had any sense at all, which he clearly didn't, ought to get himself back to whatever county claimed him and make something of his life.

Jackson, naturally, had no such plan.

"They say she cut him and that he threw her out of his bed for it," Jackson was saying, watching Sophia Grey as she passed through the crowd.

"A reasonable response, certainly," Aldreth replied, letting his gaze settle on Sophia Grey for a moment. She was a beautiful woman and certainly knew how to make herself the center of attention, a useful talent for any woman to possess.

"The wagering is to exactly *where* she cut him," Jackson said, with rather more enjoyment than the remark required.

It was entirely too lurid a remark and Aldreth was in the entirely wrong frame of mind to enjoy it. Aldreth was, in that precise moment, done with Jackson.

"Why don't you find out?" he said. It was not so much a question as a command. He was a duke, after all, and he was quite accustomed to having his desires made facts.

"A wager?" Jackson said, with entirely more eagerness than was in good taste. Jackson owed him a hundred pounds and was logically eager to reduce a sum that he likely could not pay.

"If you like," Aldreth said. "Find out where Sophia cut Westlin, by whatever means you find necessary, and we shall call your debt to me met." It was a generous offer and had the benefit of being simple to accomplish and of getting all ties to the tiresome Jackson severed, once and for all. "I shall watch, naturally, to make certain that it is from Miss Grey herself that you gain the information and from no other. A matter of form, you understand."

An entirely insulting statement, obviously, and one that had the added benefit of being amusing to deliver. In his more quiet moments, moments he avoided with rare talent, Aldreth was aware that he was becoming a rather hard man and in some lights, even cruel.

It was with delight and some relief that Aldreth was able to drown his thoughts in the noise and activity of the Theatre Royal at Drury Lane.

MR. JACKSON approached Sophia with the exact degree of directness to which Sophia was accustomed. In fact, some might say that he almost ran to her side. Certainly Sophia was inclined to say so.

"Miss Grey, may I introduce myself to you? I believe we have a mutual acquaintance."

Sophia could hardly keep from laughing in his face. What an ill-conceived start to their conversation.

"If you mean the lovely Miss Chester, then you are correct, which is entirely why I have no desire to speak to you, Mr. Jackson. Good evening," she said, dismissing him in the exact way that a man most detests and that would ensure that he refuse his dismissal. Men were so very predictable about these things and it was so very convenient of them to be so.

"But," he said, recovering as quickly as he could, "I loved her, Miss Grey."

"You loved her?" Sophia said sweetly, moving her fan languidly in the general region of her bodice. Jackson's attention strayed there and remained, reliably fixed. "Or was it simply that you were overcome by passion and Miss Chester was the convenient cure?"

Jackson lifted his gaze briefly and attempted to impale her with a look of rebuke. He failed. Impaling was not in Jackson's catalog of skills.

"You mock me, but I did think myself in love with her. Gaining her regard became my sole purpose."

"Until you attained it," Sophia said.

"Surely you will grant that nothing is as simple as that, Miss Grey," he said.

In that he spoke the truth. Nothing at all was simple, except perhaps revenge.

"As you say," she said, with a nod of acknowledgement. "You loved her. It was not simple. And now you seek me out. There is nothing simple in that, either, is there, Mr. Jackson?"

"I am a man, Miss Grey. You are a woman impossible to ignore."

"I am aware of both facts, Mr. Jackson," she said, with a half smile of invitation. He was making it so simple and it was really quite pleasant of him.

"Then you are amenable to a friendship between us?"

Dear, simple Mr. Jackson.

"Mr. Jackson, I am not adverse to making new friends, though, as you have pointed out, nothing is quite that simple. I was not aware that you had the funds necessary to pursue an alliance with me."

"I had not thought it would be a friendship of that sort, Miss Grey," he said, growing slightly flushed about the ears. As he was excessively blond, it did not suit him in the least.

"Between men and women, what other sort of friendship is possible, Mr. Jackson?" she asked. "To be truthful, I have made my fortune on that particular point of fact."

"I only thought to know you, Miss Grey, in the most cordial of ways."

"That does not sound at all profitable, Mr. Jackson."

Mr. Jackson stepped closer to her, which was not at all enjoyable, and whispered, "I am involved in a wager, Miss Grey. Aid me, and I will share the profits with you."

"Profits?" she answered softly. "I'm listening, Mr. Jackson."

He swallowed heavily and, casting a glance about the theater, said, "Everyone in Town is laying odds on precisely how your alliance with the Earl of Westlin came to an end."

"And I care because?" she said.

Jackson swallowed again. "Because of the drama with which you disposed of him, Miss Grey. How many women have exited relationships such as the one that you shared with Lord Westlin?"

"If they shared the relationship with Lord Westlin, all of them, I should say," Sophia said sarcastically.

Jackson looked about and swallowed again. He was becoming most tedious. How he'd ever managed to find his way under Emma Chester's skirts was becoming the question of the hour.

"But Miss Grey," he said, "you know you are spectacular. You cannot walk across Piccadilly without being commented upon and emulated. Do not think I mean to flatter you. I only speak the truth."

"But of course you mean to flatter me, Mr. Jackson. I enjoy it completely. Do continue."

"It is because of who you are, how you've captivated London, that everyone wants to know everything concerning you," he said.

"Then they are destined to be disappointed, Mr. Jackson."

"But I have made a wager, Miss Grey, a wager with the Duke of Aldreth that I would discover where and how you injured Lord Westlin. If I can discover this, from you . . . a hundred pounds is the wager."

Of course his wording was too careful. He did not say that he would win one hundred pounds. Still, it *was* a wager and as a wager could so easily be made to humiliate Mr. Jackson. What was there to lose? Indeed, because it involved the Duke of Aldreth, it might be in Zoe's best interest to pursue it. Zoe's stumbling across Aldreth's path would look so much more innocent that way. Men did seem to enjoy a certain degree of innocence where women were concerned, as long as it did not inconvenience them in the least particular.

"I'll take fifty pounds of that wager, Mr. Jackson," she said. "But you must do your part. You will be my artist's model, shall we say? I shall require your body to illustrate. You agree?"

Mr. Jackson looked alarmed, but he did not look as if he were going to refuse her. How convenient.

"Shall we begin? Here and now? I am so eager to have my fifty pounds. Money is always such a sharp motivator, is it not? Show me your goods, Mr. Jackson," she said, closing her fan gently and staring up into his eyes. "Kindly unbutton and show me all. Then I shall show you precisely how Westlin was disposed of."

THREE

Zoe watched the Duke of Aldreth watch Sophia as she toyed with Jackson and was more than slightly alarmed. Aldreth was not supposed to be watching Sophia; he was supposed to be watching her.

Men did so rarely do as they ought. If Aldreth were not so very rich and she so very desperate, she would not bother with him at all, not if he were going to make a habit of being contrary. Unfortunately she was in no position to be particular and Aldreth was the best man to improve her situation. Also, far from being a necessity but so very tempting, Aldreth happened to be a most beguiling looking man. He was tall, lithe, dark, and slightly dangerous in appearance. He was also extremely well turned out, which was the very best a man could be since it bespoke wealth in abundance.

Actually Aldreth was watching both Sophia and Jackson from a not-too-discreet distance. Watching them *both*. It was really too irritating. Zoe had done almost everything she could think of, which was quite a bit as she was from Paris, after all, to capture Aldreth's attention. *Almost* everything. The only thing left to do was to catapult herself into the duke's line of sight, which meant, obviously, that she was going to have to join Sophia and Jackson in whatever game they were about.

She could do that.

The thing to do, of course, was to ignore Aldreth completely while putting herself directly in his path. Men did so abhor being ignored completely. Actually she had yet to meet a woman who found being ignored a benign experience. She certainly had no liking for it.

Zoe swished her pale pink silk skirts, filled her bodice to bursting with a nice deep breath, and sauntered over to where Sophia stood with her back against a wall and her front almost indecently close to Jackson's cravat. It was very nearly indecent. Very nearly as she *was* from Paris and she therefore found very little indecent when men and women were involved.

Of course, that was a new perspective entirely. Her upbringing had strongly, almost violently, encouraged her to see any interaction at all between men and women as indecent, but that was in the irretrievable past and much had happened in the last year. She had made her adjustments and would continue to do so. She had to eat, did she not? She would pay for her sins later, at a more convenient time. Perhaps when she was very old and could indulge in the luxury of repentance. Now she was too occupied with trying to survive.

As to survival, there was no better tutor than Sophia. She had mastered the skill and wielded it expertly. Just look at how she had so quickly managed Mr. Jackson into a circumstance ripe with humiliation.

Jackson seemed to be fussing with the hidden buttons of his breeches. There was only one reason for that. Casting a discreet glance to where Aldreth stood, Zoe could see that he was observing the activity of Jackson's hands with as much interest as was decently allowed. Most strange, unless Aldreth's interest happened to swing in that unprofitable direction? That would be most inconvenient. Still the only point that mattered at the moment was that

Zoe needed to throw herself in the way of Aldreth's interest and if that meant throwing herself at a man in the throes of exposing himself in the Theatre Royal, well then.

"Good evening, Miss Auvray," Sophia said in pleasant invitation.

"Good evening, Miss Grey," Zoe answered. "I hope I am not interrupting?"

"Not at all," Sophia said, to the obvious irritation of Mr. Jackson. It was a most peculiar way to manage a man, but English women were a strange lot, though now that she considered it, Zoe was not at all certain that Sophia was English. "Please join us, Miss Auvray. I am quite certain that Mr. Jackson would not mind in the least the addition of a beautiful woman to our party."

Upon which Mr. Jackson, his expression indicating complete fury, said, "Naturally not. Miss Auvray? I am most pleased."

"Oh, Mr. Jackson, how you continue to flatter. Why, one cannot fail to see your enthusiasm and appreciation. I'm certain that Miss Auvray can see how pleased you are," Sophia said. "Or can't you? This light is most uncertain, Miss Auvray. You can, can you not, see how very pleased Mr. Jackson is by the sight of you?"

Which could only mean one thing and they each knew exactly what that was.

Most peculiar. Yet it must be admitted that Mr. Jackson did not so much as sniff in outrage. English men were, clearly, a strange lot as well. She must remember that when dealing with Aldreth, who was, remarkably, still watching Sophia and Jackson with avid eyes. Well, some men *did* like to watch.

But how had Sophia arranged for Jackson to display himself so, and in a matter of minutes? Most impressive, though how it calculated as a revenge she could not quite fathom.

"I can see very well that Mr. Jackson is a most attractive man," Zoe said carefully, walking a very uncomfortable line between Sophia's revenge, Jackson's exposure, and Aldreth's possible jealousy. Jealousy, properly managed, could be a most effective spur.

"Yes, he certainly is," Sophia said, waving her fan in a most attractive manner. "Yet I do wonder if he displays the obvious virility of French men. Would you say he does?"

Mr. Jackson, his hands twitching at his buttons, looked almost angry. Which was certainly a reasonable response. What precise form was Sophia's revenge to take? Certainly behavior of this degree of oddity could not have been the source of her success in London. Yet there was a certain something, a certain glimmer in Sophia's eyes that called her to play in the particular field she was creating with Mr. Jackson. With Aldreth watching, Zoe felt no inclination to decline the offer, no matter what Sophia had in mind.

"You are familiar with . . . French terrain?" Zoe asked Sophia, closing the distance between them until Mr. Jackson was neatly snuggled within the generous fabric of their panniers.

"But of course," Sophia said, laying a hand on the hem of Mr. Jackson's waistcoat, "and I enjoyed my time there, and the men, immensely. Of course, I am speaking of Paris specifically. You are from Paris, are you not, Miss Auvray?"

"Yes, I am," Zoe answered pleasantly, laying one of her hands on Mr. Jackson's coat pockets, fingering the embroidery. It was a bit dirty, but one was not supposed to notice details of that sort in this type of situation so she revealed nothing. But she was not impressed. "It is the city of my soul, but I think that London will become the city of my heart. Do you think this is possible, Mr. Jackson?" Zoe asked loudly enough for the Duke of Aldreth to hear, for she was naturally asking *him* this most important of questions.

"Anything is possible, Miss Auvray," Jackson answered. "London is the source of dreams."

"Or nightmares," Sophia said pleasantly, "but pray continue, Mr. Jackson. You can see I have provided you with every advantage. Miss Auvray is so very pleasant, so very lovely, is she not? And she is so very discreet. You are protected, Mr. Jackson. Unless one is looking very carefully, your privacy is assured."

Zoe did not waste a bit of effort in paying attention to Mr. Jackson for it was perfectly plain that Sophia was the source of everything that was happening between them all, and that included the Duke of Aldreth, who had drawn closer to them by a foot and was not just watching, but listening to them with avid attention. Sophia had managed it, by every measure, effortlessly, and it was then, perhaps for the first time, that Zoe truly understood what it was about Sophia that made her the source of so much pointed interest and speculation. Sophia was a woman who turned every word and every action to such a precise and well-executed purpose that it was quite impossible to thwart her. Zoe could not possibly have made a better friend and she was wise enough to know it.

But as to pointed interest, was this exercise in seduction merely to determine the measure of Jackson's . . . point?

"I did think that we had an agreement between us, Sophia," Mr. Jackson said. "A private arrangement."

"In a public theater?" Sophia said. "I thought that surely a man in your particular situation would be delighted to entertain two women of such pleasant aspect. Or am I mistaken?"

Zoe watched with interest the play of emotion that crossed Mr. Jackson's pretty features; it was most remarkable. Sophia was having her revenge, but what was Mr. Jackson having? Certainly Aldreth had some part in the affair, and to judge from his interest, he was very much involved. Naturally that decided the matter for Zoe. She was going to ensnare the duke and the sooner the better. If Mr. Jackson was the lure . . . Zoe indulged in a mental shrug and kept her expression pleasant and only mildly curious. It seemed appropriate, given the question Sophia had asked of Mr. Jackson.

"I'm not at all certain Miss Auvray would be interested in our private arrangement," Mr. Jackson said.

"I can be as interested as you'd like, Mr. Jackson," Zoe said.

"How very accommodating you are, Miss Auvray," Sophia said. "Small wonder everyone speaks so highly of you."

"You are too kind," Zoe said, with a nod of her head. "But as accommodating as I do try to be, what is the exact nature of this private arrangement?"

"Only the most simple of wagers, I assure you," Sophia said, cutting off whatever reply Jackson had been on the verge of making. "There is a small wager afoot as to the manner in which I removed Lord Westlin from my bed. I am to demonstrate on dear Mr. Jackson. Naturally, for my cooperation, I will receive half of the winnings, a sum of fifty pounds. Simple, yes? Mr. Jackson, being a man of some virility, which does defy some small rumors of him, has risen up in the presence of two attractive women. Which is so very flattering, is it not? The wager, after all, was not in any way a measure of Mr. Jackson's point of interest, yet his tackle is impressive."

Tackle? Tackle was a word with which Zoe was not familiar. Her confusion must have shown on her features, for Sophia, without any hesitation whatsoever, laid a very firm hand on Mr. Jackson's private parts and . . . squeezed. "Tackle," Sophia said.

Mr. Jackson groaned and lurched a bit.

Zoe bit back a smile and tried to look interested in a most scholarly fashion. "Ah, yes, I do enjoy learning new words. Thank you."

"Not at all," Sophia said pleasantly. "If you would continue, Mr. Jackson? I would so love to collect my fifty pounds. Who is to pay it out? I do think Miss Auvray would find that of interest."

As the Duke of Aldreth was hovering so close, it was completely obvious who had made the wager. How very wonderful. It put her in exactly the right place with exactly the right person.

Aldreth was listening to every word and she wanted him to know that, at least for the moment, she was entirely available. Of course, it would not do at all for Aldreth to think of her as terminally available since it was universally known that men preferred to struggle for what they attained. It was very odd, to be sure, but that did not change the facts in the least. She was available, but only just. Somehow that point must be made to Aldreth in the next quarter hour.

She was quite certain she was up to the challenge.

"I do not believe that information is necessary to our arrangement," Jackson said stiffly, not able to quite stop himself from glancing at Aldreth, who stood not six feet away and was wearing the most intriguing look on his face.

And so it was that Mr. Jackson unbuttoned himself fully and allowed his manhood to tumble out and be displayed for their pleasure. He was fully erect, though he did not look at all happy about it, which surely was most unusual for a man in any situation.

He looked at Sophia with something very much like challenge in his gaze and said, "And now you will perform your part, Miss Grey?"

"But I am so distracted, dear Mr. Jackson," Sophia said, standing back and studying his *tackle* with extreme care, "by this display of manly prowess on your part. I had not thought to find you so, for such cause. Is this not all of wagers? I do think now that you might have misled me and want to pursue another course with me entirely. Your point, dear Mr. Jackson, can mean nothing else, can it? And yet . . ." she said slowly, studying him overtly, "and yet, I do confess that I had expected a man of your height and obvious health to be a bit more . . . impressive. Do you agree, Miss Auvray? Is this not a display of manliness that is altogether . . ."

At which point, Zoe, understanding the gist of the exercise now, held up her little finger and wiggled it about before letting it fall in a drastic arc of disappointment.

"Altogether," Zoe finished, "lacking, yet just as rumor tells of it. How very sad for you, Mr. Jackson. I am so very sorry."

"You're a cunning bit of baggage," Jackson said, keeping his blue-eyed gaze upon Sophia, "but our bargain was that—"

"That you display yourself for me, Mr. Jackson," Sophia interrupted coldly. "You wanted to be shown how I disposed of Lord Westlin. Is this not sufficient? Does it require more elaborate measures than this to toss a man from my bed?"

Aldreth snorted in laughter.

Jackson lunged at Sophia, brushing Zoe aside, and put one hand on Sophia's throat in a chokehold and the other at her waist, forcing her against the wall. Zoe was stunned into speechlessness, stumbling where Jackson pushed her, tripping backward until a hand caught her and steadied her. She looked back and caught her breath; Aldreth had her securely, his gaze dipped down to hers briefly. She was caught by the intensity of his startling light blue eyes and held securely as his arm wrapped around her waist.

While Zoe did nothing to right herself, keeping herself very firmly in Aldreth's grip, Sophia had acted. A very long, very shiny knife was in Sophia's hand and being pressed against Mr. Jackson's dangly bits. Sophia was almost smiling and looked not at all alarmed by the situation.

The same could not be said of Mr. Jackson.

"Shall I cut it off?" Sophia hissed softly. "Would you survive or bleed away? I confess to being just a bit curious."

Jackson's hands did not move. He seemed scarcely to breathe. His blue eyes were wide as he whispered, "You wouldn't. You couldn't."

"I would," Sophia answered him softly, her voice almost gentle. "I have."

At that bit of information, which could hardly be credited, Mr. Jackson paled.

"Did you forget who I am, Mr. Jackson?" she said. "Did you forget that I am my father's daughter? My father cut off a man's head for insulting me. I kicked it through the grass just like a ball. The eyes fell out first. Then the teeth were broken off. The ears mangled until just bloody holes remained. The nose ripped free."

"I'll see you hang," Jackson said, his upper lip coated in sweat.

"If you live," Sophia whispered, "you can try."

Zoe believed every word Sophia uttered and as a result, her own lips were quivering and a line of sweat was forming between her breasts.

Jackson removed his hands from Sophia's body and tried to step back; Sophia followed him, her blade resting against his soft flesh. Obviously Jackson's rather unimpressive point was lying timidly between his legs.

"He'd make a pretty gelding, I'll give you that," a male voice said from the shadows. Sophia did not so much as blink.

Zoe did blink and saw an exquisite-looking man, tall and dark haired and beautifully dressed in a suit of pale green and brown ribbed silk embroidered elaborately in amber and ivory silk thread. The Earl of Dalby. He looked decadently rich and ruinous to a proper girl's reputation.

It was such a relief that there were no proper girls in the immediate vicinity.

"Have you a use for a gelding, my lord?" Sophia asked, not moving her knife, but shifting her gaze ever so briefly to Lord Dalby.

"Fortunately for him, my tastes do not run to geldings," he said mildly.

"Your Grace," Jackson said, addressing the duke, "I do beg your assistance with this wench."

The Duke of Aldreth shrugged his lovely broad shoulders and said, "I must insist that you manage your own affairs, Jackson."

"You'd be best served by asking Miss Grey for mercy. She is the wielder of the knife, after all," Lord Dalby said, in a soft voice ripe with laughter.

Whereupon Sophia gave the delectable Lord Dalby a most blatant look of appreciation. Lord Dalby seemed to be enjoying himself completely. How very lovely for Sophia. All that was left was for Jackson to be disposed of, though he had served his purpose brilliantly. Was she not still leaning against the remarkable Duke of Aldreth, struggling to gather her composure? Poor, dreary Mr. Jackson would never understand how brilliantly he had facilitated events this evening. And dear Miss Chester, when she heard of this night's events, for how could she not, would have her revenge as well.

Such a lovely way to begin an evening. How could it fail to progress to something even better?

Seeing no chance for aid from either the Duke of Aldreth or the Earl of Dalby, Jackson snarled at Sophia, "When this is done, I'll see you whipped from one end of London to another."

"How very medieval," drawled Sophia. "Is that quite the thing now?"

"It could be arranged," Aldreth said, setting Zoe on her own two feet, with some reluctance. Things could not be progressing more beautifully, unless one were Mr. Jackson, of course. "For a price," Aldreth added.

"But naturally," Sophia said, her dark eyes glittering, "anything may be had for a price, Your Grace. But who would pay it? Would you?"

It was not said playfully and the mood shifted downward, which did not serve Zoe's purpose at all. She would have said that it did not serve Sophia's, but she suddenly was not quite as certain as she had been what Sophia's purposes were. There seemed almost to be some history between Sophia and Aldreth that was not of the most cordial nature. Certainly between men and women, all dealings must remain cordial for them to remain profitable. It was most odd and Zoe did not enjoy things being odd in the least.

"No, Miss Grey, I would not," answered Aldreth solemnly.

"And speaking of price," Dalby said, breaking the mood, "you have duly won the wager for me, Miss Grey. I thank you most heartily."

"Wager?" Aldreth asked, watching Sophia with rather more interest than Zoe found complimentary.

Dalby shrugged. "I assume you've heard the gossip about Westlin and Miss Grey?" Zoe hadn't heard a thing, which was so completely like Sophia. She took a step closer and pricked up her ears. Aldreth nodded and Dalby continued. "I merely wagered with Lord Westlin that I would discover from Miss Grey where she managed to cut him. I must assume she has just done so; is that not true, Miss Grey? Have you just now scarred this unlikely fellow in approximately the same fashion as the annoying Lord Westlin?"

There was something so devious and yet so likeable about the handsome Lord Dalby that it was quite impossible not to want to agree to everything he said. Zoe found herself grinning before she completely understood what he had been saying and when she had fully translated his remarks, she grinned even more fully.

Sophia was clearly in more control of her responses than Zoe, for Sophia only smiled fractionally and said, "Approximately, Lord Dalby, approximately."

Dalby clearly fought against a most unrefined grin. He almost lost. "How very . . ."

"Satisfying?" Sophia offered, moving her knife away from Jackson's sac, whereupon Mr. Jackson took his first full breath in five minutes.

"Satisfying," Dalby echoed, giving into his grin completely. "Very."

"Besting Lord Westlin does lift the spirits, does it not, Lord Dalby?" Sophia asked, with a gleam in her dark eyes. "I am so delighted to have helped you win your wager against him. What has he lost? His estate, one hopes?"

To which Lord Dalby laughed outright.

It was a most peculiar conversation and was made more so by the blatant delight reflected in Lord Dalby's dark blue eyes. Was Sophia going to use Westlin as a lure to attract the Earl of Dalby? It certainly appeared so. And it appeared that Westlin was a very compelling lure.

How perfectly odd.

Englishmen might be more difficult to manage than she had first thought, which would be singularly inconvenient as it was imperative that she lure Aldreth and his very deep pockets to her immediately, at the very latest.

"Besting anyone lifts the spirits, at least for the moment," Aldreth said. "It is too bad that the relief does not last longer than an hour, at most. But I must confess that Mr. Jackson has afforded me some small satisfaction as well. I, too, had a wager and it concerned the dispute between the Earl of Westlin and Miss Grey. I do believe that Mr. Jackson, in a method he had not anticipated, has met the terms of our wager. You have won, Mr. Jackson."

It was perfectly obvious that Mr. Jackson did not at all feel he had won anything worth winning as he was now and perhaps forevermore to be the laughingstock of Drury Lane.

"If we are to make confessions," Sophia said, her knife having mysteriously disappeared somewhere upon her person, "then might I add my own? I am not at all pleased that Lord Westlin has managed to intrude himself upon my evening at Drury Lane. Is his reach so very far, then? Can none of us escape his influence?"

It was precisely the sort of comment to arouse aggression and animosity in the most ordinary of gentlemen. That these two were not ordinary in any sense of the word made it all the more inexplicable that Sophia would chide them so.

"I believe, Miss Grey," Dalby said, "that the very heart of the wager was exactly how thoroughly and how aggressively you had escaped Westlin's influence. Very well done, by the way," he said, bowing slightly to her. "We should all heed your example and, indeed, your methods."

It was completely charming of him. Sophia had certainly chosen well, but how did she expect to induce the lovely Earl of Dalby to the altar? To bed a man was one thing, but to tie him up in marriage was altogether another.

"Of course," Sophia said pleasantly, checking the arrangement of her dark hair, "I will happily accept any and all compliments, Lord Dalby, but it does seem to me that while I have been directly responsible for the winning of two separate wagers, each concerning the tedious Lord Westlin, I have won nothing for myself. It is perfectly obvious to me that Mr. Jackson, feeling himself to be needlessly abused, will refuse to pay me the fifty pounds he offered. Furthermore I am distinctly suspicious that Mr. Jackson is not in possession of fifty pounds cash in the best of circumstances."

To which Mr. Jackson, still pink about the ears, said nothing. It was a most illuminating silence.

"You had something in mind, Miss Grey?" Aldreth asked, his light blue eyes twinkling dangerously.

"Naturally, Your Grace," Sophia said, with the barest smile. Aldreth seemed to take Sophia's chill in stride. What history did they share? It was becoming almost imperative that Zoe find out, though she rather suspected she would not find out from Sophia. "As Lord Westlin has made himself the man of the evening, at least as pertains to wagers, I have an axe of my own to grind upon his large red head. Would you help me, Lord Dalby? I can assure you that it will not be onerous duty and that you may even find your own desires well served in the process. What say you? Have we an arrangement?"

"Tell me more, Miss Grey. You have intrigued me," Dalby said, dipping his head intimately toward hers.

"I can see there is no part for me in this wager against Lord Westlin," Aldreth said. "If you will excuse me?"

Zoe felt her heart skip a beat and, unable to think of a reason for Aldreth to stay, looked to Sophia.

Without hesitation, Sophia replied, "Miss Auvray is far too modest to admit how very much her presence induced Mr. Jackson to draw out his manhood for scrutiny. As such, she is certainly owed a certain consideration, my lords?"

"Of course," Dalby said, bowing politely to Zoe.

Aldreth did not bow. Aldreth merely looked at her. To be more precise, he looked her over.

Zoe did not mind in the least. She was a likely enough looking girl, possessed of a stellar figure, chestnut hair that leaned toward auburn, and eyes of a very specific shade of golden brown. In short, she was an exotic beauty and she knew it.

"And how may I assist Miss Auvray, canceling my debt to her?" Aldreth said, his black brows drawing down into a very seductive scowl over his ice blue eyes. He did not put her off in the least. Men of Aldreth's rank and power often scowled as if life itself were very tedious indeed. It was most amusing of them as life was not at all tedious.

"How very gracious you are, Your Grace," Zoe said, not at all certain of how to make use of the appealing duke. Again Zoe looked at Sophia. Sophia, thankfully, looked completely certain of exactly in what manner to use Aldreth.

"You are familiar with Miranda Sinclair?" Sophia asked, her look encompassing both gentlemen. As Miranda was at that moment on the stage, saying her lines very woodenly, both men looked to where she was posed, and nodded. It was not an untrue observation to say that many, *many* men were intimately familiar with Miranda Sinclair. "Of course you are," Sophia said mildly. "You are likely not aware that Miss Auvray, new to Town and a quite accomplished actress, was making her way very nicely upon the stage, which would not be in Miss Sinclair's best interests, obviously. A fresh face, a voice of singular clarity," Sophia said, with a shrug, "Miss Auvray certainly could not be allowed to inhabit the same stage as Miss Sinclair, could she?"

The gentlemen looked at her expectantly. Zoe shrugged. "Am I to deny it? I cannot. I have the voice of a lark."

Aldreth came very near to smiling. She felt the warmth of his look down to her spine and suppressed a shiver of sexual awareness.

"As we have helped the two of you to win a wager tonight, is it not in the spirit of fair play that you help us?" Sophia asked.

"I am never against helping a woman," Aldreth said.

"Is that so, Your Grace? A new philosophy, surely," Sophia said stiffly, her eyes cold and dark.

"New or old," Zoe said into the stilted silence, "it is a useful philosophy and I intend to take full advantage of it, Your Grace."

Aldreth's gaze was turned almost gratefully from Sophia to her and he let out a short breath, almost a sigh. There was definitely some unpleasant history between Aldreth and Sophia. She was most determined to find out what it was and at the earliest opportunity. Being new to Town, it was of utmost importance to learn every alliance and every *on dit*; how else to survive?

"I am currently available to be taken advantage of, Miss Auvray," Aldreth said.

"Then I shall make good use of you, Your Grace," Zoe said, with a sultry look.

"How enjoyable that sounds," Dalby said. "Am I to be made good use of, Miss Grey?"

"Do you think you can bear it, my lord? I believe I have a reputation for using a man hard," Sophia said, with the barest smile. "Lord Westlin would certainly claim so."

"I have never given anything Lord Westlin has to say much weight," Dalby said. "In fact, I would enjoy proving him wrong about many things. Is that not what you had in mind for tonight?"

"For tonight, yes," Sophia said, her smile warming slightly. "Are you available, my lord?"

"Completely, Miss Grey," Dalby said.

"You know how you plan to use His Grace, Zoe?" Sophia said. "I do believe Miranda is quite overcome with curiosity at the moment. She seems to have forgotten her lines entirely. In fact, a good part of the audience appears most interested in our conversation."

At that observation, Zoe looked around and saw that Sophia was correct. At least half of the actors on the stage were staring down at them, Miranda included, as well as fifty or sixty or so of the audience, Lord Westlin most specifically.

"How lovely," Zoe said. "I almost don't know what more I can do to punish her. Do you have any ideas, Your Grace?"

"I do, Miss Auvray," Aldreth answered smoothly. He was going to be such a pleasant man to seduce. She could hardly wait.

FOUR

It was quite impossible for Aldreth not to know what was in Miss Auvray's mind: She wanted him between her legs. The look she gave him was simple enough to translate, no matter her point of origin. In fact, being French made her more eminently readable in these sorts of things.

He was not adverse to the idea, but neither was he excessively eager. While Aldreth had sought his pleasures under skirts other than Martha's and while he had also made something of a habit of it, he did not do so frivolously. No, in fact, he did it almost morosely, which was quite ridiculous enough. He was a duke. He was in the prime of his life. And he was afraid to have relations with his wife.

"I think I have lost you, Your Grace," Zoe Auvray said softly. "Is that not so?"

Aldreth pulled his attention back to her. She was a lovely little thing, all amber and honey, lushly drawn. So petite, so blatantly feminine, quite decidedly French.

The timing was off. Talking with Sophia had reminded him of

things he had no wish to be reminded of, Westlin first and foremost. Had Sophia somehow aligned things to work out in this fashion? But how? She could not have known who would be in the theater tonight and who absent. She could not have managed his meeting Miss Auvray.

Still the feeling he had been manipulated into this situation tugged at him.

"Unfortunately, yes, Miss Auvray. Another time, perhaps," he said.

"Running, Your Grace?" Sophia said quietly. "What of your new philosophy?"

Zoe gasped. Dalby's head snapped around to stare at Sophia. Aldreth stared into Sophia's dark eyes and said nothing. There was nothing to say. Nothing that would make the slightest difference.

"I mean that in kindness, Your Grace," Sophia said softly, answering him even though he had said nothing. "I am quite certain that you have it within your power to aid her in the most lovely fashion. Do not miss the opportunity to do so. Help her."

"How?" Aldreth said, his gaze intense.

"Certainly that is for Miss Auvray to explain," Sophia said, looking more at Zoe than at him. He could make no sense of it, but then women were such difficult creatures to make sense of. In truth, they made little sense at all. Such melodrama over a quick tumble behind the scenery. All this talk of running and of aiding . . . Aldreth felt his stomach tumble against his ribs and avoided Sophia's stare. Between Sophia and Westlin his night at the theater was going quite sour.

" 'Tis too much philosophy for me," Dalby said, breaking the mood. "I came tonight to see a play, nothing more."

"Dear Lord Dalby," Sophia said, smiling up at him, "please do not think to dissemble so early in our acquaintance. You came tonight to play, not to *see* a play. Such an important distinction, don't you agree?"

"Do not dissemble?" Dalby said, with a grin. "How then should men and women rub along together with any sort of equanimity at all? Brute honesty will have them wielding knives against each other in minutes."

"And is that so terrible a fate?" Sophia said, one sable brow arrogantly cocked.

"Excuse us," Dalby said to Aldreth in abrupt answer. "I wish you an evening's pleasure, Aldreth, wherever and upon whomever you may find it. Now, Miss Grey, I will not share you for another moment."

With not another word, Sophia and Dalby blended into the crowd, by every appearance making their way to the side of the theater near the stairs. So very many delightful things could happen in a stair hall. If only Zoe could manage to negotiate Aldreth into one.

It had been a lovely beginning, but one had to proceed swiftly or the delightful duke would escape Zoe altogether and that would be a perfect disaster. She had the man literally by the coat sleeve and she had the means to keep him. She was, after all, in the full flush of her beauty and, as any woman knew, that rose-pink flush of plump perfection did not last forever. Indeed it barely lasted a decade. All she needed to do was to convince the changeable Aldreth of her perfect allure, which would be a challenge as his attention had wandered quite astray, but it was a challenge she was entirely capable of surmounting. She had more than a little experience and she was Parisian. What else could possibly be required to ensure success?

"You appear to have ensnared me, Miss Auvray," Aldreth said, looking down at her hand upon his arm.

"And didn't I do it neatly, Your Grace?" she said lightly. "Whatever shall I do with you now?"

"Miss Auvray," he said, with a completely sober expression, which was perfectly dreadful and entirely off point, "I fear I am unable to accommodate you this evening."

He looked so sad, so truly sad, that it was quite remarkable. What on earth could a duke have to be sad about? Certainly he had a roof and a meal, and he clearly had his looks and his health. It was blatantly ridiculous. What to do but tell him as much?

"Your Grace, I am quite certain that you do not understand how very perfectly able you appear to accommodate me completely, this evening or any other. Aside from your obvious melancholy, of course. You look, if I may say so, completely without hope, and that cannot be possible, can it? England cannot be so very different from France, can it? You are a man who has everything, everything except joy. Why is that, Your Grace?"

"I must confess that I think this is more of Miranda than of me. Am I mistaken, Miss Auvray?" he said, his expression gone dark and chill. She didn't care in the slightest what he looked like at the moment; there was something about this very handsome, very sad man that touched her heart.

Zoe shrugged in pure Parisian fashion and said, "I may wound her unintentionally, but if she is pricked, am I to pretend distress?" She was rewarded by a brief and shallow smile from Aldreth. She continued, "But no, I had forgotten her in studying your very downcast expression, which is very negligent of me. One cannot achieve an ideal revenge without complete concentration. I do hope she didn't notice."

And Aldreth chuckled.

Such a lovely sound from such a melancholy man. She quite liked the sound of it and she liked very much that she had been the cause of it. She liked it so much that she almost forgot how alone in the world she was.

"You are very French, are you not, Mademoiselle Auvray?" he said, still smiling. It was a remarkable thing to experience as Zoe was almost completely certain that the duke's smiles were quite rare.

"I am most exquisitely French, Your Grace. How complimentary of you to notice."

"You delight in being French. I do wonder that you came to England at all."

"I like to eat, Your Grace," she said. "It grows difficult to eat in France now."

"So it does," he said, serious again.

The government of France had no money, for how could they when they spent everything on wars that they then lost? All very interesting, of course, but what it did to the cost of bread was the only thing that truly mattered in the end. But what would a duke know of the cost of bread? When he wanted food, food appeared, which was precisely how it should be when one was hungry.

"We shall not speak of food if it distresses you, Your Grace. I myself have never found the topic to be troublesome, but then again, I am not accustomed to English food."

There, he smiled again. The Duke of Aldreth's smiles were hard won, yet so very lovely. He had quite a nice smile, the sort of smile that made one want to smile with him. And so she did. Smiles were free, which was such a lovely thing in a world where everything cost so much.

"You are quite unlike any other woman, Miss Auvray, I must confess," he said softly. "I do wish I could aid you in your revenge against Miss Sinclair, but—"

"You are married," she interrupted, "and petite entanglements are not permitted in England, Your Grace?" she said quietly, looking boldly into his pale blue eyes. "Can two countries be as different as all that? I did not think to find it so. I did not think," she whispered, "to find anyone quite as tempting as you."

"You speak not of revenge? Of Miranda? Is it possible you have a wager with her?" he asked, looking quite boyish all of a sudden and quite vulnerable. Such a silly thing for a duke to be. Was not vulnerability a terribly costly thing for a duke to indulge in? The thought struck her that he might need protecting, her dark duke. Yet from what? What did he need that he did not already possess?

Hope.

The dark Duke of Aldreth lived without hope, she was instantly and intuitively certain of it. Of all the things she did not have, she still had hope. Let them share that, at least.

"No, Your Grace. This is all of you," she said in a near whisper of raw emotion, "and of me. Of us. Of what we might share between us. Of what we might find together."

It was an odd, unexpected moment between them and it seemed to grow straight out of the ground, entwining them, catching them up. It was tender and fragile and almost completely unwelcome. She did not want to feel tenderness toward this man.

Zoe had never before felt any such emotion for a man. Men did not require tenderness. What would they do with it? It had no currency for them. They wanted only beauty and power and if a woman would not feed those indulgences, she had no value at all.

Certainly he knew that as well. He was not an uncultured man. He knew and would follow the rules regarding affairs such as these.

But the look in his eyes, for just a moment or two, was so unguarded and so full of longing that she did not quite know what to make of it. She could only hope that she had not been so unguarded with him. Men did not like that. Men did not like to think of anyone but themselves in moments such as these. Had she not learned that? Had she learned nothing since leaving France?

"You are not speaking of a meal, are you, Miss Auvray? You look very much in need of a meal, shared or not," he said, with a small dose of sarcasm, shielding his vulnerability, shifting his gaze to the crowd around them.

"Are you offering a meal, Your Grace?" she said, matching his tone, both saddened and comforted by the return to the normal sort of bantering that went on between men and women who spoke together without revealing anything of import. But she knew she was telling him something more, something about not betraying his unguarded moment, and she did not quite know why she was being so careful of this very powerful duke. He did not need protection and she could provide none. He was supposed to be offering protection to her, which was the entire point of this exercise.

Why did she have such trouble remembering that? Certainly Sophia would not be so distracted by a pair of pain-soaked blue eyes.

"I'm very much afraid that I can offer you nothing, Miss Auvray," he said hoarsely.

It was at that precise moment, a moment when she very poetically felt something rip free inside of her, that Miranda Sinclair saved her. It was completely accidental, of course, but she did it, nonetheless.

"But *look at her,*" Miranda said from the stage, her voice putting the accent on the words she wanted the world to hear. "She is so frail, so wan, *not a morsel of food* can she swallow. How much more can she bear before she is in the grave? *I told you* she was ill."

Aldreth looked up. Miranda, posing on the stage, smiling cruelly when the scene called for no such smile. Zoe held herself regally still. Aldreth took her by the arm and draped it through his own. Smiling coldly at Miranda, he said, "I think we have been challenged, Miss Auvray, and must stand and deliver a volley to Miss Sinclair with the only weapon she understands. Are you willing?"

The look in his eyes was so very cold and determined that it gave her a thrill of sensual foreboding. All vulnerability, every whisper of despair had been erased. All doubt was gone from him. And Miranda had done it.

Zoe smiled up at him. "Yes, Your Grace. Very willing."

The Duke of Aldreth, with complete mastery and grace, led Zoe away from the tumult of the ground floor of the theater and up to his box. They did not speak. They did not so much as look at each other, but it was not necessary. She would perform beautifully and then he would . . . and then he would, do what? Buy her a pastry? Buy her a diamond clip? Buy her a house in Town?

She was a fool. He would use her and he would leave her. She would get nothing, nothing but a man between her legs and she had no need for that, not when men were so abundant.

The duke's box was beautifully positioned to see the stage below and much of the theater crowd. Sophia's box was on the same level, but over two or three; Zoe could not be certain. The one thing she was certain of was that, if they were very near the edge of the box, Miranda would have a clear view of them. Aldreth led her to the very edge of his box. Aldreth, with a dark smile and an icy gleam in his pale eyes, tipped up her chin and kissed her on the tip of her nose and then the very corner of her mouth.

It was ridiculous, but she had not been expecting it. His scent, the touch of his lips, they caught her by surprise and she gasped slightly and stiffened fractionally before forcing herself to relax and melt into him. But it was too late. He pulled back, sat down, and pulled her onto his lap.

It was done in less than a minute, less than half a minute. It had not gone at all as she had intended it, and she did not quite know how to repair the situation.

Aldreth did it for her.

"I do apologize, Miss Auvray, for my boyish awkwardness, but I did think it best to give something for Miranda to choke on at the soonest opportunity."

Perched on his lap, her skirts hiked ungracefully, Aldreth took her hand and snaked her arm around his neck, nestling her against him. It was quite remarkable. Was the Duke of Aldreth snuggling with her?

"I think, Your Grace," she said, trying not to squirm, "that you have a battle of your own against Miranda."

"I do know her," he said, caressing her hand softly, staring out over the theater. They were being watched. It was inevitable and she hardly minded, but where would it lead? Perhaps nowhere.

"In the biblical sense, I assume?" she said, studying his face and the shadow of his beard beneath his skin.

"Why would you assume that?"

"Because, being a man, is there any other way to know Miranda?" she answered. "I don't mean to be harsh, but I do not think she knows any other way to communicate. Or am I wrong?"

"No, probably not," he said, the faintest whisper of a smile drifting over his lips. "I do know her in precisely that way. History now, of course."

"History," Zoe said, leaning against Aldreth with a sigh of pleasure. It was very comfortable. He was very comfortable, which was not at all what she had expected of an English duke. "I have a fascination for history. Tell me all, and if you can, make Miranda the villain of the piece, if you please, Your Grace."

Aldreth chuckled and pulled her nearer, her hip tucked into the curve of his loins. He was aroused and it aroused her to know it. A sign of her inexperience, surely. Sophia would not be aroused by so little. She could not be as unsophisticated as all that, not now, not with this man. He would lose all interest. Once the flower was plucked, men liked experience and ease with a woman. Zoe let out a slow breath and tried to appear easy.

"Very well. If you insist, Miss Auvray," he said, his voice a lovely rumble in his chest. "I met her. She was willing. I was willing. I enjoyed her company until . . . I no longer enjoyed it. We parted."

Zoe turned on his lap and stared into his eyes. "You are not a gifted historian, Your Grace."

"Am I not?" he said stiffly, but his eyes were twinkling in amusement.

"You are not," she said. "Your description of events lack all detail, all color. One must paint a picture, Your Grace. One must draw the audience in."

"Drawing in," he said softly, staring at her mouth. "I like the sound of that. Perhaps you could tell it better?"

"But of course," she said, leaning forward to kiss him briefly on the mouth, tracing her tongue over his lower lip. She wanted more, a deeper kiss into his tantalizing mouth, but she did not allow it. Teasing ease, a light and experienced touch, that was what the duke would want and she was determined to be all that he would want. Zoe leaned back and crossed her arms, assuming a serious mien. "In act one, you see Miranda on the stage. She is lovely. She is compelling. She is—"

"Act one? Is this a history or a play?" Aldreth cut in.

"A historical drama, Your Grace, much in the vein of *Richard II* by Shakespeare. There will be blood, death, disgrace."

"Will there?" he said, grinning.

"Why not?" she said, with a swift smile. "The play continues even tonight. Anything may happen, may it not? But I will continue," she said, looking down at Miranda, who was looking daggers up at her. It was quite lovely. "She lures you. Being a man, you succumb. You cannot resist, can you? You should not be blamed. A man," she said, with a shrug, "he is like a child where women are concerned. No resistance. His wants devour him and he struts upon the world stage seeking only to feed his many appetites."

Aldreth was no longer smiling. Gathering her composure, Zoe realized that she was not smiling, either. Stupid, stupid girl. This was no time to lose the thread. This was to be an amusing tale of Aldreth's history, not her own.

"And so Miranda swooped you up," Zoe continued before Aldreth could interrupt her with some awkward questions about her particular history. Making a game of his history with Miranda was one thing, but delving into her story would not be at all amusing. "She is beautiful, in a somewhat tawdry, insignificant way. And she is very old, is she not, Your Grace?"

"I believe she is above twenty," Aldreth said, his eyes dancing in amusement again. "I am above twenty myself. I do not feel particularly old."

"But it is very different for a man, of course, Your Grace. With a woman . . ." Zoe shrugged and made a face. "She has much experience, naturally, and she uses it with extreme determination."

"Determination? I think you might mean vigor."

"Vigor?" Zoe said, quirking her head to look at him. He looked amused, which was ideal. "Of course, you would know. Vigor. Yes, Miranda has much vigor. But what does she do with it? She turns it this way and that, first for you and then against you. What is a man to do? He does not engage a woman to have her turn against him; he must deliver himself of her. He must find a woman who pleasantly engages him. A younger woman who is not so . . ."

"Vigorous?" Aldreth said, grinning.

"Is that the word, Your Grace?" she said. "I do not think so."

"Old?"

"Yes, certainly, he would want youth," Zoe said. "Youth is king in matters of love, walking hand in hand with beauty. What man would not welcome both into his life?"

"And his bed?" Aldreth said, kissing her neck, sending a shiver down her back.

"With men, are they not the same?" she teased.

But he did not react as a man teased. These English men, they were so very backward in affairs of the heart, not knowing how to play at seduction. They were so very serious about something so very pleasant and temporary. It was exhausting.

"How old are you, Miss Auvray?" he asked.

"I am not above twenty, Your Grace," she said, leaning into him, kissing his ear where it met his neck. He smelled lovely, like fresh linen and lavender.

"Below twenty? How far below?"

Oh, dear, this was becoming too serious, like being questioned by a lawyer.

"Are you thinking of Juliet, Your Grace? It is the wrong play, is it not? Juliet was a maid of less than fourteen years. I am not a maid. I am above fourteen and there is no murderous cousin waiting in the wings. All is as it should be, Your Grace."

"And you came to England because of our balmy climate?"

Worse and worse. It was almost an inquisition and for what? This was play, especially for him. For her, it was work, but he should not be quite so aware of that.

"I am seventeen, Your Grace. Young enough, yet old enough, am I not?"

"It is very young, Miss Auvray, though old enough, as you say. Certainly there are younger girls than you on the streets of London."

"I am not so very old, Your Grace!" she said in exaggerated stiffness, causing him to smile. "In France a man does want a woman who is green on the vine. I am perfectly ripe, as you can plainly see."

"Very plainly, Miss Auvray," he said, taking her chin in his hand and kissing her lightly on the mouth. The kiss lingered, lengthened. Zoe felt something unravel in her belly and then Aldreth stopped abruptly, frowning.

"And how is it that you are in England, Miss Auvray? It is unusual for a woman in your position to travel across continents and seas."

"Is it, Your Grace? I had no idea you were so well versed in the travel habits of French women of a certain age. What a broad education you English enjoy."

"Yes," he said, with a smile, "I suppose we do. But it is expensive to travel, I know that well enough."

"You know many things, Your Grace, most well enough," she said, kissing his throat, threading her hand underneath his waistcoat. The duke was very lean and very hard. She liked it very much. "Is there a reason why you do not want to share the depth of your knowledge about female anatomy with me?"

"And leave off this fascinating exploration as to why you came to England?"

"I came to England because I had the chance to come. Is not travel an ideal way to broaden one's experience of the world?"

"Yes, I suppose it is," he said, his expression still somewhat somber. The duke's moods were as dark as his hair. He was not the easiest man to manage, though dukes seldom were.

"Are you very curious about me, Your Grace?" she said softly, her lips against the lobe of his ear. "It is most courteous of you. I shall return the courtesy, shall I? You are very sad for one so very high in the world."

"Am I?" he said, leaning away from her kiss and turning to face her. "You think I am sad?"

"I do."

"Perhaps it is that I have lost my heart to Miranda and pine until she gives it back."

Zoe burst out laughing. "I am not an idiot, Your Grace. No man could lose his heart to Miranda. She is a bedmate, nothing more. And, if I had the coin to wager, I would wager that she is a most disappointing one."

"But you do not have the coin."

"I do not."

"But you have a duke?"

Zoe looked at him as playfully as she dared. He looked almost enraged, but his anger did not flow outward but was suppressed, swallowed. It was most peculiar. If she were a duke, she would rage and bellow whenever she wanted. Who would stop her?

"Do I? So soon? Why, I did nothing to win for myself a duke. How easy it was. If I had but known earlier, I would have snared myself a duke long before reaching the age of seventeen. Could I have managed it at fifteen, do you think?"

She grinned at him, her fingers toying with the hair on his nape. He had very thick hair, very glossy and black and quite lovely. Aldreth's cold blue eyes looked at her in that odd pained fashion he had and then the tiniest spark lit them from deep within. She had done it again, pulled him back from whatever brink called out to him. Such a sad, hopeless man. It did not make any sense at all.

"I have no doubt of it," he said, "but have we not forgotten Miranda and our punishment of her?"

Before Zoe could say a word, Aldreth arched her over his arm and kissed her soundly on the mouth. His arm held her fast while his mouth ravaged hers almost violently, and she was shocked to discover, it caused the most volatile reactions in her. Her stomach lurched, her heart hammered, and her breath caught in the vicinity of her borrowed necklace. It was not what was supposed to happen; she ought to have been more urbane, more bored by it. But she was not. She was most alarmingly not. As to Aldreth, it was not quite what she had expected of him, but given his volatile moods, she should not have been surprised.

Aldreth was a man beset by demons she could not understand. Of course she did not need to understand them, she only had to please him in the precise way a man most sought pleasure, but there was something so fragile about him. It called to her. Had she not once been fragile? Had she not learned to bury that part of herself in the mud of the Seine?

"Is she watching?" Aldreth murmured, his mouth trailing down her throat to the swells of her breasts.

Zoe was jerked out of her pounding desire, which was a good thing as she was supposed to be seducing Aldreth, not the other way around, and plunged back into the present moment. Miranda. Yes, he was asking about Miranda.

"I believe so, Your Grace. You are very convincing," she said. How very true that was. He had almost convinced her that he wanted her for herself and not some strange revenge against Miranda. "What did she do to earn your anger, Your Grace?"

"Nothing serious," he said, kissing the tops of her breasts, his hands cupping her through the silk of Sophia's dress. Her nipples throbbed in response, and she suppressed a gasp of pleasure, entirely unsuccessfully, she was afraid. "She merely made a wager with Sheridan that she could find her way into a duke's bed. I was the fortunate duke."

So that was it. If there was anything a man detested it was playing the fool for someone else's wager.

"Why Sheridan?" Zoe asked, arching her back and lifting her breasts into Aldreth's hands, entirely without meaning to.

"He used to manage this theater."

"Ah, that would mean that Miranda warmed his bed," Zoe said, struggling to keep their conversation light and sharp, ignoring the ache between her legs. "She would do no less for a place in the theater company. But what did she win from Sheridan for seducing you, Your Grace? What could ever be worth more than forming an intimate attachment to you?"

Aldreth jerked her up roughly and snapped, "Don't play me for a fool, Zoe. Have I not admitted that Miranda already did that? I am not likely to allow myself to be played again."

The look in his eyes was glacial. He was hurt. He had been hurt.

Aldreth was more than a duke. He was a man. Perhaps, like her, he was not as jaded as he liked to appear.

She laid a hand against his cheek and looked deeply into his eyes. "I will admit to certain things, Your Grace. One is that I hoped you would call me by my Christian name, though I had hoped in the passion of desire and not anger. I will also admit to . . . to . . ." she stammered. Oh, this was difficult.

"To what?" he asked. "I know you want to prove something to Miranda and you're using me to do it."

"I am not using you, Your Grace," she said, her eyes not meeting his. "I am only here for you to use me, in the way a man likes to use a woman. Miranda is a part of this only in that she made certain I would lose my place in the theater company. To see you take me up would annoy her, nothing more. I need . . . I want . . ." She could not say it. It was too horrible, too awkward. Men so disliked awkward moments.

"You need and want what everyone wants," he said. "A place."

How very nicely he put it. How very chivalrous he was.

"Yes," she said, straightening her bodice, not looking at him, "a place. That is it precisely, Your Grace."

"And where was your place before London, Zoe? The truth."

Why did it matter? What man cared what had gone before or even what after as long as he had his place?

"Paris," she said.

"Yes, but where."

"A convent," she said, staring into her lap. She was behaving like a child, she knew it, and she could not stop.

Aldreth expelled a breath softly. "You have strayed far from that life, Miss Auvray."

"Yes, that is true, Your Grace, but there is no going back, and this life I find myself living could have its happiness. Could it not?"

She said it with more wistfulness and hope than she should have revealed, but did it matter now? He knew all, or at least all that mattered to a man.

"You are a Catholic? A good Catholic convent-bred girl of Paris, in London, alone," he summarized, his gaze on the distant stage below them. "And you lost your position because of a very nasty bit of work by the name of Miranda. She took something from you that you could ill afford to lose, a situation I can well understand." Aldreth sighed heavily and scanned the theater, avoiding her eyes. He looked far more serious and reluctant than he should have looked, given that she was sitting on his lap and very near to begging him to debauch her. Staring off into the distance, he said softly, "Miss Auvray, shall we punish Miranda fully? Shall we show her you can acquire a most virile duke on your first foray into the world of men?"

"But why would you do this, Your Grace?" Zoe asked. "It can mean nothing to you. Miranda is nothing. I am nothing. You are a duke. What can touch you?"

"You can touch me, Zoe," he said. "Touch me." His hands ran

up her back and he pressed her against his chest, his mouth seeking hers. "Hold me, and hold nothing back."

THE Earl of Westlin watched it all from his box with a very jaded gaze. Jackson's disgrace at Sophia's hand, Sophia and Dalby disappearing amid smiles into the stair hall, Zoe Auvray and the Duke of Aldreth seducing each other, all plain to see, all very intentionally plain to see. He was going to lose another wager if things kept on, and Sophia had had a hand in both.

The thing that most intrigued, obviously, was how Sophia could be humiliated in what was certain to be a very disagreeable and highly entertaining scene of the first water. She was on easy terms with Zoe Auvray, that had been made obvious, though she was not on easy terms with Aldreth, which he knew for a fact because of his own mismanagement of their affair. Nasty bit of business, that. He remembered every bit of it in disagreeable detail even if he still could not reason out just exactly why it had gone so terribly wrong. He had been deeply in his cups, certainly, but that did not erase any of the details of that day.

Westlin shrugged off whatever lingering whispers of discomfort the memories of that day engendered and pulled himself back to the present moment. Whatever happened tonight, indeed whatever happened for as long as he lived, he was determined that Sophia be punished for rejecting him. He had begun with Zoe Auvray. That Sophia had taken Zoe into the house he had paid for, sat her in the box he had paid for, in clothes he had . . . the point obviously being that Sophia and Zoe be made to pay him back. Somehow.

Westlin's gaze was trained on Aldreth's box. Any means at all. Wagering did have such interesting results, even when one lost.

FIVE

It wasn't as if the stair hall provided any real privacy, but Sophia and Lord Dalby were out of the direct gaze of the theater crowd, if one discounted those making their way up and down the stairs, which Dalby was inclined to do and Sophia was not.

"Now that you have me alone," she said, holding her fan to her chest, "what did you think to do with me, Lord Dalby?"

"Caution you, for one," he said in complete seriousness. It was completely charming. He wanted to protect and advise her? Could he be more accommodating? "Mr. Jackson could have caused you trouble tonight. I would not see you so served."

"Is that what you were doing tonight, Lord Dalby? Protecting me?"

"Saving you, Miss Grey," he said softly. "Taking a blade to Mr. Jackson was—"

"Extremely enjoyable," she said, interrupting him.

"Extremely dangerous," he said, looking quite solemn. "There could have been serious consequences for you."

Sophia smiled. "My lord Dalby, I cannot think of a thing worth doing that does not involve serious consequences. Certainly the scent of danger should never tether us. What sort of life would it be, chained and domesticated?"

He lost his serious mien and the mood lifted between them, just as she had intended it should. "And you are not domesticated?" he asked.

"Do I look it?" she replied, lowering her fan.

His gaze moved leisurely over her body. She lifted her chin and invited his perusal. Why not?

"No, Miss Grey," he said, his lovely eyes shining down at her, "you do not look domesticated in the least. Quite the opposite."

"Thank you, Lord Dalby. That is quite the nicest compliment I have received all evening. Now shall we take the next step in this dance we have so pleasurably begun?" At Dalby's amused nod, she said, "You have saved me. I have been complimented. Lord Westlin, I do suspect, is at the heart of much of this. Will you admit as much, my lord?"

"I will admit to nothing without the proper inducement," he said, grinning.

"Such as a blade pressed against your skin?" she asked, with a smile.

"*Something* pressed against my skin, but are you not tired of using blades when other means are more pleasurable?"

"I am by no means convinced that other means are more pleasurable, my lord. A knife is so very useful, is it not?"

"You prefer the metallic scent of metal to other more enticing scents, Miss Grey?" he asked. Lord Dalby was so very pleasant, so very reasonable, and yet so very uncooperative. There were things she must know and if Lord Dalby could be induced to reveal them, well then, it would serve her plans very well indeed.

"I prefer, above all things, a man who can speak plainly. Is that not within your abilities, Lord Dalby? I must confess that, according to Lord Westlin, plain speaking is beyond you." Sophia closed her fan and laid it against her throat.

"Lord Westlin?" Dalby said, his expressive eyes revealing perhaps more than he was aware. He straightened slightly. "I must confess to having believed that plain speaking would cause you to recoil, Miss Grey."

"This belief as reported is from Lord Westlin?" she asked mildly.

Dalby said nothing, which did recommend him. There was little worse than a man who could not keep his tongue between his teeth, unless it were a man who did not know when to deploy his tongue to best advantage, by which she meant to *her* best advantage.

"At least you are confessing something, my lord Dalby," she added, looking him over with obvious delight. He was a most attractive man, quite tall and well formed, his eyes most expressive, his brow positively poetical.

"Miss Grey, if confession is the key to charming you away from the use of your knife, I will confess all," Dalby said, with an amused half smile.

"I await with pleasure, my lord. Please, do begin."

He moved a step closer, leaning his head down to her. Sophia was not a small woman, but Dalby was a very tall man. His height and breadth of shoulders created a wall of privacy for them that she found strangely enticing.

"Speaking plainly," he said, "I have a history with Lord Westlin, a rather unpleasant one, and I had hoped that, between us, we could corner the rat in his hole, in a manner of speaking."

"You have the most delightful manner of speaking, Lord Dalby," she said softly. "How remarkably similar our goals are, as I suspect you know. Shall we not only corner the rat, but turn the blade in his deserving hide?"

"As you wish, Miss Grey," he said, with raised brows and a quirked smile.

"How best to achieve our shared goal, Lord Dalby? Does any plan spring up within you, my lord?" she said coyly.

"Most assuredly," he said.

"I did hope so," she said, smiling, knowing full well what exactly had sprung up on the lovely Lord Dalby.

She did not lean forward and allow him a glance down her bodice. She did not move closer and allow him to enjoy the delicate scent of her perfume. She did none of the things that women did to entice a man because, quite simply, she suspected that Lord Dalby would be more intrigued by following a different route entirely. He was a man accomplished at seduction and at being seduced, that much was more than obvious. For Lord Dalby, an entirely different sort of seduction was required, and as each moment passed in his enjoyable company, Sophia was more than certain that she was going to get far more from Lord Dalby than merely a cash settlement or a diamond necklace. He would, by all appearances, make such a pleasant husband.

"Lord Westlin?" she prompted when Lord Dalby seemed entirely too distracted by her bodice even without her enticement. How very charming of him.

"Yes, Lord Westlin," Dalby said, his dark eyes losing some of their twinkle. Lord Westlin was remarkably consistent in his ability to untwinkle the most sparkling of moments, even as a mere reference. "It is not necessary for you to be aware of my grievance against Lord Westlin," Dalby said, but naturally she was very aware of it as Lord Westlin had boasted of it repeatedly, disagreeable man that he was, "but I have just cause to want to see him abused in any way possible."

"As to cause," she said, "that is your own concern and certainly no one should interfere or, indeed, comment upon it. Is it not entirely a matter for your singular discernment? One does not take one's causes up for a vote in the House of Lords, my lord. As indeed, my own grievance against Lord Westlin is also a matter of private concern to me and to no one else."

"Miss Grey, your causes are your own," Dalby said softly, his eyes quite large in empathy, which clearly meant that he had heard at least some version of events as they had transpired. How very like Lord Westlin to be so indiscreet.

"Lord Dalby," she said, casting her gaze downward in a motion of feminine distress, "I do believe that Lord Westlin has wounded each of us in the precise manner to cause the most anguish. Should we not do him the same service? Do we dare to repay him in the precise manner to cause the most harm?"

"What sort of harm, Miss Grey?"

"Lasting harm, Lord Dalby."

"A blade?"

"Of a fashion."

"Miss Grey, you do intrigue me."

"Lord Dalby." She sighed, tracing a finger over her lower lip. "I had hoped for just that."

"Then we are allies?"

"Soldiers in arms would be a better description, my lord, don't you agree?"

"Are we to be as martial as all that, Miss Grey?"

"I am armed, my lord. Had you forgotten?"

"Regarding you, Miss Grey, I have forgotten nothing." She was entirely afraid that was true and there were certain things she did not particularly care for Dalby to know, the reason for her war against Westlin to be first among them, naturally. "But I do wonder if you have it in you to display restraint. Didn't someone very wise say that discretion is the better part of valor?"

"Certainly no one of *my* acquaintance," she said sweetly, fanning her face artfully. "If you have fears, Lord Dalby, you can trust that you need not fear *me*. I shan't harm you. Overmuch."

"I am deeply reassured." He breathed heavily, reaching out and taking her fan from her. It was most bold of him and long past due. She had begun to wonder if Lord Dalby was quite up to scratch in seductions after all. "But my concern was that you might do yourself an injury in trying to injure Lord Westlin. I could not allow such waste. He is not worth it."

"Lord Dalby," she said softly, "I would not have guessed it. You are a gallant, ever determined to rescue me from all sorts of perceived injuries. I am most deeply flattered."

"And I am most deeply determined, Miss Grey," he said, leaning down to kiss her on the top of her lightly powdered cheek. "Damaging Lord Westlin is not worth your destruction."

"Darling Lord Dalby, is not the point to destroy Westlin? Will you not play to win?"

"I would rather win you than destroy him."

"But, darling, why not do both?"

"Win you and destroy Westlin?" the Earl of Dalby asked, his breath brushing her temple in delicate and deliberate seduction. "You have a plan, I suppose?"

"But of course, my lord," Sophia answered. "I do nothing without a plan in place. How else to get what I want?"

Dalby dipped his chin down and considered her very seriously, perhaps for the first time of the evening. Men did not often take women seriously and it was in their profound worst interests not to do so, which was so very convenient for a woman with her wits about her.

"Your plan includes me?" Dalby said.

"Most definitely," she said.

"Dare I assume that you want me?"

"My lord," she said, with a smile, "how could you assume otherwise?"

With a flutter of her fan, she turned and walked up the first flight of the stairs, certain that Dalby would follow her. He did. It was upon the stair to the second floor, dingy and smoky as it was, that Dalby let slip his restraint. He grabbed her by the waist from behind, held her hard against his twitching manhood, and cupped her sex through her skirts.

"And isn't this what you want from me?" he said against her ear. "More than revenge against Lord Westlin?"

"My lord Dalby, dark corner gropings are not to my taste."

But with this man, perhaps they would be. He was a bit different from the other lords of London, a bit more observant and a bit more gallant. Certainly that could not be said of most of England's aristocracy.

"You do not want me? This?" he said, holding her hard against him. "You feel nothing?"

"I feel all the future earls of Dalby bursting to be free very well, my lord. Was there more I was to feel?"

She taunted him. He had to know that she would not be as easily won as all that, not even in the name of a mutual revenge. What was truly lovely was that he knew he was being taunted and laughed softly in response. Humor in a man? Lord Dalby jumped even higher in her estimation.

"You're a savage bitch, Sophia," he said cheerfully.

"You've noticed," she answered cheerfully. "How sweet. But shouldn't we be concentrating on Lord Westlin and our mutual loathing of him? Or have I distracted you?"

In answer, he tipped her chin up and kissed her, his manhood still grinding into her from behind. It was not at all unpleasant. In fact she liked it more than was in her best interests. Passion, which she kept on a thick leash, would not be let loose tonight and certainly not upon this man. Passion running rampant could confuse the best of plans.

"We share a mutual *something*, Sophia. It is more than loathing Westlin, I think," he whispered, adding, "I hope."

It was entirely unexpected, this glimpse of tenderness, of hope. The expression in his eyes coupled with the taste of him on her tongue resulted in a tingling in her breasts that galloped down to make her moist and twitchy where men most wanted women to be moist and twitchy.

Passion growled for release. Sophia let the leash slip.

She turned upon the stair and kissed him on the mouth. Softly, at first, but so quickly descending into urgency. She breathed into him, their breath mingling as fully as their plans, twisting through their hearts and lungs until they breathed as one, panting against each other, opening to each other. Plans for revenge misting away in the blaze of starved desire.

Dalby twined his tongue with hers and clasped her arse in his hands, pulling her into him, sliding his bent knee between her legs. She rode him briefly, trying to find the leash, trying to pull it all back into her hands and into her control.

"Hot for me. I knew you would be." Dalby breathed into her mouth, his hands at her breasts.

And then she pulled away from the glorious friction and pulled his kiss from her by a hard yank on the back of his hair.

He grunted and released her, his mouth still open with want, his throat deliciously exposed, his jugular vein throbbing. It was a sight to make her nipples tighten and tingle.

"I have a blade, my lord. I will use it," she whispered hoarsely. "Would you like to be the next wager on White's book?"

"You'll need no blade with me, Sophia. I'll only give you that for which you ask."

He did not move. He did not pull his hair from out of her hands or try to overpower her. He could have done so, if only until she unsheathed her blade. Perhaps he knew that. Or perhaps he was not afraid of her, no matter the blade she carried to protect herself. Whatever his reasons, she could see no fear and no impatience in his eyes and that was a sight so unexpected and so frightening that she punished him for it.

Holding him by his hair, his chin lifted, his throat exposed, she pulled free her blade from the scabbard sewn into the centerpiece of her bodice. It was a narrow blade, but as sharp as a snake's tooth. Sophia held it to Dalby's throat, to just below his ear, and pressed it as lightly as a lover's kiss. A small dot of blood appeared.

The Earl of Dalby did not flinch. He regarded her calmly and with something close to sympathy. She did not want sympathy, never that, and not from an English lord who likely knew more about her than she wished him to know.

Damn Westlin for everything.

"I have not asked, my lord," she said, her voice sounding harsh to her own ears.

"No, you have not asked," he said softly. "Yet you will."

"You first," she said in whisper, hearing the roar of desire trying to break free, tempted to put them on the savage back of untamed passion and let it run away with them both. "Untie your cravat," she commanded.

Dalby obeyed, slowly. His hands were very well formed and large, the fingers straight and long. She watched him and kept her breathing slow and even, commanding her heart to beat at peaceful intervals. But she was not peaceful and neither was Dalby, no matter the calm that carefully painted his features. His manhood strained against his breeches, always the true measure of a man's thoughts.

His cravat, untied, lay docile and limp against his coat.

"Where should I mark you, my lord?" She struggled for a playful tone, certain by the pounding in her blood that she was failing.

"Shall I tell you, Sophia?"

"Do you dare?" she asked, pressing the blade deeper, knowing he would wear a scar there for the rest of his life and delighting in that fact.

She wanted to mark him, in every way. She wanted him to remember her. That was the deeper truth: that she wanted to be remembered.

She had no time for deeper truths. She had only this moment and the will to best him. He was just a man, another man. He could be managed like any of them. That he made her feel things, remember things, was of no import. She would win. She always won.

"With you, I believe I would dare anything," he said, staring down into her eyes.

"Brave words," she scoffed. "You know I cut Westlin. You can hardly conceive of where or how."

"Can't I?" he said. "What did he do, Sophia? What did he do to you?"

Sophia took a deep breath and smiled herself back into composure, leashing the beast within. "It is none of your concern. I can take care of myself."

"Clearly," he said, still studying her too closely, the net of desire slipping from him as thought and speculation returned. "But the question is, can you take care of me?"

He said it lightly, even frivolously, but there was something, some thread of intensity that he could not mask. They were so swiftly moving onto ground that could not hold them, not yet. Only their desire to punish Westlin bound them and that, however meaningful, was not enough. She wanted more from Lord Dalby than that. Every minute spent with him confirmed it.

"You can't mean you want your throat slit, Lord Dalby," she said, tilting her head to look at him coyly. "I know the English aristocracy has little to live for, still . . ."

"We've been known to live for revenge," he said lightly. "I think you understand about that, don't you, Sophia?"

She did not want to look into his eyes any more, and more importantly, she did not want him looking into hers. She withdrew her blade from his throat and, leaning up, ran her tongue over the wound, licking up the blood, trailing her mouth down his throat until she found the hot beat of his jugular and there she set her mouth and bit him, sucking hard at the heat beneath her lips.

She held him hard by his hair, holding him precisely as she wanted him while she sucked at his throat.

He wrapped his arms around her waist and pulled her hard against him.

They stayed that way, entwined, her mouth on his throat, his hands gripping her hips, for more minutes than they had to spare. Westlin would not stay in the theater all night and this was still all of Westlin. She was almost certain of that.

"I understand," she said, watching as he tied his cravat clumsily, "that the best way to punish Lord Westlin for his various and never-ending crimes against us is to cut him with the same blade."

Dalby looked at her, his brows drawing down into a small scowl. He had the cleanest, straightest brow, like a statue of marble in perfection, and quite the most beautifully shaped nose. It was nearly a pleasure just to look at him, though she normally measured pleasure by the size of the jewel or the weight of the silver.

"What blade do you mean?" he asked.

Sophia slipped her blade inside the sheath in her bodice and took a breath before answering him. When she looked at him again, it was with her composure and her plan fully in place.

"The finest and sharpest blade of all, my lord. A woman," she said, with a smile. "Me."

"You would use yourself to wound Westlin? Have you not been hurt enough by him?" Dalby said.

Sophia kept her expression stony and said, "I don't know what you *think* you know, Lord Dalby, and I would say that if you are foolish enough to believe anything Lord Westlin tells you then you deserve to be the butt of his jest, but Lord Westlin did not hurt me. I am here, am I not? I have a home and Westlin gave me the means to keep it. What harm has he done me? It is he who bears the scars, is it not? Is that not what you set out to prove tonight?"

"There are many kinds of scars, Sophia," he said tenderly.

"The only scars that matter are those that come from the edge of a knife, my lord," she said. "If you believe otherwise then you are too civilized to be of use to me."

Dalby snarled softly, saying, "You despise civility? Very well, then."

He grabbed her, clasping both of her hands in his, pressing them to his tackle, pressing his body against hers and trapping her against the wall. She was not truly trapped. She could use her legs or her head to defeat him. She knew how to fight. She knew how to survive. She had learned those lessons long before London had claimed her.

Freeing one of his hands, Dalby pulled her blade from her bodice and held it to the base of her throat.

She did not make a sound. She did not allow her breathing to quicken.

"A silent captive," Dalby said in admiration. "I should have known."

She did not answer him, but her gaze was calm and her posture arrogant. He would not cut her. He liked her skin too much to scar it.

Dalby released her hands, the blade still at her throat, his arm fully extended. It was a wise decision as he had removed himself from her easy reach. Still she knew how to disarm a single man with a single blade. Dalby was no threat to her, not physically.

"Take down your bodice," he commanded.

She obeyed. This was an old game between men and women, and she understood how to play it. She was still in control. If she wanted to stop, she could do so, but she did not want to. Where would Dalby take this? How far would he go? What would be unleashed in him by seeing her so?

Her bodice was perfectly fitted to her, which meant it was quite snug. She managed to free a single breast to nearly perfect nakedness and stopped, awaiting his next command.

"You do not fear the blade," he said, tracing her bosom with the tip of the knife.

"I fear no man's blade, my lord," she said, staring into his eyes.

"Did your father teach you that?" he said, still tracing her, laying the flat edge of the knife against her erect nipple, the chill steel warming against her heat.

"No," she said. "My mother did."

Dalby froze, his gaze locked with hers, the knife pressed against her nipple.

"She was a captive?" Dalby asked.

"Yes."

"Of which tribe?"

"Mohawk."

"He married her?"

"Eventually."

"Why did he marry her?" Dalby asked. He wanted to ask more; he wanted to ask why her English mother had married her Mohawk father. Sophia answered truthfully, though she did not know why.

"Because he would not live without her," Sophia said softly, her voice carrying in the hall, the words lingering. "The very same reason that you will give for why you want to marry me, Lord Dalby."

Dalby, to his credit, did not drop the knife. He did, however, lower it.

"This is to be our revenge against Westlin?" he asked.

Her breast was still bared, a single breast to entice him. She suspected she looked exactly what she was: a Mohawk woman wearing English silk.

"It is the perfect revenge, my lord. He took your woman. Take his."

Dalby shook his head and motioned for her to rearrange her bodice. "He told you?"

"He tells everyone," Sophia said. "Did he not tell all why I left him? What happened at his estate? How I was used?" Sophia laughed sharply, tucking her breast back underneath silk, hiding as much of her Mohawk training as she could. "To think that you would want me and take me in such a way, in marriage. I'm not at all certain he would recover from it. But it is only a rumor you start, my lord. I would not marry you. You must know that."

Dalby's dark head lifted, his pupils dilating dangerously. "*You* would not? Why not?"

Sophia shrugged. "You are too . . . English, my lord. Far too civilized."

It was exactly the prod to his pride that he needed. Sophia knew then that, at some future date, Dalby would beg to marry her, perhaps even kill for her. It was what her father had done to win her mother, after all. It might even become a family tradition, if Lord Dalby was agreeable.

She would be entirely surprised if he was not perfectly agreeable to almost anything, eventually.

SIX

"Most certainly, Your Grace," Zoe said agreeably, her heart pounding. "I shall touch you. I will hold nothing back. What else would you have of me?"

"I would have all of you, mademoiselle," he said hoarsely, his voice only just loud enough for her to hear.

"But of course," she answered, thinking quickly, "but piece by piece, I think. The palate can be so quickly overwhelmed, the appetite gorged. It is best to savor the meal, is it not, Your Grace?"

"You are truly willing?" he asked, his gaze growing quite seductive, his sadness fleeing like the outgoing tide. "Here and now? You would do that?"

"I would," she said, looking deeply into his eyes. What hesitation was there and why should a duke balk at such a little thing as this? Men plunged themselves into women upon the merest notion and did they think to care if the woman was willing?

Of course she was likely biased in her view of things, but one worked with the information one had.

"Are you not frightened, Miss Auvray?"

"I can be frightened if you wish," she said. "Shall I run? Shall you catch me? There is not much space here to run, but perhaps you should like me to slap you?"

"Stop it, Zoe!" he said in suppressed fury. "You cannot be as experienced as all that."

"I can be as experienced as you like, Your Grace," she said softly. "Shall I prove it to you?"

"Certainly," he said, his anger like a taunted cat, silent and twitching and ready to claw.

And now the play truly began. Zoe moved in such a way that Aldreth was visible from the stage below. Miranda stumbled upon the hem of her skirts, her pose ruined.

Zoe smiled and ignored Miranda. She knelt at Aldreth's feet, though she could hardly afford to abuse this gown so. Running her hands up his silk encased legs, around the back to his buttocks, which were quite nice and firm, and up to his waist, she looked up to Aldreth's face.

"A sumptuous feast," she murmured. "I know exactly where I shall begin. The meat course, obviously. I am quite hungry and refuse to deny my urges. Your permission?"

"Continue," he said, his voice low and rough.

And so, with as much theatrical flair as possible, she unleashed his tackle from within the collar of his breeches and, giving every indication of ravenous hunger, proceeded to swallow him whole.

He did not appear to enjoy it, which was peculiar. Most men did. The poor Duke of Aldreth did need some cheer in his life. Licking him along his length, pausing now and again to sigh, a kiss upon the tip, a nip along the side, her hands delicately clasping his arse . . .

"Enough!" he snarled, dragging her to her feet by her arms, forcing her mouth away from him. Zoe stared at him, her eyes filling with tears. "You are not such a wanton as you pretend, Miss Auvray."

"If I failed to please you, then teach me how," she said. "I know I can please you. I know I can give us both what we surely want."

Standing, Zoe pressed herself against him, putting her mouth on his and whispering, "Kiss me and taste what I have tasted. A fine meal you make, Your Grace."

He grabbed her a bit roughly and, clearly against his better judgement, devoured her mouth with his own. His kiss was passionate, almost desperate.

Aldreth's hands were demanding, his mouth hungry. Running her hands over his shoulders, she slipped his coat partly off, trapping his arms to his sides.

"Dessert course, Your Grace," she informed him, and pushed him into a chair, straddling him before he could say a word. Zoe lifted her skirts and positioned herself just over his eager point. She did not lower herself. She did, as it happened, have a lovely view of Miranda, who appeared to have forgotten her lines entirely. Zoe smiled at Miranda, redirected her attention to Aldreth, and said, "I am ready for you. Take me, Your Grace, and I shall prove to you that I am as wanton as you need me to be."

His kiss was a violent thing of longing and hunger that shocked her. His tongue swept in and scoured her mouth, hot and driving, starving. Her poor duke was starving. She moaned and opened to accept him, her tongue dancing against his, enticing him, welcoming him.

It was so difficult to play this game to win. She could not lose her way, forgetting everything in the blaze that defined desire. Aldreth was capable of arousing that in her. Even so soon, he was capable of it. Men enjoyed the hunt, not the meal. They lost interest and wandered off as soon as their lusts were fed, their bellies full. Through the haze of passion, her loins throbbing with need, she made herself do what she must to keep him intrigued.

It would be all too simple for him to forget her name an hour from now. Was that not the way of things with men? French or English they were, after all, only men. Yet was she not a woman? Could she not tame this man even for an hour?

She could and she would.

He thrust his hips upward to impale her and made some small headway, but she raised herself up and he lost ground. He thrust again and she let him in a bit more, stay a bit longer, and then she released him.

"You want me," she said in French, half certain that he would understand her. "You want this, even now. You are angry. Yet you burn. In life and in death, we burn. Let us burn together and make a fine blaze."

Aldreth scowled at her and tried to reach her, to lift her from him, she suspected. She plunged down upon him, impaling herself, capturing him, riding him when he would have thrown her from him. Like an angry stallion, he bucked and snorted. He wanted, yet he fought at every point.

He yanked his arms forward, ripping the tiny stitches of his jacket. Yes, that was only right. He must fight, even a little, for his pleasure. How else to fully enjoy it?

"I will not do this!" he said. "I will not use you this way!"

"And yet you are," she said. "We both know that you can release yourself. All you must do is to lose your desire. You will fall away, leaving me empty. Can you do it? I do not think you can."

"I can do anything," he snarled. "Certainly I can resist you."

"Can you? I do not think so. I will not make it easy for you, that is certain. You need this, Your Grace, I think. This wild ride within the heat of a Frenchwoman. Let me give you this," she whispered, taking his face in her hands. "It is a small thing."

"It is no small thing," he whispered in response, his breath fanning her face. "It is because you think it small that it must not be done. You must stop this, Zoe. Stop."

As an entreaty it was ridiculous. He could have overpowered her at any moment, yet he did not. He needed this and he needed to be free of the guilt of it. She did not understand why, but she did recognize guilt when she saw it, even in the eyes of a duke.

"No, no, Your Grace. I will do all, but I will not release you. Can you not remember passion? Can you not ride the crest of it and let it abandon you where it will?"

"Who taught you that? Who turned you into this?" he snapped, the veins on his forehead and throat extended as he fought passion and lost.

"It matters not. The lesson was learned. The past is dead. We live only now," she said. "We must convince Miranda that you are irresistible to women, a task that falls to me. When I am done with you, then you may prove your insatiability, a task that will fall to you. Are we in agreement, Your Grace?"

"This is not what you learned in the convent, little Zoe," he said, "and you did not live long on the streets of Paris."

"No?" she said, with a seductive smile. "I do not think you know Paris as well as I do, Your Grace. It is the city of learning, is it not? Now are we in agreement? Yes?"

But, in fact, he was more right than wrong. Life, as was often the case, had spun wildly out of control and left her here, in a London theater with a duke held firmly within her folds. One made of life what one could. A salty tear or two to mark the divergence of a course and then a smile and onward. What else? Life must be lived.

"Agreed," Aldreth said hoarsely. "But nothing of Miranda. Just us. Just now."

She ground herself abruptly onto him, impaling herself sharply and marking it with a loud gasp of unbearable pleasure. She was quite certain Miranda heard it, but she did not care about Miranda now. Miranda might have propelled them together, but she was fading away into the past. In a week she would be forgotten completely. Aldreth was consuming her, inside and out. This strange, intense man, wounded in some way she could not quite see.

Zoe looked down at him, at his earnest and slightly desperate face, at the intensity that shimmered from his eyes, at the deep loneliness that hovered in the air around him.

"It *is* just us," she said, taking his face in her hands, Miranda and all that she had caused forgotten for the first time that night. "It is just *you*," she whispered along his cheek.

He shuddered and released his seed into her.

"Just you," he whispered, his coat in place, his arms wrapped around her, his hands buried in her hair. He lifted her and placed her on her feet, pressing her back against the dark wall of the box, far away from the edge and the open theater below them.

Her heart tripped. His eyes told her that he spoke the truth, but could it be that simple? But what was simple? She felt empty and alone, as she always did at the end of passion. Aldreth had spoken the truth. She had not known this life long enough to be at ease in it. When she had the luxury of time, she would admit that she did not want to be at ease. She wanted something else, something lasting, something tender and careful and kind.

But she did not have the luxury of time. She could admit nothing. She could not even admit that Aldreth and his sharp, sad eyes made her want only him.

"Stay," Aldreth whispered to her, his eyes beseeching.

"Yes," she said eagerly.

"Leave," he commanded, not taking his eyes from hers.

A man grumbled something. Zoe blinked and looked. She had not heard anyone enter Aldreth's box. It was that horrible man, Sophia's enemy, Lord Westlin.

"You win," Westlin said. "I didn't think you'd do it, not this quickly, but she's pretty enough, if you like the type. Is that it, Aldreth? Was Sophia too dark for your tastes?"

"I won every term, met the wager," Aldreth said coldly, shielding Zoe as much as he could. "Did you expect otherwise?"

"You know what I expected, what I thought after that . . . after . . ." Westlin stumbled.

"After what?" Zoe said, pushing Aldreth away from her. He did not push easily.

"This is a wager that does not concern you," Westlin said dismissively. "But as it is amusing, I will tell you. I wagered that the duke could not pleasure himself with a woman tonight, yet there you are." Hideous man, little wonder that Sophia hated him so.

Sophia.

Westlin.

Aldreth. It all came together in a flash that made her wince in pain.

"This has something to do with Lord Westlin and Miss Grey, does it not?" she demanded of Aldreth, ignoring Westlin.

"You don't understand," Aldreth said.

"You use people with a careless hand, that I understand most well," she said. "I can only learn from it and, with fortitude, prosper. Good evening, Your Grace," she said, and with a stiff smile made to leave his box.

"As the wager has been met," Aldreth said swiftly to Westlin, holding out his arm to stop her, "I will expect the French clock to be delivered as we agreed. Good evening," he said, and he practically pushed Lord Westlin out of the box. Lord Westlin did not go easily, but Aldreth was a man at his most ducal and most rigid. Perhaps they were synonyms.

"A night of wagers. I suppose I might have made my fortune, had I known," she said. "Thank you for yet another lesson, Your Grace. I am becoming extremely learned."

She was delighted to see Aldreth wince.

"This had nothing to do with you. At the start," he added.

"But of course," she said, smoothing her skirts. "English dukes, much like French ones, do as they please. Explanations are never necessary, are they?"

"I didn't intend—"

"Yes, you made that very clear. Repeatedly. I suppose I am to blame for overpowering you and forcing you to do that which you most expressly did not want to do. I apologize. There. You are satisfied?"

She eyed him coldly, her expression stiffly polite, her posture regal. But her heart, her heart wept.

"I will explain and—"

"And what will you do with your French clock, Your Grace?" Zoe asked, her arms crossed over her chest. She did not want to hear his ridiculous explanations. Why was he even bothering? She was a French whore. No one ever felt the need to explain anything to a French whore.

"I will give it to my French mistress, Mademoiselle Auvray," Aldreth said. "If she will accept it."

"If you mean me, I will accept it. I have earned it," she said. "I bid you good night and farewell, Your Grace. It has been a memorable evening."

"Zoe, listen to me," he said, taking her by the arms and staring down at her.

Zoe pushed against him, her head down, her eyes filling with tears. Where was her Parisian sophistication now? Like all illusions, it had evaporated at the first hard shake of reality. She was not sophisticated. She was a destitute girl from a long way off and she had just lost her best chance at everything.

"Listen!" he said sternly.

She stopped pushing. He was a duke. He was very adept at being stern and getting his own way. He also could likely have her arrested for any reason at all.

"I will listen, Your Grace. What will you tell me? Some story about Miranda having disgraced you?" she said, walking away from him to stand on the other side of the box. It was not a very big space, but she put every inch of it between them.

"What I told you about Miranda was true," he said. "What was not quite as true was my reaction to it. What an actress of very certain reputation says about me is far beneath my concern."

"But naturally," she said. "We are all far, far beneath you, Your Grace."

She sniffed.

"Just listen and try to keep your insults to yourself for the time being," he said, pacing to the front of the box and staring down at the theater crowd below them. It was fair to say that fully half of the crowd was staring back up at him, Sophia and the Earl of Dalby included. "While I do not care what Miranda says about me, I must have a care what the men with whom I socialize say. It is a matter of honor, of prestige, and I cannot allow my reputation to suffer in their company and by their testimony."

"I was not aware," she said loftily, "that a duke had to care what anyone thought."

"I was not aware," he parroted, "that you knew very much of anything about dukes. Or am I wrong? Who was it who lured you out of your cloister, Zoe?"

She felt her cheeks pinken and she whirled away from him. She felt his hands on her shoulders, a gentle entreaty.

"I blame no one but myself," she said softly. "I was very naïve. I am no longer naïve, as you may have noticed, Your Grace."

"You will not tell me. You are very discreet. Very few people are," he whispered. "It is a trait I place a high value upon."

She turned to face him. His face, still so severe, loomed above her. He was a very tall man, very beautiful in the way of a man, very dark and . . . alone. Those icy eyes, how they pierced her. She felt so tender toward him when he turned those eyes upon her.

The easiest solution to avoid feelings of tenderness was to walk away and never look into his eyes again.

Zoe did not move. Perhaps she was still a bit naïve, after all.

"I . . ." he said softly, "I have a wife. She has given me a girl."

"My congratulations," she said, trying very hard to be sophisticated.

"She is not strong," he continued as if she had not spoken. "But I must have an heir. She is a good wife to me. She is a fine woman. But I cannot," he said in a hushed voice, turning away from her to face the theater crowd again. "I cannot go to her as often as I should like." His voice was stronger. Facing the crowd, his audience, he was stronger. How very like a man. "I don't want to hurt her, but I must have an heir."

"Of course, Your Grace," she said. She understood. She didn't want to, but she did. "And how does this need for an heir connect to Lord Westlin and to Sophia and to me?"

Because that was the point, was it not? She was not going to be so stupid as to forget the point.

Aldreth turned to face her, his eyes blazing in mute appeal. "You are discreet. I am trusting in that, Zoe."

She nodded, unable to find a single word to say.

"I avoid my wife as much as I can," he said. "It is noticed. I do not often sow my seed upon other fields because I . . ." He shrugged and looked down. Zoe knew without his having to say it. Because he did not want to give to other women what he withheld from his wife, just as he had not wanted to give that to her. "And when a man has developed a reputation for not . . ." he said woodenly, "and he attends a house party and does not partake of what is readily available, it is wondered . . . and then gossiped . . ."

"It was Sophia," she said in a rush of understanding. "You did not partake of Sophia, and they mocked you and so you had to prove that you could perform and you performed tonight upon me."

He nodded stiffly. "Approximately."

Approximately. She was learning to hate that word.

"But you are a duke," she said in disbelief. "Why does it matter what a few men say about you? You know what is true. That is all that matters."

"I have a daughter," he said, staring down at her. "She must marry one day. My name must be protected or she will have limited prospects among the sons of these very men."

Of course. It was no different in France. Perhaps it was no different anywhere.

"And your reluctance?" she asked. "What part did that play in this wager?"

"No part at all," he said, staring hard at her, his gaze as hot as coal fire. "Miranda mocking you was the last straw. I wanted to see her punished for your sake, even in so small a fashion. You wanted it as well. I tried to make certain of that."

"I did," she said quietly. "Your Grace," she said, dipping her head, "you have your reasons and as long as they are good to you, then they are good enough. You need not explain yourself to me. Now I must go. I have the night before me and I must make my way through it."

"No."

She looked up at him. He looked fierce and hard and resolute.

"I must make my way *in* it?" she said.

"*No,*" he said, with the smallest and most fragile of smiles.

"My English is not perfect, Your Grace, but my meaning must be clear enough."

"Is *my* English not clear enough for you, Zoe? You will not go. You must not go."

He looked as determined as a knight facing a dragon and as frightened.

"I must not, Your Grace? Why not?"

He walked across the box toward her, reaching out a hand to her. Without thinking, she reached out her own hand to him. They touched and she shivered. He felt it and smiled. Such a rare thing, Aldreth's smiles. Such a sad and lonely man. He needed someone in his life to tease smiles from him.

Could she not do that for him? Could she not allow that revenge could be a road to a pleasant destination as well as desperation could be? In fact life being what it was, this night of wagered seductions would be something to laugh about in a few weeks or months. She did so hope for months. She was so very tired and Aldreth was so very compelling.

"Did you forget about the clock, Zoe? We won it together. It is a French clock."

He was almost grinning now, a lopsided grin that had almost no shadow of melancholy in it. How very good it looked on him.

"It is a very pretty clock?" she asked, cocking her head up at him, pursing her lips in speculation. "As it is French, I suppose it could be little else."

He was smiling, an air of relaxation about him that she decided she was wholly responsible for. She smiled and felt a spring in her step as they left his box together, arm in arm, and walked down the stairs to the ground floor.

"It is a *very* pretty clock," he said.

"A woman would be a fool not to accept a French clock, Your Grace. I am quite of the opinion that French clocks are the best to be had. But where shall I put it?"

"Upon the mantel, Zoe," he said lightly. "Wherever do they put mantel clocks in France if not upon a mantel?"

"And where is my mantel to be?"

"In a very nice house in a very respectable part of Town. I do not make it a habit to visit disreputable parts of Town, and as I am paying for it, I will be visiting this house regularly."

His smile faltered and a scowl crept upon his brow. He scowled too often. She would have to break him of that.

"If you agree, of course," he said. "I hope you will."

"A woman would be a fool not to accept a duke, Your Grace," she said softly, her eyes brimming with unwelcome tears. "Particularly dukes who are as lonely and lovely as you."

Aldreth's head came up sharply and he scowled in earnest. "I am not often referred to as either lonely or lovely, Miss Auvray. I am not flattered."

"Your Grace," she said, with a smile, "if you are insistent that you be constantly flattered then we shall run out of conversation very quickly. On the other hand, if you want someone prepared to charm you then you shall be lonely no longer. And if you want to fall into bed with someone who will demonstrate how lovely you are, then you have found her." Aldreth stopped upon the stair and looked deeply into her eyes. He had such lovely eyes in such a lonely face. It was not at all right for a duke to be so unhappy.

It was not at all right for a man to be so alone.

"For you, I think I could even make do without a French clock," she said, laying her hand upon his cheek. "As I am profoundly French, that is, you will admit, quite a sacrifice."

To which the lovely Duke of Aldreth laughed. And then he kissed her.

SEVEN

East Sussex, 1792

He kissed her again, a lingering kiss of considerable warmth and tender familiarity.

Zoe and Aldreth stood in the middle of the lane to Iden Place and kissed. The wind swept down the sunny lane, charming the moment with the soft scent of summer green, infusing their kiss with more sweetness than heat. It was the right sort of kiss for this exact moment. The lane curved away before them, a curl of sandy white dirt, the borders of the lane tinged with pink and purple and gold. They stood wrapped together, Aldreth's strength a prop against the gusty wind.

"I never tire of kissing you," Aldreth said, moving his mouth so that his lips brushed her cheek.

"And why should you? Am I not delightful to kiss?" Zoe said, looking up at him. "I always make it a point to be delightful. It is something of a habit with me."

"I thought *I* was your habit," Aldreth said.

"I am most certain I am allowed more than one habit. To have only one habit, is that not the essence of a bore? How very limiting. I would be ashamed to be so scant in my habits."

"Zoe," Aldreth said, grinning fully down at her, "you know you don't need to flirt incessantly with me. I am yours, most devotedly. I am won."

Zoe flicked a curl of hair back over her shoulder and stepped back from Aldreth. The wind took her curl and sent it skipping across her shoulders. "I like to flirt, Aldreth, and *almost* exclusively with you."

"*Only* with me, you French vixen," he growled good-naturedly.

"Only because you insist," she said on a laugh, "but you are denying me one of the chief joys of a French woman. How can I improve my technique upon only one man?"

"Even if that man be a duke?" he said.

"Oh, yes," she said, smiling, teasing him. "Being a duke does make up for much of it."

"And the rest?"

"You, my dearest Aldreth, make up for all of it. I have quite lost the heart of coquetry as a form of civilized entertainment. You have stolen every urge I ever had. Save one."

"The best one to keep," he said, grinning, pulling her into his arms to kiss her deeply.

His kiss swept her away, as it always did, even now ten years after their first kiss on that dark and desperate night in London. She had hoped for this, planned for it, yearned for it. Yet, truly, not quite this, only a place to lay her head and some small measure of safety. What she had found in Aldreth was so very much more.

She had found love.

She had not dared dream of finding love. But Aldreth dared what other men only dreamed. He had dared much to love her and in loving her, he had given her a new life.

"Mama!"

Most definitely, a new life.

Aldreth lifted his head and scowled mildly, his look more amused than annoyed. "He has infallible timing. And a wretched nurse. We must hire someone slightly more savage, don't you think?"

Zoe smiled and swatted Aldreth on the shoulder before turning to face their son as he ran down through the sunlit lane toward them, his nurse huffing for breath behind him.

"Ah, your competition arrives. He does have flawless timing, much like his father," Zoe said. "And he is too old for a nurse, my dear. He requires a man of very long leg and able arm. Who else could possibly keep up with him?"

Aldreth scowled in earnest now, poor dear, and said, "Long of leg and able of arm? Is that any way to describe a tutor? You torment me, you French witch."

"But of course, Your Grace," she answered silkily. "Who else is there to do it? A man must be tormented with some regularity or he becomes impossible. You have far too much inclination to be impossible as it is. I must do my part to keep you. . . ."

"To keep me what?" he said, smiling in spite of all his best intentions.

Zoe leaned up on tiptoe and kissed his very lovely chin. "Just . . . to keep you. That is all."

"Mama! Father!" Jamie said, reaching them. He was James Caversham, after his father, but unlike his father, without title. But not without love and that was more than enough for any boy. "We have guests!"

Ah, yes, for a boy of almost nine years, guests would be a thing of great import. They had guests rarely, which was only to be expected. Zoe was not Aldreth's wife, Jamie was his natural son, Iden Place was where Aldreth kept them and kept them very well. That Iden Place was only fifteen miles from the south coast was a clear measure of Aldreth's consideration for Zoe; she could travel to France almost at will, which was far more than she had ever expected when she first left France ten years ago. But as to guests, whom would she entertain? A duke's mistress had very few reasons to entertain anyone other than her duke. A situation she found entirely restful, likely a holdover from her days in the convent. Iden Place was quite as large as the convent, better furnished, and she didn't have to perform penances. A lovely situation from any perspective.

"Hold, boy," Aldreth said, ruffling his son's dark hair. Jamie was almost an exact copy of Aldreth from the thick dark gloss of his hair to his light blue eyes to the angle of his jaw. It gave Zoe an immense amount of pleasure for it to be so for even when Aldreth was busy at his affairs in Town, she had Jamie and having Jamie was very near to having Aldreth. "Guests or merely a messenger?"

"Guests, sir," Jamie replied, clearly outraged that it should be supposed he not be fully aware of the distinction. Boys of almost nine were quite savage about protecting their reputations. Zoe smiled and readjusted her hair. She was without bonnet because Aldreth preferred it that way. It was not quite the way to receive guests, however.

"What sort of guests, boy?" Aldreth said, quizzing him.

"Reputable, sir," Jamie answered. "A family of distinction, I should say. Husband and wife, two children, and a coach, sir, a coach of immense proportions of red lacquer with yellow leather and drawn by four black horses very nearly matched."

"Oh, very *nearly* matched," Aldreth said in mock severity. "Not so very reputable then, to have only very nearly matched horses."

"Aldreth!" Zoe said on a laugh. He did so love to tease Jamie, and Jamie was not always certain when he was being teased.

"But, sir," Jamie insisted, his small body trembling with excitement, "the coach was crested! They must be reputable, musn't they? To have a crest?"

Oh, dear. That did not bode well. It might signal some disastrous news of Aldreth's children by his late wife. Aldreth had two children, a daughter and a son, his heir. Zoe could only feel compassion and concern for those two as they had no mother to ease their way in the world. She knew too well the emptiness of being a child without a mother's love and care.

Aldreth lost all desire to tease his son at that news and, without pause, made his way down the lane to their home. Jamie ran lightly just behind his father while Zoe, still organizing her hair, walked perfectly reluctantly at the rear of their family parade.

There was indeed a perfectly magnificent coach pulled up in front of the sprawling manor house that was Iden Place. The crest on its side was not Aldreth's, nor was it a crest she knew, which hardly spoke to the point as she had not made it a priority to learn the family crests of England. She did know fifteen or twenty of the crests of France, however, which did not help in this situation.

She did wish that her hair looked more artfully styled and that she had worn a better gown. When one went walking the fields and lanes with Aldreth, one did not wear one's best. Aldreth did have the most consistent habit of tumbling her in the most unlikely places, which was completely delightful and immensely flattering, but was most hard on one's clothes.

She did not suppose it was required of her to make an appearance. Whoever was calling upon the Duke of Aldreth at his most private of residences would have no need of her.

Before she could act on that impulse, a voice called to her.

"Zoe, you look marvelous. Aldreth clearly agrees with you completely."

Zoe turned at the sound of that familiar voice and smiled.

"Sophia, or should I say Countess? You are welcome to Iden Place indeed. Most welcome. You look marvelous as well. Clearly being a countess agrees with *you* completely."

Sophia, who did indeed look as beautiful as she had ten years ago when Zoe had first met her, smiled and said, "But of course it does, darling. Whoever could be dull enough not to enjoy being Dalby's countess? He is able to make even membership in the English aristocracy bearable, for they are an insipid lot, are they not? How wise of you to avoid them so devoutly. But I do hope that you will tolerate us for an afternoon."

"I'll do more than tolerate, Sophia, I'll press you for every *on dit* and promise not to reveal the more scandalous bits to Aldreth.

He puts such a fine point on decorum. I do, at times, find him a bit of a handful."

"I should say you do," Sophia said, "and look not at all put out by it. Most wise of you, darling Zoe. You always did have the most delightful outlook on life and just look where it has landed you."

They were about to enter the drawing room, a perfectly convivial room fitted out in mellowed oak paneling with plentiful leaded French doors and done up in pale gold silk damask, when they were interrupted by Jamie and the two children of the Earl and Countess of Dalby. The boy was slightly younger than Jamie, perhaps by as much as two years, and the girl younger still. Nevertheless, no matter their ages, they possessed a poise and dignity of carriage that bespoke their exalted position in life.

"My children," Sophia said softly, the affection clear in her voice. "Dalby's heir, Lord John Markham Trevelyan, and my heir, Lady Caroline Trevelyan."

"Oh, Mother," Lady Caroline said in slight exasperation. "You know perfectly well that I am not your heir. Mark is the heir. I am the daughter."

"You are *my* daughter, Caro, and that is what makes you my heir. You will have to allow me some latitude. I made up my mind long ago not to be bound by arbitrary English rules."

"They are not arbitrary," Mark said. "They are tradition, Mother."

"Tradition, as you will one day learn, can be completely arbitrary and ridiculously illogical," Sophia said lightly.

Jamie looked them over, clearly astounded by the level of intimacy shared by the Trevelyan family. Of course he would be. Aldreth, while his father, was not a man of easy familiarity, and it was beyond obvious that Jamie was not and never would be Aldreth's heir.

Did Sophia's children understand that? It seemed unlikely that Sophia would have explained it to them as she found these notions of English heritage and succession arbitrary and illogical.

They were a lovely gathering, these three small proofs of an enduring affection. Did Sophia actually love Dalby? It was more than clear that she loved her children. Markham was tall, though very slender, dark of hair and eye, and with quite a nice brow. Caroline looked more like Sophia than Markham, her hair nearly black though her eyes were a deep blue. She had the most adorable little mouth, quite the shade of a summer rose. With that mouth and those eyes and her father's title, Caroline's future was assured.

Zoe's gaze drifted back to Jamie. What a handsome boy, what a startlingly handsome boy, but no title was waiting for him. It hardly mattered. Aldreth had secured his future. He would lack nothing, nothing except the legitimacy of his father's name.

"Will you inherit *your* father's title?" Markham asked Jamie. "He is the Duke of Aldreth, is he not?"

Zoe and Jamie nearly flinched.

"I am not his heir," Jamie said evenly, his pale blue eyes unblinking.

"I am not an heir, either," Caroline said without pause. "We'll hide, shall we, and the heir of Dalby must seek us out. Markham, you're it!"

And with that, Caroline Trevelyan ran out the door into the garden, her black hair trailing out behind her. After only a moment's hesitation, Jamie ran after her, grabbing her by the arm when he caught up with her and pulling her toward his favorite hiding spot, which Zoe knew from experience was under a spectacular camellia that was becoming less spectacular with each passing day enduring Jamie's favoritism.

"I'm always it," Markham said to his mother. He did not look at all excited by the idea.

"You'll just have to hunt them down, Markham," Sophia said, taking his chin in her hand and caressing his face. "That's what the men of my family do. One day, you'll meet them and you'll be well prepared. Think on that."

"I should have a knife," Markham said, his dark eyes sparkling.

"No knives," Sophia said, shaking her head.

Markham sighed dramatically and walked purposefully out the
door and into the garden.

"No knives?" Zoe said. "How staid you've grown, Sophia."

"And cosseted," Sophia said. "I hardly have any need at all for
knives now."

They moved to the open doorway and watched their children play
in the safety of a sunlit garden surrounded by green hedges and stone
walls. The symbolism was not lost on them, not these two women
who had experienced so much of the dark belly of the world.

"You are content?" Zoe asked.

Sophia looked at her, her dark brows slanting against the sun-
light, her dark eyes unchanging pools of mystery. "More than
content. And you, Zoe? Are you merely content or more than content? Or have you reached beyond contentment and found happiness?"

Zoe smiled and said, "I am happier than I ever imagined I could
be. Did you wonder? Is that why you are here?"

Sophia turned her face back to the garden. Markham had found
Caroline under the camellia shrub, but Jamie still eluded him.

"It is known in Town that Aldreth has a mistress and that he is
devoted to her," Sophia said. "But his mistress is rarely seen and
so it is wondered if she is more prisoner to his passions than heart
mate. Those who know the Duke of Aldreth have a very difficult
time imagining him to be blissfully in love, you understand."

"And you know the Duke of Aldreth," Zoe supplied, staring at
Sophia's delicate profile. "Were you worried that I might need help
in escaping my luxurious jail?"

"One of the rumors is that he keeps you in a crumbling old ab-
bey with a single servant to provide you with a single meal," Sophia said, turning again to face her, smiling again.

"And that single meal is bread and cheese," Zoe said.

"How very French you still are, darling Zoe. Of course in English tales of this sort, the meal is moldy bread and stale water."

"How unappetizing. It hardly makes being slave to a man's desires worth anything at all," Zoe said, with a chuckle.

"But being a slave to Aldreth's desires is . . ." Sophia prompted.

"Dear Sophia, but of course Aldreth is my slave fully as much as I am his. He is . . ." she said, her voice trailing off, her eyes gazing mistily at the yew hedge, "he is . . . not what I expected and certainly not the man his reputation makes him out to be."

Sophia nodded. "He is in love. He is transformed. At least with you."

"As love demands," Zoe said, with a tiny shrug.

"And your son?"

"Is well loved and well provided for. Aldreth would do no less."

Sophia nodded again, her gaze thoughtful, her tongue stilled.

"But what of you? Is your Dalby a slave to your whims?"

Sophia laughed lightly. "Darling Zoe, I do not indulge in whims. I have intentions, and Dalby is both adept and willing to succumb to all of them."

"I did not think it would work out this well," Zoe said softly when the laughter between them had faded into the scented air. "I did not dare to think that, from that night, something as wonderful as this could come."

"Did you not?" Sophia said. "It was my intention that precisely this would be the result. And I was right. I do so enjoy being right."

Zoe laughed at that, for it was so completely like Sophia, and they linked arms and walked into the drawing room where Aldreth and Dalby awaited them, and by the looks on their faces not at all patiently, which was exactly as it should have been.

HUNTER'S MERCY
Shiloh Walker

To my husband and my kids, always.

And to a strange duck that kept asking when I'd write a historical . . . Not sure if this is what you were asking for, but here you go.

Dear Reader,

Although I love history, I've always been more interested in the people, the conflicts than the details . . . like the Revolutionary War. When a Patriot went off to the war, what happens at home? Questions like that, and the answers, have always interested me more than technical details and factual data.

While researching for *Hunter's Mercy*, I used mainly two resources, listed below, and I tried to be as accurate as I could while keeping true to the story my characters had to tell me. My characters have always driven the story and that hasn't changed with my occasional foray into historical paranormal romances.

While my focus is always on the characters, I tried to be as accurate as possible . . . hopefully, I succeeded. And I hope you enjoy *Hunter's Mercy*.

Always,
Shiloh Walker

- *The Complete Idiot's Guide to the American Revolution* by Alan Axelrod
- *The Writer's Guide to Everyday Life in Colonial America from 1607–1783* by Dale Taylor

ONE

November 1783

"What are you doing here?"

There was nobody there to answer, but he'd been speaking to himself anyway. Jack Callahan was alone as he rode through the quiet town. It was past midnight and most of Williamsburg was asleep. Jack had wanted to reach town earlier than this. No—in truth, he didn't want to be in Williamsburg at all. So many memories here, memories of those who he had lost. Memories of those he had failed.

He had enough death and darkness in his life, but even though the war had ended, all the death and darkness wasn't going to end for him. Jack just wanted some peace before it encroached on his life again—peace, a nice soft woman, a nice soft bed, and some good hot meals.

If he was lucky, he could get that soft bed and a good hot meal here very shortly, but it would be a time before he could seek the soft woman. It had been three years since he'd made a promise on a bloody battlefield in South Carolina. Three years since he'd given his word as his dearest friend lay dying in his arms.

Look after my sister, Jack—she has no one else.

Sourly Jack muttered, "She will not be happy to have me looking after her, old friend."

No, Mercy Harper hadn't ever cared for Jack Callahan and she'd made that more than clear. Her delight throughout childhood had been to be a thorn in his side, following her brother and Jack around, running to her father to get the boys in trouble, pulling pranks on any girl Jack spoke with, anything she could to cause trouble for him. The girl had probably danced the day he left to fight in Washington's army. And if he'd been killed at Camden or any of the other battles that followed, she would have cheered.

It had been her brother who died at Camden, though, and now Jack had the unpleasant task of watching after the little hellcat. Even if she was alone in the world, she wasn't going to be happy to have him looking after her.

The newly recognized United States of America had won the War for Independence, but it had cost untold lives. Jack himself had lost many people that he held dear—not just in this war, but throughout his life.

Yet none of them had left this same mark on him. Richard had known him better than any other person alive, knew what Jack was and had accepted it. That acceptance was such a rare gift. Although no true witch had died during the Salem witch trials, people like Jack had learned a harsh, ugly lesson.

Mortals weren't ready to accept them. He wondered if they would ever be ready for that. In Salem, innocent people had died for no reason. How many people would die if mankind saw that there really were things hidden in the dark?

They wouldn't understand and what humans didn't understand, they feared. What had happened in Salem was proof enough of what came from fear and hysteria.

Richard, though, Richard had been unique. They'd known each other since they were boys. Jack's parents had been farmers from Ireland, coming to America seeking land and riches, just like most of the colonists. They'd gotten the land, but the riches hadn't come as easily as hoped.

The land, though, the land had been the most important thing. Jack came from a long line of shape-shifters on his father's side and there could only be so many of them in one place before hunting became difficult. Simply existing became a treacherous thing, because the more they numbered, the greater the risk that some mortal would encounter one of them.

In a new place, they'd hoped for a bit more freedom. They'd found it, of a sort, only to have the laws of the land impose even more structure on them. Unless they wanted to live completely apart from mortals and seek out some unpopulated place, they had to adapt and live as mortals. Which meant they were faced with the same injustices as any other family struggling to live under English rule. The ridiculous laws, the excessive taxes—and choosing sides in a war.

Jack had been thirteen years old when he came into his gift. His parents had spent most of his young life preparing him for it, but even with all that his father had taught him, all the times his mother had told him he was special, none of it could have prepared him for the first shift. The shock of it, the thrill of it, the pure, undiluted power—Jack could understand how that power could drive some of his kind insane. How it turned some of them into bloodthirsty monsters.

Monsters. Aye, monsters existed in the world and not all of them had fangs or howled at the moon once a month. Some were simply human. They were the hardest monsters to face because all of Jack's life, he'd been raised on the belief that he must protect the humans. Protect them against one another—and the things that lived in the shadows.

Jack had come face to face with his first monsters when he was all of fourteen. Barely a year into learning how to control his abilities, he had heard somebody scream. Richard. A familiar voice, with an even more familiar scent called to him as he ran through the woods. He'd heard his father moving through the woods and vaguely heard the order that he was to go back to the house.

The need to obey his father was strong. Obedience to the stronger creature was instinctive, a drive that wasn't easily controlled. But it faded when compared to the need to follow that scream for help. It was as though it pulled at him, somewhere deep inside. He'd gotten to Richard just as two vampires shoved the boy back and forth between them, laughing as he struggled. Bite marks marred his neck and the crook of his arm and though Richard had been pale, still he fought.

Even when one of the vampires backhanded him across the face and sent him flying into a tree, Richard hadn't stopped fighting to get away. Rage made a shape-shifter's control shaky and the fear and rage of seeing his best friend hurt was enough to shatter Jack's control, and he had attacked.

If his father hadn't shown up, both Richard and Jack would have died. A furious fourteen-year-old shape-shifter was no match for two feral vampires. He'd known, though, after that night what he was meant to do with this strange ability. He'd known, his father had known, and he wasn't even sixteen when a Hunter came looking for him. He spent the next three years roaming the colonies with George Whitlow, a werewolf. Where Jack's father had worked to teach him how to control his gift, George had trained him to use it.

He returned home to his family, to a friend who understood and knew Jack's every little secret. Jack had been ready to settle on his father's small farm and live a normal life. Or as close to normal as he could. But his life was governed by those in need, and when he was called, he had little choice but to act. The urge to protect the weak was as powerful as his need to shift and it would keep him from living in peace for too long.

Then his parents died. A damned cooking fire—Jack had been working in the field with his father when they saw the smoke and if Richard hadn't ridden by when he had, Jack would have followed his father into the house. He would have died along with his mother and father.

But Richard had been there. Strong for a mortal, Richard had tackled him when he tried to run into the house and Jack would have thrown him off, but he'd punched Jack in the jaw. The shock of it had broken through the terror in Jack's mind. "It is too late, Jack."

Yes, too late.

Jack had been too late to save his parents then, and a few years later in the Battle of Camden, he had been too late to save his friend. Richard was shot in the leg and the ensuing infection killed him. He had lain on the bed, out of his mind from the fever, and held Jack's hand as he died. He'd died in a filthy, packed tent, surrounded by other dying men and he'd begged Jack to look after Mercy.

It had taken Jack three years to return home and fulfill that promise, but he was here now. Though he'd been serving in Washington's army, it didn't ease the guilt over how long it had taken him to return home so he could fulfill that promise.

Now that the war was over, nothing else would interfere.

Jack passed by a tavern, and he thought longingly of some ale, a bowl of stew, and warm, fresh bread. Something other than hardtack and dried meat. He should have stopped earlier when he scented that buck. No soldier had fared well in the army, but shape-shifters had more trouble than the typical soldier. The foodstuffs available to them weren't fit to keep a child well nourished, much less grown men. Or grown shape-shifters who needed to eat twice as much as a mortal male.

He wondered idly if the small cabin he had once called home was still standing. It wasn't much, one room that served as both bedroom and kitchen. The house he had grown up in had been a bit nicer, but Jack had no desire to try and rebuild that home.

Jack murmured to his horse and the chestnut obediently sped

up. The sooner he got home, the sooner he could rest. He didn't give a damn if the building still stood or not, so long as he could find a place to lay his tattered bedroll. Just long enough that he could get a few minutes of sleep before he had to seek out Mercy Harper.

He only hoped that the past five years had improved her disposition a bit.

He was so tired that at first, he couldn't quite make sense of what his brain was telling him. Out on a battlefield, fighting to stay alive and fighting to keep his friends alive, he hadn't heard the call for help in months. The low-level burn settled within him and it hovered there, waiting for him to acknowledge it. Once he did, he forced the exhaustion out of his brain and tried to focus.

The scent of blood, sweat, and fear surrounded him, and the knee jerk response to the blood was telling. Too damn hungry. The response to the sweat was visceral—female, soft, scented female. A soft, clean woman was a pleasure he hadn't had in months and if he had caught that scent anywhere other than here, under any other circumstance, he knew he would have acted on it.

But the circumstances were of the dire kind, not the sex and sport kind.

Her fear knotted inside of him and turned his blood to acid. It was like burnt flowers. Bringing his horse to a stop, Jack dismounted in silence and left the horse alone, following the scents on the wind. He heard the voices long before he caught sight of them and the genteel feminine voice didn't seem to fit what Jack's senses were telling him.

Courageous little thing, she didn't sound afraid at all. She sounded madder than bloody hell.

"You worthless bastard."

Her tone, her manner of speech, was so polite, so softly spoken, the speaker should have been reciting poetry, not swearing. He worked his way through the thick, concealing undergrowth and hoped the wind didn't change. He could be as silent as death, but if the wind changed on him, his silence wouldn't matter. He scented feral werewolves with that woman and if they became aware of his presence, all hell would break loose.

Jack hadn't lived through Eutaw Springs, Camden, and God only knew how many other battles and raids, not to mention freezing his arse off all these winters, just to get taken down by ferals. Not yet, anyway. Not until he kept his promise.

One thing was certain: if he lived through this, the first thing he was going to do was send word back to Brendain. This was the second pack he'd encountered in the Virginia countryside in the past year. The Council needed more than a few random Hunters in the newly formed United States of America. They needed some sort of authority on this side of the world as well.

He only hoped the animosity between England and the colonies hadn't filtered into the Council. Most of the Hunter's Council may no longer be mortal, but most of them had been at one time and the discord among humans too often worked its way into the Council ranks.

Judging by the mocking voices he could hear just ahead of him, ferals had infiltrated the British ranks as well as the Continental Army. The first pack he had dealt with a few months back had been American, and they were using the battlefields as a feeding ground. Jack couldn't figure out which bothered him more— werewolves feeding and terrorizing the enemy as they lay dying, or werewolves terrorizing a woman.

Damned fools, what are you doing around here anyway? The Treaty of Paris had called for the removal of all British soldiers, but then again, ferals had little use for political and government machinations. Most nonmortals sought to blend in, but ferals thrived on the chaos, fear, and despair their kind could bring. Blending in wouldn't suit them.

They'd live to regret that, though. Jack hadn't just been trained on the battlefields—he'd also been trained by veterans of a war so old, it predated England. Predated history. The battle between good and evil. The Hunter inside of Jack was furious that any feral would dare come this close to his home. He was dismayed and worried, as well. How long had they been around here and how much damage had they done?

Regardless, it stopped now. Cautious, he edged around one towering oak and peered into the night. It was dark. The only light was from a lantern that lay on the hard-packed dirt and the moon filtering through the trees overhead. Still he could see well enough. The redcoats were gathered around their fallen victim. At first, he thought perhaps his ears, even his nose, were playing tricks on him, because he saw no woman.

He saw a skinny lad, little more than a boy, lying on the ground. The woman he had expected was nowhere to be seen. One of the soldiers kicked the lad and the soft, feminine cry of pain aroused every protective instinct he had. His nostrils flared and he tested the air again. His eyes narrowed and he focused on the boy. He could smell the human over the muskier scent of the werewolves and that soft, delicate fragrance didn't belong to any male. Women simply smelled different—granted, those who didn't bathe often didn't smell quite as enticing as this one did, but bathed or not, a woman did not smell like a man. Or a boy.

Another brutal kick to the woman's unprotected body and the tricornered hat she wore went flying, along with the short, powdered wig. Under it, he saw thick, dark hair, braided and wrapped around her head like a coronet.

Shite.

Something about her scent teased a forgotten memory but he didn't have time to chase it.

He studied the ferals in front of him then looked down at his rifle. The pistols he wore would be every bit as deadly as the rifle this close. He had silver bullets—no good Hunter left home without weapons of silver. Jack was no different. But the rifle wasn't a good weapon for combat and the pistols, though fast and accurate, were loaded with regular lead, not silver.

Getting either of them loaded with silver in silence would be impossible.

It left him with only one choice.

He tossed his hat to the ground and propped the rifle against the tree, lay his pistols and several knives down as well. He sent one look toward the dark sky overhead and said a silent prayer of thanks. The full moon had been seven nights ago—long enough for the power to have waned. Although he was outnumbered five to one, those men were dependent on the moon for their strength to be at its fullest.

Jack, on the other hand, needed nothing but desire.

He stepped away from the tree and closed his eyes. The power built low in his gut, heating his belly the same way good whiskey, or a woman, did. It stretched his skin and flowed through him like water. His vision altered, going from the slightly-better-than mortal sight he had in his human form to the highly refined vision of a giant cat.

As his form shifted, he bent over. Jack pressed his hands to the dirt and the scent of it, ripe and earthy, filled his head. The sensation of the dirt under his hands changed as his bones reshaped and formed themselves into claws. Those claws, black and curved, dug into the earth. His vision cleared completely and he lifted a dark, sleek head. His black hide would blend with the night and he planned on taking down some of the English bastards before they even knew what was coming.

Under a gleaming black coat, muscles flexed and bunched. He threw back his head and roared. For the briefest moment, the ferals were silent. And then he lunged out from behind the tree, crossing the distance between himself and the closest werewolf in one bound. He took the startled feral to the ground, ripped out his throat and focused on his next target before the rest of them had fully realized what was happening.

Two jumped for him and he caught the glint of silver in the faint light. He twisted away with the liquid grace only felines possessed.

He managed to avoid the blade, taking another feral down with his bulk. Under one paw, he felt a soft, unprotected throat and he flexed his claws, effectively ripping it out. Blood gurgled and sprayed. The man fell to his knees, choking and grasping at the gaping wound. Whether the feral lived or not would depend on whether he was strong enough to heal the wound before he bled out.

The man with the knife swung again and Jack darted under his arm and pivoted. He clamped his jaws down on the weapon arm. A scream of pain and fury filled the air. Jack shook his prey back and forth like a rag doll. Bone crunched and the man fell down, screaming as blood fountained from the stump where his arm had been.

Power danced through the air and alarm trickled through Jack's killing rage. He saw the flash of gray fur just before a giant clawed hand swiped at him. Wicked, black-tipped claws dug furrows down his side. He backed away, growling low in his throat. He stared up at the wolf-man's face, saw the hatred gleaming in glowing yellow eyes. "Mangy cur. I'll teach you to interfere."

Out of the corner of his eye, Jack saw the fifth and final feral moving, trying to circle around behind. Lightning fast, Jack shifted and turned so that he had both of them in his line of sight. He screamed defiantly as the fifth man, still in mortal form, lifted a musket at him. Hunters rarely went anywhere without silver on them—likewise ferals did the same. If there was anything other than regular lead in that bloody musket, Jack was dead.

A resounding crack echoed through the air. A smile spread across the wolf-man's face but it faded as his partner was the one to collapse to the ground, missing half of his head. *Well, that one is dead,* Jack thought inanely. Then he lunged, using the distraction to charge for the wolf-man. He closed his jaws around a heavily furred, thick neck, working until he had the throat between his teeth. Big, clawed hands struggled to rip him away. Jack dug his claws into the furred pelt and held on. He clamped down. Blood filled his mouth but he didn't let go.

There was another crack and a fiery hot pain tore through his side. Another crack and the wolf-man's body slumped. Sensing the werewolf's death, Jack dropped him. Blood flowed down his side as he turned to stare at the woman. Smoke was still drifting from the muzzle of the pistol she held in her right hand. The one in her left hand was held at ready. She was slender and the weapons she held should have looked bulky and unwieldy.

But she looked entirely too confident.

His surprise though died as he stared into familiar golden eyes. Mercy Harper.

She didn't look much like her brother, dark where Richard had been fair, slender graceful curves where Richard had been big and broad, built like a battering ram. But their eyes were the same.

Mercy Harper—the girl he had returned home to watch over, had just pumped him full of silver.

THE big cat didn't fall the way Mercy expected. No, she hadn't shot him square in the heart, but that bullet should have had some impact on him. He gazed at her with eerie eyes that reflected back the glow of her fallen lantern. Her heart seemed to lift in her throat, choking her when the cat dropped low to the ground, powerful muscles coiling.

This is it—Mercy was staring into the jaws of death and she knew it. Oddly she didn't feel the relief she had expected to feel as time slowed down to a crawl. It felt as though she had stepped outside herself to watch as she stood before the demon creature and waited for him to kill her.

All she felt was emptiness. Just a void. She felt nothing. No relief, no fear, no regret.

Just emptiness.

Then the cat lunged and time sped back up. Instinctively she jerked her pistol up. She tightened her finger on the trigger and then all but sagged to the ground as the cat dove for the underbrush instead of her throat. She heard barely a sound as he disappeared into the woods, leaving her alone.

Mercy sagged a little as the tension drained out of her body. It seemed a bit anticlimactic, this sudden, still silence. She took a deep breath and it sounded terribly loud in the small clearing.

In death, the demons reverted to human form. Clothes hung in tatters around their bodies. One of them was still alive but just barely. The man was missing his right arm, and even in the dim light, Mercy could see the pallor that came from blood loss.

She'd seen the unnatural acts these monsters performed, though. She'd seen them heal wounds that should have ended their lives, seen them take a chest full of lead and still survive. She wasn't taking the chance. Drawing one of the pistols from her waist, she leveled it at the man's face. He had probably been a handsome man. Now though his face was twisted with hate and his eyes were mad with hate. ". . . Bastard hunter . . ." he whispered as he stared up at her.

His rambling made about as much sense to her as his existence. Expressionless, she lifted her pistol and fired. She lingered only long enough to make sure he was well and truly dead.

Then she gathered her hat and her wig and took a deep breath. It made a sharp pain shoot through her side and she winced. Gingerly she pressed a hand to her side and probed the tender flesh. If she was lucky, the ribs were bruised and nothing more. But she wasn't certain she would be that lucky, and come morning she suspected she wouldn't feel the slightest bit lucky. Already, she ached all over and by morning, she would feel like one big bruise.

She lifted her fingers to her lips and whistled, hoping that Samson hadn't been frightened enough to go home. A few minutes passed.

"Now why would I expect to be lucky?" she muttered. She was injured, alone in the forest, and running preciously low on ammunition—and her horse had deserted her, leaving her to walk home on foot.

It was going to be a long walk.

TWO

"Ohhhh . . ."
Whoever it was banging at the door ought to be shot. She glanced at her window and saw a sliver of light had managed to penetrate the thick curtains and considering how warm it already was, she suspected it wasn't as early as it seemed.

But she hadn't fallen into bed until well past midnight. That made it far too early. A headache pounded behind her eyes and her body was sore from the past night. She'd been lucky, Mercy knew. As it was, she would have a few bruises, maybe a cracked rib.

She was alive, and even though her head felt as though it would split in two, the pain wasn't as bad as she had anticipated.

"I don't feel lucky," she whispered. She had thought, for a brief moment, that perhaps it would finally be over. Then that cat had emerged from the woods. Big and gleaming black, it was unlike anything she had ever seen before. It had gazed at her with watching, waiting eyes.

Too intelligent, those eyes. Too human.

Another demon, Mercy knew. It had killed the other demons

with an ease that should have made Mercy shudder with fear. Nothing frightened her though. Nothing excited her. Nothing seemed to truly affect her at all. Until last night, she would have believed the only thing that interested her beyond killing those demons was to have one of them finally kill her.

But when that cat had been so very close, the promise of death interested her about as much as that of life. Not at all.

Odd, that. She chased after death with the same determination that she had once used when chasing life. She would have expected a bit more enthusiasm.

But there was just this—emptiness.

Mercy rolled over so she could press her face into her pillow. The fresh, clean scent of lavender filled her head and the pounding there eased just a little. Only a little though and considering that her head still felt as though it would split in two, that small relief was just a little too small.

Distantly she heard voices and she knew that somebody had answered the door. Judging by the deep voice, whoever it was hadn't gone away. Theo's voice had a different cadence to it, soft, slow, and comforting. This new voice was deep, but that was where the similarities ended. "Whoever you are," Mercy muttered. "Go away."

It was most likely another would-be suitor. Ever since she had buried her husband a year ago, men had been presenting themselves to her in a display that was rather appalling. Theo, bless him, managed to keep most of them at bay. But every once in a while, some tenacious man slid past the big black man who had worked on White Oak since before Mercy was born. Theo had been one of several slaves being sold off at an auction nearly thirty years ago. Mercy's father had purchased him, along with several others, and then he'd freed them. Slavery was something that had gone against William Harper's deeply religious beliefs and those beliefs had been passed onto his children.

Theo had stayed and worked at White Oak as a free man and

his daughter, Lydia, was only a few years older than Mercy. They'd grown up together. Lydia and Theo may have been servants in the Harper household, but they were also friends of the Harpers. When Richard left to serve in the Continental army, Theo had been a silent source of support as Mercy struggled with running the plantation on her own. When word came back that Richard had been killed, Theo and Lydia had cried with her. When Mercy lost her husband, it was Lydia who sat up and held Mercy while she wept.

For the past year, Theo and Lydia had been her only family. There were other servants in the house, but none of them brought back the safe, happy memories of Mercy's childhood. Before she made the fool mistake of falling in love and before her brother had gone off to fight in a war that didn't seem like it would ever end. A war that had killed him.

The crumpled, tattered letter telling Mercy of Richard's death was tucked inside the Bible that lay beside Mercy's bed. A Bible she hadn't read once in the past year. God had taken her brother and not even two years later, He had taken her husband. She had no desire to pray to that God, or read His word, not after what He had taken from her. Not after she'd learned the sort of evil that God allowed to live.

Thinking of that, she smiled a little. There were now five fewer of those monsters in the world. Five might not seem like much, but those five, added to the four she'd killed over the past year were that many that couldn't harm another soul. Couldn't kill another husband.

Her headache hadn't fully receded but her vague memories of last night had her in a brighter state of mind. Enough so that she decided her headache might ease up a bit if she ate something. She shoved herself up in bed and saw Lydia sitting beside her, her dark hands folded over the swollen mound of her belly.

And just like that, her mood soured. Envy curled through her but she struggled to bury it. Lydia would soon be giving birth to her second child and Mercy was a widow with no desire to ever remarry. But what she wouldn't give to have her own child, to hold a little baby against her breast and rock until they both fell asleep. Something of Simon.

"You look better," Mercy said. Mercy had insisted Lydia retire early the previous night. The girl's color hadn't looked good and the swelling in her feet and ankles had been markedly pronounced. Mercy couldn't see Lydia's feet but her color was once more a warm, dark brown and the grayish cast was gone.

Lydia replied tartly, "You don't." She held out a delicate china cup and Mercy accepted it. The strong, lukewarm tea eased the burn of thirst and she drank half of it before putting it down. She watched as Lydia hefted her bulk out of the chair and moved to the windows, drawing back the curtains to allow the breeze into the room. It was warm and muggy—Mercy suspected they'd have rain before nightfall.

"What time is it?" Mercy asked, looking outside. The sun was hidden behind a thick bank of clouds, but she suspected it was nearing noon. Out by the barn, she could see her horse, Samson. He stood with his nose inside a feedbag while Lydia's husband, David, ran a curry comb over the big bay.

The knot of fear in her chest loosened just a bit. Something had spooked the big bay and he'd bucked. Startled at the horse's sudden change in temperament, Mercy hadn't been paying attention to the horse and he'd thrown her. By the time she had pushed to her feet, Samson was long gone and Mercy realized she wasn't alone.

There had been a couple of British soldiers she'd seen a few days ago. She'd come looking for them, but she hadn't planned on coming face to face with them on her bottom in the forest while they gathered around looking much too eager. A sudden, overwhelming urge to run had taken over. Run far and fast and hard and not look back.

Those men, it wasn't the way they watched her that bothered her. Not that she cared for those sly smiles and lewd comments. But they had made her skin crawl, just looking at them. Not just a woman's fear when faced by a number of strange men, but a deeper fear. Gut deep and instinctive. The need to run.

It wasn't her fear, though. It was something these monsters caused. She hadn't truly felt anything since she'd buried her husband. She'd felt that kind of fear before, though. The night she watched monsters tear her husband apart before her very eyes. Demons—monsters like these had taken everything from her. It had been a year, but Mercy felt as though she had aged thirty years. Twenty-two years old, widowed . . . "Stop feeling sorry for yourself," Mercy muttered.

Her parents had raised her to be stronger than this. She might be a Greene now, but she had been born a Harper, born into one of the most affluent families in the Virginia colony and she was her father's daughter. William Harper had ignored the rules of polite society most of his life. He'd raised her to be strong, and that was exactly what she would be.

Strong enough to survive this, and strong enough to keep living when all she wanted to do was die. Strong enough to keep searching for the things that had killed her husband.

She had the determination, and, thanks to Richard, she also had the skills.

Mercy had spent many long summer days trailing after him and his friend Jack Callahan, begging and pleading for the older boys to teach her how to hunt, how to track.

Girls never got to do anything fun. Her grandmother had despaired of Mercy, claiming the girl would never be a lady. *She will not wear her stays. She will not wear her petticoats. One of the servants found her swimming.*

Grandmother never did learn, but Richard finally gave in and did as she asked, teaching her how to hunt, how to track. They'd spent many hot summer days in the Virginia forests and Mercy learned how to spot a deer trail, how to find water, how to build a fire. By the time she was ten, she could shoot as well as any boy her age, if not better.

As a child Mercy hadn't ever had to use the skills Richard had taught her, other than for her own amusement. But when the time came and she needed those skills, they came back. It had been the day after her husband and some of her servants had been so brutally killed. What had been done to the men and the woman who had lived in the cabins behind White Oak had been beyond brutal, beyond senseless. It had been pure evil, evil that mauled and violated and destroyed.

Lydia had brought her a steaming cup of tea, liberally laced with opium. While the oblivion seemed enticing, instead of drinking the tea, Mercy had left it sitting on the small table by her bed and she had stared outside.

People from all over town had come to White Oak. Some to help with the preparations but some had come just out of morbid curiosity. All of them seemed to press in on her, just as the walls had seemed to close in, suffocating her. She had slipped outside and saddled Samson, intending to take a ride in the forest.

There, under the cool green canopy of the trees, Mercy had seen the blood trail and she had followed it for nearly a mile and then the trail of bloodied footprints had changed. Literally and inexplicably changed, from the footprints left by a man to the paw prints of one very big wolf. She would have followed the wolf trail had Theo not found her. He had taken her back to the house, despite her protests.

Since then, she'd refined the skills and she'd gotten better at evading him. He followed her, she knew that. Or at least she thought he followed her. Mercy never saw him, but there had been many nights when she felt a silent, watchful presence as she sought out the bloodthirsty demons.

She shook the thoughts away and glanced over at Lydia who was making Mercy's bed. "Lizzie can take care of the bed, Lydia. You really do need to be resting. It won't be long before the baby comes."

Lydia grinned, her nose wrinkling and her eyes laughing. "You really expect me to do nothing but stay in bed all day, Mercy?"

"I expect you to take care of that baby," Mercy returned.

Lydia rolled her eyes. "And if I start feeling tired, I'll go lay down. Now do you want to come down for breakfast or do you want me to bring you something up?"

Although she had intended to have something to eat, the thought of food in front of her was less than desirable. She sighed and shook her head. "I'm not very hungry right now."

Gazing at her with sad, serious eyes, Lydia murmured, "You're never hungry, Mercy. You don't want to eat. You hardly sleep." She eased her bulk down on the edge of the bed and Mercy saw the brush and comb in her hand. "Your pretty hair is a mess."

Mercy reached for the brush and said, "I can do it, Lydia. I keep telling you that you need to rest."

Lydia laughed. "Brushing hair isn't hard work, Mercy. Now be still."

If her head didn't hurt so bad, Mercy might have tried to argue. But her head throbbed in time with her heartbeat and if the ache got much worse, Mercy feared she would be ill. Lydia's gentle, capable hands unwound the thick braids she had wrapped around her head. She'd been so tired, so sore from last night's ride, she hadn't bothered releasing the braid but she imagined the weight of her hair and the tight wrap of the braids wasn't helping her headache.

Finally Lydia had Mercy's hair free and she started to pull the brush through with slow, steady strokes. On occasion, the rhythmic strokes stopped so Lydia could work on a tangle. After the third or fourth snarl, Lydia spoke up. Her voice was carefully flat but Mercy caught the disappointment all the same. "You started sneaking out of the house again, Mercy."

No. I didn't start. I never stopped so it's hard to start again. But she kept that to herself.

"You can't keep doing this. It's too dangerous," Lydia continued.

Mercy said nothing.

"It's been a year. Whatever or whoever killed your man is long gone." When she continued her silence, Lydia sighed. She gave Mercy's hair a final brush and the bed shifted a little as Lydia got to her feet. "Come on now. Let's get you something to eat."

Mercy opened her mouth to object only to close it without saying a word. Lydia was glaring at her, her dark eyes narrowed. "You are going to eat something. You ate no dinner. You need to eat."

Mercy's retort died on her lips as she heard a voice from outside her room. A deep voice—her unexpected visitor and judging by how loud the voice had gotten, he was coming to her room. "I will leave after I've spoken with Mercy, Theo."

That voice—it was familiar. As the doorknob turned, Lydia grabbed a wrap from the foot of Mercy's bed. Mercy shoved her arms into it, swearing under her breath. Lydia grinned. "Your mama would blush if she could hear you right now."

Mercy retorted, "If some strange man was about to intrude on her while she was wearing nothing but her bedclothes then she would have done more than swear." The door opened and Mercy turned to face the intruder. Her hands, in the act of tying her wrap closed, fell limp to her side as she met deep, dark green eyes. She knew those eyes—Lord forgive her, she had dreamed about those eyes for more than half of her life. Even when her husband had been lying in bed beside her, she had dreamed of him.

"Jack."

He cocked a brow at her but said nothing. Instead he studied her, that faint, mocking grin on his lips as he started at the top of her head and went down. His gaze lingered on the loose neckline of her shift. Mercy felt a blush start, low along her breasts, right where he seemed to be staring and as his gaze went lower, her blush climbed higher, along her collarbone, up her neck, until her cheeks felt painfully hot.

Once he'd finished his perusal, he looked back at her face. "A strange man, Mercy? Does that mean since I am no stranger, I'm allowed to intrude on you while you're in a state of undress?"

Undress? Mercy thought wildly. *I'm practically naked.* Her hands shook as she reached for the belt of her wrap and tied it tightly around her waist. She hoped he couldn't see just how much they shook, but there was little Jack didn't notice. His forest green gaze locked on her left hand, on the wedding ring that she simply couldn't part with, and he glanced around the room. "And where is your husband, Mercy? Should I fear being challenged to a duel for interrupting your privacy?" He didn't look at all concerned about it as he sauntered into the room and settled his long, lean frame in one of the chairs placed by the fireplace. "I hadn't realized that you had wed."

Mercy closed her eyes. She wasn't going to cry, not in front of Jack Callahan. "Simon was killed last winter," she said. Her voice was husky but it didn't shake.

Jack winced and that ever-present mocking smile faded. "I am sorry, Mercy. In the war?"

Turning away from that penetrating gaze, Mercy moved to her dressing table. As though realizing that she needed a few minutes to compose herself, Lydia came up behind her and started once more to brush her hair. "No—Simon wouldn't fight in the war. He didn't believe in violence."

Bitter irony moved through her, followed by the same sense of futility. He hadn't believed in violence and he'd died the most violent way imaginable. Simon had moved to Virginia from Maryland shortly before they'd met. He had been Catholic and Mercy knew that alone had given the men and women in town just one more reason to shake their heads—Mercy Harper, marrying a Catholic.

Simon had once told her he had considered entering the priesthood for a time. Then he'd given her that wide, wicked grin. "But I loved women too much to give them up for the cloth," he had teased her. "And a blessing that was, because if I had taken vows, and then met you, I would have forsaken all of them."

Funny, a gentle but strong man, his love had warmed her soul as much as his touch had warmed her body. While he believed in the causes the Americans fought for, he hadn't been able to join the war, not with a clear conscience. Sometimes Mercy wished his values hadn't so strongly governed his life. Losing him in battle might have been a little bit easier than losing him to monsters. And he could have lived through the war. After all, Jack had.

But no—Simon had stayed home, worked his small farm, met Mercy, and they'd fallen in love. He'd been a man of God—a devout and true believer. For him to have died at the hands of creatures straight out of hell, it wasn't just heartbreaking. It was so very wrong.

It was little wonder she hadn't spoken to God since He had taken Simon from her. Her faith had crumbled under her grief and nothing could give her solace. Not her faith, not her friends—often, even Simon's memory couldn't console her. Not after that night—

No. I will not think of it.

She felt the weight of Jack's gaze on her and she met his eyes in the mirror's reflection. The sympathy she saw there would undo her, if she let it. She could turn to him and cry on those wonderfully broad shoulders, and somehow, Mercy knew he wouldn't think less of her. Perhaps if she hadn't spent so many years thinking of him, dreaming of him, then she might have done just that.

She'd been faithful to Simon and she loved him, so completely, so much that she wished Theo hadn't been so quick to respond when he heard her scream. If Theo and the other men had taken just a bit longer, then perhaps she could have died along with Simon.

Had that happened, she wouldn't have to deal with the onslaught of guilt assailing her. Mercy hadn't seen Jack in nearly five years. There had been nights when she woke from dreams, dreams so hot, so erotic, she had been trembling on the verge of climax when she opened her eyes—and it hadn't been Simon's hands on her body in those dreams.

Simon had been the man to introduce her to carnal love—he

had been the first and only man to kiss her, the only man to lie beside her in the night and bring her such pleasure she wanted to weep.

But she had dreamed of Jack Callahan. To cry on his shoulder over her dead husband wasn't just weak—it was wicked. Guilt turned her heart to lead and she looked away from him. "I received your letter about Richard."

"I am so sorry, Mercy."

She nodded. "You were his dearest friend—I know you must miss him as much as I."

It was a stranger looking back at him, Jack thought.

A lovely stranger. The sadness in her eyes told Jack that the years he'd been gone hadn't been kind to Mercy Harper, but it only showed there. She'd gotten a bit taller and although she would never be as lushly curved as some women, a woman's body had replaced the gangly girl he remembered. That tightly belted wrap couldn't hide the swell of her hips or her breasts. He watched, almost mesmerized, as Lydia combed through Mercy's hair. Her hair was dark, thick and straight, the ends of it hanging to her hips.

Jack had a hundred memories of her when she was a child, tagging along after him and Richard, that long dark hair tangled and unkempt, hanging around down her back. While other girls were working on samplers, Mercy had been outside, demanding that Richard teach her how to hunt, how to swim.

"Was he laid to rest with your parents?" he asked, although he already knew the answer. He had stopped briefly at the small family plot before coming to the house. The graves were well tended and each one had fresh flowers. The gravestones hadn't had the grinning mask of death so common—instead, there had been cherubs. More fitting, Jack had thought. He could remember seeing a grave for a man he didn't know—a Simon Greene. He suspected then that Mercy Harper had wed and felt some sympathy that she was already a widow.

Mercy Greene—no longer Harper.

"Yes."

Lost in the morass of his thoughts, it took Jack a moment to recall what he had asked. Oh, yes. Richard. "Perhaps you could accompany me out there so I can pay my respects," he suggested.

Her only response was a noncommittal little *hmm*. Lydia stood behind her and continued to comb through Mercy's dark gleaming mass of hair. The black woman's belly was full, round with child. "You're looking well, Lydia."

She smiled and paused long enough to pat her swollen belly. "I look enormous." With a proud grin, she added, "Our second baby."

"Congratulations."

"Thank you." Lydia lay the silver-backed brush aside and bent down to murmur into Mercy's ear. Mercy started to shake her head, then stopped. She sighed, pressed a hand to her forehead and nodded.

"Would you care to join us for a late breakfast, Jack?"

The polite question was so unlike the termagant who Jack remembered. Mercy had been seventeen when he left and she had been so untamed and wild then, he never would have believed it possible for her to become the woman he saw before him now. The people in town had despaired of her ever changing. While most women her age were either married or looking to marry, Mercy had continued to dress like a boy and spend her days riding Samson or fishing.

From that—to this. The lady in front of him was lovely, amazingly so. But the life from her was gone. Jack didn't like it. *She'll never be a proper lady*—it was something he'd heard murmured about Mercy before. He'd always agreed and while the curious, impatient child he remembered had been a thorn in his side for years, she'd also made him smile.

He almost refused her polite invitation for breakfast. If it wasn't for the promise he'd made Richard, he would have left. This quiet,

sad woman bothered him. But instead he murmured his acceptance, and excused himself long enough to find a washbasin.

The tepid water did little to wash the cobwebs from his mind.
Jack was so damned tired. He stared at his reflection in the small
mirror hanging on the wall and was surprised that he didn't seem
a good twenty years older than he truly was. Jack felt ancient—the
war, fatigue, hunger, and grief had aged him. But he looked just a
bit thinner, perhaps a bit more harsh than he had when he had left
home five years earlier.

Regular meals and rest would help some, but he knew he'd
never be the reckless youth who had left Williamsburg five years
earlier. There was a knock on the door, pulling him from his
thoughts, and he crossed to open it, smiling as he saw the clothes
Theo had. The older man offered them to Jack with a smile. "I
thought perhaps a fresh change of clothes might help. You do look
tired, Mr. Jack."

"Just Jack," he corrected as he accepted the clothes. Grief knotted his gut and his hands tightened on the garments as he recognized the scent on them. Faint and faded after five years, but it was
Richard's all the same. He set the clothes down but made no move
to undress. "Mercy—is she well?"

Theo's gaze slid to the door and then back. He held up one finger
and turned away to close the door. When he looked back at Jack,
his expression was troubled. "No, sir. No, she isn't well at all."

He said nothing else but Jack could sense there was more the
man would say. Jack rubbed the back of his neck and sighed. Not
home even a day, and already the trouble with Mercy had started.
It wasn't just how much she had changed—Jack had expected her
to change, to grow up. Perhaps he hadn't been prepared for her to
be an entirely different person, but that wasn't what was so heavily
weighing on him.

The memory of her from the night before loomed large in his
mind, the way she had stood in the dark of night, surrounded by
creatures that could tear her apart in so many ways, and enjoy it

thoroughly. The way she had stood before them and faced them down as though she didn't give a damn about how easily they could kill her.

"Tell me, Theo."

"I don't know what I can tell you, Mist—Jack," he corrected when Jack gave him a narrow look. "After her man died, she was just different. There's so much anger inside her. So much grief."

"How did he die?"

The look on Theo's face made the hair on the back of Jack's neck rise and his skin started to crawl. Theo was no stranger to violence. Before Mercy's father had freed him, Theo had been a slave. Jack had seen the scars on his back. Life in Virginia wasn't as brutal now as it had been a hundred years earlier, but there was still violence.

But the look on Theo's face was the look of a man haunted, the look of a man who had seen something that had left scars inside. Theo shook his head and murmured, "I don't like to talk about that, Jack. Not at all. I haven't ever seen anything like that before and I hope I never see it again."

"I need to know what happened, Theo."

"Men came. I heard Mercy scream. I came running. A few of the other men came, but not all of them. Some of them had been killed, too." His gaze fell away and he sighed. "I think they came looking for the women. There was a girl, Susie, who helped in the kitchen. She was missing—we found her a few days later, raped and beaten. She lost so much blood. By the time we found her, she was already dead.

"And Miss Mercy . . . Lord . . . that poor girl."

The nausea roiling in his gut disappeared, replaced by the hot, powerful wash of rage. "What happened to Mercy?"

"She saw it," Theo replied, his voice just a bare whisper. "Men came into their room. I don't know what happened in that room and she won't speak of it." He paused and took a deep breath. His big shoulders slumped.

Jack wasn't sure he had ever seen the man look so broken. "They hurt her." It felt as though each word was made of broken, jagged glass that cut into his throat as he spoke.

Theo gazed at him sadly. "Not like that. They would have. But we heard the screaming. We got there but not in time to save Mr. Simon. Dear Lord, what they did. . . . Men can't do things like what they did. It was something evil in that room. I saw—"

He stopped speaking, and then he shook his head. He opened his mouth to speak but then he closed it without saying anything. But Jack didn't need to hear the words to know what Theo had seen— or why he couldn't form the words to explain. Theo had seen something that many mortals whispered about, but not all of them believed in.

Most mortals never saw the monsters that lurked in the dark. Men like Jack were there to protect them from the monsters, but this time, when the evil had encroached on the land that Jack called home, he hadn't been there to protect the innocent.

He hadn't been there to protect Mercy.

"How much did she see?"

Theo looked at Jack with grim eyes. "I don't know, Jack. She won't say. There were four of them, but Mr. Simon, he killed one of them before they got him. We killed two of them. Shot one of them in the head. The other one, Jonah shot him in the gut. Shot him again in the chest. He kept on breathing. Looked at us and laughed. I saw Mr. Simon's rifle and grabbed it and I shot him again. In the head. He fell down and didn't move. The third one ran. Took off running and jumped through their window and hit the ground like all he did was jump over a piece of wood or a water puddle. He disappeared into the forest and some of us went after him, but—" He broke off and rubbed a hand over the graying hair on his scalp. "You going to think I'm crazy. We found his tracks where he ran into the forest, but then his footprints, they turned into something else."

"Something else?"

In a hushed voice, Theo answered, "Wolf tracks. His footprints stopped, the path got all disturbed and then there were the paw prints of a wolf. A big one, bigger than I ever seen."

HOURS later, Jack stood at the window of Richard's old room. He hated being there. Even though it had been years since Richard had been here, Jack could still faintly scent his old friend. Especially on the bed. Although the bed was clean and soft, he wouldn't be sleeping on it. He'd already made a pallet on the floor.

In the morning, he would speak with Theo about sleeping elsewhere. He couldn't sleep in Richard's bed, but he'd be damned if he continued to sleep on a hard wooden floor when a soft bed was available. The brief stay was going to be longer than he'd originally anticipated. Jack had planned to go to his own small piece of land across the river, but he couldn't see himself leaving, not with this new knowledge weighing so heavily on him.

Ferals had been on his land and Jack hadn't ever realized. "Lousy Hunter you make," he muttered. Jack had thought he couldn't possibly feel any guiltier, or any more bitter, but he had been wrong.

He could still hear Theo's sad, horrified voice. *It was something evil in that room.*

Evil, yes. Jack doubted Theo understood just how evil. Ferals didn't just hunt their prey for sport. They hunted for food and for sex. One of the sickest experiences in Jack's life had been when he interrupted a couple of feral shifters that had been enjoying both on a young woman, at the same time.

Mercy had seen them feeding on her husband.

It explained so much, the dedication that had her leaving the safety of her home to hunt monsters. More, it explained how she had known what to look for. Shape-shifters had a strange feel, be they of the werekind that required the moon's power to shift, or natural shifters that needed nothing more than the desire. Most mortals were aware of the difference, even if it was only on a sub-conscious level.

There were still many questions—Theo had claimed that Simon killed one of the men. How had a mortal killed a shifter? How had a mortal known how to?

But he didn't need to know the answers to those questions. He knew what he needed to know about Mercy, or at least as much as he could know, without her talking to him. He knew the why.

Vengeance was a powerful thing. It could drive a man, or a woman, to do most anything.

What Jack needed was to find some trace of the girl he'd known. Find her and see if he couldn't convince her that her life was worth so much more than vengeance.

THREE

No, Jack decided as he looked for some sign of the girl he remembered, Mercy wasn't well at all. She sat in the parlor, a delicate porcelain tea cup held in one hand. She'd been holding it for some time and had yet to take a drink.

Mercy stared outside, but Jack suspected she wasn't seeing the lovely gardens or the vast sprawl of land. She just sat and stared and the lack of movement was almost as disturbing as the lack of emotion.

In all the time he had known Mercy Harper, he'd never seen her go more than a few minutes without jumping out of her seat or running around or chattering like a blue jay. The stillness and the silence bothered him a great deal. She was too contained, too controlled.

He'd expected her to try scalping him when he had told her that he was there to watch over her. But instead of lashing out at him, she had politely smiled. "I appreciate the intent, Jack, but I am perfectly fine." It was too—polite. Mercy didn't trouble herself with niceties.

"Regardless, I gave Richard my word," Jack said. He sat on a silk-covered chair that seemed as though it would break under his weight. Mercy sat across the room. In the pretty, feminine parlor, she should have looked out of place in her breeches and waistcoat.

She didn't, though. There was something innately feminine about her, something that had just been beginning to bloom when he had left. The swell of her hips and the curve of her backside drew his eye and he kept having to remind himself that he was here to watch over her, not ogle her.

It wasn't something he had counted on. In the years since he had left Williamsburg, he hadn't often thought of Mercy, but when he did, he thought of the wily, demanding child with tangled hair, big eyes, and a mean streak. A *wide* mean streak.

It was taking some time to acclimate himself to this sad, solemn-eyed woman. With the loss of her husband and brother, that sadness was to be expected. And if she hadn't plugged him with silver, he could have accepted that sad, somber exterior without a qualm.

But she had leveled a rifle at him, pulled the trigger, and he still had a nasty, slow-healing wound in his left side, thanks to her skill with that rifle. If she hadn't used silver, it would have already healed, but the silver would make the wound heal almost as if he were mortal.

She'd held that musket with a skill that would have done her brother proud. But it wasn't just her skill with a weapon that had him so confounded. It was *how* she had managed to wound him—by using silver.

How had she known? There was a logical explanation, but Jack didn't like to think of it. But that was a question he would have to have answered. Looking after Mercy meant more than making sure she was safe—Richard would want her happy. More, Jack wanted her happy. Even if it meant she was the thorn in his side that she had been as a child. He would take that curious, demanding waif over the heartbroken woman any day.

"I'll be needing to go out to my parents' land here shortly. I have been gone so long, I imagine there's a great deal of work to be done."

Mercy glanced his way, but her eyes skipped over his face as though she wasn't truly seeing him. "Not so much work, Jack. Theo has taken care of your land."

"That wasn't necessary." He winced mentally. If Theo had done any work on Jack's land, then Jack would owe him for the work. But Jack had no way to pay, at least not for some time. In his foreseeable future, he saw many a scant meal before him while he tried to get his parents' farm back into a place that could at least maintain him, if not turn a profit.

"Don't be silly. Of course it wasn't necessary, but we are neighbors." Her voice was soft, so polite. She could have been any one of the polite ladies she had used to make fun of. Jack had to fight the overwhelming urge to grab her and shake her. This calm, emotionless mask she wore was going to drive him insane.

It might not be so hard to deal with if he hadn't seen her, stared into her eyes the night she shot him. It had just been a few brief moments, but it had been long enough to let him see what lay below the surface.

Pain, rage—passion. Emotions she had buried deep inside, and the previous night, they had worked their way through to the surface—emotions she kept hidden except to hunt. She let them out long enough to kill and while Jack couldn't fault her for that, it would surely lead to her death.

Truly it was a miracle it had not yet happened. He had to keep her safe, but keeping her safe was going to present a problem. If she cared about her safety, she would never have started tracking down creatures that could kill her as easily as they breathed. Bloody images danced through his mind and he wondered how often she had slipped away from the safety of White Oak to hunt monsters. How many had she killed and how often had she evaded death?

The way she had handled the rifle, her confidence when she had faced down the werewolves and then Jack suggested she was no stranger to the odder side of life. That had Jack worried, very much so. She had luck on her side to have come through the past night unharmed, but luck wouldn't last forever. He didn't want to think of what awaited her if she were caught.

I will not let that happen, he thought to himself. *I won't.*

His protective instincts weren't the only concern, though. His duty was as well. Not all of his kind were evil, and those innocents, he was bound to protect. Not just the shape-shifters, but the weres, the vampires, and the witches, as well. He'd done this for too long to fool himself into believing that Mercy could discern the difference between the real monsters and those men and women who had simply been born different.

Brooding, he stared into the delicate tea cup. He was going to have his hands full. He would protect Mercy. But he must also watch after those who were under his protection and he had a feeling that he would have to protect them from Mercy.

Without letting her realize it. It was a tricky game he had before him.

MERCY didn't have to turn around to know who was standing behind her. Jack's shadow fell over her as she continued to pull the weeds from Simon's grave. She'd already cleared the graves of her parents and brother.

"I thought you were going to spend the day at your farm, Jack," she said without looking at him.

"I did plan to." On soundless feet, he moved up behind her and crouched down next to her. "I thought it would take the day, or more, to see what needed to be done. But there is very little. Someone has been working the farm for me. The house has been tended to."

Glancing at him, she murmured, "That would be Theo's doing.

I told you that he was tending things in your absence. But thanks
are not necessary. He's been working your fields and I've been paying him from the money your crops brought in."

From the corner of her eye, she saw Jack smile. "I feel I owe him
much. Even when my parents were still alive, that little piece of
land wasn't so well cared for."

"Theo takes pride in his work." Mercy brushed a few more
weeds aside and then she reached for the flowers she had brought.
"Simon's mother loved roses. He did not care for flowers, but he
did enjoy the roses. He told me that they reminded him of her."

"How did you meet?"

"In town," she murmured. Her thoughts drifted as she remembered the day she and Lydia had gone into town with clothes the
women on the plantation had made for the soldiers. "We were
sending clothes to the soldiers. There was a woman, Abigail Greer,
who had moved here from Georgia after her husband was killed in
battle. We were at the mercantile and she claimed that Lydia had
stolen from her. She had the nerve to strike Lydia when Lydia denied it." She smirked a little, recalled the look on Abigail's face
when Mercy had punched her. If Simon hadn't dragged her away,
Mercy would have done a great deal more.

Lydia might be a free black woman, but she couldn't strike a
white woman without facing serious consequences.

Mercy, however, could. Could, did, and immensely enjoyed it,
too. Then she had looked at the man who had dragged her off
Abigail and she had fallen in love. Hard and fast. She had looked
into Simon's gray eyes and known she would marry that man.

Marriage by choice was a luxury, Mercy knew. Many of the
girls she had known in childhood were already married, already
mothers, married to unite families and expand their lands. While
many men had attempted to court Mercy, she had no desire to marry
for anything short of love.

Her parents had loved each other. Mercy wanted to love the
man she married. And other than Jack Callahan who didn't even

realize that Mercy was female, Simon was the only man who made her heart race.

"If that smile of yours is any indication, then I would wager that you struck her back," Jack said, with a wide grin.

"Was I smiling?" Mercy murmured. She reached up and touched her lips, unaware that she left a smudge of dirt on her chin. She was indeed smiling. It felt strange. She wondered how long it had been since she'd smiled.

Jack was staring at her—at the fingers she had touched to her mouth. Blood rushed up her neckline, heating her neck and her face until it felt as though her skin was on fire. Nervously, she lowered her hand and focused her attention back on the grave. She brushed a few stray leaves off and then smoothed a hand down the grass that covered the grave. "Simon kept me from strangling her—none of the other men would dare touch me."

Jack laughed. "Oh, I would imagine not." More than one man had been on the receiving end of Mercy's ire and none cared to experience that more than once. "Simon Greene—I don't know that name. He wasn't from here, was he?"

She sighed. There was a tremendous weight on her chest, almost like Lydia had laced her stays far too tightly. Except Mercy hadn't put on those bloody stays today. She was wearing breeches and a waistcoat—men's clothes were far easier to move in than women's and she didn't care to tend to the grave sites while wearing skirts, petticoats, and stays.

Tears burned her eyes but she blinked them away. She did not wish to weep in front of anybody, but most especially not in front of Jack. "He moved here from Maryland."

"Then that would explain why he had no qualms about interfering. Tell me, did he pull you off in time or is this lady now in need of a wig?"

Unable to stop it, Mercy laughed. "She already wore one. Silliest thing I've ever seen. It fell off when I hit her and under it, her hair was so short and thin—I've seen newborn babes with more hair than she had on her head." Then she slid him a sidelong glance. "Since when have you ever known me to pull hair? I am much more likely to hit somebody than pull hair."

She pushed to her feet and arched her back. She had spent the past hour bent over the graves and the muscles in her lower back were tight with pain. She felt Jack's gaze slide over her. Something shimmered in his dark green eyes, but by the time Mercy had realized it was a look of pure male interest, he was no longer looking at her and his gaze went from heated to hurting. She turned her head and saw the tombstone.

The first year after Richard had died, seeing his name on the tombstone had hit her like a fist in the gut, with enough force to take her breath away. It had eased a little, going from that visceral knifelike pain to a residing ache that would never fully fade.

But she suspected that for Jack, that pain was as fresh now as it had been when he had held a dying Richard in his arms. Seeing a name on a tombstone made the death all the more real, inexplicable as it was. A muscle in his jaw jerked and she watched as his eyes went from grass green to near black.

Understanding, Mercy stepped aside. He barely seemed aware of her as he moved to stand beside Richard's grave. "I'm sorry I didn't watch over him better, Mercy."

"That wasn't your job, Jack. Richard knew what he was doing when he left home. He was going to fight in a war. In war, people die." A soft breeze, warm and sweet with the scent of honeysuckle, blew through the little cemetery, catching a few stray strands of hair and tugging them free from the loose braid that hung down her back. She brushed them back from her face and tucked them behind her ear. The glint of her plain gold wedding ring caught her eye, and she held her hand out in front of her, staring at it. It was loose—too loose. Protectively she closed her hand into a fist.

"You can't take it off, can you?"

She looked up to find Jack watching her once more. "Do you think I'm silly? Many women who were widowed in the war have already remarried. With the men returning home, those who haven't wed will likely do so within months, even weeks. But I can't imagine taking this ring off—can't imagine marrying another man."

"Perhaps. It sounds as though you married for love, instead of convenience. Love isn't so easily replaced." He paused and then asked gently, "You did love him?"

The tears were harder to hide this time. She looked at him through a veil of tears and whispered, "Yes. I adored him." She rubbed her thumb over the smooth surface of her ring.

"Can you tell me what happened?"

"No!" Mercy said, her voice harsh. Covering her mouth with her hands, she shook her head. It was too late, though. That question, meant to help, brought it all back, the memory she tried so hard to forget. It played out behind her closed lids and she couldn't tear herself free.

Not until two hard hands came up and closed over her arms, shaking her. "Mercy . . . Mercy, look at me."

Grateful for the intrusion on those hated memories, Mercy looked up at Jack's face. He brushed her hair back and murmured, "It is all right, Mercy. You don't have to tell me."

"I can't," she whispered, forcing the words past her tight throat. Sometimes, at night when the memories wrapped themselves around her and she thought she might lose herself into that madness, she wished she could share them. Holding them inside, they seemed to fester and Mercy wouldn't be surprised if that nastiness killed her.

But she couldn't talk about it. "I wish they had killed me, too." She had thought it so many times but she hadn't ever said it. This time the words slipped out of her before she even realized it.

Jack cupped his hand over her clenched fist. "Don't wish for that, Mercy."

Hot tears spilled over and ran down her cheeks. "I do wish it. I want it. He's gone and it's as though I died with him."

"You aren't dead—you are far from it." He lifted her hand and pressed a kiss to her knuckles and then he let go of her hand. But instead of stepping away, he cupped her chin in his hand, angling her head back so that her gaze met his.

He dipped his head. Mercy's heart stuttered to a startled stop and then started to race within her chest as he kissed away her tears. "Grieve for him—if he was a good man, then he deserves that grief. He deserves those tears. But do not wish for death." He pulled away, but just a bit. He remained so close to her that his face was all that she could see, those compelling eyes. A dark mysterious green, like the forest just before dawn when mist hung in the air like a shroud.

What had they been talking about? she wondered dimly. She wasn't sure. Her mind had gone blank and the only thing she could think about was Jack. His dark eyes, his gold-streaked brown hair—and the way he smelled. She couldn't quite define it, but like his eyes, it made her think of the forest. Wild and free.

When Jack's lips touched hers, everything inside her stilled. Her heart stopped beating for the briefest moment, her breath froze in her lungs, and she didn't move. Not even to breathe. Her chest started to ache and she opened her mouth to gasp for air. It was as though that desperate little breath pulled him closer. His chest pressed against hers. His hips nudged hers. Through the layers of their clothes she felt him, the muscled wall of his chest, his lean, flat belly—and more, the thick, hard length of his sex, pulsing in rhythm with her own ragged heartbeat.

The heat exploded through her and she desperately, *desperately*, wanted to strip away her clothes, then his. It had been too long since she had felt a man's body against her own, felt the warmth of a man's touch. Too long since she had known the sweet agony of taking a man inside her body.

Too long—the words circled through her mind and she pushed onto her toes, leaning into him. She slid her hands up his chest, over his shoulders. His hands came up to her waist and tightened, almost painfully. "Mercy," he muttered, his breathing unsteady, as ragged as her own.

"Hmmmm . . ." Blindly she sought out the scrap of leather he had used to tie back his hair. She jerked it free and then slid her hands through his hair. It was thick and soft.

Jack had only meant to comfort her—he was still trying to adjust to the changes in Mercy and the last thing on his mind was this. Although he would have a hard time convincing himself of that. He was starving for her. He'd gone from uncertain he even wanted to reacquaint himself with Mercy to dying to fully know her, in the most basic way. All with the simple press of his lips to hers.

Perhaps not so simple, he admitted to himself as Mercy groaned into his mouth, pressing her long, slender body against his. He could feel each subtle, sweet curve in glorious detail. It should be outlawed for a woman to wear men's clothes, he thought weakly.

He was acutely aware of the warmth of her skin. He could feel her body through their clothes and all too well. Once more, Mercy hadn't bothered with stays and Jack knew just how easy it would be to slide his hands up until he could cup the soft, warm weight of her breasts.

She kept making soft, demanding little whimpers deep in her throat and she rubbed herself against him in a manner that was slowly destroying his ability to think. Even to breathe. If she kept this up, Jack's willpower was going to shatter into pieces.

He needed more, more of those hungry little moans and whimpers and soft, shaky sighs. But instead of taking more, he eased back from her. "Mercy . . ."

It didn't make it any easier—all she did was follow him, her body moving toward his as though she yearned for more. Yearning, oh, Jack could understand that. He had always thought that to yearn for something was simply to need something. But yearning wasn't just need. It went deeper than need but he hadn't ever felt anything like it until now.

He yearned to keep kissing her. Needed it more than he needed to breathe. Instead he wrapped his fingers around her upper arms and held her still as he eased away. "Mercy."

She hummed low under her breath, her lashes lifting slowly. She stared at him. Her gaze was fogged with desire, the black of her pupils so huge they nearly eclipsed the pretty burnished gold of her irises. If Jack was convinced that it was his face she saw when she looked at him, he would have hauled her against him and finished it. He didn't even care where they were.

But she would care, and in her mind, it wasn't Jack she'd been kissing. He knew exactly when she realized what had happened. Her face went death white and she tore away from him so fast, she ended up stumbling. He caught her arm to keep her from falling but she hissed at him. Actually hissed. With tormented dark eyes, she whispered harshly, "Do not touch me."

"Mercy—"

She shook her head, staring at him. A soft moan escaped her lips and she muffled it with her hand. Tears glinted in her eyes and that one pitiful moan turned into another, and another. For a brief moment, he thought she might break. He thought all that grief he sensed inside of her was going to break free. But instead she spun away from him and rushed to her horse. She mounted Samson so fast, it was a wonder the big bay didn't throw her.

He wanted to grab her, haul her off the horse, and hold her against him. Jack realized he was even reaching his hands out to do just that. But the torment he saw on her face froze him. Helpless in the face of that grief, he let his hands fall and stood there, unmoving, as she pulled the horse around and rode away.

SAMSON ran so fast the ground blurred beneath them, and still Mercy couldn't escape the guilt inside. It was choking her. It wasn't so much that another man had touched her—it was that she had responded. Quite passionately. Jack had touched her and it was as though he had set flame to something inside her. Something frozen and long dead, or so she had thought.

One touch from him had thawed her. Warmed her so completely she had all but melted into a puddle at his feet. Melted her so that everything inside her felt soft and liquid. Samson's smooth rocking gait was sheer torture, making her breeches and underclothes slide back and forth against the delicate, sensitive flesh between her legs. She ached, deep inside and it was an ache only one thing could ease. A man's touch.

She had woken from her dreams with that ache so often, yearning for Simon. Yearning for that sure and certain touch. But now it wasn't Simon she needed. It was Jack. Mercy must be truly wicked—kissing him so.

Ever since she was old enough to dream of a man in that way, she'd dreamt of Jack. Even while she had been married to Simon, she'd dreamt of Jack. Now she knew those dreams paled next to the reality, and somehow, that made her betrayal so much worse.

Mercy bent low over Samson's neck, until the wind had his mane snapping back into her face. *Run, Samson.*

As though he sensed her desperation, the bay's speed picked up. The wind tore at her hair until long strands worked free from the braid and her eyes were watering. It made no difference.

She couldn't outrun this, but even that knowledge wouldn't keep her from trying.

FOUR

D amn.

Hours had passed since Mercy had run away from him, but he could still feel her long, slender body, so soft and strong, pressed against his own. And her taste—it was going to haunt him. Those soft, hungry moans, he would hear them in his sleep.

Not that he expected to sleep much tonight.

The moon hung in the sky, a pale sliver against the star-dappled sky. For the past two hours, Jack had done little more than stare up at the moon and brood. He'd left the house shortly after supper, roaming through the woods, even taking a swim in an attempt to cool off and exhaust himself.

It hadn't worked. Now sitting in the cool darkness of the woods, he was restless. His skin itched, his muscles were tight and drawn, and he wanted little more than to run. Well, there was one other thing he craved. Sliding into Mercy's room and joining her on her bed.

The night was hot and muggy. If he looked back through the woods, he would see the house and the occasional flicker of candlelight, although Mercy's window was dark. She wouldn't be bundled under the covers. Her skin would be dewed with sweat and her eyes heavy with sleep. Jack's body tightened in anticipation and he surged to his feet with a brutal curse.

If he continued to sit there and brood, he might do something he'd regret. Better to take that run than to risk losing what little remained of his control. Methodically he stripped his clothes away, stacking them in a neat pile by the tree. But as he started to shuck his breeches, he heard something.

Soft footsteps, certain and swift, moving through across the thick carpet of grass. Someone who moved with a light tread, someone who knew the land. There was a soft creak of metal hinges as somebody entered the stable. Even as he strained to hear better, he knew who it was.

Mercy.

He snarled and grabbed his shirt, jamming his arms into it. "Damn fool girl, what is she up to?" he muttered.

The answer to that came to him as he reached for his boots. Another noise. This one was farther off. A howl, distant and faint. It was followed by a second one and although mortals would have a hard time telling the difference, his ears easily detected it. Two wolves—and they were on the prowl. He glanced up at the moon and swore. It didn't bode well, two shape-shifters out this long after the full moon. Only the strongest were could harness the power to shift outside of the full moon. And this wasn't just one wolf, but two.

Jack didn't bother stripping out of his clothes again. He just shifted and the clothes ripped as muscles tore the well-worn seams of his clothing. The shredded garments fell to the forest floor in pieces. He gritted his teeth against the pain as his bones broke and realigned. Along his hands, the skin rippled and he watched in the dim light as fur grew, spreading upward from his hands, down from his neck, all over his body until even the barest bit of skin was obscured by a thick, dense coat of black hair. He fell forward and reached for the ground. He reached out with hands that looked human, but by the time he sank his claws into the earth, even the last vestige of humanity had fallen away.

He threw back his head and stared up at the nighttime sky. There was a defiant scream building in the back of his throat, but he wouldn't let it free. Not yet. No sense in warning the enemy, now was there? He scented Mercy on the wind and knew that if they hadn't scented her yet, it wouldn't be long.

The wolves were dead already, but if they hurt her, they were going to pray for death for a good long while. Who were they? Where had they come from? More, why hadn't Jack realized there was a threat until it was nearly too late to deal with it?

He had nearly intersected them when he realized why he hadn't sensed a threat.

There wasn't one. The shape-shifters were doing exactly what Jack had planned on doing—taking a run through the cool, clear night and perhaps get a little hunting in. But the prey they were after wasn't the human kind. If they were hunting human prey, Jack would have sensed them the moment they entered his territory. Since he hadn't, it meant only one thing.

They weren't feral. But they would protect themselves. The muscles and healing flesh in his side screamed in agony but he ignored it and ran faster. He caught a glimpse of Samson's pale hide and he leaped out of the shadows, landing right in the middle of the horse's path. He met Mercy's gaze and screamed. Samson reared. The bay rose up on his hindquarters, whinnying in fright. Mercy's hands tightened on the reins and although she made soft, soothing noises to the horse, her gaze focused on Jack with an intensity that was a little unsettling.

He crouched low on the ground, staring at her and at the same time, he focused on the shifters who were moving closer and closer. Jack had no ability to speak directly into the mind of another shifter, though he'd heard of men and women with that talent. But this was his home, his land—if he focused hard enough and if he prayed hard enough, maybe somehow they would understand.

But Jack wasn't going to count on luck or a miracle to guide them away. He growled at her, challenging and then he crept backward into the undergrowth. She brought Samson under control and a cold, mean smile curved her lips.

That's it, my girl. Come after me. I'm closer, aren't I?

He led her through the woods, circling back and around, staying just out of her line of sight. She stayed just on his tail, so daringly close that Jack couldn't help but admire her bravery and curse her foolishness. They reached the James River before her patience wore out. The sound of her rifle echoed throughout the quiet forest and the stink of gunpowder, hot and acrid, filled his nostrils. Bark and small slivers of wood went flying just a few inches away from Jack. He growled low in his throat, tired of this game and scared for Mercy. She couldn't keep up this fool's quest. It would only end with her death.

He crouched low to the ground and then sprang, climbing a towering oak that had branches hanging low over the river. He'd jump in and swim away if he had to. Unlike normal cats, he had no dislike for water. But he didn't want to retreat yet. Mercy passed underneath him, searching for him with narrowed eyes. *Perhaps we shouldn't have taught her to hunt, Richard,* he thought. He kept silent and still, waiting for her to move on, but instead, she brought Samson to a stop and started to search the trees, from the base upward.

He padded out along one thick branch, leaves rustling ever so slightly as he passed. The sound was too quiet for humans to hear, yet as he used the pathway of branches to move from one tree to another, her gaze sought him out. She couldn't see him, not in the inky blackness so far below the canopy of leaves, but she knew where he was, nonetheless. Intuition—it was what had made her brother such a skilled hunter and it was clear she had it as well.

He dropped down out of the trees right behind Samson. As the bay reared and threw her, Jack offered a silent apology. She landed with a yelp and a curse as the horse took off for the safety of his stable. She scrambled on her hands and knees to get to her rifle but Jack beat her to it, closing his jaws around it and jerking it out of her reach. He slunk to the river's edge, watching her carefully.

The hot look of hatred faded from her eyes, ever so slightly, replaced by curiosity as she watched him. "I'm just going to keep hunting you," she said softly. "The only way to stop me is to kill me."

Her eyes widened as Jack swung his head back and forth. The butt of the rifle dragged on the ground and he dropped it.

Stop this, Mercy. Please. If he could make her hear his silent plea, he would have done so. He would just have to pray that common sense would eventually prevail. The tension in the air dragged out. Jack could no longer hear the wolves—he prayed they had decided to seek out their hunting grounds elsewhere.

Mercy stood there staring at him and he slowly started to back away, mindful of the pistols she still carried. But she made no move to reach for them and once Jack reached the water's edge, he turned and dove in. He swam with the current, letting it carry him away. Every second, he expected to feel the burn of silver again.

SHOOT, Mercy.

The heavy musket seemed to feel heavier with each passing moment. She held it level, focused on the dark spot in the river that was the demon cat's head. But she couldn't pull the trigger.

Slowly she lowered her gun and just watched until she could no longer make out the dark shadow of the cat from the darkness of the water.

Part of her was furious. *You let it get away. When that demon kills again, it will be on your head.*

But the rest of her was so confused. She'd faced the demon creatures down before. They stared at her the same way a cat would watch a mouse, with hunger and greed. But this one, if she was fool enough to think that demons could suffer human emotion, she would have thought she saw sympathy and sadness in those oddly colored eyes. There had been intelligence, for certain.

Mercy had been sure of her death this time. The cat had frightened Samson intentionally. She might even dare to say that he had been waiting for her with just that plan in mind. To kill her. That was what demons did. They killed.

But that one though . . .

She turned away from the river and started back toward White Oak. Each step sent a ribbon of fire shooting up her right leg and into her back. This was the second time in a week that Samson had thrown her and she wasn't sure her body could take much more of that abuse.

By the time she was halfway home, she was gritting her teeth against the pain and fighting not to cry. Blood pounded in her head and she was caught up in the chore of just placing one foot in front of the other. She never heard the hoof beats until a dark, tanned hand appeared in front of her.

She blinked, startled and looked up to find Jack sitting on Samson's back, staring at her with worried eyes. "I heard Samson come back and I couldn't find you. Are you hurt?"

Automatically she started to shake her head, but then she took a step toward his outstretched hand and her abused leg buckled. She stumbled forward but before she could fall, Jack had managed to dismount Samson and catch her up against him. He moved so fast, it seemed to blur, but Mercy wasn't certain that she was thinking straight. As he stood there, looking down at her, his eyes seemed to glow—for just the faintest moment.

No. Not thinking well at all. Her voice hitched a little as she answered, "He threw me. I think I may have hurt my back."

Jack's dark green eyes got even darker and his face tightened. He looked positively furious, but when he spoke, his voice was soft and gentle. "Can you ride?"

"Certainly better than I can walk," she said, forcing herself to smile. She cast one last look behind her. Jack's hand, warm and strong, curved over her neck. Oddly that touch made her feel safe, secure—and it made her aware of something she hadn't allowed herself to acknowledge.

She was frightened.

Terrified. Not necessarily over the encounter with the demon cat, but something she couldn't quite define. Something about the way the cat had watched her. It was not just the intelligence she had seen in his gaze, but the emotion.

Surely demons couldn't feel the emotions like what she had thought she'd seen in his face. None of the ones she had faced before had displayed anything beyond malevolence, malice, and hunger.

"Mercy."

The soft, husky murmur intruded on her thoughts and she focused on Jack's face. He was staring at her. She flushed as she realized he had been speaking to her. "I'm sorry, Jack. My mind was wandering."

"You look scared. Has something frightened you?"

Mercy forced a smile and shook her head. "Don't be silly, Jack. This is my home—whatever would I be scared of?"

Jack glanced around the dark, shadowy forest and then he shook his head. "Your horse throws you in the middle of the forest, it's well past midnight and dark, you're alone. But no, nothing could possibly frighten Mercy Harper, now could it?"

"Greene," she corrected, her voice faint. She glanced down at her wedding ring and said louder, "It's Mercy Greene. And you're right, of course. Foolish of me to come out so late, and alone, too. I'd like to go home now."

"You will not tell me what scared you?" Jack asked, with little hope of a response. The only answer he received was a smile. Jack was certain that if he saw that false, polite smile once more, he would do something foolish. Shout at her. Grab her and shake her and tell her to stop placing her fool neck in danger. Something. Anything. But instead of responding, he guided her to Samson and lifted her up on the horse. She frowned at him when he mounted behind her and then lifted her onto his lap. "If you've hurt yourself, I do not wish to make it worse. Be still now," he told her.

It was even partly true. He was responsible for that look of pain he'd seen in her eyes and he would like nothing more than to undo it. But he wasn't holding her on his lap for purely selfless reasons. He wanted to hold her. Wanted to hold her close and perhaps keep her there. Maybe even forever. Jack wanted to see Mercy Harper—no, Mercy Greene—smile again, smile the way she had when she had been younger, before life had been so cruel to her.

Unconsciously he lay a hand on her thigh. He let Samson set his own pace through the forest while he stared at Mercy's downcast head. Her hair was coming free from its braid again. Jack wanted to untie the scrap of cloth that bound the braid and comb his hands through the dark, shining strands. She smelled sweet, like water and honeysuckle. "Do you still swim in the river?" he asked abruptly.

Mercy glanced up at him. In the dim light, he could just barely make out the faint blush that crept up her cheeks. "It was a hot day."

"We have a lot of them," he said. He attempted a teasing tone, but it fell flat as he imagined the way she would look, swimming in the shallow bend just a little north of here. There was a place where the James River dipped inward and the trees bent low over it where he loved to swim. He'd spent nearly an hour there earlier before admitting that a cool swim would do nothing to ease the fire inside him.

It was a lovely spot. Honeysuckle grew thick and the river bed was sandy. He could see her there, swimming through the water, the air sweet with the scent of flowers blooming—and with her.

Need surged inside him, hot and demanding.

"Jack . . ." Her voice was shaky and her scent was changing.

Jack's eyes narrowed down to slits as he realized why—she wanted him. He could smell it in the air and when she tipped her head back to stare at him, he could see it in her eyes. He realized he had slid his hand higher up her thigh and he looked down and stared—so very close. If he slid his hand up just a bit more, he could cup his hand over the heat of her. She would be wet.

His cock jerked demandingly inside the breeches he had hastily pulled on after returning to the house. He hadn't had time to mess with stockings or underclothes, just his breeches and the long-tailed shirt that he hadn't bothered to tuck in. It would be an easy matter to dismount and strip both of them naked. In a few heartbeats, he could be inside of her and he would love her until that emptiness faded from her eyes and she screamed out his name. He'd bring her to orgasm over and over and when it was done, she would cuddle up against him and fall asleep with a smile on her face.

But instead of doing that, he pulled his hand from her thigh and tried to find something else to think about. Anything else.

He didn't succeed. By the time Samson had them home, Jack was all but dying from the needs inside of him. He helped Mercy dismount inside the stable and carried her over to sit on a bale of hay just outside Samson's stall. "I'll come back out here and comb him down after I get Lydia for you."

Mercy shook her head. "Do not disturb Lydia. She needs her rest. It's close to her time."

"You need a hot bath and you need to have somebody look at you, make sure you aren't injured badly."

"I'll tend to it myself, Jack. There is no need to wake Lydia." Mercy may have grown up dressing like a waif and running wild, but she had a streak of arrogance in her that would have been more in place on a princess. She lifted her chin and even though she was seated on a bale of hay, she managed to look down her nose at him.

Jack shook his head. "Fine. Stay there. I'll take care of Samson and then I'll help you to your room."

She opened her mouth to argue but he narrowed his eyes at her. "You can either allow me to wait until you get in bed so I know you aren't seriously hurt, or I can wake Lydia. It is your choice, Mercy."

Mercy pressed her lips together and then folded her arms. She gave him an impatient look and Jack managed, just barely, to suppress his smile. For a girl who had been born in America, she had the haughty demeanor that would have done the English proud.

Thirty minutes later, he wasn't so amused. In the time it took him to care for Samson, the desperate rush of energy that had kept Mercy going had faded. Each injury made itself known. He saw the pain tighten her face as he moved toward her and when he lifted her into his arms, the pain kept her from fighting him too much.

"Perhaps now you will allow me to wake Lydia?"

Jack had no idea how she did it, but she stiffened in his arms until she barely touched him. She lifted her chin, and although he held her cradled in his arms with her head level with his shoulder, the woman managed to look down her nose at him. "I am fine. Perhaps a bath . . ." Then her voice faded away.

It was the middle of the night and Mercy was clearly in no shape to take care of drawing the bath. But Jack suspected that a long hot soak was the only thing that would ease the pain enough for her to sleep.

"I'll draw the bath," he said in a flat tone. It wasn't as though he would sleep anyway. Even if his gut wasn't knotted with worry, he would be thinking of Mercy. And now, he would be thinking of a wet, naked Mercy, soaking in a tub of steaming, scented water.

She shook her head. "It isn't necessary, Jack. Drawing a bath would wake everyone."

"Mercy, sweet, hush. Your arguing would wake them just as well and you know that you will not be able to rest with your leg hurting you so." When she would have continued her argument, Jack narrowed his eyes and said, "You will take the bath, Mercy.

Willingly or not. Make no mistake, I'll drop you in there fully clothed if need be and I care little if I wake everyone in the house."

She fell silent, but he suspected it was to keep from disturbing the others. He didn't bother to tell her it was a waste of time—Jack could already hear movement from inside as he carried her along the cobbled walkway between the house and the stables. People moving around and oh so faintly, he heard water sloshing.

A faint smile appeared on his face as he rounded the corner. Both David and Theo were awake, Theo walking toward the house, carrying two massive wooden buckets filled with steaming water while his daughter's husband, David, carried his emptied buckets. "It would appear they are drawing a bath," Jack said mildly.

The door opened and he looked up to find Lydia glaring at them in the faint light of the full moon. She gave him a dismissive glance before focusing on Mercy's face. The woman propped her fisted hands on her hips and her dark eyes glinted with fear and worry. "That horse done threw you again, didn't he? Why do you keep running off in the middle of the night?"

She fell back to let Jack enter but she was by no means done fussing at Mercy. She followed Jack up the back stairs as he took Mercy to her room, her voice rising and falling as she alternated between fussing and praying for patience. "Lord, what am I going to do with her?" Lydia mumbled.

Under his breath, Jack muttered, "If you get an answer, share it with me."

"Out in the middle of the night." Lydia shook her head, muttering in a voice too low for Mercy to hear, but Jack heard her fine. "She's trying to get herself killed. Lord, what am I going to do?" In a louder voice, she said, "It was a terrible fright to wake up and realize you had crept out of the house again. One of these days . . ."

"One of these days, nothing," Mercy interrupted, her voice gentle and consoling. "Lydia, I am fine. You need to go back to bed."

"Ha! Mr. Jack, you just put her down right there." Lydia gestured to a chair by the steaming half-filled tub. He did so and the moment he did, Lydia pushed a steaming cup into Mercy's hand.

They both recognized the scent and Jack almost felt sorry for her. Mercy shook her head. "I don't need this. Just the bath and some rest and I shall be fine."

Lydia narrowed her dark eyes. "You hurt so that you can barely move with it. You're not fine."

Mercy took one small sip and Jack grinned as she shuddered. "How do you know I'm hurt?"

"Samson threw you, didn't he? Falling like that, it's going to hurt," Lydia snapped.

Mercy took another small swallow and grimaced. "Truly, Lydia, I am fine."

She started to set the cup aside but Lydia chose that moment to rub her swollen belly. With a mournful shake of her head, she murmured, "I just don't know how I can get any rest, worrying about you. Every night, I lay there wondering if you going to disappear into the forest, if you'll be hurt, if you'll be safe. Makes me half sick."

Well done, Jack thought admiringly. Lydia kept her face averted, but Jack could just barely make out her pleased smile as Mercy lifted the cup and drank every last drop of the opium-laced tea. Satisfied, she moved toward Mercy. She waved her hand dismissively toward Jack. "Let's get you into the water so you can soak away your aches."

"I'll see to my own bath," Mercy said, her tone edgy. "You will go rest now, Lydia, or I will not step one foot into that water."

"You need that bath," Lydia returned. "You going to stand there hurting so just to be stubborn?"

Mercy blinked. "Me? Stubborn?" Then she sighed and rubbed a hand gingerly against her injured hip. "I'll get into the bath, I promise you, Lydia. Then I'll rest. But I'll sleep better knowing you aren't hovering around me when you should be resting."

Apparently using guilt to obtain something was an art form both of the women had perfected. Lydia left reluctantly and Jack followed her. They passed by Jack's borrowed room and he saw David waiting at the end of the hall for his wife. He gazed at her with a love so naked, and there was a possessive pride in his eyes as Lydia rubbed a hand over the swollen mound of her belly.

Theo emerged from the shadows as Lydia and David disappeared around the corner, taking the back stairs down to their cabin. Jack welcomed the intrusion. He could hear the soft little splashes as Mercy climbed into the tub. He could even hear the ragged catch of her breathing as she lowered her body into the steaming water.

"How often does she do this, Theo?"

"Too often." The older man had a worried look on his face. "There's too much grief inside of her, Mr. Jack. Too much grief and too much anger. It's going to tear her apart. This has to stop."

With a sigh, Theo left. Jack stood alone in the hall, Theo's words echoing through his mind. *It's going to tear her apart.*

"No," Jack murmured. "No, it's not."

He watched Theo and continued to stand where he was until the man disappeared from view, following his daughter's path down the back stairs. He heard a door close gently and then he looked back at Mercy's room.

It was well past time that she stop hiding from her pain. Well past time that she stopped hiding from life. She only allowed herself to feel anything when she was out hunting monsters that would sooner kill her than look at her. She needed to grieve, and she needed to realize that her life wasn't over.

He heard the water splashing and he paused for just a moment. Waiting until she had dressed, perhaps rested, would be the wiser course of action for him. A naked, vulnerable Mercy Harper Greene was going to be a test on his will. But if he waited, she'd retreat back inside herself again and it would be that much harder to draw her out. Best to do this now, while she was still shaken over the events of the night and before she had a chance to close herself off again.

FIVE

The door opened and Mercy shivered a little as some of the heated air from her room escaped and the cooler air from the hall drifted in. Without opening her eyes, she murmured, "Lydia, do go get some rest. I promise I shall soak in the water until my skin shrivels and then I'll sleep. Please do the same."

There was no answer. The air in the room seemed to heat and she took a deep breath. Under the illusory shield of the water, she felt her nipples tighten and her belly knot. She opened her eyes to see Jack standing by the door. He stared into her eyes for a long moment and then his gaze drifted down.

There was a flash of emotion on his face, a harsh, demanding hunger but then it was gone and his features were unreadable.

"Jack, have you gone mad?" she asked, and she immediately wished she hadn't said a word. Her voice was shaking.

"No, although if this continues you shall drive me mad. It must stop, Mercy."

He was once more looking into her eyes, but Mercy's skin burned with heat, and she couldn't help but feel he could see her far too clearly as she sat in the bathwater. She folded her arms protectively over her chest and forced herself to speak, to think past the heat that rose to the surface any time he was near. "I do not know what you are talking about, Jack. I went for a ride. I had an accident."

"Don't take me for a fool, Mercy." His voice was soft, deceptively so. "This ends, Mercy. It ends tonight. It must."

She narrowed her eyes. "I have no idea what you mean. Would you leave me to finish my bath, Jack? I am tired."

"No." He crossed over to her and crouched down by the wooden tub. He reached out and instinctively, Mercy pulled away but not fast enough. He cupped a hand over the back of her neck and held her still as he leaned close. "If you continue these little midnight raids, Mercy, you will end up on the receiving end of a bullet—or worse. What do you think could happen, if the wrong man sees a lady out in the dead of night, one as pretty as you? Would your husband want that? Do you?"

Her eyes narrowed. *Midnight raids.* He knew. Somehow he knew what she was doing. She cocked a brow at him and said in a cool voice, "I am hardly helpless, Jack."

"This stops, Mercy."

She just stared at him. It didn't stop. It couldn't. Not until she managed to forget what she had seen, what had been done to her husband—what she'd seen him do. . . . Those hated memories rose inside of her and with a cry, she jerked away from Jack and stood, uncaring that she stood naked before him. Ignoring the pain in her back and leg, she stepped out of the tub and grabbed her wrap. Her hands shook so hard she could barely put it on. As she fumbled, Jack moved up behind her. He took the wrap from her with gentle hands and slid it over her shoulders. His hands lingered there and she caught a glimpse of his eyes in the mirror. That hunger was back, burning there, burning nearly as bright as his anger.

But there was also concern. He didn't let go. Instead he pulled her back against him and slid an arm around her waist. "Tell me about that night, Mercy. Tell me what happened."

Wordlessly she shook her head. But the concern she heard in his voice worked its way inside the icy walls she had built around her heart. Like a flame, it grew and grew until the ice melted. The ice had hidden so much inside. Fear, grief, anger, and pain, emotions she had struggled to keep pent up since that night. On rare occasion, something slipped and the emotions would blind her for the briefest moment. But she had never broken. Not once.

Not until now.

The raw scream of pain hurt her throat. Jack lifted her in his arms and she was scarcely aware of it as he carried her to the bed and sat down, cradling her in his lap. She cried for what seemed like ages and Jack merely held her, stroking her back and murmuring to her under his breath.

"You shouldn't keep your tears hidden inside, Mercy," he said softly once the storm had eased. "You need to heal, but you cannot heal until you let yourself grieve."

"I fear that if I let myself fully grieve, truly cry, I may never stop," Mercy whispered. Her voice was husky and thick from the tears and when she looked up at him, her eyes were diamond bright. Her nose was pink and she sniffed a little. Jack pulled a handkerchief out and tucked it into her hand. She mumbled a thank you and tried to pull away but he wouldn't let her. So she blew her nose there, blushing a furious shade of red. She held the kerchief clutched in her hand, and again she tried to pull away from him but Jack just tightened his grip.

She tipped her head to look at him, her mind forming the words to demand he let her go and leave. She had humiliated herself enough. But as she met his dark, mysterious eyes, all thought escaped her. His hand came up, cupping her cheek. He wiped away a tear with his thumb and the feel of his callused flesh sent something hot and hungry streaking through her. "You keep so much buried inside, Mercy," he whispered.

But his words made little sense. She couldn't focus on his words. She was too focused on his mouth. The hard, sensual curve of it, desperate to feel it pressed against hers once more.

Mercy missed a man's touch. In the still of the night, she ached to feel a man's hands on her body. Only now it wasn't just a man's touch she yearned to feel, but Jack's. She turned her face into his touch. He stilled and then he rubbed his thumb over her lower lip. Mercy opened her mouth and bit down gently. Jack's breath hissed out of him. Then he pressed down, opening her mouth a little more. She sucked his thumb into her mouth and he groaned. "Mercy."

His voice was rough and hoarse, almost a growl. It shivered along her flesh and made something deep inside her start to burn. She had one hand resting on his shoulder and she flexed her fingers, then tightened them so that she had the thin, worn cotton of his shirt clutched in her fist. She was painfully aware of how warm he felt. She could feel his heat through his clothes as though they weren't even there and the cloth of her wrap didn't seem to provide any protection at all.

Her heart skipped within her chest and she wanted to rise, strip away her wrap, and then climb atop him, rub against him and beg him to touch her. She'd dreamed about him so often but none of those dreams could compare to the hunger and need she felt for him now. It was devastating in its strength, all consuming and powerful. Worse, she felt naked and vulnerable after sitting in his embrace while she cried.

Turn away, some small sane voice inside her whispered.

But she didn't want to.

He stared at her, his breathing harsh and erratic, his face dark with hunger and his eyes—his eyes seemed to glow. She took a deep breath and tried to find some calm inside her. But that deep breath made it worse. She could smell him and it was intoxicating. He smelled of the forest and the night and it seemed to get stronger, wrapping itself around her. "Mercy," he muttered. His lids drooped and he shook his head as though he felt as shaken as she.

He reached up and rubbed a hand over his eyes and she realized his hand was shaking. "You are shaking," she whispered softly.

He lowered his hand and stared at it. A rueful smile curled his lips upward and he whispered, "You make me weak, Mercy. How can I speak to you, how can I talk sense into that stubborn head of yours when I cannot even look at you without wanting to kiss you?" He stood up, edging around her but as he would have walked past her, she reached out and caught his arm.

"I would like for you to kiss me," she said quietly. She stepped closer, pressing her body against him. "I would like for you to touch me."

"I fear that if I touch you, I will not stop with just a touch, Mercy." His eyes were shadowed. He reached up and wrapped his fingers around her upper arms, easing her back just a little so that she wasn't pressed against his chest.

She smiled. It felt good, allowing herself to feel something besides the anger and the pain. Mercy knew that come morning, she may regret this choice; for now, she knew what she wanted. "I do not wish for you to stop, Jack." She eased away from him and his hands fell to his sides. Mercy held his gaze and reached for the tightly knotted belt at her waist. She loosened it slowly and although she never looked away from his face, she could still see his hands, hanging loosely at his sides. They curled into fists so tight his knuckles went white. "Touch me, Jack. I am tired of sleeping alone and I am tired of waking alone. I am tired of not feeling. I want to feel something, Jack." She stepped up to him again and reached for one of his clenched fists and lifted it, pressing it to her chest.

His fingers uncurled and curved over one breast. He circled the nipple with a light, deft touch. "Mercy . . ." His voice faded away.

She mimicked him teasingly. "Jack." She lifted onto her toes and pressed her lips to the cleft in his chin. "I want to feel, Jack. I want to feel you."

A stronger man could have walked away, Jack knew.

But Jack wasn't that man. He brought up his free hand and shifted so that he could curl them both around her waist, holding her steady as he drew her close. The scent of her filled his head, honeysuckle, roses, and the night. It was intoxicating and Jack imagined himself pressing his lips to her cheek, her chin, her neck, kissing every last bit of skin until he'd found the source of her sweetness.

"Will you regret this in the morning?" he asked.

Mercy lifted her head and smiled at him, a confident sultry curve of her lips that managed to be both seductive and demure. "I do not know, Jack," she whispered, rising on her toes so that she could press her lips to his as she added, "But I do know that I would regret it more if I let you walk out of here. Make me feel, Jack. Take away this emptiness."

The last of his control vanished as she slid her hands under his shirt and pressed her palms against him, her hands cool and soft against his skin. She leaned forward and pressed her mouth against his chest, left bared by his hastily donned shirt. Her mouth seemed to mark him, branding him. Hunger rose inside him, swirling through his system, demanding. Demanding so much more than the light touch of her hands on his side or the whisper-soft kiss she pressed to his chest.

Out of self-preservation, Jack caught her hands and pulled them up. He pressed a kiss to each of her palms and then he stooped, lifting her body into his arms. "Your eyes haunt me at night," he whispered against her mouth as he lay her back on the bed. "I remember a girl who laughed and joked and seeing you that first time was like seeing a stranger. You had such sad eyes and all I wished to do was take the sadness away." He moved his lips over her jaw, kissing her, nuzzling her neck, making his way so that he could murmur in her ear, "Tonight there will be no sadness."

He covered her body with his without bothering to strip his clothes away. If he pressed his naked body to hers, this would be nearly over before he even began. He rested his weight on his elbows and cradled her head in his hand, stroking the tangle of her hair back from her face. He kissed her, keeping the contact gentle, easy.

He wanted to keep it slow, keep it gentle, make love to her softly. But he realized soon that both of them were far too hungry for slow or gentle. Her mouth warmed under his and he could scent the strength of her arousal. It perfumed the air around them and when he tried to take a breath to clear his head, the scent of her flooded his being. Warm, hungry woman—one who didn't fear a man's touch or her own pleasure. Her hands clutched fistfuls of his shirt and she tugged demandingly. "I want to feel you against me," she murmured, tearing her mouth free.

Need made his hands clumsy. He shoved up onto his knees and tore at his shirt, cursing as the excessive material seemed to tangle around his hands. In the end, he tore it, shredding it and shrugging away the scraps of material. Mercy's eyes widened and he swore silently at his loss of control. Her gaze slid over him and when it touched on the still-healing injury on his side, he watched her eyes darken with worry. "What happened?" she murmured, her fingers tracing the red, healing mark.

"Nothing," he replied, lying through his teeth. "It is nothing."

He moved back over her and dipped his head to kiss her, hoping to distract her from the injury she'd inflicted on him. Jack settled his hips between her thighs so that the thick, aching length of his cock was pressed against her sex. He could feel the wet heat through his pants. It was a sweet, painful pleasure.

Her breasts were small, but incredibly full and round. Often when he saw her, she did something that bound her breasts flat to her chest. Perhaps it made it more comfortable when she went riding. Why ever she did it, Jack did not know, but he knew he'd never again see her without remembering what lay hidden under her clothes. The sweetly curved breasts were topped with small, deep rose nipples and when he cupped them in his hands, she fit so perfectly. Her waist was narrow and trim, her hips delicately rounded.

No, he would never see her without thinking how she looked just this moment, with her mouth swollen and red from his, her nipples stiff and hard and begging for his touch. He dipped his head and caught one in his mouth, licking it, tracing it with his tongue while Mercy slid her hands up and fisted them in his hair. She rocked under his hips and cried out his name in a harsh, hoarse voice.

He shifted to the side so he could reach down and cup her in his hand. Her core was shockingly hot and so slick and wet. He pushed one finger inside the snug satin sheath. To his amazement, he felt her come, just from that light touch. She came hard, each rippling little caress squeezing his finger tighter and tighter. "Shite," he muttered under his breath, pulling up and shifting so that he could sprawl between her thighs and press his mouth against her sex.

Hot, sweet as wild honey, and Jack knew he could start to crave this, crave the sound of her ragged cries as she screamed out his name, crave the silken soft feel of her body under his, and her satiny wet heat. He groaned against her flesh. Mercy jerked in reaction, bringing up her thighs and squeezing them tightly around his head. "You're sweet. So tight and hot . . ." He lifted his eyes and stared up the pale curve of her torso. Candlelight danced on her flesh, turning it a warm gold. Her eyes were half closed and she had caught her lower lip between her teeth, biting down so hard he could see a small bead of blood welling there.

The sight of it pushed him to the edge, so hard that he could feel himself teetering on the edge of climax as he fought to free himself from his pants. Even the light touch of his hand as he freed himself was sheer agony. He grimaced and tried to find some small shred of control. He didn't wish to spill his seed like a boy with his first woman, not here, not with Mercy.

He covered her body with his and bent his head, pressing his mouth to hers. She opened for him but Jack didn't deepen the kiss yet. He licked her lower lip, catching the drop of blood on his tongue and then stroking his tongue over her abused flesh. Then he lifted up and whispered, "Open your eyes and watch me, Mercy. Let me watch you." Their gaze held as he settled his hips between her thighs.

He pushed inside, exquisitely aware of how tight, how wet she was. She arched up against him and her hands tightened on his shoulders so that her nails bit into his flesh. The scent of her flooded his head and he could hear her heartbeat, erratic and strong, pounding wildly. He could see the pulse fluttering in her throat and he dipped his head to press his lips there, then he licked her slowly.

He set his teeth against her neck and bit down gently. Beneath him, Mercy screamed out his name and lifted her hips, trying to take him deeper. She slid her hands down his torso, grasping his hips. She was hungry and demanding and soft pleas fell from her lips. Jack slanted his mouth against hers and caught her hands, pinning them down in an effort to slow her down a little.

But all it did was press them closer together. With a ragged groan, Jack pulled out and then thrust forward, pushing deeper and deeper until she had taken all of him. He swallowed her shattered screams and rocked against her, shifting his grip so that he held her wrists in one hand. Then he used his freed hand to lift her higher against him. That small shift had him rubbing against her in the sweetest way. She stiffened beneath him. Jack rolled his hips against hers, slow and teasing. She shivered. He did it a second, a third time, and she climaxed, hard and wild, the walls of her sex closing around his cock and squeezing, milking him, and pulling his own orgasm from him before he had time to stop it. So hard, so wild, and so fast but when it ended, he was still hard and throbbing inside her and she continued to move and rock against him. Still demanding. Still needy.

She thrashed beneath him and Jack pressed his body to hers, trying to use his weight to still her. He wanted to go slower than this, but if she kept moving around so, he would continue to have the control of a green boy with his first woman. He pressed her into the bed and caught her head between his hands. "Shhh," he muttered against her lips. Jack pressed a soothing, soft kiss to her mouth, nuzzled her cheek and muttered in her ear, keeping his voice soft and gentle, waiting for her to still.

"Jack, please," she begged.

"That is what I wish to do, to please you. Make you moan. Make you scream. Make you forget every lonely, unhappy moment in your life," he whispered against her damp flesh. He nuzzled her neck and pressed a kiss to her breastbone. Licked a circle around one nipple. Kissed his way back up to her mouth and wished there was a way he could have more of her. All of her, tasting her, fucking her, listening to her scream endlessly even as he took her breath away. He could not get enough of her, could not touch enough, could not feel enough. She shifted and squirmed upward, tried to wrap her legs around his hips and pull him tighter. Jack reached behind him and unwrapped her legs, pushing her knees up to her chest. "No," he said softly. "You cannot do that. You do that and I will not be able to take my time, go slow with you and touch you and kiss you until you sigh out my name."

He pushed onto his knees and cupped her rump in his hands, tucking her up close against him. He brushed the small bud of her clit, stroked her with firm pressure. "I need to feel it again, feel it as you lose yourself and scream out my name."

It took so very little. It seemed as though Mercy's body had been made just for him, reacting to the smallest movement, burning with the same heat that consumed him. He pushed her again and again, until his body was shaking and sweating from the need to lose himself inside her again. The slick, swollen walls of her sex clenched around him, tightening, rippling, and kneading his flesh. His balls had pulled up tight against him and he ached with the need to spill himself inside her.

When her hands slid slickly from his arms and fell limp to her side, he knew he couldn't hold back any longer. He bent low over her body, gathered her up close. He started shafting her with a hard driving rhythm—one stroke, two, three. By the fifth stroke, he felt his climax building. On the sixth, he lost himself inside her and roared out her name. His cock jerked, wrapped in the satin heat of her pussy. He drove in, deep and hard and erupted, spilling his seed deep inside her.

FAINT moonlight streamed in through the open window. They could hear the call of crickets and the rustle of the wind moving through the trees. Jack lay on his back. Mercy lay cuddled up against his side, tracing her finger over his chest in a senseless pattern. "Will you tell me something?" he asked.

Mercy looked up at him. She had a smile on her pretty lips, a rather feline looking smile that heated everything inside of him. He shouldn't be able to feel this heat, not after the past few hours. It was nearing dawn, and since he had taken her in his arms, they had made love six wonderful times. The last time, he had pulled her atop him so that she straddled him. She'd blushed and he pulled her down against him so he could kiss her. "You love to ride, so ride me," he'd whispered.

After that last time, he would have thought he would need time to recover but there he was and just one smile from her had his sex swelling. He focused on her face though. They did need to talk and Mercy needed some rest. He'd ridden her hard. Jack had been years without a woman, and he could take her endlessly and collapse after, but he didn't want to bruise her soft body any more than he already had.

She reached up and touched her finger to his lips and murmured, "What would you like me to tell you?" Then she gave him a naughty smile. "After tonight, I haven't many secrets. You know what a wicked, wanton woman I am."

"Hmmmm. Wanton, perhaps," he mused, combing his fingers

through her tangled hair. "But you are not wicked. I think perhaps you are an angel fallen from the heavens." Then he shifted, rolling her onto her back and leaning over her. He laced their fingers together and lifted her hand to his lips. "I want you to tell me what happened that night. I need to know."

Mercy needed not to ask him what night. She went cold inside, the heat and pleasure of the past few hours fading away until all she felt was icy grief and sorrow. She shook her head and pulled away, struggling to get free but Jack simply tightened his arms and held her locked against him. One hand cupped the back of her head and the other rubbed her back in slow soothing circles.

But Mercy couldn't be soothed. She squeezed her eyes closed, desperately trying to block out those awful memories. It was too late though. With that simple question, Jack had opened the floodgate of memories and Mercy was lost in them. Lost and terrified, like she hadn't been since that night. Even as often as she chased death, she hadn't been this frightened.

As though he understood her internal struggle, Jack cupped her chin and lifted her face to his, his grip gentle but unyielding. "You will not get past this loss until you face it. You cannot keep running from it, or keep trying to chase it down and destroy it. You must face it as it happened, or you will never heal."

Hot, salty tears leaked out of her eyes. "I cannot face it. I will never heal."

He kissed away the tears on her face. "And is this what Simon would want of you? Living your days, hiding from yourself, while you chase after death in the night? You never were a coward, Mercy."

"I am," she responded, her voice bitter. "I am a horrid coward. They killed him, right in front of me. And I was too terrified to do anything about it." But that wasn't even her greatest shame. Suddenly, as though the secret had become too great for her to bear, she said it. After keeping it hidden inside all these months, she told Jack what had happened.

"He turned into a monster—right in front of me," she whispered.

An abrupt stillness took Jack. She darted a glance upward at his face but in the darkness of the room, all she could see was the faint glitter of his eyes. For some horrible reason, it reminded her of that night. That night when Simon changed from the man she loved into a monster that could only have come straight out of hell, one of the devil's own demons. Men didn't turn into giant wolves. Surely it could be nothing but the devil's work.

"Men came," she said, her voice halting. "It was like they came from nowhere. They were everywhere. I could see them outside the window. I could hear screaming coming from the servants' cabins. Simon got out of bed and he grabbed me, carried me to the clothespress and told me that I must hide. But before he closed the door, they were in here. They looked at him, at me, and they laughed. He jumped for them and right before my eyes, he—he just changed. His body . . ." Mercy's voice trailed off. "You will surely think I am mad. He stood beside me, looking as he always had. Then he moved so quickly, I could hardly see him. And as he moved, his body changed. When it was done changing, Simon wasn't there.

"It was like something trapped between a wolf and a man, and he was so tall, he could have reached up to touch the ceiling. His eyes glowed." She swallowed. "I screamed. I was so scared. I screamed and I screamed. I couldn't stop it. He killed two of them but there were so many. I saw him go down—heard him call my name. Then there were gunshots. Theo was there, along with some of the other men."

She pushed insistently at his chest but he wouldn't release her. "Jack, I need to move. I can hardly breathe." His arms fell away, reluctant somehow, as if he didn't want to let her go. Mercy pulled away, scrambling off the bed. Away from Jack, she suddenly felt cold, chilled to the bone. Although the wind blowing through the window was warm, Mercy was shaking. She grabbed her wrap and pulled it on, but it did nothing to warm her. She moved to the window, staring into the night. "He died trying to protect me and I was too terrified to even look at him."

She cast Jack a glance and murmured, "You must think me insane."

"No." He rolled from the bed and moved to stand close. He didn't touch her, but she could feel the heat of his body so close to hers. She yearned to press against him and let him warm her again. "I do not think you are insane."

Mercy laughed bitterly. "Do not patronize me and do not lie just to be kind. If I hadn't seen it, I would certainly think myself mad. Sometimes I do. Most times, though, I simply wish I *were* mad."

He touched her then, lightly, just his hands resting on her shoulders. But that light touch shook her more thoroughly than it would had he done anything else. He dipped his head and murmured into her ear, "I am many things, Mercy, but rarely have I considered myself a kind person. Certainly not kind enough to lie to a woman simply to make her feel better. I trust that you truly saw what you say and I cannot imagine the burden you have lived with since then."

Slowly she turned in his arms and looked up at his shadowed face. Only the faintest light lit the room but she couldn't doubt in the intense sincerity she saw in his gaze. The young man she had remembered hadn't been a cruel man, but neither had he been a man who would say something to appease others. He spoke what was on his mind and said what was in his heart.

"You truly believe me."

He cupped her face in his hand. "Yes. I believe you." Then his grip on her chin tightened. "You cannot continue as you have, Mercy. I do not know if you do this to ease your guilt for not saving your husband, to ease the guilt for being frightened when you saw him change, or to avenge his death. But you cannot continue like this. You will die if you do, and I will not let that happen."

Troubled, she gazed at him. "I cannot rid myself of the guilt, Jack. But I do not know what troubles me more—that I fell in love with a man who was a monster or that I grieve for him still—love him still."

He was quiet for a time, his hands resting on her shoulders. Then he drew her closer and softly said, "What makes a man a monster? How he looks? Or what he does? Had he treated you cruelly, I would think him a monster. But he treated you well, did he not? You were not wrong to love a good man who loved you."

He kissed her then, hard and furious, almost desperate, as though that alone could keep her safe. When he lifted his head, he rubbed his thumb over her swollen mouth and sighed raggedly. "Mercy . . ."

She reached up, stilled the apology she knew was on his lips. "No. You needn't apologize, Jack." He'd warmed her inside when she had thought she would be chilled for hours. Days. That he believed her, that he cared enough to worry, it only widened the crack in the ice that enshrouded her heart. She was coming back to life inside and part of her hated it, dreaded it. The memories she had managed to keep buried for months were resurfacing, but oddly, Jack's presence made them more bearable.

She'd always loved him. Always. He had been the prince of her childhood dreams and as she grew older and those dreams became more impassioned, he had remained the center of her world. He had always made her feel safe, even when she had been trailing after him and Richard like a waif.

If there was a soul alive who could make her want to live, it would be Jack.

He said her name and his voice sounded odd, stilted. She stared into his troubled eyes. Lifting a hand, she touched his cheek. "When you promised Richard you would look after me, you had no idea what that was going to mean, did you?"

He caught her hand and pressed his lips to it. "It would not have mattered," he whispered. His mouth was warm on her skin and she felt a responding heat inside. "Mercy, there is something I need to tell you but I do not know—"

The scream split the night air. It shattered the silence like a piece of fragile glass and Mercy's heart stopped as she realized where the scream had come from. A man's voice followed and Mercy swore under her breath.

She spun away from Jack and moved to the wardrobe, grabbing the first pair of breeches she saw. Behind her, she heard Jack laugh. "What would your mother think if she heard you speaking like that?"

Mercy laughed. "I heard her speaking worse on nights when she woke to pounding on the door. It's Lydia. It must be the baby."

Jack watched as Mercy dressed quickly, pulling up those men's breeches over her sweet, soft curves. The knee-length shirt she pulled on did little to hide the full breasts underneath. He imagined she was too focused on Lydia to realize that any man with eyes could see the soft ripe curves and the stiff nipples that pressed into the cotton. She didn't bother with boots and paused only long enough to find a strip of leather with which to bind her hair.

After finding and lighting a candle, Jack dressed as well. He only had time for his own breeches before she headed to the door. There was a satchel by the door and he reached it just before she could lift it. She gave him a faint smile. A real smile, one of the few he had seen from her since returning. She was worried, tired, and her eyes were still reddened from her tears, but the smile lit up her face, and he was struck by how amazingly beautiful she was.

There was another scream and halfway down the stairs, they encountered David. He held a fat candle in one hand, the wax dripping down and pooling on his hand, but he did not seem to notice. The two candles were the only source of light and the flickering light cast shadows on David's worried face. "It's Lydia."

"The baby?" Mercy asked, her voice calm.

But David shook his head. "I don't know. She was sleeping.

Then she started to scream and she won't wake up." His soft, slurred drawl was so thick with his worry that Jack barely understood him but Mercy did.

Her eyes narrowed thoughtfully, a frown tightening her features. "Well then. Lets go." Jack followed behind them, watching as Mercy spoke to David, her voice gentle, firm, pulling answers out of him even though the man seemed half sick with concern.

Jack hadn't quite reached the cabin where Lydia and David slept when he felt something in the night. It chilled him to the very bone. Off in the distance, he heard a warning howl. Though there were no words, he recognized the warning for what it was as some shape-shifter miles off felt the same evil of which Jack was just now aware.

Close, too. Too close.

Some dark magic must have hidden their presence because Jack would have sensed it before now, even as preoccupied as he had been. *Preoccupied.* Bitterly he thought to himself, *Preoccupied, my arse.* Preoccupied didn't quite explain how he had felt when he had lain sprawled between Mercy's pretty white thighs or the sickness that had twisted his gut as he realized just how deeply Mercy's scars ran and why.

Looking back, Jack knew he should have uncovered the secrets of that night before he took her but how could he have known? He knew she had seen ferals, knew in his gut that those nasty, evil bastards were behind her husband's death. But he hadn't expected to find out that Simon Greene had been a shape-shifter. No, it was an unexpected complication, and it had already been a mess without that added weight.

No, preoccupied didn't describe his state of mind for the past few hours any more than *fear* described what was coursing through his veins right now. Terror, rage, guilt, all of them threatened to choke him, threatened to swamp him, and he had to curtail all of them, forcing them down deep inside so he could deal with the threat that pushed closer with every second.

Another scream rent the air and this one was more terrified than the last. "They're coming. . . ." He barely made the words and he didn't like it all. Lydia recognized it. Somehow. He broke into a run, beating Mercy to Lydia's bedside, shouldering her father aside, as well as the others who had come running when they heard the pregnant woman screaming.

Touching her brow, he whispered her name, although he didn't know how much good it would do. Her father and brother had surely tried to wake her. Why would she wake for him?

She did, though. Her eyes, dark as the night, stared up at him and she reached up, clamping her hands tight around his wrist. "They're coming, Mr. Jack. I feel them. There's a woman with them; she's hiding them. Making it seem like they aren't there, so you can't find them."

He didn't waste time trying to figure out how Lydia had known. She was no shape-shifter, no vampire and although it was harder to detect a witch, he sensed no magic about her. But she knew nonetheless. He rose and turned, running straight into Theo's big body. Theo shoved a rifle into his hands and jerked his chin toward the door. They moved outside as the others rushed in.

"It's loaded with silver," Theo said, keeping his voice low.

"Silver." Jack studied Theo's grim face in the faint light. "That is how Mercy ended up carrying a rifle with silver instead of lead bullets."

Theo nodded once. "It's the only reason Mercy's alive. Those wolves would have killed her as well as her man."

"How do you know?"

A mean smile curved Theo's lips. "I just do. Always have. Lydia, she's the same way. She feels people who are different. We both do. But none of that matters now. They're coming and they don't plan on leaving anybody alive."

Jack shoved the rifle back into Theo's hands. "Give this to one of the men, one that's steady and doesn't frighten easily." The mystery of how Theo knew, and just how much, that would have to wait for later. Jack disappeared into the night and tried to focus, focus on something other than the wild scents of fear that permeated the air.

Over the distance and through the rough wooden walls of the cabin, he could hear Lydia's erratic breathing and Mercy's soft, calming words. He scented the smell of blood in the air and he knew Lydia's baby was coming. All around the small cabin, men gathered while inside the women rushed to prepare for a birth. The whole place was rife with life and emotion.

That was what the ferals were coming for. White Oak was secluded, away from town and far away from neighbors. Had Lydia not woken screaming, had Jack not been there, he suspected that whatever dark magic protected the enemy would have kept them hidden until it was too late. It would have been a slaughter.

It still might be, but not if Jack had anything to do about it. Focusing on his territory was bloody hard with the fear that choked him. Jack hadn't done it before—he hadn't had a chance to establish himself, even though this was his home, his land. He'd been too focused on Mercy and now he had to worry what that was going to cost.

Finally he was able to focus on something beyond the rage roaring inside him. He reached out, and like it had been waiting for him, the land reached back. Jack focused on the land, the sense of home, the sense of strength that flowed out of the earth and into him. He felt it, felt them—he could feel all the gifted creatures, the evil and the innocent.

It was what made a Hunter into a Master, that ability to link with the earth and connect with those under his protection. Jack had heard about this, that enigmatic bond between Master and land, but he hadn't expected this—the strength and certainty of it, and the confidence and power that came from it.

There was so much life. It flooded through him. As though those lives somehow added to his own, Jack felt a renewed strength and a sense of calm settled around him.

He could also feel the warriors. He touched on the presence of the wolves he'd sensed earlier. They rejected his presence at first, but then they yielded as the lesser always yields to superior strength. He called them, wordlessly, a simple summons that no amount of words could explain. And they came. He could feel them racing to him as he reached out, searching for others. The response was weak, precious little, but he could only hope it was enough as vampire, shifter, and witch came rushing to him on the night.

As he shifted his focus back to the enemy prowling ever closer, the land continued to feed itself to him, and it flooded him with strength, clearing his own fear and in turn, he shared that calm with those who would aid him.

If death was waiting for him tonight, Jack wouldn't go alone.

He tipped his head back to the sky. The growling scream that came from him was one that no mortal could make. In the distance, he heard lupine howls and feline growls rise up to answer—some in support. Others in challenge.

Come—come to me.

SIX

Mercy heard the scream outside, and it sent a shiver racing down her spine. It was unlike anything she'd ever heard before. She had heard the calls of mountain lions, but this—this sounded different. An eerie cadence of howls and screams drifted to her on the wind and her belly went cold with fear.

She looked down at Lydia, the woman's dark face contorted with pain and gleaming with sweat.

"They comin', Mercy," Lydia repeated for the third time. Whether the girl was delirious or whether she sensed the same evil in the air as Mercy, Mercy didn't know.

Candles cast their flickering light on Lydia's face but it was still much too dark. She wished she had brought more candles out from the house but she would not send for more. Not now. Outside the cabins something evil lurked and Mercy wished she had brought her rifle and her pistols.

"Nobody is to leave this cabin," she said over her shoulder. She glanced at the door and then over at Beth. The heavyset woman took care of the kitchen and she was as level, as steady, and as calm as they came. She spoke, and others listened. "Beth, I want you to tell the men to get inside the cabin. This moment."

But Beth shook her head. "They won't do that, Miss Mercy. Theo and the men, they out there with rifles. Something strange is out there. Something strange." In the dim light, Beth looked frightened but her voice was calm and flat.

Jack . . .

Fear turned her belly to ice and she wanted to get up, find Jack and force him to stay with her. He wasn't in the cabin, she knew without even looking for him. But she couldn't leave Lydia.

The baby was coming fast, almost too fast, as though something inside of Lydia had sensed the danger and nature was trying to get the slow, laborious task of childbirth done before the danger crept too close. Pressing a cloth between Lydia's thighs, Mercy saw the bloody fluids on Lydia's thighs. Too much blood.

Unbidden, she found herself praying. *Holy Father . . . please . . .*

What she prayed for, whether it was herself, Lydia, or Jack, or all of them, she didn't know.

Outside she heard a loud crash, like something huge had crashed into the ground. A yipping sort of snarl, followed by guttural laughter that made Mercy's gut clench with fear. Then she heard that same odd scream again.

Her eyes narrowed as she realized she *had* heard a scream like that before.

The cat. The demon cat that she had allowed to escape. Squeezing her eyes closed, she hoped she hadn't damned them to hell by not killing the cat.

Lydia's face contorted. "Too quick, Mercy."

"Shhhh," Mercy murmured, stroking a hand down Lydia's face. "All will be well. All will be well."

She just prayed she was not lying.

❧

JACK heard the scream of a newborn babe. Surrounded by three werewolves, he snarled at them and swiped out with one huge paw. Two evaded him. The third went to his knees, squalling as blood sprayed from one thigh. The scent of the blood was rich and Jack knew he'd cut a large vessel.

Hope you bleed to death, he thought, and he focused on the other two wolves.

One was still in human form.

The other had shifted into a giant wolf-man and Jack knew instinctively that this was the leader. This was the one he needed to kill. Most feral packs had an alpha and killing that alpha would leave them confused.

There had indeed been a witch with them but that witch now lay dead.

A man unknown to Jack had killed the witch, a man with a shaved head and near-black eyes. He'd looked at Jack with hostility and Jack had understood why. The Indian didn't like answering the call of a white man, any more than Jack would have liked answering the call from a redcoat. But theirs was a duty that went deep, too deep to ignore. The Indian had killed the witch and with her gone, the rest of them had been able to pick off the ferals that would have massacred every living soul at White Oak.

Jack had no idea how much time had passed as he continued to struggle with the wolves. Distantly he was aware that some of the wolves around him fell and that some ran. Time lost all meaning and as the dim light of predawn slowly bled into morning, he scarcely noticed.

All that remained to fight were two dominant feral wolves who continued to fight because running wasn't an option for them.

He heard the crack of a rifle and smelled the stink of gunpowder only a split second before one of the wolves still in his mortal form collapsed dead. Blood stained the front of his shirt red and the scent of burnt flesh drifted upward.

Victory punched through him, heady and intense. The second feral fought in the halfling form, his body caught between shifts so that he looked more wolf than man, yet he walked upright. The wolf-man's lids flickered and then he lunged for Jack, one last desperate attempt to win. Desperate—and useless. Jack ducked under the wolf-man and turned his head at the last second, clamping down on the muscles in the back of the wolf-man's massive thigh. The wolf went down. The flesh was already knitting back together but Jack used those few seconds wisely, going for the throat—and the kill.

The blood that filled his mouth was bitter and acrid. It sprayed all over him as he tore the wolf-man's throat out. He retreated two steps and lifted his gaze to see Theo standing near, his rifle up and ready. The gunshot echoed through the clearing as Theo fired the killing shot directly between the wolf-man's eyes.

Relief hit him hard, and desperate to get rid of the blood that was in his mouth and staining his clothes, Jack shifted back to mortal form. Theo's eyes widened just a little. A few of the other men reacted a little more vocally, but it wasn't them that caught his attention.

It was the soft, female gasp from behind him.

He turned and saw Mercy standing behind him. She stared at him, her gaze wide and tortured. She shook her head and even over the distance that separated them, he heard the wild beat of her heart.

"Mercy . . ."

She turned on her heel and ran. She ran as though the devil himself was on her heels, fleeing to the cabin at her back and throwing herself inside as though it was the only sanctuary left in the world.

Looking down at himself, Jack stared at his naked, bloodied body, and then he closed his eyes and swore.

NOT again.

Mercy managed just barely to swallow the sobs, but now they

threatened to choke her. She pressed her back against the door of Lydia and David's small cabin, staring at the women in front of her.

A few had left when she had, venturing out to help the wounded and begin the grim task of caring for the dead. Beth was among them, calling out orders with a skill that would have done Washington well. Trapped inside the small cabin, Mercy tried desperately to think past the fear and pain that swamped her.

"Mercy?" Lydia, her face exhausted but at peace, looked at her from the small bed, her newborn son swaddled and held close to her breast. David was at Lydia's side. He must have slid inside when Mercy went out for those few brief moments. "Are we safe?" she asked softly, her voice thick with exhaustion.

Safe? Mercy thought hysterically as she recalled what she had just seen.

No wonder Jack had known about her midnight raids, as he called them. He had followed her. He'd had the audacity to appear concerned over her safety. Perhaps it had been his own safety that concerned him, though. She'd tried to kill him twice and perhaps he feared that she might actually succeed.

How could we possibly be safe? But she didn't say that. Too many years of caring for new mothers kept her from saying anything that might frighten Lydia.

David bent down low, pressing a kiss to Lydia's brow and saying the strangest thing. "We safe, Lydia. You saved us, girl."

Saved us? Mercy thought, almost hysterical. But then she remembered the odd words that Lydia had said to Jack when they came to the cabin just a few hours earlier. A few hours. It seemed like days. Weeks.

Lydia had been lying there, her breathing harsh and her body shuddering with the birthing pains. Jack had knelt by her side and Lydia had opened her eyes, stared at him with a fever-bright gaze. *They're coming, Mr. Jack. I feel them. There's a woman with them; she's hiding them.*

She'd known. Somehow Lydia had known. More—Mercy had a horrid suspicion that Lydia had known about *Jack*.

As though the exhausted new mother had heard the chaotic spin of Mercy's thoughts, Lydia whispered, "Jack—is he safe?"

The hysteria building inside Mercy finally broke free, and she started to laugh, doubled over and giggling until her sides ached. "Safe?" she managed to gasp out. "Is he safe?"

In her mind's eye, she saw how he had looked when he changed from that demon cat back into the man she'd made love with during the night. He'd been smeared with blood and on his side was the wound she remembered from last night.

Now she knew how it had happened. She'd done that, firing silver into the feline body he'd worn that night.

"Oh, God." She moaned. She covered her mouth with her hands and started to shake uncontrollably.

When she heard him through the door, she bolted upright and shoved away from the door, desperate to get away. Lydia and David stared at her with wide, puzzled eyes and she flinched.

I must get away from here, she thought desperately. She had to.

The door creaked as it swung open and Jack stood there, wearing a pair of breeches and nothing else. The blood still streaked his body and now she realized that some of the blood was his, flowing from deep gashes on his side, his shoulder, even his face. Yet as she stared at him, the wounds seemed to get smaller and smaller—the ones on his face closed up before her very eyes.

"Mercy—"

"No." Her voice was a sharp, angry crack in the air and she shook her head.

He came inside the small cabin and she edged away, circling around the perimeter of the room, keeping as far from him as she could manage.

His voice was husky and soft as he whispered, "Mercy, please. I would never hurt you—you must know that."

Blinded by her tears, she could no longer see him clearly. But

when he started toward her, she knew. "Stay back!" she shrieked
and then she turned, running out the door. Her bare feet pounded
down on the soft carpet of grass as she fled toward the forest, not
knowing where she was running. Pain jolted through her, but fear
and the need to escape were stronger than the pain.

All that mattered was getting away. Getting away from Jack,
getting away from the pain. She only wished she could run away
from herself so easily.

She stumbled over an exposed tree root and fell to her knees.
Her injured back was screaming at her and pain tore through her
hands as she threw them out to break her fall. Something jagged
and sharp cut into her knees but she got back to her feet.

Once more, she started to run, but it was a shuffling, limping
motion, and each step sent renewed agony through her. She felt
something wet trickling down her leg, but Mercy didn't dare slow
down, not until the pain became too great and then she stumbled.
She landed on a carpet of mossy green and lay there, her face buried in her arms and her shoulders trembling with the force of her
sobs.

That was how Jack found her, lying on her belly beside the
James River in that little alcove where he'd swum earlier. Was it
only yesterday that he had imagined seeing her in this place?

It hardly seemed possible. His body ached from the battle and
his heart burned with grief as he stared at Mercy. He shouldn't
have taken her. He knew it now, and in his heart, he knew he'd
done even more damage to an already damaged soul. Yet he
couldn't find it in him to regret their night together.

He knelt beside her and reached out to touch her hair. He knew
that she was aware of him, he could tell it by the way her sobs cut
off abruptly and by the way she stilled, as though she feared to
breathe. He braced for her to pull away as he stroked a hand down
her hair, but she did not move.

"Mercy, forgive me."

She moved then, scrambling on her hands and knees away from

him, crawling over to a massive oak and cowering against it. She looked at him with fear in her eyes and it was as though someone had gouged him with a hot poker. "Please don't fear me, Mercy," he whispered gently. "I would never hurt you."

She shook her head. "You're a monster, Jack. How could you *not* hurt me?"

"I am no monster, Mercy. This is simply how I was born. This was no choice I made." He searched for words to explain it to her, but considering how deep her scars ran, he knew there were no words that could make this right. Bloody hell, if he had known . . . *No, it is too late for that.* He hadn't known about Simon until it was too late and now, he would suffer for it.

More—Mercy would suffer for it.

He wanted to reach for her. Wanted desperately to cradle her against him. But he knew he couldn't. Not now. Not ever again. "Forgive me," he said again. And then he stood, straightened, and walked away, leaving her alone in the forest.

IT was already difficult, getting through the days alone. In such a short time, Jack had come back into her life and made himself a fixture. Less than a week. And now, less than a week since he had left her alone, Mercy wondered if this pain would ever ease.

She sat by Lydia's side, watching as Lydia nursed her son, a handsome boy with a head full of tight black curls and large liquid eyes. They'd named him Richard. Mercy's eyes had teared up when they told her.

"Mercy."

She blinked and looked up to find Lydia gazing at her with worried eyes. "I'm sorry. My mind was wandering."

Lydia watched her knowingly. "I think I know where it wandered to. Go to him, Mercy. He is not what you think."

She swallowed and shook her head. Lydia hadn't seen—she couldn't know.

Except it seemed that Lydia did know. "Jack's the way he was meant to be, Mercy. He's the way the good Lord wanted him to be. That don't make him a monster."

Unwittingly she remembered what Jack had said. *What makes a man a monster? How he looks? Or what he does? Had he treated you cruelly, I would think him a monster. But he treated you well, did he not? You were not wrong to love a good man who loved you.*

You were not wrong to love a good man who loved you. He'd spoken of Simon, Mercy knew. And deep inside, she'd yearned to believe that was true. Was Simon a good man? Her heart had always insisted he was. It had been her head, the logical part of her, that commanded she believe otherwise.

"Go to him, Mercy."

Daring a glance at Lydia's face, Mercy shook her head. "I cannot."

Lydia's face softened. "You can. He's a good man, Mercy. He loves you."

At that, Mercy laughed, a sad, bitter laugh that hurt her deep inside. "He doesn't love me. . . ."

Lydia reached up and lay a hand on Mercy's cheek. She made Mercy look at her and when Mercy finally met Lydia's dark eyes, Lydia smiled, a knowing smile. "Doesn't he?"

You were not wrong to love a good man who loved you.

What makes a man a monster?

Indecision and doubt churned inside her and it kept her awake late into the night. Hours had passed since she had left Lydia in Beth's capable hands and returned to the main house. A thousand chores awaited her, yet she couldn't focus on a single one and the day passed without her accomplishing anything.

She paced, her room dark save for the moonlight that fell through the windows. A cool breeze stirred the night air, a promise of autumn.

What makes a man a monster. . . .

The skin on her spine tingled and she shivered, feeling as though eyes were watching her every move. She stopped in the middle of the room and without moving, shifted her gaze to the window.

Jack.

He was far, far away, just a shadow lost among shadows, but she knew he was there. She could all but feel him even though she couldn't see him. And somehow she felt his grief.

What makes a man a monster. . . .

Swallowing, she finally let herself answer that question. A man's actions made him what he was, not how he looked. Jack had fought the monsters that night, fighting to keep her safe while she stayed by Lydia's side to deliver the child. And he had saved her that first night from the real monsters, the redcoats who would have killed her when they were done with her.

You were not wrong to love a good man who loved you.

No. She hadn't been wrong to love Simon and she wasn't wrong to love Jack.

EYES gritty with exhaustion, Jack remained under the tree where he had slept for the past week. He'd spent the days working his land on his own, preparing for the coming harvest, and the nights, he'd spent here, watching over Mercy just as he had promised.

She might not want him in her life and he wouldn't be surprised if she came hunting him, but it mattered little. He'd made a promise—and more, he'd fallen in love with her. He would sacrifice whatever it took to make sure she was safe and cared for.

The big house was quiet and he felt nothing in the air around him so as sleep crawled closer, he let himself relax. At first he was sure he had fallen asleep and that he dreamed of Mercy.

Certain of it, until she came to stop before him and reached out to touch his face. The cool, gentle touch of her fingers on his flesh convinced him that it was no dream and he stared at her face in the light of the moon, hardly able to believe what he saw.

She stared at him, and the hatred, the fear, and the disgust he would have expected were not there.

"How many nights have you spent watching over me?" she whispered. "You look exhausted."

Jack didn't dare move, hardly dared to speak. "I am where I should be."

She glanced back at the house and then at him. "Are you?" She shifted a little, settled down on her bottom and folded her legs. She wore her breeches again and a long-tailed shirt that seemed to swallow her.

He said nothing. He didn't know what he could say or why she was here.

"You were born . . ." Her voice trailed off and she bit her lip, as though she searched for words.

"I'm a shape-shifter, Mercy. I was born this way. It was nothing I did or that was done to me. It is simply what I am," he said wearily, and he looked away, unable to keep staring at her while she stayed so close. If he continued to stare at her, he would have to touch her. "I would have told you that night but . . ." This time, it was his voice that trailed away and he ended with a restless shrug of his shoulders. "If I could undo how that night happened, Mercy, I would. Believe that, if you believe nothing else."

"Why?"

He turned his head, staring at her. "Why? Because there is little I wouldn't do if it could ease the fear I saw in your eyes."

"And why does it bother you that I was afraid, Jack? If you were born like this, surely you've encountered fear before."

"But not from you," he rasped, his voice harsh. Yes, he'd encountered fear and it hadn't concerned him overmuch, not until he saw it in her eyes. "I hate for you to think of me with fear in your heart."

Persistent little termagant, Jack thought as she again asked, "Why?"

"Mercy, what is it you want of me?" he demanded.

She shrugged. "I want to understand. I want to know how Lydia knew what you were, and I want to understand why my husband never told me what he was, and I want to know why those demons killed him like they did. I want peace." Then she reached out and touched his cheek. "And I want to stop crying over you at night. Surely if you were a monster, I wouldn't continue to miss you."

He caught her hand. "Mercy . . ."

He almost stood up, almost walked away. But then he made himself look into her eyes. What he saw there was more than he would have allowed himself to hope for. It wasn't just the absence of fear or a need to understand. It wasn't even acceptance, although he had yearned for just that.

It was Mercy as she'd been before grief destroyed something inside her.

"Do you miss me, Jack?"

For a moment, it was as though he'd forgotten to breathe. "Miss you?" he repeated, his voice hoarse. "The past week, it has been as though I died inside. Yes, Mercy. I missed you and I've ached to see your lovely face again and I dreaded each day because I knew it would be another day that passed when you wouldn't be near me. So yes, I've missed you."

He caught her hand in his, brought it to his lips. "I cannot give you peace, Mercy. I cannot give you an understanding of what I am, because I do not even know. I cannot help you to understand why you lost your man as you did." Then he took a deep, steadying breath. She no longer seemed to hate him. That would be enough. Slowly he released her hand. "But I can promise you that no harm like that shall ever come to you. I will protect you with every last bit of strength I have in me. Believe in that."

He surged to his feet, determined to walk away before he grabbed her to him and demanded more than he knew she could give.

"Is that all?" She stood as well and tipped her head, gazing at him in the moonlight. "You will keep me safe? What about happy? Don't you think Richard would want you to see me happy?" She closed the distance between them and pushed up on her toes, brushing her lips against his cheek. "Did you know that I was terribly infatuated with you when I was a girl? Just a girl's sentimental dreaming, I always thought. And then I saw you again."

His voice was a harsh growl as he whispered, "Mercy . . ."

A smile edged up the corners of her mouth. "Jack . . ." She mimicked his voice. Then she touched a finger to his lips. "What makes a man, Jack, is his actions. And if I were bold enough, I would dare say that your actions last week made you mine—and mine would make me yours."

Hope was almost as debilitating as fear, as pain, Jack discovered as the strength drained from his legs and he fell to his knees before her. Slowly, almost hesitantly, he reached up and wrapped his hands around her narrow waist. Fearful that he had heard something she hadn't truly said, he lifted his gaze and stared at her. "Yours?" he whispered.

"Hmmm." She sank down and straddled him, planting one knee on either side of him. "You wanted me to come back to life, Jack. I want it as well—but only if you would be in it." Mercy leaned forward and pressed her lips to his. "I do want to understand, Jack. But more than understanding, I need you. Just you."

THE MEN AND WOMEN'S CLUB
Robin Schone

Author's Foreword

London, England, in 1887 was hungry for sex. It vicariously fed off the private lives of men and women who were unfortunate enough to capture the public eye. Reputations were butchered in the courtrooms and dished up in newspapers where respectable citizens could dine at their leisure. In a few more years, the great Oscar Wilde himself would be brought down in such a manner.

It was also a time of great repression and censure, a time in which the mere propagation of birth control was punishable by imprisonment.

No one was safe. No one was sacrosanct.

Imagine that you live in such a society, and are called as a witness in a notorious trial where your private life will be put on public display. Imagine that you are the founder of a club in which men and women discuss their most intimate desires.

Imagine now that on the eve of this trial that you neither instigated nor approbated but which will surely destroy you, you are locked inside a museum with the one person who can force you to confront your past and the fear that is more terrifying than truth. Because some secrets are meant to be shared. . . .

Read about the private lives of Ardelle Dennison and Joseph Manning . . . *before* their story hits the London papers.

ONE

"*Vive memor leti,* Miss Dennison."

The harsh greeting ricocheted around the twilight-blackened cornices, Latin words pulsing and throbbing over the muted grind of turning wheels.

"Mr. Manning!" The feather-tipped silhouette whipped around, startled motion eliciting a kiss of cool air.

She did not see him.

A muffled gong pierced the thickly carpeted floor.

Rare uncertainty quavered her voice. "Is that you?"

Silently he perused the pale outline of a nose and chin, all that the v-ed light bleeding through the boardroom door revealed of the twenty-nine-year-old woman's beauty.

She had been twenty-seven when he had first approached her, flushed with success at becoming the first female publicist for the London Museum. He had been thirty-three, confident in his professorship at the University of London.

It was within their power to create a new order, he had told her. A modern society of freethinkers unimpeded by conventional dialogue.

Together they had drafted rules for the Men and Women's Club. Together they had pored through professional journals and handpicked prospective members.

Together—he sitting at the head of the twenty-foot-long table where he now sat, and she sitting to his right—they had for two years weekly presided over men and women who coldly discussed sexology while overhead gaslight blinded them to their arrogance.

But tonight there was no light to blind him. Tonight there were no men and women to redirect the desire that pumped through his groin.

Joseph Manning ignored Ardelle Dennison's question.

" 'Live mindful of death,' " he translated instead in that harshly grating voice that came from his throat. Immediately her head jerked toward the head of the table, blurred outline becoming an oval face pitted with black-eye holes. Joseph glanced down at the gavel in his right hand, a darker shade of shadow. "My students interpret Persius's words as a motto to live each day as if it were our last. A license to sin, they argue. But I think his words are cautionary, a warning that if we aren't careful in our day-to-day activities, we will suffer, and we will die."

Herded, sexless voices wafted up from beneath Joseph's feet: men and women he did not know, but who would soon know him.

"You take pride in masculine reason, Miss Dennison." Purposefully Joseph looked up; behind the feather-tipped silhouette, light slashed a squat credenza, turning anonymous black into gleaming mahogany. "Do you believe Persius's words are a warning or an invitation?"

"I believe it's late." Ardelle Dennison was frigidly forthright. There was no sign of the vulnerability she had for one infinitesimal moment revealed. "The museum is closing. Why are you sitting in the dark?"

Through the v-ed door and down the dimly lit corridor, metal banged metal, the sliding gate of an elevator.

Memory gouged the throbbing twilight.

One man questioning. One woman responding.

What does a woman desire?

Yet the woman had not asked what it was that the man needed. And now they must each appear—every single member of the Men and Women's Club—in a court of law.

"Tomorrow we stand before a judge and jury." Cold mahogany wood pulsed against Joseph's fingers. "What do we tell them?"

The feather-tipped silhouette visibly stiffened, even as distant laughter mocked his impotence, everything he had ever wanted lost in this room: his reputation, his position at the university.

The hope for love.

"Do we tell them about the French postcards we didn't look upon?"

Naked men and women doing things he had imagined but never performed.

"Do we tell them about the pornographic shop we refused to visit?"

In his mind's eye flashed the print of a woman who sat backward across a man's hips, wearing only a smile of unfathomable mystery.

"Do we tell them we sat here while five men and six women flaunted every decent moral known to man"—the first in a series of dull bass bongs, Big Ben spitting out the hour, underscored his words—"and we did nothing to stop them?"

"We did everything in our power to direct those meetings," shot through the deepening gloom.

Joseph was not fooled by the publicist's righteous indignation.

"Do we tell them, Miss Dennison," he asked, fingers choking the gavel that he had as president of the Men and Women's Club wielded unsparingly, but which on the morrow would be used to direct jurisdiction in a court of law, "that when I had you on this table two years earlier, you were not a virgin?"

One final bong fell onto the sudden silence: It was seven o'clock.

A shudder vibrated the air, the public doors shutting. The singsong hum of passing carriage wheels emphasized the dead stillness permeating the museum.

Ardelle Dennison's voice, when she spoke, was arctic: "How dare you bring up that night, sir!"

Joseph would dare many things this evening.

"Did I give you no pleasure at all?" he rasped.

In the thickening dusk he could for one fleeting second make out two shadowy figures: a man . . . a woman.

Reaching. Embracing.

He knew that Ardelle Dennison also saw the two ghostly figures, a professor and a publicist who had for one brief moment dared to be a man and a woman.

"This lawsuit is a farce!" she lashed out with sudden anger. "We cannot be held responsible for men and women who cannot control their animal lusts."

"Like us?" Joseph rejoined.

The silence was explosive. But once again she regained her composure.

Surprise did not faze her. Desire did not distract her.

She was everything he thought he had wanted, this woman who could match a man's cold intellect. He now realized he knew nothing whatsoever about Ardelle Dennison.

"Please state your business, Mr. Manning," she curtly rallied. "You rang you wanted to see me; here I am. What do you want?"

Joseph wanted back the life that had been ripped away from him—*all because of one man and one woman's reckless pursuit of passion*—but more than anything, he wanted back that which had been stolen from him two years earlier.

"You took something from me," he said bluntly.

"I never took anything from you," she instantly denied.

"But you did, Miss Dennison." It had taken a subpoena to make him realize just exactly what it was that he had lost. "You unfastened my trousers—"

The rebuttal was swift. "I will not discuss that night."

But this evening she was not being offered a choice.

"—and you grasped me," he baldly continued, reliving the memory of chill air chased away by warm fingers, "and you guided me, and you took me into your body—"

"I told you this topic is not open for discussion—"

Joseph talked over the icy admonition. "—and you took something from me, Miss Dennison."

Into the charged silence broke the distant patrol of footsteps.

Each impact of a wooden heel beating a wooden floor jarred his memory.

Another night: Saturday rather than Monday. Another year: 1885 rather than 1887.

Joseph studied the faceless woman who with each pounding heartbeat . . . with each jarring footstep . . . was fading into darkness.

Slowly, succinctly—his engorged penis throbbing in time with the blood that thrummed inside his temples—he enunciated: "And I want it back."

It was the publicist who spoke, voicing the scorn of a woman who had fought in a man's world against unbeatable odds, yet had won. "And just what do you think I took from you, Mr. Manning?"

What could a woman take from a man, she inferred, when all the time men took from women?

"My virginity," Joseph said flatly. And remembered how it had been.

Before Ardelle Dennison had touched him, he had been content to hoard the memories of his past and furtively jerk his own flesh for release. Now every night he sought to duplicate her touch, either with his hands or in his dreams.

A closing door sliced through the pulsing tension.

"There ye be, Mr. 'Armon!" echoed down the corridor; *now*, not then when Joseph had still been young and full of hope. The pale sliver of light delineating the mahogany credenza dimmed. "All's well, sir. Just a few more cocks, and I'll be out o' 'ere."

"Very good, Mr. Bonnen." Ragged breathing rang out over the aged curator's praise; it matched the bellowing of Joseph's lungs. "Have you seen Miss Dennison? I thought she said she was meeting with a business associate, but she's not in her office, and her cloak is gone."

Instinctively Joseph's gaze sought out the darker shadow clasped before the feather-tipped silhouette.

"I 'aven't seen 'er, sir." The guard's hollow voice penetrated wood, flesh, and bone. "Shall I look for 'er?"

The breathing inside the boardroom quickened, faster than the air tunneling through Joseph's own lungs; it almost drowned out the curator's response: "No, no need, Mr. Bonnen. No doubt she finished her business early and is already on her way home. She's a capable woman, is our Miss Dennison."

"That she is, sir," gently trailed down the corridor. The streak of dull mahogany faded to black, another gas cock screwed shut. "Shall we take the lift tonight?"

Tensely Joseph waited: for Ardelle Dennison to alert the curator and the guard of their presence. Or simply for her to turn around and walk out of the boardroom. As she had walked out two years earlier.

She did neither.

Two pairs of receding footsteps traversed the corridor, one set firm, the steps of a healthy young man, the second halting. Each fading, faltering heel tap was accompanied by the sharp stab of a cane, until even the retreating *click . . . click . . . click* was swallowed by darkness.

Metal grumbled, a cab climbing a metal cable. Metal clanged, a gate opening . . . closing . . . elevator descending . . . Leaving behind Joseph Manning and Ardelle Dennison.

They were not the same man and woman they had been two years earlier.

Deepening twilight shone through a solitary window. Faint chimes announced the quarter hour.

Between one accelerating breath and the next, a remote side door slammed shut, sealing together the two shadows they had become.

"*'Business* associate,' Miss Dennison?" Joseph hoarsely goaded.

"We are associates, Mr. Manning." A disembodied whistle penetrated the darkness, a bobby in pursuit of authority or a boy in innocent play, neither with whom Joseph could identify, his childhood ripped away by the very people paid to protect it. "I apologize if that disturbs you."

"I don't want your apologies, Miss Dennison," Joseph baited, and did not know if it was anger or lust or fear that spurred him. He did not know what would happen on the morrow, but neither did he know what would happen this night. "But I am curious."

Without warning, the feather-tipped silhouette turned in a flurry of rustling wool. The *v* that had minutes earlier been filled with light but which now admitted only darkness, burst wide in a crash of metal stopper and wooden door; simultaneously a wall of chill, musty air slammed into him.

She did not escape quickly enough.

"Who is the animal?"

Animal hurtled through the void that was the emptiness of their lives, an emotive ball of pain.

Ardelle Dennison halted—a black silhouette framed by even blacker shadow—and lied. "I don't know what you're talking about."

"You said, 'If we felt desire,'" Joseph quoted, capturing her every inflection those forty-four days past, that day they had voted into their club a woman who dared to be honest, and for whom they would now all pay the price, "'we would admit it. But we are guided by a higher moral ground,' you said. '*We* are not animals,' you said."

"Git your evenin' news 'ere. . . ." wearily drifted up from the street below. "*Globe*'ll tell you all. . . ."

Fleetingly Joseph wondered if, come the morrow, the evening

newspaper would carry their names, perhaps even their like-nesses.

"Who is the animal, Miss Dennison?" he repeated, question rasping his throat.

Ardelle Dennison—the only woman he had ever allowed to touch him—remained frozen in the doorway.

"You, for taking my virginity?" The precariousness of their future crawled on Joseph's skin like electricity. "Or me, for giving you my virginity?"

TWO

"You are insulting."

"I am inquiring," raced up her spine.

"I didn't know you were a virgin," echoed past doors Ardelle could not see, every one of them closed to a woman who could not claim moral superiority.

"Did you not?" mocked her lie.

For one heart-stopping moment Ardelle remembered the passionate man Joseph Manning had been two years earlier, convinced that men and women could be advocates rather than adversaries.

Immediately the vision died, bringing with it the reality of the man who waited behind her.

"I attended every meeting." She closed her eyes against the throbbing black curtain that was the corridor; pinpricks of light danced behind her lids. "I supported your every hypothesis. When you voted, I voted. When you abstained, I abstained. What more do you want from me?"

"The truth," pierced wool and flayed her spine. "I want the truth, Miss Dennison."

"And just which *truth* do you desire, Mr. Manning?" Eyelids snapping open, Ardelle compulsively swirled around in a flare of wool and bouncing bustle. Murky gray-green light splotched the boardroom. Unerringly she focused on the man who sat at the head of the conference table. He was so deeply shrouded by shadow that all she could see of him was an indistinct blur of skin topped by black hair darker than night. "Do you want to know if I regret not looking at French postcards? Or do you want to know if I regret I will lose my reputation, because the other members of the club looked at them? Or perhaps you want to know if I regret the fact that I, too, did not break the law and visit a pornographic book shop?"

"Do you?" was the harsh rejoinder.

Bitterness rose up like bile inside Ardelle's throat. "As you so astutely reminded me, I have seen a naked man and more. I do not need to imperil my reputation by ogling obscene postcards. Nor do I need to purchase a leather phallus. I have experienced sexual coition, and quite frankly, Mr. Manning, it's not worth discussing, let alone duplicating."

The triumph she expected, uttering the hurtful words, did not come.

"So you felt no pleasure when you took me inside your body."

His voice was strangely flat over the singsong whine of carriage wheels.

Cold, sticky sweat coated her palms.

She was afraid, but she did not want to be afraid.

Ardelle gripped her cloak and reticule more tightly. "I have never taken pleasure in any man."

"Then you're a virgin."

She blinked. "I beg your pardon?"

"Or a liar."

Anger swelled the twilight. "You wanted the truth, Mr. Manning; I have told you the truth. I assure you, if it were in my power, I would gladly give you back your virginity."

"But it is within your power, Miss Dennison."

There was only one explanation for his behavior.

"You're inebriated," she said contemptuously.

"Not at all," Joseph Manning replied, speaking in that strangely grating voice that did not belong to him, but which reverberated throughout her entire being. "You obviously remember the meeting in which a dildo was introduced."

Ardelle stiffened at his deliberate use of vulgarity.

"Surely, then," he baldly continued, "you also remember Mr. Stiles' suggestion that it is not abstinence that makes a man or a woman virgin, but the lack of sharing pleasure. Prove to me we did not share pleasure, Miss Dennison, and you will give me back my virginity."

"You do not believe that nonsense."

Virginity—like innocence—could not be regained.

"Don't I?"

What did Ardelle Dennison know of Joseph Manning? his voice implied.

"No," she replied with conviction. He was—and always had been—a man of unquestionable intellect. "You do not."

"I remember how slick and wet you were, Miss Dennison."

But this evening he was not talking like a member of the intelligentsia.

Curtly Ardelle returned, "How do you know I was—"

He did not allow her to finish.

"I was inside you," whipped the darkness. "Don't you think a man feels a woman?"

"Yet, Mr. Manning," she sharply riposted, "for a man who has 'felt' me, you seem strangely uncertain as to whether or not I took pleasure in your touch. Are you so certain it is not your memory rather than my person that provided this 'wetness' of which you speak?"

"No."

A harsh sough of air punctuated the taut silence: Dimly Ardelle realized it was her breathing that she heard.

"But neither do I know it is."

"And you want me to prove to you that my body is not affected by your touch."

Her voice was equally harsh.

"Yes."

"So you hoped, by luring me to this room and keeping me here after closing hours, that I would lift my skirts and grant you access to my sex."

"If that's the only way you can prove you do not desire me, yes."

Ardelle struggled to hold back anger. It was emotion that made women weak. But Ardelle was not a weak woman.

"I *told* you I do not—"

Desire was drowned out by hard speculation: "Because I have to wonder, Miss Dennison."

Heart beating against the cage that her corset had inexplicably become, Ardelle asked in the sneer that intimidated men, *all* men, young and old, single and married. "What do you wonder, Mr. Manning?"

"I have to wonder why a woman would take a man into her body if she did not desire him."

"Perhaps I was curious to see how you would compare to my"—she could not stop the biting emphasis—"*former* lover."

"I have to wonder why"—the relentless, driving voice did not falter; it was as if she had not spoken—"in the two years that the Men and Women's Club convened, you attended every single meeting."

"I, too, had an investment in the club," she quickly pointed out.

"I have to wonder why every week you sat *here*, at the head of the table, at my side."

Her breathing quickened. "It was the position we had agreed upon."

"I have to wonder why you voted when I voted," he said, deliberately mocking the words she had earlier spoken, "and abstained when I abstained."

"The other members looked to us for leadership," Ardelle said forcefully, determined to make him listen to her.

But still he did not listen.

"I have to wonder, Miss Dennison, why you are standing here . . . *tonight* . . . in this room . . . if you do not desire to be alone with me."

"You could have made me pregnant!" burst out of her throat.

Pregnant shot up the twenty-foot-long table upon which she had made the sacrifice that had allowed them to similarly use it two years earlier, and at which she had sat every week thereafter. Always beside him. But never with him.

Never a part of his life.

Joseph Manning did not move.

Distant chords sliced through the quivering tension: Westminster Chimes played the half hour.

The shadow of light illuminating the boardroom abruptly faded.

Night would not come at five minutes after the hour of eight, as predicted in the morning paper: It had arrived here, *now*, in this room where it had all started and where tonight it must inevitably end.

Feeling as brittle as the thin metal inserts reinforcing her corset, Ardelle confronted the man for whom she had risked everything, yet who now accused her of stealing from *him*.

"For three weeks I woke up in the grip of a nightmare, unable to breathe for fear I was with child." His sperm had erupted inside her body, filling her womb; emotion, equally dangerous, spewed from her mouth and filled the darkness. "Did you once stop and think about the consequences of that night?"

"I would have married you."

Ardelle could not halt the accusation: "Even though you do not find me worthy?"

The words he had uttered—*I have not found a woman worthy of marriage*—vibrated in the air between them, as if spoken now instead of in the disastrous meeting that had occurred forty-four days past.

Into the throbbing silence dropped the clang of a muffin man.

It was Joseph Manning who spoke first. "Those words were not directed at you."

Ardelle's lips curled in a cynical smile. "Were they not?"

For two years that one illicit night—no, not even a night, their entire affair had started on the strike of the quarter-hour and ended with a half-hour chime—had simmered between them, waiting for this moment of reckoning.

"There are preventive checks," abraded her skin, the darkness a living, breathing entity that would swallow her whole if she did not soon escape.

"I am fully aware of what contraceptives are available," Ardelle countered. "We have discussed them ad nauseam in our meetings. But we didn't use any checks, did we? And what if we had? How many women become pregnant, despite these 'preventive' measures?"

"Nothing is fail-safe," came the harsh response.

As if it were men who paid the consequences of a woman's indiscretion.

"You are a man." Derision spilled from her mouth while injustice squeezed her chest. The darkness that bathed Joseph Manning throbbed in time with the pulse that beat inside her eyes. "A man, I might add, who is chair of Latin at the University of London. Have you given any thought to what position I would now hold, had it been necessary for me to marry?"

Her question was rhetorical. They both knew what would happen were she forced to wed: She would become a wife and mother, with no life outside that of home and children.

It was why they had been subpoenaed: To condemn a forty-nine-year-old widow who had succumbed to the very trap Ardelle had narrowly avoided: marriage, children. Subservience to men. And Ardelle *did* condemn her.

She condemned the widow for having a son. She condemned the widow for suing her son.

All for *sexual* liberation.

"No," pierced the emotion churning her thoughts.

"No?" Ardelle repeated on a sharp intake of breath. "Then let me educate you—"

"No," he reiterated. "It's not pregnancy you fear. You had a lover; you knew the risks. Yet you still took me into your body. Why?"

Memories like kaleidoscopic images flashed before her eyes.

Dripping sweat. Grunting satisfaction.

A deflated rubber condom dangling from a shrunken knob of a penis.

"Why, Mr. Manning, is it so important I take pleasure in your cock?" Ardelle deliberately parried, hurt, and angry, but she could afford to be neither. Yet it seemed she could control neither, drunk on the tension that seemed to grow with every breath they shared, inhaling darkness, expelling pain. "That *is* what they called it during the meeting to which you referred, is it not? A *cock*?" she repeated, vividly recalling the meeting in question. Every obscenity spoken—*diddle, cock, jizzum*—had further alienated Ardelle from the other members, each one of them so painfully innocent in their ignorance.

"Is that how you referred to your former lover's member?" Joseph Manning unexpectedly demanded, focusing on her past rather than the vulgarity with which she had hoped to distract him.

Ardelle swallowed; she had no saliva. "One could wonder, Mr. Manning, about a man who asks for intimate details of a woman's former lover."

"One could wonder, Miss Dennison, about a woman who takes one man merely to compare him to another," momentarily snatched away her breath. "Was your lover the animal to whom you referred?"

Ardelle commanded her lungs to draw in air. "You are strangely obsessed with this lover of mine."

"And you are curiously reticent."

"What shall I tell you?" The darkness burned her eyes, there a sliver of white shirt, there the curve of a shoulder darker than night. "That you compared favorably to him?"

"Did I?"

Ardelle was fast running out of lies.

"I don't remember."

"Did you get wet for him?"

Remembered pain—hard, driving—pierced her pelvis.

"I don't remember."

"Did you unfasten his trousers?"

Ardelle squeezed shut her eyes to block the memory of sausage-like flesh framed by black wool.

"I don't remember."

"Did you reach inside his small clothes and take him into your hands?"

Cold air crawled up her thighs like giant slugs.

"I don't remember."

"Did you steal his virginity, like you stole mine?"

THREE

Ardelle's eyelids jerked open. "I did not steal his virginity."

The sharp report was instantaneous. "Did he steal yours?"

Heart gorging her throat, she tautly asked: "Why are you doing this?"

"I want to know why you—a woman of experience—took me into your body without benefit of a condom."

A fingernail dug into wool, snapped on a wooden button. "Are you concerned my former lover was diseased?"

"I want to know why you wanted sex so desperately you risked pregnancy."

"I did not want sex!" broke free of her too-tight throat.

Instantly he took advantage of her weakness, a sexual man in pursuit rather than a sexless associate in discussion. "What *did* you want?"

A pale glimmer shone through the darkness: A pupil.

It occurred to Ardelle that she, facing the sole window inside the boardroom, was far more visible than Joseph Manning.

"I wanted to feel you inside me," she said tightly.

"You wanted to feel me ejaculate inside you?"

"I thought your pleasure would—"

Ardelle bit her lip to stop the damning words.

"You thought my pleasure would . . . what?" the relentless voice prompted.

A fine tremor started deep inside her stomach, everything she had ever accomplished unraveling in the deepening gloom.

"What did you think to accomplish by making me ejaculate inside you?" he pursued.

"This wouldn't be happening," Ardelle said, forcibly holding on to the disintegrating threads of her life, "if it weren't for that woman."

"Did you think to gain confidence, by demonstrating how powerless you could render me?" Joseph Manning probed.

But she could not answer without destroying that which she had worked so hard to gain.

"I sacrificed every feminine desire," Ardelle said instead. "Every frivolous weakness."

"Did your lover hurt you, and you hoped to take comfort from me?"

There had been no comfort in taking Joseph Manning's sex, only an ache to explore the promise of pleasure too soon ended.

If only the Westminster Chimes had not sounded. If only the footsteps had not approached.

Then perhaps she would not now be "wet," as he had so crudely described her, and wondering what it was she had missed out on.

"When you asked me to help you build a platform on which to hold rational and empirical discussions"—determinedly Ardelle delayed the inevitable; remembered pride swelled her breasts—"for the first time in my life, I felt like a woman who had value."

"Did . . . your . . . *lover* . . . hurt . . . you?" sharply, clearly enunciated the only man Ardelle had ever wanted.

The spark of pride gave way to the coldness of reality.

Joseph Manning wanted the truth, and suddenly, knowing the consequences, Ardelle wanted to give it to him.

"He was not my lover."

The dark silhouette, more felt than seen, remained motionless.

She took a deep, steadying breath; damp, chill air filled her lungs even as her nipples stabbed her chemise. "He was *never* my lover."

"What was he then?"

Ardelle was familiar with vulgar language; no one single word existed to name what she suddenly needed to describe.

"He didn't steal my virginity." The coldness congesting her lungs settled inside her stomach, confessing what she had never before admitted. "I sold it."

"For what?" it skidded down Ardelle's spine.

"For this, Mr. Manning." Both her mirthless smile and her sweeping arms—reticule swinging like a pendulum—were hidden by the pulsing darkness. Or perhaps not. "I sold my virginity to a sweating, grunting pig so I could become publicist to the London Museum."

An electric current of shock rippled the air.

"To Mr. Harmon?"

The kindly, aged curator who called her "a capable woman." But he, too, answered to a greater authority.

"No." Ardelle's vagina burned and stung in denial; there was no denying the truth. "The chairman of the board. I met for an interview, and he wanted me, so I gave him what he wanted. So I could have the position I wanted. I lifted my skirts, and he took me here, in this room, on this table, where I took you."

Disbelief clouded Joseph Manning's voice. "You took my virginity that same day he took yours?"

"I was already the publicist when we met," Ardelle bluntly corrected.

"You took me when he dismissed you as his mistress."

The masculine deduction was no less blunt.

"I wasn't his mistress." The darkness squeezed her chest until she fought to breathe. "I was his whore."

And a whore is exactly how the chairman of the board had treated her. Once monthly for six months she had paid for her success.

"Yes." Her voice tore through the suffocating darkness. "I took you that day he dismissed me, because he took me. He told me to bend over the table, and I did, and he—" Ardelle swallowed air; the memory remained all too vivid. Inanely she repeated, "I wanted to feel you inside me."

" 'Ot pies! . . ." wafted up from the street below; immediately the vendor's cries faded into the whine of carriage wheels, a London constant, hunger and commerce.

"You told her," broke the frigid silence permeating the boardroom. Joseph Manning referred to the woman for whom they had been subpoenaed. "When you were introduced, you said it was because of your position that we were allowed use of this boardroom. But what you really meant to say, is that it was because of your sacrifice."

Ardelle did not pretend to misunderstand. "Yes."

"But she didn't understand."

"But she *should* have understood," Ardelle retorted. The childishness of her accusation singed her ears. More reasonably she added, "She sold her virginity in marriage. She knew the price women pay for position."

Ardelle had convinced herself that she sold no more than what millions of other respectable Englishwomen annually sold. She now knew better.

"But she gave something in return," was the double-edged response.

Protest welled up inside Ardelle; it lodged inside her throat. "Yes."

The widow had given her husband children and had given his children her love.

Now, on the morrow, they would all stand trial at the Old Bailey: Mother, son, and the members of the Men and Women's Club.

And Ardelle could not forgive her.

"Who is the animal?" Joseph Manning abruptly repeated. "You? The chairman of the board? Or me?"

"I don't know what you mean," Ardelle lied, dying a little with each question.

"Is it desire, Miss Dennison, that makes us animals?"

For one paralyzing moment she had the curious sensation of looking down at a man and a woman, two black shades.

"Or is it lack of desire?" Joseph Manning continued, as if each word did not stab her to the very core. "Were you an animal when you lifted your skirts for the chairman of the board?"

Ardelle's broken fingernail ground into the wooden button buried inside worsted wool.

"Or were you an animal when you took my cock into your body?"

"Don't say that word!" escaped her lips before she could swallow the protest.

"Which word?" Joseph relentlessly pursued. "Animal? *Cock?*"

"I am *not* an animal!"

A dull thud of impacting wood vibrated her spine.

"Show me."

The unexpected command was hoarse.

Ardelle hugged her cloak and reticule. "What?"

A chair creaked; simultaneously a shadow that was darker than the pending night stood up. "Bend over this table—where you bent over for him—and show me which of us is the animal."

"Joseph—" His name slipped out unbidden.

"Isn't that why you're here, Ardelle?" Joseph rasped. "To find out which of us three is a sweating, *grunting* animal?"

A low groan wormed through the century-old walls, wood shifting, the past never buried.

"Are you so certain you wish to know?" Ardelle whispered.

There was no hesitation—none of the fear that immobilized Ardelle—inside his voice. "Yes."

"What if that truth, Joseph"—slowly, slowly the noose that

comprised countless lies tightened around Ardelle's throat—"had the ability to destroy your entire life?"

There was no compromise in the harshly grating voice. "I will not allow you to walk away this night."

A distant noise . . . more vibration than sound . . . prickled the blackness that cloaked them. Ardelle recognized it as the first strike of Westminster Chimes.

As a child—on a piano—she had pecked out the notes that every night she lay awake listening to, waiting: *E, C, D, G . . . G, D, E, C . . . E, D, C, G. . . .*

She waited for a fourth bar, followed by nine strikes; it did not come. It was seven forty-five in the evening, not the appointed eight for which she had awaited as a child.

Ardelle looked away from the looming shadow that stood over the table and stared out the window. A pale pink thread dissected the flimsy curtain.

In twenty minutes night would reign, but the sun had not yet set.

She glanced away from the ribbon of hope. Purposefully—stiffening her legs to still their trembling—Ardelle stepped toward the black silhouette that monopolized the end of the conference table.

A medallion-backed chair—no less solid for its invisibility—slammed into her.

Her hands . . . still gripped the reticule and cloak.

Clumsily Ardelle leaned over the chair and dropped the twin leaden weights; a coin bag heavily clanged. Stepping in front of the black shadow, she raised her head and met the pale gleam of impenetrable eyes.

"It was not my intention to cause you pain, Joseph."

Hot, moist breath seared her cheek. "Then take it away, Ardelle."

But some things could not be undone.

Right heel catching in the thick carpet—ankle wobbling, stabilizing—Ardelle turned away.

The twenty-foot-long mahogany table was black with shadow.

For one heart-stopping second, she stared into thirteen pairs of eyes: The pale green eyes of a widow who had not judged her, the hard hazel eyes of a barrister who would question her, the cornflower blue eyes of a woman who had a husband but no son, the gunmetal-gray eyes of Joseph Manning. . . . Her own amber eyes were among them.

She had lied to each and every member of the Men and Women's Club, those eyes said. It was time to face the truth, the amber eyes said.

Between one serrated breath and the next, the ghostly eyes disappeared. Hands trembling, Ardelle grasped cool, unyielding wood and slowly bent over.

There were no rough hands or sudden deluge of coldness; instead there was a slow rise of tickling cloth and cool, spring air.

She closed her eyes against the coming night and waited, breasts flattened, lungs laboring.

"Did he expose you?"

The voice behind her was as rough as unlined wool.

Her fingernails gouged ungiving wood. "Yes."

Slowly the seamless vent in her drawers was peeled back until she was fully revealed to the darkness. Hot, hard hands cupped her naked buttocks—Ardelle forced her body to hold still and not leap off the table as it dictated—and slid downward to the jointure of her thighs.

"Spread your legs."

Ardelle clumsily shifted her weight . . . right leg—her right breast bore into the tabletop—left leg. . . .

Icy air lapped the unprotected lips that suddenly seemed weighted with lead, so full and engorged they would surely burst like overripe fruit.

Forbidden fruit, her parents' pastor would claim.

Unwanted vulnerability washed over her.

She felt young, but she had never been young. She felt innocent, but she had never been innocent.

"Did he touch you?" crowded the darkness of the past.

Hard, hot fingers trailed down the naked crevice between her buttocks.

Remembered sensation superimposed current sensitivity.

Past shame. Present fear.

Mounting desire.

Lightly he grazed the narrow bridge that separated the two exposed orifices.

"Not with his fingers," Ardelle managed to answer, heartbeat accelerating, body straining, memories trickling like tears behind her eyelids.

Thick flesh. Long flesh.

Pulsing.

Piercing.

Pounding.

One man an animal. One man a virgin.

But Joseph was a virgin no more.

Between one short inhalation and the next, the hard, blunt fingertips sank into the moisture she could not hide and plugged up the need she could not deny.

"You're wet."

His voice was flat, closer now than it had been a heartbeat before. It did not sound as if he derived joy in the discovery.

"Yes," she admitted.

"Were you wet from him when you came to me?"

An ache commenced inside Ardelle's breasts—lifting up her torso when she inhaled, lowering it when she exhaled—and spread deep into her chest.

"No."

She did not lie.

A muffled shout wafted up from the street below.

Ardelle braced herself for Joseph's next question.

"You said he didn't touch you."

His fingertips pulsed in time to her heartbeat.

"Yes," she said, breasts rising, falling; vagina contracting, expanding.

"Because he didn't want to"—Joseph's breath was ragged over the pounding of her heart—"or because *you* didn't want him to?"

Cold, hard wood gouged her cheekbone. "Both."

"You didn't want him to touch you," he hoarsely pressed, "here?"

There was no escaping the darkness that writhed behind her eyelids. "No."

Or had she?

Would she ever know the truth?

The fingertips annexing her body trembled.

Joseph had trembled when first she had cradled him between her hands, Ardelle remembered with sudden clarity, and again when she had cradled him deep inside her vagina, sharing the air she breathed, his gray eyes alight as if her sex was a precious gift.

"Do you want *me* to touch you?" he probed with his voice and his fingertips.

The truth.

"No."

Immediately the trembling fingers tensed, poised to give pain instead of pleasure. "What do you want, Ardelle?"

What had Ardelle ever wanted from Joseph Manning?

FOUR

"I want you to fuck me," glanced off the wooden table and slammed into Joseph's face. "Just like he fucked me. With no touching. No gentleness. No sentiment. *That* is what I want, Joseph."

He had asked: She had answered.

Ardelle's vagina—a small fissure buried between slick folds of flesh—throbbed against his fingertips. A matching pulse throbbed inside his testicles.

"You want me to be an animal," Joseph said. "And take you like a whore."

"I am a whore."

The loathing in her voice exacerbated the rawness of his emotions.

Joseph remembered how easily her body had accommodated his sex. Instantly his middle finger was enveloped in liquid heat.

For one heart-pounding second her vagina fluttered around him, as if in welcome; immediately the tiny contractions stilled.

Involuntarily he reached out to find the evading homecoming;

instead he grasped the yielding globe of a buttock. "What are you doing?"

"I'm relaxing my body for you."

As she had relaxed her body for the chairman of the board. An *animal.*

Joseph teetered on the precipice of humanity.

Firmly gripping her left buttock, he deliberately slid free of her body—inwardly crying at the loss of her heat—and sent two blunt fingers deep into her vagina where she had taken another man. For *position.*

A small intake of air pierced the darkness.

He hurt her.

But Joseph didn't want to hurt Ardelle. And knew that he lied to himself.

She had hurt him with her honesty: He wanted to hurt her with his strength.

He wanted to gouge and pound his way into her body and explore every secret inch of her vagina and womb. He wanted to penetrate her so deeply she would never turn to another man.

He wanted to make her ache with the same solitary desire with which he had ached for two years.

And still the heat and the wetness of her squeezed his chest.

Carefully he investigated what felt like a fleshy cap deep inside her body.

The realization of what he touched jolted up his arm.

"This is the opening to your womb," he said rawly.

She involuntarily gripped his fingers.

Her vagina was surprisingly strong.

Instantly her flesh relaxed around him, creating a receptacle rather than a sanctuary.

He had ejaculated against this small, fleshy cap, he thought—stomach knotting, penis flexing—and had not once wondered what would happen if his seed should take root.

But Joseph wondered now.

"Did you not worry that your chairman of the board would make you pregnant?" he asked, and found a tiny heartbeat, *there*, right in the center of the fleshy little dome where Joseph's seed had penetrated.

"He wore a machine."

His ears pricked at the strain in Ardelle's voice, uttering the euphemism for a condom.

"But I didn't," he said hoarsely. Trying to piece together the puzzle that was Ardelle Dennison. Seducer. Associate. *Whore*. Gently he pressed there where her vagina and womb met. His ring finger dug into damp hair and moist, tender skin; it could not be comfortable for her. Quickly he readjusted his position, two fingers becoming three and she did gasp, vagina unabashedly milking his flesh while he pressed deep into her flesh, *lightly* . . . harder . . . lightly . . . harder, needing to know what it was that this woman needed from him. "Did you want my child, Ardelle? Did you want me to give you a child that night?"

"I wanted"—she audibly sucked in air; her buttocks, that had been soft and quiescent, stiffened—"I don't want you to touch me there."

"Why?" Joseph pressed, lightly, *harder*. The fleshy little cap softened against his fingertips, as if inviting him to enter, there where only his seed had ever penetrated. "Does it hurt?"

"Yes," wafted over the never-ending grind of metal-rimmed wheels and cobbled street.

The wetness and the softness of Ardelle's flesh was layer by layer peeling away every emotional barrier with which Joseph had armed himself. "Did he hurt you like this?"

"No."

"But you stole my seed."

"I gave you pleasure," she quickly refuted.

"And he gave you pain."

"Joseph—"

"And that's what you want me to do," he forcefully interrupted, pressing harder, *harder*, deserving more from this woman than an impersonal *fuck*. "You want me to give you pain, so you can prove to yourself that you're not an animal."

"Yes."

Her affirmation throbbed in the darkness. Joseph's cock jerked as if it had a will of its own.

"Then why, Ardelle," he murmured, sex aching, chest hurting, "don't you want me to touch you here"—gently he pressed, soothing as well as arousing—"if it causes you pain?"

"This isn't how it happened," she evaded, pelvis involuntarily arching into his touch.

"How what happened?" Joseph pressed, lightly . . . *harder*.

"When he dismissed me."

"He didn't hurt you here?"

"No."

"Where did he hurt you?"

"You know where."

Images superimposed themselves inside his mind's eye.

Ardelle sitting on the edge of the table, taking Joseph. Ardelle bending over the table, taking the chairman of the board.

"But I want you to tell me," Joseph said. Wanting to work past their anger and their pain. Needing to know how he could reach this woman who by turns spouted polite euphemisms and raw, earthy language. "What did he do to you?"

Her heart beating against his fingertips counted off the passing seconds. His penis pulsed a matching rhythm against the barrier of his small clothes.

He did not think she would answer. Then she did.

"He told me to hold my buttocks open," Ardelle whispered, her confession magnified by bare, glancing wood.

Joseph pictured her buttocks naked underneath the five gaslights suspended over the conference table, her fingers—long, white, beautiful fingers—spreading wide the soft white globes of her flesh.

"Did you?" he prompted, knowing the answer, his fingers sinking more deeply into warm flesh, wet flesh, giving flesh.

"Yes."

"What did he do then?"

"He took me."

Like a whore.

With no touching. No gentleness. No sentiment.

But the pain in her voice had not been caused by the chairman of the board.

"Do you want me to fuck you there, Ardelle?" Joseph whispered, voice so low he could barely hear it over the pounding of his heart. For emphasis he gently pressed against the inner wall of flesh that rhythmically squeezed his fingers. "Is that what you want from me?"

"Yes." Her voice was as taut as her body.

"You want me to hurt you."

"Yes."

"Like he hurt you."

"Yes."

"Because you like to be hurt."

"Yes."

Joseph knew what it was like to crave pain; it was not pain that Ardelle desired.

Without giving himself time to think—no, he'd had two years of thinking, nightly thrashing to ease the flesh that would not be eased—Joseph took back his fingers and his idyllic dreams of simple, normal pleasures.

The audible slurp of hard, masculine flesh withdrawing from the wet, clinging flesh of a woman pierced the night.

Joseph heard it. Ardelle heard it.

Standing upright, he unfastened his bottom trouser button, fingers slippery, carved wood resisting.

Two pale half-moons shone between the double frames of black night and even blacker wool.

"Hold your buttocks open, Ardelle," Joseph said, voice hardening. And freed a second button.

Wool rustled. Wood creaked.

He could more sense than see the hands that reached back to grasp her buttocks. . . . *There,* he could just make out dark lines striating pale, plump mounds.

Joseph imagined Ardelle holding herself open for the chairman of the board.

To be *hurt.*

He unfastened a third button, easier than the first two, each swirl of chill air, each brush of cloth wiping away the warm slipperiness of desire. "I have condoms."

This night he had been prepared.

But she didn't want his protection.

"I don't want you to use a machine."

The coldness inside his chest a discordant contrast to the heat pumping through his sex, he reached through the placket of his wool trousers and into the softer wool of his small clothes. His flesh was hard, familiar; the engorged crown beat to the same rhythm of his heart. Firmly grasping himself—his pubic hair was more crinkly than hers—he stepped closer.

The slick head of his sex skidded off tensed knuckles. Simultaneously the black lines striating the plump half-moons jerked.

Straining to find his way through the darkness, Joseph followed a narrow burrow of ever-widening, ever-deepening dimensions.

He locked his knees, notching puckered flesh.

Emotion bolted through him, touching the only woman he had ever possessed in a place he had never thought to possess.

But still the past stood between them.

"Did you relax your body here"—he pressed into the tight, resistant flesh; it had neither the elasticity nor the wetness of her vagina—"when he touched you with his cock?"

"Yes."

But she was not relaxed for Joseph. Nor was her voice that of a cold, frigid publicist. She spoke with the voice of a woman who teetered on the dark edge of pleasure.

"Did you get wet for him?" Joseph tautly pursued, pressing, lightly, *harder,* lungs expanding, contracting.

"No."

Her denial was too quick.

Joseph had never served as a juror, but he knew that if Ardelle stood in the witness box now, not one man would believe her.

Not the jury. Not the judge.

Not the barristers who would question her. Not the reporters who would print her answers.

"But you desired him," Joseph probed.

"No."

The truth yet not the whole truth.

"But you desired what he did to you," he said inexorably, carefully, relentlessly smearing her body with the liquid heat that flowed from his body.

Her resistant flesh softened, like the little cap annexing her womb.

Joseph bunched his muscles and leaned forward.

Without warning, her flesh opened up—as hot as her vagina, as soft as her vagina, as welcoming as her vagina had been two years earlier—and swallowed whole the turgid, swollen crown that had become the sum of his existence.

"No." There was pleasure as well as pain in the raw, primal cry that pierced the darkness. The black shadow beneath him convulsively arched; he sank into Ardelle so deeply she squeezed his testicles. "I do not desire this!"

The pulsing heat surrounding him said differently.

Sweat stinging his forehead, Joseph leaned over and roughly worked his hands between wood and wool, digging deeper . . . his hands, his cock . . . until he anchored the taut, rounded curve of a stomach with his left palm. With his right hand he found her sex. She was wet and slick and open, everything he had ever wanted. Feeding her three fingers—the hard bulk of his cock crowded his knuckles—he whispered into her ear, "I think you're lying, Ardelle."

"No." She struggled, trapped, her hands caught between their bodies. Fine hair tickled his nose; it smelled of ginger, Ardelle's scent. The hard hump of a bustle and wadded wool dug into his stomach. "Why would I lie?"

For the same reason Joseph had lied to himself, trying to be what he was not.

"I think you got wet for your chairman." He pushed his fingers more deeply inside her . . . deep . . . deeper yet until his wrist worked apart slippery lips and he could feel a hardness pulsing against the veins that fed his fingers while a matching hardness hammered his knuckles. "As wet for him as you are for me."

"You don't know," was her muffled response, head rearing back so that his forehead abutted warm, silky hair and prickly pins.

But he did.

"I think"—Joseph pressed the little cap hidden deep inside her vagina, a woman's private place: lightly . . . *harder,* matching the pulsating rhythm that seared his wrist and his knuckles—"you got wet because you wanted to be touched."

"How do you know . . ." Every shuddering breath, every squirm of her hips implanted him more deeply between her buttocks and her thighs, forcing him to ride her while the little mound that was as stiff and erect as his sex rode his wrist. ". . . what I want?"

How could a man whose only knowledge of sex came from books and their one brief affair—a night in which they did not even exchange a simple kiss—possibly know a woman's secrets?

"I think"—Joseph pressed lightly . . . *harder* . . . needing to reach that place where innocence was born—"when the chairman took you that last time, you thought about me."

"You don't know that," Ardelle retorted, buttocks rising when he descended, table groaning with their combined weight.

"I think, Ardelle, that for two years you've wanted me here"—Joseph thrust as deeply as he could reach with his cock—"just as you wanted me"—he circled the fleshy little cap, pressing, *lightly*, harder—*"here."*

"No." A fine thread of tension coiled deep inside Ardelle's body, there against the tiny opening to her womb, a tension that reso-nated inside his very marrow. "I do not want you like this. I have never wanted you like this!"

"Like what, Ardelle?" Joseph pressed his fingers and his cock, left hand curving around her lower abdomen to shield her from the man he was and the pain he would inevitably bring: with touch, with gentleness, with sentiment. "You didn't want me to fuck you this hard?" He reached higher up inside her; impossibly her body stretched to accommodate him. "You didn't want me to fuck you this deeply?"

A short gasp skidded across the table. "This isn't love."

Her fisting flesh squeezed his chest. "Do you love me, Ar-delle?"

"I can't love you."

With each rhythmical press . . . with each rasping breath . . . with each creak of protesting wood . . . the distance between their two bodies narrowed until only a thin membrane separated them.

"Why not?" Joseph's testicles tightened; a familiar burn inched up the base of his spine. "Why can't you love me?"

"I can't love any man."

"Because we're animals?" he pressed. Heart pounding against his fingertips, knuckles, and wrist.

"You're not an animal."

"Is your chairman an animal?" he pushed more deeply.

"He's not my chairman." She pushed back, taking him more deeply.

"But is he the animal?"

Ardelle struggled to take more fingers. More cock. "No."

Joseph struggled to give her more fingers. More cock. Testicles tightening. Sperm readying. "Who's the animal, Ardelle?"

FIVE

"**M**y *father*!" pinned Ardelle to the table.

For long seconds she could not breathe for the fingers and the male appendage that stuffed her, and the heavy weight that bore her down into the unforgiving truth.

Between one heartbeat and the next, a deep groan split the night, and scalding liquid spurt deep into her body. She could not stop the fist that her vagina independently became. Milking the fingers that gorged it. Buttocks lifting high, higher to take a second . . . third . . . fourth jet of sperm while her womb contracted—bearing down as if to allow entrance to the pushing, prodding fingertips—and a thin cry of agony ripped free of her chest.

For an infinitesimal moment she flew high above the two black shadows that had, impossibly, become one; the next moment she plummeted downward and could not breathe for the reality that was Joseph Manning.

Hot, gusting breath feathered her throat above a tight, banding collar.

Ardelle squeezed her eyes shut to block her confession: *Father* continued to reverberate inside her ears.

Faint, familiar chimes infiltrated the boardroom: *C, E, D, G . . . C, D, E, C . . . E, C, D, G . . . G, D, E, C. Bong . . . Bong . . . Bong. . . .*

With each distant, vibrating bong, Joseph shrank until the long, thick flesh piercing her heart became a soft bud needing her protection.

"It's eight o'clock," Ardelle whispered, opening her eyes. Unable to hold back the past.

The rasping sough of breathing filled the silence.

His. Hers.

"My father is the animal," she repeated, accepting what the widow—with her uncomplicated desires—had forced her to acknowledge.

The muted whine of carriage wheels underscored each gasping hitch . . . each slowing outtake . . . of air.

"I didn't understand." Hot moisture slid down her temple, pooled underneath her arms and breasts, trickled from her vagina. "I was 'Papa's girl.' Every day he brought me gifts and hid them in his desk. Every night I slipped down to his office, clad in my nightgown, and sat on his lap. He wiggled until his face turned red and his breathing quickened." The memory of noisy, labored breathing superimposed the hot bursts of air that branded her neck. "I laughed, thinking it a game. And that was how she caught us."

"Who?" penetrated starch, cotton, and flesh.

An ache that had nothing to do with the weight of Joseph or the hardness of wood permeated Ardelle's breasts.

"My mother."

"How old were you?"

"I don't remember." Ardelle did not lie. "Six, I think."

The fluted fingers filling her vagina flexed. "What did she do?"

Ardelle gripped his fingers. "Nothing."

Through the eyes of a child, she had done nothing.

The past juxtaposed the darkness.

"'Mama, look at Papa!'" Ardelle whispered. "'Isn't he funny?' I asked. My mother and father looked at each other until their silence killed my laughter. The Westminster Chimes played, such a pretty sound. Big Ben struck the hour . . . eight bongs . . . and they still stared at each other. I remember thinking they looked like cardboard dolls, with Papa's rouged face and Mama's pretty blue dress."

Warm fingers cradled her lower abdomen. Hot, moist air caressed her neck. "Did he touch you?"

But Ardelle was not yet ready to answer that question.

"I was never alone with my father after that," she continued, as if Joseph had not spoken. "But I wanted to be. I wanted him to hug me, to kiss me. I wanted to sit on his lap and watch his face turn red. I wanted the little gifts he brought me. I wanted my father's love. And my mother knew it. She brought him to my room. Always at eight. He would stare down at the floor—never once did he look at me—and bid me good night. But she looked at me. She stared at the disappointment on my face, that he did not hug and kiss me. Every night she brought him to my room, until I understood what had happened when he wiggled underneath me. Then she brought him to my room, to punish me."

The bittersweet aftermath of orgasm flooded Ardelle.

"I wish he had touched me," she said into the cold press of wood. "I wish he had hurt me, because then I wouldn't yearn for the love I had felt, sitting on his lap. I wouldn't wonder—when you touch me, Joseph—if *this*"—she squeezed his fingers and his penis—"is what I secretly wanted from my father."

"Ardelle." Her name was a warm sigh.

"I understand your natural disgust." The heavy weight pinning her to the table suddenly shifted. Simultaneously the fingers filling her and the soft bud nestling inside her jiggled. Ardelle wriggled free her hands—fingers stiff from being trapped between their bodies—and grasped at his hips that lifted to give her freedom. "But please don't leave me."

Not now. Not when she was at her most exposed.

Instantly the heavy weight settled, blunt fingertips shielding her womb while the soft, nestling bud plugged up the warm fluid it had jetted deep inside her. "I don't want to hurt you."

Even though she wanted him to do just that.

"You're not," she said, and swallowed past the lump inside her throat.

She had not once cried during those long years of nightly visitations. She would not cry now, discussing a past she could not change.

Gently Joseph traced her cervix. "You're not a whore, Ardelle."

The tenderness that flooded Ardelle was far more painful than any physical hurt.

Flattening her palms against the conference table where she had sold her virginity for position and had then stolen Joseph's virginity for recompense, she closed her eyes against prickling tears. "I know what I am, Joseph."

"What are you?"

"I am a frigid bitch." Ardelle repeated the words she had frequently overheard, and in which she had even taken pride. "I don't think I'm capable of love."

"I don't know if any man or woman is truly capable of love." Gently, gently Joseph teased the tiny opening deep inside her body. "But when I touch you here, I feel that it is possible."

"What about"—Ardelle involuntarily squeezed her buttocks; the bud of flesh instantly expanded in girth—"*here?*"

He buried his face into her neck, cheeks surprisingly bristly, there above her collar. "You didn't want me to touch you there."

"But you gave me your sperm."

"I gave you my sperm two years ago."

The memory of his essence spurting deep against her cervix clenched her womb.

Joseph pressed and prodded, as if he could feel the deep contraction. "Did you want my child, Ardelle?"

Scalding fluid trickled down her temple and leaked onto the wooden table. "Yes."

She had wanted something that had not been corrupted by animal lust.

The rise and fall of his chest rhythmically pressed her breasts into the hard, unyielding table that had witnessed the loss of their innocence. "Did you wake up in the middle of the night, afraid you did not conceive?"

For three weeks she had slept with her hands cradling her stomach, clinging to hope.

"I realized," Ardelle said, each breath, each word jostling anew the flesh that filled her, "when I started my courses, that having your child would not change who I am."

The singsong career of wafting carriage wheels and the reverberating creaks of the aging museum filled the silence.

"When I was sent away to school, a don there liked to discipline young boys," abruptly broke the bittersweet serenity that surrounded them. The fingers inside her tensed, as if expecting to be expelled. "He came to our dormitory one night—there were five of us—and ordered us to drop our trousers and peel down our drawers. And we did, because we were ashamed and frightened and did not have the authority to protest. He went down the row, paddling each one of us until we grew hard and erect. 'My little peckers,' he called us.

"When he finished, we pulled up our clothes and got ready for bed. We could not look each other in the eyes, for what had been done to us. In bed, my penis—which I had never before paid much attention to—burned and ached so dreadfully I couldn't leave it alone. When I ejaculated, I felt both relief and terror. Relieved that the throbbing pain had abated, but afraid I would be discovered abusing myself. The next morning the dorm smelled faintly like green chestnuts. I realized each one of us had masturbated."

Ardelle stared at the darkness, night now instead of twilight. "How old were you?"

"Eleven."

She tried to remember when she had first started counting the Westminster Chimes—that day she had realized *why* her father turned red and breathed hard when she sat on his lap—and could not.

"The don came the next night." Joseph's voice drew her from the past. It was removed, as if his childhood belonged to someone else. "And the next. And the next. Each night we crawled into our narrow little cots and frantically worked our flesh. After awhile we didn't even bother holding back little grunts and groans when we ejaculated. Some nights the don didn't come. I still worked my flesh, but the release wasn't as pleasurable. I liked the pain, Ardelle. I liked how stiff it made my 'little' pecker. I liked how with each paddle my bum swelled and my testicles tightened. By the end of term, the mere sight of the paddle was enough to make me erect."

Ardelle squeezed his fingers and his penis, the only comfort she could give him.

"We did not discuss it, the other boys and I," Joseph said into her neck, words hot and moist, through her collar, above her collar, "not in private, certainly not in public."

Sudden insight illuminated the blackness veiling the boardroom. "And so you thought to create a club for men and women, where such things could be discussed."

"Yes."

"But we did not encourage personal exchanges," Ardelle said.

"Because we did not confront our own desires," Joseph agreed, voice blunted by starched cotton.

But exactly what did they desire?

"I don't think"—Ardelle swallowed—"they would understand my actions."

"I think Mr. Stiles would stare at his drawing pad and say that men who take women for no other purpose than to satisfy their own selfish needs are the whores, not the women who grant them release."

For one fleeting second Ardelle saw the architect's electric blue-green eyes; instantly they winked back into the inky blackness of night.

The faint smile that touched her lips vanished just as quickly.

"And what would he say about the fact that I still live at home with the father who lusted for me and the mother who punished me for his lust?"

"He would say that it is now you who punish yourself."

"And my father," Ardelle realized. Paying for every bauble she had ever wanted. The price for her silence. "And my mother."

The pink ribbon that had been the sun shone no more.

"I *did* desire what the chairman did, Joseph."

"And I still get hard when I remember the pain, Ardelle."

"But pain didn't touch me."

Each time the chairman withdrew from her body she had been as cold as before he entered her.

"But I did," reverberated deep inside her body, an ache that was both pleasurable and painful.

"What do you fear, Joseph?" Ardelle whispered, squeezing his fingers and his penis, hands clenching against unforgiving wood. "Pain or pleasure?"

His fingers curved to fit her stomach on the outside; inside he prodded her cervix, there where he had planted the seed that her womb had rejected. "Being alone."

Ardelle forced her body to hold still for his exploration instead of pushing him away out of fear as she had done two years earlier. "Do you have family?"

They had discussed their goals and ambitions for the Men and Women's Club, but they had never broached personal matters.

"My family is best left undiscussed."

Ardelle's breath quickened, from him, *for* him. "Why?"

"My parents are more concerned about the appearance of a family than they are about the welfare of children."

Slowly, carefully, she asked, "Did they hurt you?"

No childhood pain lingered in his voice. "They, like many parents, believe children should neither be seen nor heard. I and my sisters were shipped off to school as soon as humanly possible."

But school had not protected him from hurt.

Her throat tightened. "I will lose my position."

Joseph's fingers curled around her womb, *inside,* outside.

Ardelle knew that he, too, would lose his position at the university.

After the trial, they would no longer be deemed respectable in a society that prized the illusion of respectability above all else.

Regret sliced through her. "This is the last time we will have use of this room."

"There will be no more club meetings regardless."

Ardelle squeezed her vagina in protest. "Why?"

"They don't need us."

His words throbbed deep inside her.

Ardelle remembered the intimacies exchanged between the members of the Men and Women's Club during the last four meetings—the fears, the secret desires—while she and Joseph looked on. Denying their own fears. Hiding away their own desires.

But one woman had seen both Ardelle's fear and her desire.

Suddenly the night was clear.

"A license to sin," Ardelle said.

The sex that plugged up her body flexed, growing harder. "What?"

"*Vive memor leti.*" Ardelle repeated the Latin phrase he had greeted her with an hour earlier. "I grant you a license to sin, Joseph."

The body blanketing her suddenly tensed, fingers crowding, penis elongating. "And you, Ardelle?"

SIX

"I grant myself the same license," Ardelle said.

"And tomorrow?" gusted hot and moist into her ear.

Tomorrow they would stand in a witness box and testify against a widow whom every decent, law-abiding man and woman would condemn.

"I don't know what will happen on the morrow."

Without warning, the fingers and the sex that held the future at bay withdrew.

Ardelle had never felt so cold. A cold that not even the *swooshing* fall of wool petticoats, bustle, and skirts could block.

Shakily—breasts slowly reforming into their natural shape instead of the squashed mounds the table and their combined weight had made of them—Ardelle straightened. Her breath caught in her throat.

"What is it?" sharply pelted her.

"You," Ardelle said unevenly. "I need to attend to personal matters."

"I need to wash up, too."

The street lamps below faintly shone on the ceiling; they did not provide any useful light.

"There are candles in the credenza," Ardelle offered. She had been headed in that direction—to procure safety matches to light the overhead chandelier—when Joseph had spoken. "I'll get them."

With each step she took, Ardelle felt as if her body were dissolving. Everywhere he had penetrated her, she was wet. Naked.

Vulnerable.

Fingers shaking, she struck a small, thin stick against the side of a metal box. Blue light flared, instantly turned to yellow.

Joseph stood beside her; his semihard sex protruded from his trousers.

Would he still desire her come the morrow? she wondered on a small catch of oxygen.

Leaning down, Joseph grabbed a candle from the opened drawer; straightening, face darkly lit by dancing fire, he stuck the wick to the burning match.

Dual flames leapt up, bounced off a thin mustache and short black hair.

Intimacy had been so much easier in the blackness of night, Ardelle thought, when they had been ignorant of each other's past.

Heat seared her skin; immediately it was soothed by a hot gust of moist air.

Joseph blew out the match that flamed dangerously close to her pinched fingers. Silently he took the smoking, blackened stick.

His fingers were sticky . . . from *her,* she realized, pupils dilating.

Scooping up her cloak and reticule off the twenty-foot-long mahogany table, Ardelle walked out of the room that had borne so many dreams and destroyed so many lives.

The corridor was a windowless pit. Each step she took was preceded by a black shadow cast from the burning candle held high behind her.

The lavatory was as dark as the corridor.

When Joseph followed her into the small, private facility, her heart threatened to leap out of her chest.

He wore a dark gray bowler hat; his gray wool coat dangled over his arm.

While she had stepped through the doorway—leaving the boardroom—he had veered to grab his hat and coat off the brass coat tree.

Still without talking, the brim of his hat hiding his eyes, he tilted the candle. Hot wax spilled onto veined marble; adeptly Joseph set the candle into the cooling wax.

Ardelle hooked her cloak and reticule over the doorknob. Joseph took off his hat and hung it and his coat on the brass hook behind the door.

Unwittingly she gazed at shadow-shrouded memories.

She had ordered the cream-colored soap that matched the veins striating the dark blue marble counter. She had chosen the porcelain commode—Joseph lifted up the seat; the toilet flushed—so that no customer would be knocked in the head by a swinging pull.

Liquid splattered liquid.

Heat stained her cheek.

She had taken two men into her body, but she had never before witnessed a man using the lavatory.

Hurriedly Ardelle swirled around in a flurry of petticoats and skirt and grabbed off the marble countertop a neatly folded linen towel.

But Joseph was suddenly there, standing in front of the cabinet. He twisted a brass and enamel faucet. Steam roiled up from the primrose-patterned basin. He lathered his hands and impersonally washed the flesh she could still feel deep inside her body.

The shaft was lined with blue veins. He peeled back the foreskin that semicovered a purplish-hued crown.

"Have you told the university?" she asked over the pounding gush of water.

Carefully he rinsed off the clouds of soap before answering, "No." Turning, water dripping from his fingers and his sex, he asked, "Have you told Mr. Harmon?"

Hesitantly Ardelle cupped his penis through the folds of the towel and dried him. "No."

He would learn soon enough about the trial.

"Your family?"

Deliberately she concentrated on the fluid that leaked out of his hardening sex. No matter how thoroughly she dried the tiny ure-thra, it continued to leak a clear, thin stream of lubrication.

"I do not discuss my affairs with my parents," she said over the falling drum of water.

"When do they expect you home?"

"Whenever I arrive."

One moment she was busily drying him, the next moment the towel was tugged from her hands.

Joseph wet the linen and wrung it dry, water like diamonds dripping through his fingers. Twisting off the faucet, he purpose-fully turned to face her. "Lean over the sink and I'll wash you."

"That isn't necessary."

"But it is, Ardelle." There was no degrading lust inside his eyes, only honest need and masculine curiosity. "I want to see you."

Forgotten emotion twisted deep inside her.

He knew the sins of her past, yet he did not turn away from her.

"What do you see in me, Joseph?" she whispered.

Flickering shadow danced around the twin bands of his gray irises. "I see a woman who is afraid to hope."

"What did you see two years ago?"

"A woman who was not afraid to take what she wanted."

Ardelle—both fearful and hopeful—could no longer meet the honesty inside his eyes. She turned around and leaned over the primrose-patterned basin, arms bracing her torso. An amber-eyed woman with straggling brown hair topped by a black felt hat and wilting ostrich feather watched her inside the steam-misted mirror.

Many claimed the woman was beautiful; Ardelle had never seen beauty in her reflection.

The candle to her left alternately flamed and cringed at the chill draft that crawled up her thighs. Goosebumps marched across her exposed buttocks.

Cold amber eyes watched Ardelle's every reaction.

The bowed head that topped her own suddenly dropped out of the mirror.

Hot breath serrated her icy flesh. "I dream of you."

Warm, wet fingers drew apart her buttocks. Cool air was chased by the touch of moist, warm linen.

"Are they pleasant dreams?" she asked.

Water crawled down her left buttock.

Ardelle's muscles involuntarily clenched.

A towel-tipped finger gently cleansed her, there where she had opened herself to the darkness. "Sometimes."

Hot, moist flesh—his tongue—licked off the droplet of water that dripped down her left cheek.

Sympathetic moisture dribbled down Ardelle's thighs.

And still the woman in the mirror watched her.

No desire shone inside the cold amber eyes.

"And when they're not?" Ardelle asked.

The flesh he held open snapped together.

"Spread your legs."

Arms straining, Ardelle spread her legs.

Bare fingers glided between her buttocks . . . slid past her empty vagina.

Moist heat seared her thigh. "*Kleitoris*"—a blunt finger found her clitoris—"is Greek, while vagina is of Latin origin."

Ardelle knew the basic rudiments of Latin; she did not know Greek at all.

Warm lips grazed her left buttock. "When the dreams are not pleasant, I pump my cock and pretend my hand is your body. Do you touch yourself?"

"I try not to," Ardelle said, voice remote, staring into those cold amber eyes.

Joseph explored the folds of her clitoris as thoroughly as he had explored her cervix, weighing it against his palm, pinching it between his fingers—Ardelle's breath hitched inside her throat; the woman in the mirror remained stoic—circling the very tip with the tips of his fingers. "But you do."

"Occasionally."

When her flesh would not lie quiescent, despite the long hours she worked each day.

"It shames you." A slow, burning sensation crawled up her clitoris to her spine. "Do you think of your father when you touch yourself?"

Ardelle jerked. "No."

"*Vive memor leti,* Ardelle."

A warning. A license.

Just when the hardened bud of her clitoris leapt against his fingertip, Joseph stood.

Chill air unwarmed by his breath bathed her.

He dropped the damp linen into a wicker basket.

Scratchy wool abruptly abraded her buttocks. Inside the mirror, gunmetal-gray eyes snared the cold amber eyes.

"Tonight there's no need to lie," Joseph said. Leaning forward, he slipped his left hand underneath the heavy woolen skirts. A hard, warm palm fanned her lower abdomen at the same time that sharp knuckles brushed her buttocks.

A blunt instrument nudged her vagina.

Ardelle sharply inhaled. And instinctively tightened her muscles. "You're wearing a machine."

The head of his penis had felt large in the dark; in the flickering light it felt as big as a fist.

"Look at me," he said.

"I am looking at you," Ardelle returned, breath quickening.

She forgot to breathe when the thick knob of flesh squeezed past her clenched muscles.

Thicker than his fingers.

Ardelle involuntarily tilted her pelvis.

Longer than his fingers.

The gray eyes watched the amber-eyed face in the mirror, searching for Ardelle knew not what. "You let the chairman do whatever he wished."

Ardelle gripped cold marble; it did not stop the slow retreat of the large, thick stalk that was his penis.

"Yes."

"Will you let me do anything I wish?"

The long column of flesh reversed, tunneling into her so deeply it crowded her cervix to the point of pain.

"Yes."

She did not remember him being this large two years earlier.

But she had not wanted to remember the night that had proven she was not indifferent to desire.

The long, thick flesh slowly withdrew; her vagina collapsed behind it, inch by inch.

"Did you enjoy my cock inside your bum?"

The impossibly large crown hovered there at the opening to her vagina, not quite in, but not quite out.

"Yes."

"Did it burn dreadfully?"

The gray eyes in the mirror were older than time.

"It still burns," she admitted.

"Did it make your clitoris hard?"

"Yes."

He pressed against her lower abdomen, compressing her flesh. At the same time, he thrust forward, forcing open the collapsed walls of her vagina.

Heat flashed up her spine.

Thick lashes and flickering flame shadowed his face.

"Does this make your clitoris hard?"

The five fingers fanning her abdomen pulsed in time to the fist-sized flesh gouging her cervix.

"Touch it," she said, voice strangely hoarse, "and see."

The thick dark lashes lifted; the thin band of gray had been swallowed by the black of his pupils.

He held her gaze. Left hand sliding round the curve of her hip. Fingers combing through damp pubic hair. Reaching lower. Finding her. Swollen.

Hard.

"My cock wasn't much larger than your clitoris." His shadowed face briefly contorted with pain. Gently he grasped the engorged little bud that pulsed and throbbed against his fingertips as if preparing to ejaculate. "I was afraid I wouldn't be able to get hard for a woman. That I would only be able to enjoy sex if a man paddled me."

The tightening of her vagina and buttocks spread to Ardelle's chest.

"But when I took you into my hands," she said, "you got hard."

The spasm of pain passed from his face; it lingered inside his eyes. "Yes."

"And then I took you into my vagina," Ardelle continued, body crying for the pain she had inadvertently caused. Because of her past. "And we both took pleasure."

"But I thought I disappointed you."

Because of his past.

Slowly, inch by inch, the hard flesh gorging her slid free; his right hand pressed her stomach inward, aiding the collapse of her squeezing flesh.

He paused just a heartbeat inside her vagina, eyes alternately gray then black in the flickering candlelight.

Wanting. But afraid to want.

"Make me burn, Joseph, like you burned," she said, bracing herself. And did not know if she braced herself against pain or pleasure. "Make my clitoris harder."

As he had been made to get hard.

Joseph gave her every inch of his penis.

Hard. Thrusting. Groin pounding her buttocks while he worked her clitoris as if it were a little cock, *his* cock.

Squeezing. Pulling.

Pounding. Pushing.

Hurting. Pleasuring.

Neither of them responsible for the past that had shaped their desires.

"Look at me, Ardelle."

A red aura surrounded the flickering eyes.

Ardelle studied the peculiar phenomenon.

With each grinding thrust of his penis—with each scalding arch of sensation—the red aura hazing his eyes spread. Painting taut cheekbones. Combing through a thin, dark mustache. Flirting with a chiseled top lip. Kissing a generous bottom lip. Caressing a shadowed chin . . .

A surge of pure, unadulterated heat blocked the watching eyes.

Her body contracted: womb, vagina, buttocks, clitoris, breasts, *lungs*.

Massaging fingers pulled her back from the dark abyss of pleasure.

Slowly, struggling for oxygen, Ardelle opened her eyelids.

Gray eyes caught her gaze. They were curiously tense.

"Who did you see in the mirror, Ardelle?"

Warmth flowed from the hand that massaged her abdomen. Tiny ripples of heat continued to arc from his depleting penis.

The strength that orgasm had stolen surged through her anew.

"You, Joseph." Ardelle stared into his gray eyes. And realized she had not once thought of her father when Joseph filled her. "I see you."

The flickering light shadowed his face. "You didn't come when you took my sperm."

The past.

"But I"—she gulped chill air—"came now."

The present.

The light in his eyes nearly blinded her.

"I don't think either of us are virgins," she said unsteadily.

Burning. Aching.

Vagina yawning. Buttocks throbbing.

There was no regret in either his eyes or his voice. "No, we're not."

Impulsively she asked, "What do you think they would say if they knew how we had used the conference table?"

"I think they would say it was a fitting finale." Joseph slowly lowered his lashes—the woman in Ardelle briefly envied their thickness—and gently pressed her abdomen, low where he was still lodged inside her, rubber housing his sperm.

Fleeting regret gripped her, for the child she had not conceived.

The thick black lashes abruptly lifted. "Will you come home with me?"

SEVEN

"We've never been together outside the museum."
    "Are you frightened?"
Ardelle clinched her vagina to keep his penis from leaving her. "Yes."

Head bending—she lost both his penis as well as the band of his fingers—Joseph stepped back. Heavy wool promptly cascaded down her buttocks.

A shiny, crumpled condom dropped into the wicker basket.

Briefly she wondered what the cleaning lady would think when next she collected the soiled towels.

Ardelle twisted the brass water faucets and stepped aside.

Water gushed. Steam rose.

Carefully Joseph lathered his penis. Dark head straightening, he met her observing gaze. "Is your hair salvageable?"

"Oh." Ardelle involuntarily raised her hands. "Of course."

Standing beside him—fresh, hot mist steaming the mirror—she deftly pushed back tangled hair and secured it underneath wire pins.

Joseph twisted off the faucets. Ardelle froze, arms poised in the air.

"What?" Joseph alertly asked.

"My eyes."

"What about them?"

Ardelle stared at her amber eyes through the gently wafting steam. "They're not cold."

"Should they be?"

She caught his watchful gaze inside the mirror. "Ever since I realized what it was that my father took pleasure in, Joseph, I've been cold."

So cold.

But now she was warm and that was more frightening than the cold.

Certainly less familiar.

There was no light inside the shadow-blackened eyes. Once again he asked, "Will you come home with me?"

Heart skipping a beat, Ardelle dropped her arms. "Yes."

Joseph plucked another linen towel off the counter and dried his penis.

Impulsively she turned and reached for him.

His penis was warm and soft, slightly damp. A tiny vein pulsed in the deflated shaft.

Carefully she tucked him back inside the dark placket of his trousers . . . the woolen undergarments that were almost as soft as his penis . . . and buttoned up the gray trousers.

"I'm glad it was me who took your virginity," she said.

Out of the corner of her eye, she glimpsed the ascending gray wool of a sleeve; immediately warm fingers more firmly pushed a strand of hair underneath a sharp hairpin.

"So am I." The hand dropped. "Shall we take the lift?"

Ardelle thought of the kindly curator who had preceded them. And blinked back sudden tears.

"Yes, please."

She grabbed her cloak and reticule. He grabbed his bowler hat and coat.

It took long minutes for the lift to rise, the grind and clang of weights and counterweights overly loud in the empty museum while the single candle valiantly battled stygian darkness.

The notching clank of the metal cage scraped her spine.

It should not be possible to be darker than an unlit, windowless corridor; the elevator was.

Ardelle took the candle Joseph offered and stepped inside the metal cage. The flame flared, first when Joseph followed her, and again when he slammed shut the iron gate.

Stomach dropping with the abrupt descent, Ardelle asked: "Do you regret we didn't go with them to the book shop?"

Metal clanked; the solid cage shuddered.

Throwing open the gate, Joseph stepped back for Ardelle to precede him. "I've been to many such shops."

Street lights shone through the glass that comprised the front of the museum.

She stepped out of the elevator into flickering shadows. "But you don't think them suitable for a woman to visit."

Her voice sharply echoed in the cavernous gallery.

"I didn't," followed her, caught up with her.

Candlelight glanced off a suit of armor.

"And now?"

"I think there are many objects that can enhance both a man and a woman's pleasure."

A Roman sarcophagus swallowed flaring light.

"You have these objects," Ardelle asked, head straight, heart pounding, "at your home?"

"Yes."

The ache deep inside her vagina and between her buttocks throbbed.

They had both lied about so many things.

"Do you have a leather phallus?"

A shadow-blackened fossil loomed ahead of them.

"Yes."

Ardelle veered off the main floor into an anteroom, heel taps sharp. "Are you sorry I wasn't a virgin?"

"No."

The side door she sought loomed ahead of them.

"Why?"

"Because you would not have touched me." His voice and his heel taps rang out in the chill air. "And I would still be afraid."

That he wouldn't be able to get hard for a woman.

Ardelle stopped in front of the side door. She would *not* turn around. "You more than satisfy me, Joseph."

"You don't find me too small?" Joseph asked flatly.

The voice of an injured child.

Ardelle turned around. The dull throb between her buttocks corroborated: "Be assured, sir, your 'pecker' is not little."

A fleeting smile crossed his lips. "I'm glad my dimensions do not disappoint you."

But it wasn't his size that caused his fear.

Ardelle took a deep breath. "I'm not afraid of pain, Joseph."

Hot wax dripped onto her fingers.

Ardelle forced herself not to flinch.

Silently he took the candle.

Hot wax dripped onto his long, masculine fingers.

Joseph did not flinch.

"The key, Ardelle."

Legs suddenly trembling, Ardelle searched inside her reticule.

She would not regret this night with Joseph.

Ardelle fitted the key into the lock.

The alley was dark. Bristling atop a metal garbage bin, a cat made gray by darkness hissed a warning.

Joseph pinched out the flickering candle flame. Ardelle shut the door and turned the lock.

Without giving herself time to reconsider, she slid the key underneath the door.

The weight of her position—the first female publicist for the London Museum—immediately lifted.

Ardelle turned to the silent shadow that throbbed with sexuality, a man *and* an advocate. Impulsively she said, "Do you know, Joseph, a man who gets erect at the sight of a paddle would have certain benefits."

Hot, hard fingers cupped her cheeks and lifted her face upward. "Why?"

You'll be prepared whenever I want you caught inside her throat.

Underneath the brim of his hat, a pale beam of light fingered a taut cheek bone, defined a black mustache.

"I don't know how to kiss," she whispered.

Her father had kissed her, innocent closed-mouth kisses. But there had been nothing innocent about her father.

"Neither do I," gusted warm and moist against her cheek.

But he did.

His lips were softer than hers. Lightly they flitted, as if searching for a place to settle. A sigh feathered her nose. The next instant her breath was sucked out of her lungs.

Instinctively she opened her mouth to the scalding press of a tongue.

He tasted hot and wet, with a flavor that eluded identification.

Lifting her arms to bring him closer . . . *closer*—briefly Ardelle registered the reticule that slammed into his back—she recognized the taste: It was Joseph, the man who knew what she was and did not condemn her.

"Thank you," she whispered into his mouth.

"For what?" he whispered back.

Bringing around her hands—the reticule a bumping hindrance—she cupped his face; stubble prickled her fingers. "For this night."

"But the night's not over."

"No." She inexpertly kissed his lips, noses colliding before finding his lips again. They clung to hers, stealing away a nervous bubble of laughter. Slowly Ardelle pulled back; his hands dropped away from her face. "No," she repeated breathlessly, "the night is not over."

The fingers that had mapped the entrance to her cervix suddenly grasped her hand.

The heat of his flesh squeezed her chest.

Her father had held her hand, meeting her at the door to his office and leading her to his desk.

But Joseph was not her father.

Ardelle forcibly relaxed. "There's a chemist around the corner."

JOSEPH took the rubber bag and nozzle from Ardelle's hands. Inquisitively he glanced down at her. "What is it?"

A sharp, cranky cry drifted from the back of the chemist.

Ardelle's womb ached in sympathy.

"A douche," she said.

"Shh . . ." wafted after the baby's cries. "Mama's here. Shh . . . Here we go. . . . That's right. . . . Take a bit o' tit, now."

Comprehension dilated Joseph's pupils until all Ardelle could see were two black orbs and a tiny reflection of a woman with warm amber eyes. "A condom is more effective."

" 'Nothing is failsafe,' " Ardelle quoted.

"Are ye about done out there?" the fretful mother asked. "It's past closing. I've a baby to tend. . . ."

"We're ready," Ardelle called out.

Expression unreadable, Joseph carried the douche to the front while Ardelle made a cursory inspection of the bottles lining the tiny shop. A vinegar label snared her gaze.

The woman—not much younger than Ardelle—came through the curtained doorway at the same time that Ardelle placed the bottle beside the syringe. A blanket covered the nursing baby; it did not hide its greedy little slurps. The blush rouging the woman's cheeks engulfed her face when she noticed Ardelle and Joseph's purchases.

Ardelle suddenly became aware of her crumpled skirts and drooping oyster feather.

"Annie." A woman near Ardelle's age stepped through the curtained door. She was taller than the young nursing mother. Her glossy brown hair was neat and her dress impeccable. Ardelle instantly recognized her: She was the chemist. "Bob will be here with the pies any second now. Why don't you go set the table?"

The nursing mother gratefully slipped through the dark blue velvet curtain.

Adeptly the chemist wrapped the douche and the bottle in brown paper. Joseph tied the bundle with the string she produced.

Ardelle stared at his fingers—long and strong—and felt a flutter deep inside her womb.

"It's best warmed," broke through her contemplation.

Ardelle's gaze quickly rose upward. She met the chemist's knowing glance.

"The vinegar is best when warmed," she repeated. And smiled slightly, a secretive smile. "It's not such a shock."

A slow smile curved Ardelle's lips. "Thank you."

A discordant jangle interrupted the feminine exchange; a rumble of carriage wheels rushed through the opened door. "Beth, I got the pies, nearly had to bake them myself—I say, can I help you?"

Bob was shorter than Joseph; the blue eyes that stared at him were not intimidated by the disadvantage.

Joseph stuffed the wrapped purchases underneath his left arm; with his right hand, he grasped Ardelle's elbow. "Your wife has dispensed excellent service, thank you."

Still smiling, Ardelle stepped ahead of Joseph and through the door Beth's husband held open. The teasing aroma of fresh baked pie and cooked beef rose up from the box clutched in his right hand.

The door closed behind them with a sharp, final jangle.

Noise and activity churned the street. Gaslit street lamps illuminated the starless night.

A bill-plastered omnibus crawled into a steady stream of passing carriages. A street sweeper—age indeterminate—plied his broom for an elderly man and woman. A young girl carried a worn basket of wilted flowers, crying, "Lavender! Fresh lavender a ha'penny!"

Nothing had changed. Yet everything had changed.

Joseph shrilly whistled at a passing hansom cab.

"I didn't realize Latin professors could whistle," Ardelle said breathlessly, stepping up onto the wooden platform.

Joseph gave the cabbie directions before joining her inside the cab. "Sometimes it's the only way to get a child's attention."

Passing street lights alternately made Joseph's face first sharply focused and then distant. Her hip and shoulder rubbed his hip and shoulder. Pressing. *Rubbing.* Like sex.

"Do you still burn, Ardelle?"

"Yes."

"Your vagina or your buttocks?"

"Both."

Hard fingers swallowed hers.

Never had she been more aware of her sexuality than when holding his hand. Her fingers felt as swollen as her sex; her palm as wet as her vagina.

His essence inside her was liquid; the thought of it spurting against her cervix liquified her legs.

"I felt my cock," pelted her cheek.

"When?" Ardelle asked, turning her head.

"In the boardroom." His mouth was only inches away from hers. "When I was inside you."

A vivid sensation of dual penetration knifed through her.

"What about when you pressed against my stomach, in the lavatory?"

"I'm not certain."

"What did you feel?"

"A slight flutter."

Ardelle's vagina fluttered in memory.

"Do you still have contact with the boys who were in your dormitory?" she asked impulsively.

"No."

The short answer did not invite further questions. The fingers clasping hers pulsed and throbbed.

"But you've kept abreast of their affairs," she essayed.

"They're not married, if that's what you're asking."

Ardelle realized there was more than pain or pleasure at issue here. Yet she could not think for the rub of his shoulder and hip and the pressure of his fingers.

She recalled the French postcards that had been passed around the table during a meeting. With each turning wheel a single image returned to taunt her.

"Would not a man feel rather infantile when suckling a woman's breasts?"

"When I suckle you"—he gripped her fingers more tightly, squeezing her vagina—"I'll tell you how I feel."

The cab turned a corner.

Ardelle grabbed a leather pull.

"What did you feel when you touched your . . ." She swallowed, letting go of false propriety. ". . . cock?"

"I realized how fragile a woman's sex is."

The left wheel of the cab dropped into a pothole.

Ardelle braced herself.

"And how strong," Joseph added, voice a dark husk.

The cab slowed.

A row of small town houses shone in flickering gaslight outside the window. Large oak trees shadowed the cobbled street.

Chest constricted, she asked, "Do you own a town house?"

"I rent a flat."

"Will they hear us, do you think?"

EIGHT

"The couple above me are on holiday," Joseph said, unlocking the enameled white door that looked and smelled as if it had recently been painted.

Ardelle entered a dark hallway lit by flickering gaslight. The interior smelled faintly of boiled cabbage and roasted beef.

Joseph lightly grasped her elbow and guided her toward a narrow staircase that climbed the far wall. A worn Oriental runner lined the wooden steps. "Up here."

"Who lives down here?" she asked, elbow throbbing.

"The landlord."

Ardelle took the first step. "Will he not object to you having a woman stay the night?"

"We'll find out, won't we?"

Ardelle took a second step. "I cried out when I reached an orgasm."

"That first time."

Ardelle took a third step, Joseph close behind her. "What if I do so again?"

"I will be extremely gratified."

A reluctant smile broke across Ardelle's face, remembering her high-pitched cry. "Let us hope your landlord is, too."

At the top of the narrow stairs, Joseph produced another key.

She waited outside the small foyer until he lit a brass sconce.

Slowly Ardelle entered Joseph's home.

He lit more sconces. . . . There a floor lamp just beyond the foyer. . . . A chandelier flared, revealing a large parlor.

Burgundy carpet covered the floors almost to the walls; polished oak gleamed on either side of the dark red wool. The walls were painted a warm gold. The furniture—what she could see—was masculine, composed of dark leather and even darker wood.

Coming back to the foyer, Joseph shrugged out of his coat and hooked it on a brass coat tree. He notched his bowler hat above the dark bundle of gray wool.

Ardelle was irresistibly reminded of the coat tree in the boardroom.

"Where is this collection of which you spoke?" she asked, slowly adjusting to the sensation of being a stranger in a strange flat.

Joseph Manning was not the man she had thought him to be. But neither was she the woman he had thought her to be.

"Through here." He reached for the buttons on the front of her coat. "Shall I take your cloak?"

His working fingers tugged at her breasts.

"Please." And then, "Shall you leave the lights burning?"

Joseph took her cloak. "Every single one."

There would be no darkness to hide behind.

Not tonight, when they exposed their desires. Not tomorrow, when they exposed their lives.

Ardelle reached up to take off her hat. "I've never seen a naked man."

She had seen a cock—the fundamental sex of a man—but she had not seen the whole. A man with fears as well as needs.

"I've never seen a naked woman," he said. And plucked her black felt hat out from between her fingers. He hooked it on the coat rack beside his gray felt bowler, abandoned oyster feather forlornly waving.

Fingers grasping hers—slowly Ardelle breathed through her nose—he led her through the large parlor to a medium-size bedroom.

A shirt lay crumpled over a leather valet. A book—opened, pages down—lay on a nightstand.

Clearly this was Joseph's bedroom.

He pulled out a trunk from underneath a large sleigh bed, and threw back the lid.

Light shone on his pomaded black hair.

She realized it was macassar oil that had made his hair strangely slick.

Straightening he glanced away from her, face flushed. "Take a look while I run us a bath."

Ardelle uncertainly glanced away from the open trunk.

The sound of gushing water and clanking pipes filled the silence.

Striding over to the nightstand, she scooped up the book Joseph had been reading, perhaps the night before, or perhaps in the early hours before dawn, unable to sleep for fear of the future. Faded gold lettering imprinted worn leather: Virgil, *Aeneid*.

Ardelle turned over the obviously well-read book and perused the two open pages. Black ink underlined Latin passages here and there.

Careful not to lose his place, she set the book back down on the nightstand.

The trunk irresistibly drew her.

There was a bottle of Rose's Lubrifiant, a lubricant. There was a stack of books: *The Lustful Turk, Nunnery Tales, The Romance of Lust.* . . .

Impulsively she picked up *The Autobiography of a Flea*. The leather-bound book—just as worn as the *Aeneid*—fell open. Curiously she read:

> '*My sweet and delicious child,*' *whispered the salacious priest,* '*my arms are around you, my weapon is already halfway up your tight, little belly. The joys of paradise will be yours presently.*'
>
> '*Oh, I know it! I feel it! Do not draw back, give me the delicious thing as far as you can.*'
>
> '*There then, I push, I press, but I am far too largely made to enter you easily. I shall burst you possibly, but it is now too late. I must have you—or die.*'

Ardelle could not help it: She laughed.

"You find Stanislas de Rhodes funny?" feathered her ear.

She instinctively glanced over her shoulder; Joseph stood behind her.

"Read further," he said intently, gray eyes dark. And read aloud for her, eyelashes fanning his cheeks:

> "'*Ambrose cried aloud in rapture as he looked down upon the fair thing his serpent had stung. He gloated over the victim now impaled with the full rigour of his huge rammer. He felt the maddening contact with inexpressible delight. He saw her quivering with the pleasure of his entry. His brutal nature was fully aroused. Come what might, he would enjoy this girl to his utmost. He wound his arms about the beautiful girl and treated her to the full measure of his burly member.*'"

The laughter seeped out of Ardelle's chest. "I'm not Bella, Joseph." Young. Ignorant. Virginal. "I know what men do. I can't pretend otherwise."

"And I am not the chairman of the board." His lashes slowly rose. "I know the difference between being an animal and being a man."

"What?" she asked, mouth suddenly dry.

"Giving."

Ardelle searched his face. "We will never be innocent, will we?"

Always pain would be mixed with pleasure and pleasure with pain.

"No. We won't." Within the gray eyes formed a question: Could she give as well as receive? "The bath is ready."

"But you said you had a dildo." A woman who had only ever taken, she deliberately held his gaze and tried to give him what he needed. "May I see it?"

Dark red tinging his cheeks, Joseph plucked the book out of her fingers. Reaching down into the trunk, he lifted up a wooden box.

Leather phalluses of varying sizes nestled within blue velvet.

Slowly Joseph took out a small phallus—it was not much larger in circumference than his forefinger, but longer, about five inches, she estimated—and laid it on the bed in readiness.

An object to enhance pleasure.

Straightening he turned and caught her gaze. "Shall we go bathe?"

"The douche—"

"Is in the bathroom." The heat inside his eyes burned; the vulnerability within them squeezed her chest. "I've put on a pot of vinegar to warm."

"Shall I"—Ardelle had lifted her skirts; she had never before undressed in front of anyone, not even her maid—"shall we disrobe in here?"

"Yes."

She could not keep from watching him, even as her fingers reached for her own buttons.

He shed black-patented shoes; she shed a jacket. He took out gold shirt studs; she dropped her skirt. He whipped a stiff white cotton shirt over his head; she untied her bustle. He slipped red and yellow embroidered suspenders over pink woollen-encased shoulders; she released the laces to her petticoats.

He pulled up the hem of the pink wool vest.

Ardelle froze, watching a tantalizing inch of skin revealed. His stomach was the same warm olive as was his face. A line of dark hair stretched from the gray wool waistband of his trousers . . . widening . . . spreading into a thick mat of hair . . . two male nipples. . . .

Suddenly the pink wool dropped out of sight, and gray eyes riveted Ardelle.

"You're very handsome," she said.

She had thought so the first time she saw him, inspecting the Roman sarcophagus in the museum.

There was no vulnerability inside his eyes now, just hard male intent. "Take off the rest of your clothes."

Fingers trembling, Ardelle one by one released the spring latches holding together her corset. The plain white cotton, metal-reinforced garment dropped to the floor.

Her freed flesh throbbed everywhere it had been restrained.

Ardelle had never before felt beautiful; she felt beautiful now, watching Joseph watch her. She pulled her chemise over her head. And felt his gaze latch onto her naked breasts, which rose and fell with her every breath. Dropping her arms, she unlaced her drawers. And felt his eyes fasten onto her swollen sex.

Awkwardly bending over—breasts elongating—she unlaced her walking shoes and stepped out of the confining leather. Laboriously she peeled down garter belts and stockings.

The wool carpeting scratched the bottoms of her bare feet.

His wool trousers had similarly scraped her bare buttocks, she remembered.

Straightening, Ardelle faced Joseph, fully naked, nipples stabbing the air. He stood before her, fully naked, erect penis flexing. And held out his hand.

His fingers clenched her entire body.

Steam roiled in the tiny bathroom. It, too, was carpeted.

The porcelain tub was encased in dark wood. A porcelain toilet with a water cistern and pull sat crammed between the narrow tub and a dark, wood-encased sink. The rubber douche was pillowed on a thick burgundy towel beside the white porcelain basin.

Dropping her fingers—she sharply inhaled thick mist—Joseph stepped into the steaming water, strong muscles flexing in his thighs and shoulders. Settling, he spread his legs—they were covered with fine dark hair that lazily swirled in the water—and held out his hand to help her.

Arching her toes, Ardelle tested the water.

It was hot.

Before she could pull back, Joseph tugged her downward until she knelt between his splayed legs.

Steaming water lapped her clitoris and probed her vagina.

"Give me your breast, Ardelle," he said thickly.

There was nothing infantile about the mouth that latched onto her dark, swollen nipple.

Carefully she cradled his head between her hands. Uncertainly she said, "Your hair is slick with oil."

Instantly he released her nipple and sank down, splayed legs arching out of the water, sex and buttocks pressing high into her waist.

She stared down at the hard penis and hair-studded testicles that he exposed.

Between one heartbeat and the next, his sex sank back into the steaming, swirling water and Joseph's head sprang up.

Water streamed down his face and shoulders.

She had not realized a woman could drown in a man's eyes; she felt like she was drowning in Joseph.

Uncertain as to what she should next do, Ardelle reached behind him for the soap dish in the corner.

Her left breast dangled in his face; gently he lifted it.

Ardelle blindly grasped the cake of soap.

Prickly skin abraded her; hard fingers guided her.

Ardelle straightened her spine, granting access but stiffly holding herself apart.

Water clung to the black stubble that prickled her. Mist encircled the reddish-brown tongue that tasted her.

Slowly, carefully, she lathered his hair while he suckled.

The simple intimate chore combined with the wet, tugging heat of his mouth brought tears to her eyes. The sudden scrape of sharp teeth caused her fingers to curl in his soapy hair. "Do you feel infantile, Joseph?"

But he did not answer, pulling and tugging and nipping until she leaned into him and they slowly sank down into the water, and the soap dissolved from his hair and her hands while he fed from her nipple. Suddenly Ardelle could not stand the emptiness inside her womb.

"I need you, Joseph," she whispered, cheek resting against hard, wet porcelain, hands pressing his prickly face into her breast.

Ardelle had never before needed anyone in her life. But she needed this man who understood her needs yet did not judge her.

His mouth pulled free with a slight slurping suction, like the baby in the chemist. "Where do you need me, Ardelle?"

"Inside me."

"Where?"

"My vagina."

Her aching, empty vagina that had tempted so many men.

"Lift your right knee."

His water-slickened leg slid between hers.

She automatically lifted her left knee to accommodate his sliding right leg.

Joseph was wet from the water; Ardelle was wet with desire.

He came into her, a gentle visitor instead of a "burly" invader. Giving instead of taking. Eyes dark with the knowledge of the secrets they shared. "I have always thought you a woman of value, Ardelle."

In his eyes, Ardelle realized, she was.

Water gently sloshing, hot steam caressing, she guided his mouth to her nipple and watched the thin, dark mustache frame his curving lips.

Ardelle traced his right eyebrow . . . the enviously thick lashes . . . a taut cheekbone.

"When you touch me, Joseph," she whispered, "I, too, feel that it's possible for a man and a woman to love one another."

But Joseph did not answer.

He suckled her until the gentle pull of his mouth and the lap of hot water dissolved her bones, and there was no Joseph or Ardelle; there was simply a man and a woman who took comfort in one another, as men and women were meant to take comfort.

To touch and be touched, and not worry where the pursuit of pleasure might take them.

Warm breath abruptly licked the aching hardness of her nipple. "Show me, Ardelle."

She traced the thin line of his mustache; his cock buried inside her prodded her cervix. "Show you what?"

"Show me how the douche works." Dark eyes stared up at her; hair blacker than night floated about his semisubmersed face. "Let me cleanse you."

"But you haven't yet ejaculated inside me."

"But I soon will." Before she could formulate a protest, he sat up, taking her with him. Water sluiced off his shoulders. Instinctively she grasped him for balance; the muscles underneath his wet skin were hard, as hard as the flesh inside her. His eyes, which only moments earlier had been beneath her, were now even with hers. Long fingers gently gripped her buttocks, holding her open to the sloshing water. "Show me how to care for you, Ardelle."

The thought of Joseph performing this intimate ablution was strangely erotic.

"I've never before used a douche," she confessed, muscles involuntarily tightening to shut out the invading water.

The gaze holding hers darkened. Water dribbled down his neck and fingered the stretched skin that gripped his penis. "Then we'll learn together."

Ardelle glanced away from the gray eyes that probed her very depths.

His legs were between hers.

Using his shoulders for purchase, Ardelle awkwardly stood up, legs straddling his knees. Her vagina futilely protested the loss of his penis, pulsing and contracting with every drop of water that dribbled down her buttocks and thighs.

Joseph lifted up out of the water and grabbed the douche off the sink.

"What do I do in your dreams, Joseph?" Ardelle asked, watching him fill the douche with steaming bath water. "When you wake up and work your own flesh?"

Disturbed yet excited.

"You touch me." Glancing up, he pinned her gaze. "Put your left foot up on the tub."

Ardelle gazed at the thin nozzle. And felt a surge of dark desire. *Vive memor leti.*

She put up her foot. He scooted in the bathtub until his water-slickened shoulder supported the arch of her thigh and he was directly underneath her raised leg.

He could see her. Smell her. Touch her. Taste her.

There was no part of her body that was not exposed to him.

A warm finger touched the gaping flesh she could not close . . . slipped inside her . . . the fingertip only. Hot breath seared her. And then the fingertip was prying apart her most secret recesses. "I never thought you were cold, Ardelle."

Water-warmed rubber nudged the side of her vagina . . . slipped into her vagina.

Ardelle's head snapped back.

The nozzle was thinner than his penis, but it was foreign, and it felt foreign.

Something hot and slick licked her clitoris.

"I thought you were free."

The nozzle slid up . . . deep . . . deeper . . . until it notched her cervix. Rubber instead of flesh.

Her muscles fisted about the man-made object.

A hot tongue kissed her clitoris.

"Free?" she managed to ask.

"I didn't think you'd been touched by pain."

A small trickle of water dribbled down the walls of her vagina.

She involuntarily pinched together the yawning orifice her body had become; it did not close. Ardelle could not stop the flow; it leaked past his finger and dribbled down her thigh.

"But I have," she said unevenly.

"Whenever you take my seed, Ardelle"—the hot tongue rimmed the throbbing bud that swelled to painful proportions—"I want to cleanse you like this."

Without warning, a hot gush of water spurted deep against her cervix.

Joseph held her open with his fingertip and licked her, and squirted her, and licked her, and squirted her until hot water spurted from her vagina and cascaded down her thigh in a continuous torrent and she exploded in a sharp cry of uncontrollable pleasure, her greatest fear.

It suddenly dawned on Ardelle what it was that Joseph needed. What it was that woke him with his cock aching so dreadfully he couldn't leave it alone.

Gazing down, eyelids heavy, body exposed, she said, "I know what you dream of, Joseph."

It was not pain.

NINE

Joseph visually mapped a thin trickle of clear water.

He imagined that it was his sperm with which he filled Ardelle to overflowing. He imagined that it was his sperm that drenched her dark pubic hair and dribbled down her thigh.

The nozzle was darker than his finger. The flesh he held open was pink and glistening wet.

Only inches away from his mouth a tiny red bud shone with his saliva.

Unfamiliar emotion burst inside him. Joseph recognized it as gratitude.

He had never thought Ardelle would allow him to explore her body the way she now did.

Slowly he withdrew the rubber nozzle—the flesh he held open fluttered around his fingertip—and kissed her flesh that was as sensitive as his own.

Water-softened pubic hair tickled his nose. The tiny bud throbbed against his lips.

Exactly as the crown of his penis throbbed.

Scalding tears prickled Joseph's eyelids. "What do I dream of, Ardelle?"

She knew only what he had told her. And he had told her very little.

"Pleasure."

Pushing back through hot water—testicles a sliding friction—he scooted backward and gazed up at her amber eyes.

They glowed with a heady combination of satiation and sexual knowledge.

"You have given me pleasure, Ardelle."

Unconscious of the miracle with which she had gifted him, Ardelle dipped her foot back into the water. Leaning over, she grasped the wooden edge encasing the bathtub. Her breasts dangled in front of his face.

Unerringly his gaze focused on the nipple he had suckled.

It was swollen and hard.

"I felt like a man," he said abruptly.

An inquisitive amber gaze rose to meet his.

He reached up and grasped her nipple.

Like the little dome of her cervix, it possessed a tiny indentation. Each tug of his lips had produced a corresponding tug deep inside her vagina.

Joseph's lashes lifted; he met her waiting gaze.

The pleasure his touch engendered shone in her eyes.

"When I suckled you," he clarified, "I felt like a man."

And not a little boy, trapped in a school far away from home with no power to stop the pain that became pleasure.

Slowly, slowly, Ardelle leaned down, gaze intent, until all Joseph could see were two amber rings surrounding a black abyss of unexplored sexuality.

Wet heat opened over his mouth; a pointed tongue licked the seam between his lips.

Joseph opened for her. Gently . . . harder . . . gently pinching her nipple with each flick of her tongue. Knowing that her womb contracted with every squeeze of his fingers.

She touched the roof of his mouth.

The tiny stab penetrated his cock.

"Shall I dry you?" pried open the eyes he had not been aware he had closed.

Ardelle stepped out of the tub and straightened.

She waited to attend to him. As he had attended her.

Joseph realized her hair was still pinned up.

An odd emotion jolted through him.

"Take down your hair," he said.

"Like Rapunzel?"

Curiosity sparked through him. "Is it that long?"

"Hardly," she said dryly. And reached up.

Shadow and fine hair created an enticing grotto.

Joseph stood up, creating an ungainly splash.

He set the empty douche in the sink and reached for the burgundy towel. With each swipe of thick cotton another lank of hair slithered down her neck.

Joseph had never seen anything more erotic in his life.

The darkness underneath her arms that matched the *v* of hair between her thighs. The breasts that alternately rose and fell with her motions. The nipples that stabbed the air, long and hard.

For *him*.

Ardelle shook her head; mink-brown hair cascaded down her neck and tumbled over her shoulders.

He felt large and awkward and ungainly, man standing before woman, wanting nothing more than she take him, love him, and accept him for what he was instead of requiring he be like the sexless, pomaded billboard images plastered throughout London.

She set the hairpins on the marble counter, marking the masculine bathroom with feminine apparel.

"The vinegar"—she caught his gaze in the mirror over the sink that housed the douche—"isn't it boiling by now?"

Joseph knew the difference between pain and pleasure.

"I would never hurt you, Ardelle."

Eyes enigmatic, she held out her hand.

He allowed her fingers—so much smaller than his own—to envelop his.

She led him to the bedroom, naked in the light.

The book on the nightstand had been moved.

A curious pang shot through Joseph, realizing she had glanced at the pages he had marked.

"Do you have something I can spread over the carpet?" she asked, naked shoulder rubbing his arm, fingers pulsing around his fingers. Amber eyes dark with knowledge.

Reluctantly freeing his hand, he opened a dresser drawer and shook out a soft wool duvet.

Ardelle leaned over and grabbed the bottle of Rose's Lubrifiant; momentarily Joseph glimpsed the dark puckered flesh he had penetrated earlier that night and in which his sperm still resided. Immediately she straightened—spine oddly stiff—and turned.

Joseph froze—flexing penis involuntarily feinting the air—and stared at the leather phallus in her hand.

"This is what you dream about, isn't it, Joseph?" stabbed through him.

Every muscle, every ligament inside his body demanded he deny the truth: He could not.

The dark excitement he had felt—awaiting his turn to be punished—flushed his face and crawled down his throat.

Joseph forced his gaze to meet hers. "Yes."

Her amber eyes were curiously watchful. "You dream that I introduce it into your body."

"Yes."

"Because that is what you wanted the don to do, when he hurt you so badly your bum burned."

"Yes," Joseph said flatly, cock uncontrollably flexing.

"Lie down."

But he could not surrender his control . . . not yet.

Joseph searched her amber eyes. "What did you feel, Ardelle, when you lay across the table, waiting for me to touch you?"

Brief emotion darkened her eyes. "I was afraid."

"Of what?"

"That you'd give me pleasure."

And he had. He had felt her every contraction.

"What are you afraid of now?" he asked, mouth dry, muscles taut, penis throbbing.

"That I won't give you pleasure."

Joseph's fear.

He lay down.

Ardelle straddled his hips, facing his feet.

"You saw the print," he said, breath rasping inside his throat.

The print of a woman riding a man, her back toward him, glancing over her shoulder with an enigmatic smile.

"I saw," she agreed. And took his naked cock so deeply into her vagina that he could not breathe.

"You taught me something tonight." She reached for the bottle of lubricant, pelvis rocking against his groin. "When you suckled me."

He watched shadow play across her vertebrae, feeling her every motion . . . the shifting of her weight, the clenching of her vagina . . . but unable to see her actions. "What did I teach you?"

"You taught me"—her right elbow extended, a graceful curve; at the same time, her vagina nipped him—"we are entitled to take pleasure in what we are."

Joseph's breath quickened.

"You said giving was what separated a man from an animal."

She set the cap down on the quilt beside her splayed thigh. Moist vulva rocking. Vagina painfully nipping.

"I gave you my pleasure." Slowly she rose up on her knees, his penis sliding inch by slow inch out of the tight, wet haven that gripped him . . . that held him, there at the entrance to her vagina. "Now I want you to give me yours."

"Spread your legs, Joseph."

Joseph stiffly spread his legs, forcefully holding emotion at bay. Cool air tickled his too-tight testicles.

"Lift up your hips."

His heart leapt inside his chest; the crown of his cock flexed inside the mouth of her vagina.

Unbidden memories flashed through his thoughts.

The pain of punishment. The loneliness of assuagement.

The desire that had prevented five boys from finding happiness in a woman.

Joseph lifted his hips; simultaneously he tunneled upward into the wet fist of her body . . . two short inches . . . not nearly deeply enough.

Ardelle leaned forward, vagina bending his cock backward.

He studied the play of shadows on her spine while she spread him, a kiss of air . . . while she found him, a burning notch . . . while she penetrated him. Watching his flesh stretch to accept the bulbous head of the phallus she fed him while her flesh nipped and squeezed the engorged crown that he fed her.

She throbbed. He throbbed.

One heartbeat . . . two heartbeats . . . three heartbeats . . .

The phallus was too big. Her vagina was too small.

Without warning, he blossomed open.

He had welcomed the fullness in his dreams, but this wasn't a dream.

His buttocks independently clenched to stop the raw invasion. To end the perverted desire that chained him to the past. But suddenly the phallus was inside him: one inch . . . three inches . . . five inches. And he could not move for the hard leather that crowded his body until there was no room for fear or loneliness. There was only room for Ardelle.

Her bowed back suddenly straightened. Joseph instinctively grasped warm, giving buttocks, needing an anchor, white-knuckled fingers exposing that part of her that matched the flesh she had penetrated.

Slowly she lowered her hips; her weight bore him downward.

Transfixed, Joseph watched as the masculine flesh that protruded from his body was swallowed by the feminine flesh hidden inside her body . . . one inch . . . three inches . . . five inches . . . each tug of her vagina nipping and squeezing his testicles while the leather buried deep between his buttocks burned and throbbed as if alive.

Without warning she stopped—his crinkly black pubic hair reached for her moist brown pubic hair; the delicate ring of her vagina stretched thin around the thick purple column of his penis—and glanced over her shoulder.

Emotion flooded Joseph.

There was no disgust on her face.

Ardelle wore the same unfathomable smile that the woman in the print had worn: knowing a man's desires, acting on a man's desires—Joseph reached for the bottle of lubrication—*sharing* a man's desires.

TEN

"Come live with me."

Ardelle stared up into the dark eyes that were hidden by the brim of a shadow-blackened bowler hat.

Joseph was shaven, pomaded, and impeccably dressed.

He did not look like a man who had given a woman access to his body. And who had then rinsed his sperm from her body with vinegar that burned just short of pain while he licked her clitoris until her entire body convulsed.

Trust.

"Until you find another position and can afford a flat of your own," he added, tensing at her lack of response, still vulnerable to rejection. "Or permanently. If you like."

The trial. Always it came back to the trial.

To accept change. Or reject change.

To deny pleasure. Or accept pain.

"Yes." Ardelle accepted change. She nodded her head; her body pleasantly burned and throbbed still, curiously clean with the passion they had shared. "I would like that."

"Shall I go in with you?"

"No." Ardelle stared out the single square window—beyond the steaming horse rump—at a row of mellow brick town houses. They were larger than the town house from which they had just left. More expensive. Her father—unlike Joseph—was very well off. "I'll just be a moment."

She had bathed with Joseph, but she needed fresh clothes.

Silently she threw open the cab door. Gray rain misted her face.

The butler swung open the door just as Ardelle took out her key.

"Miss Ardelle!" he said censoriously. "Your parents have been worried."

"Thank you, Berrimore," Ardelle said dismissively. She felt a familiar coldness crawl up her spine, vertebra by vertebra. "That will be all."

Immediately he stepped back, intimidated as she had meant him to be.

Ardelle briskly climbed the gleaming wooden stairs with the elegant, violet-patterned wool runner.

"Ardelle!" A sharp feminine voice cracked like a whip. "You have gone too far. You will come down and explain yourself immediately, miss!"

Ardelle did not slow down.

Inside her bedroom—where she had learned each note of the Westminster Chimes—a quilted rose velvet comforter was neatly turned down, revealing crisp white sheets. Four bed posts darkly gleamed in the morning light, taller than Ardelle the child; with a start of surprise she realized she was now the taller of the two.

This was the bed of her childhood.

Ardelle remembered how warm and welcoming Joseph's sleigh bed had been, cuddled safely in his arms while her body throbbed both for and from him. She bypassed the four-poster bed and reached into a massive wardrobe.

Laying out clean clothing, she quickly undressed.

The door yanked open at the same time her arms breached a fresh chemise.

Her mother stepped through the doorway; she was armored in a pink satin morning gown. Ardelle fleetingly thought she would look like her when she grew older. She possessed the same dark brown hair, the same amber eyes, the same slender build.

Deliberately she stood naked—walking shoes tilting her hips forward—so that her mother could clearly see the small marks of passion left over from her night with Joseph.

And see them her mother did. She saw the pale, fingertip-size bruises dotting Ardelle's hips. Her neck that was reddened from the scrape of beard stubble. The nipples dark and swollen. Her sex lips engorged.

Amber eyes wide, Althea Dennison brought up a manicured hand to her mouth. "You *are* a whore."

Ardelle had once thought so.

"Have a maid pack my clothes." She slid the chemise over her head, cool air rushing, breasts lifting. And remembered the heat of Joseph's hand that had cupped her left breast while he slept. Head clearing the neckline, she added, "I will leave a forwarding address with Berrimore."

"I will not have my daughter behave like a . . . a tart."

Ardelle laughed, a cold, brittle sound. A sharp pang stabbed through her, comparing the reverberating laughter with last night's cries of passion. Immediately her mirth died.

She pulled on a pair of wool drawers. "Too late, Mother."

"We have given you *every*thing," lashed Althea Dennison.

Ardelle stepped into a petticoat. "You bought my silence."

And Ardelle had retaliated by selling her virginity, convinced a woman's value could be purchased.

"I have no idea what you're talking about."

Ardelle gazed at her mother while she laced on a small bustle.

No guilt, no regret, no knowledge of the damage she had inflicted clouded the clear amber eyes.

The older woman believed what she had done was acceptable.

The hurt, angry words of a child welled up inside her throat. Ardelle, the adult, swallowed them.

Deftly she plucked off the rose velvet comforter a dark navy wool jacket. "Then there's no need to discuss it."

"This is ridiculous," Althea Dennison said. "Do you think a lone woman can make it on her own?"

Ardelle fastened up a navy wool skirt. "Yes."

For two years she had weekly sat across from two such women.

"You are in for a rude awakening, daughter."

Perhaps.

Ardelle scooped up her reticule. "Good-bye, Mother."

"You're just going to leave?" The amber eyes that were on a level with Ardelle were disbelieving. "Like this?"

Ardelle walked out the door.

Her father stood at the foot of the steps.

She remembered the man with the red, panting face.

He had been jolly in those days, Ardelle recalled. There was no laughter now in his brown eyes. He was a shrunken, shriveled old man at the age of fifty-seven.

Time had been his judge and jury, and they had found him guilty.

"Good-bye, Father."

The brown eyes stared at the newel post she grasped; they would not look at her.

He stepped back, retreating to the study where it had all begun when she had been . . . But Ardelle could not remember what age she had been when he had started wriggling underneath her small, innocent bottom. Five, perhaps. Or four.

Her past. Not her future.

Ardelle stopped by the small ornamental table that held the outgoing morning post. She scribbled a quick address and handed the paper to the thin-lipped butler who stared at her with disapproval. "Have my things delivered to this address, Berrimore."

The misting rain warmed her icy skin.

A bill-plastered omnibus cumbersomely rounded the corner of the cobbled street.

Sudden excitement curled in the pit of her stomach.

Lightly jumping up on the creaking platform in front of the waiting cab, Ardelle reached into her reticule and withdrew a florin. Hurriedly she paid the confused cabbie and swung open the cab door.

"Come with me," she breathlessly urged Joseph. A droplet of water trailed down her cheek, the rain as cleansing as a douche. "Quickly."

Instantly he stepped out of the hansom cab, knuckles white around the wooden handle of his umbrella.

"What is it?" he sharply asked. No doubt expecting a rampaging mother and father hot at her heels.

"An omnibus," she said. And grabbed his hand.

The iron step was slippery. Ardelle quickly regained her balance—momentarily she dropped Joseph's hand; quickly she grabbed it again when he stepped down beside her—and chased after the departing bus.

The painful years spent living in the house that had stolen her innocence raced past her.

Sudden laughter welled up inside her chest.

They had survived the night, and they would ride that omnibus.

Joseph did not question her mad dash; instead he hit the side of the bus with his umbrella, squarely smacking a faded advertisement for Victoria Regina, Queen of Toilet Soaps. The driver stopped.

The interior of the omnibus was only marginally lighter than had been the hansom cab. A woman occupied the front seat. A man read a newspaper on a third row seat.

It was nearly empty.

Feeling as giddy as a girl, Ardelle dropped the prerequisite two pennies into the meter and lurched down the aisle of the suddenly mobile vehicle to the back of the bus.

Joseph dropped down beside her.

Laughter trilling the musty air, she reached for the buttons lining his trousers.

A strong hand immediately grasped hers.

Ardelle glanced up, willing Joseph to share in the celebration of their freedom. "A woman once recommended that I fondle your privates in public."

Dark comprehension blazed in his eyes: Ardelle referred to the widow against whom they now traveled to stand witness.

His fingers helped her release the buttons, longer, stronger than hers.

"Did your bum burn dreadfully last night?" Ardelle asked.

His penis was as hot and hard—cradled between her hands—as it had been two years earlier. Blue veins pulsed against her fingers.

"Yes." His voice was strained, even as his flesh strained toward her.

Dual pulses throbbed inside her body. She knew that a matching pulse throbbed inside his body, penetrated where he had penetrated her.

For their pleasure. Not for pain.

Silently she played with the tiny urethra that cried slick tears.

So much would be lost today, but surely not everything.

"They will come back to us, Joseph," she whispered over the creaking groan of wood and the grinding whine of wheels.

Ardelle glanced up and watched rising pleasure tint Joseph's cheeks. "Someday the members of the Men and Women's Club will come home."

Robin Schone lives in a Chicago suburb with her music aficionado husband. She loves reading, swimming, listening to music (preferably rock and/or classic rock) and is a staunch defender of human rights in general and of women's sexuality worldwide.

Robin is a *USA Today* bestselling author whose work is translated in nine languages. All five of her novels—*Awaken, My Love*; *The Lady's Tutor*; *The Lover*; *Gabriel's Woman*; and *Scandalous Lovers*, which inspired "The Men and Women's Club"—were Doubleday Book Club Selections.

Robin loves hearing from readers. Visit her website at www.robin schone.com or write her at:

Robin Schone
P.O. Box 72725
Roselle, IL 60172

Coming in March 2009!

Don't miss Robin's exciting new novel *Cry for Passion*—Rose Clarring and Jack Lodoun's story—coming from Berkley in March 2009.